EXPLORE THE UNKNOWN

North Africa 8000 B.C. A young boy walks into a dazzling beam of light in the sky.

Egypt 1928. On the Giza plateau, near the great pyramid, a mysterious object is discovered that baffles scientists and defies all known history.

California 1994. A brilliant, out-of-work young genius Egyptologist named Daniel Jackson, whose theories are considered bizarre, is hired for an ultra-secret government scientific project. At the same time, Colonel Jack O'Neil, a burned-out operative of U.S. special forces, is returned to active duty after a long convalescence from a near total mental breakdown.

O'Neil is to lead a handpicked team of America's finest fighting men. Jackson is to guide them. These two men, who are total opposites, are barely on speaking terms. They hold the keys to mankind's most important mission.

A mission to the unknown—to discover who, or what, is beyond the other side of the . . .

STARGATE™

SIGNET

YOU'VE SEEN THE MOVIE, NOW READ THE BOOK!

☐ **DEMOLITION MAN by Richard Osborne.** Based on the screenplay by Daniel Waters and Jonathan Lemkin. San Angeles, in 2032. The city, having survived the savage riots of the 1990s, is a politically correct paradise where crime and violence are unknown. But Simon Phoenix, the most vicious criminal of the bad old days, has escaped from suspended animation. The police are powerless to stop his new reign of terror. (181026—$4.50)

☐ **THE PAPER by Dewey Gram,** based on a screenplay by David Koepp & Stephen Koepp. It can be a nasty, dirty job—but the guys and gals on the staff of the New York *Sun* are just the ones to do it and love every no-holds-barred, trick-of-the-trade way to the next explosive daily edition, in the fastest, funniest, most irresistible novel about dementedly dedicated newsies that anyone has ever seen fit to print. (182146—$4.99)

☐ **THE BODYGUARD by Robert Tine.** They are both the best in the business. Frank provides protection for pay to presidents and billionaires. Rachel is a superstar actress-singer who offers the adoring public her beauty and voice. But the killer stalking Rachel is also the best in the business. And for Rachel, no place is safe, not even the arms of her protector, who burns with passion for Rachel even as her enemy draws closer. (177770—$3.99)

☐ **THE HAND THAT ROCKS THE CRADLE by Robert Tine, based on the screenplay written by Amanda Silver.** Peyton Flanders was just what Claire Bartel was looking for in a nanny. She seemed to fit into the family so well. Soon Peyton was running everything. The house. The husband. The children. Only one thing stood in the way of Peyton's chilling, twisted plan—Claire. The movie shocked you—now read the terrifying book! (175433—$4.99)

☐ **FRANCIS FORD COPPOLA'S DRACULA by Fred Saberhagen and James V. Hart,** based on a screenplay by James V. Hart. A legendary evil inspires a motion picture event! Here is the ultimate re-telling of a story that has mesmerized readers for nearly a century. (175751—$4.99)

☐ **THE SECRET GARDEN by Frances Hodgson Burnett.** Now a Major Motion Picture from Warner Bros. With 8 pages of enchanting movie photos! When Mary discovers a hidden garden on her uncle's estate, she and her two friends not only open a door to a real hideaway, but into the innermost places of the heart. "A blend of power, beauty, and honest goodness ... If this is magic, it is good magic."—*The New York Times* (525817—$3.50)

Prices slightly higher in Canada

Buy them at your local bookstore or use this convenient coupon for ordering.

PENGUIN USA
P.O. Box 999 — Dept. #17109
Bergenfield, New Jersey 07621

Please send me the books I have checked above.
I am enclosing $_____ (please add $2.00 to cover postage and handling). Send check or money order (no cash or C.O.D.'s) or charge by Mastercard or VISA (with a $15.00 minimum). Prices and numbers are subject to change without notice.

Card #_____ Exp. Date _____
Signature_____
Name_____
Address_____
City _____ State _____ Zip Code _____

For faster service when ordering by credit card call **1-800-253-6476**

Allow a minimum of 4-6 weeks for delivery. This offer is subject to change without notice.

STARGATE™

DEAN DEVLIN & ROLAND EMMERICH

A SIGNET BOOK

SIGNET
Published by the Penguin Group
Penguin Books USA Inc., 375 Hudson Street,
New York, New York 10014, U.S.A.
Penguin Books Ltd, 27 Wrights Lane,
London W8 5TZ, England
Penguin Books Australia Ltd, Ringwood,
Victoria, Australia
Penguin Books Canada Ltd, 10 Alcorn Avenue,
Toronto, Ontario, Canada M4V 3B2
Penguin Books (N.Z.) Ltd, 182-190 Wairau Road,
Auckland 10, New Zealand

Penguin Books Ltd, Registered Offices:
Harmondsworth, Middlesex, England

First published by Signet, an imprint of Dutton Signet,
a division of Penguin Books USA Inc.

First Printing, December, 1994
10 9 8 7 6 5 4 3

*Special thanks to our
mischievous and often mercurial Poltergeist,
Steven Molstad*

1

8000 B.C.

All that remained was the eye of the beast, and when that was done, it would see him, it would live. The animal's hide was painted orange and black, the hooves and horns scratched onto the wall with chalk. The image was crude, but it captured the gazelle's panic—the terror of being hunted. The mouth screaming, the torso twisted in flight, the legs clattering for a way to escape.

The boy had camouflaged his dark skin with stripes and odd symbols, using the same paint he had used to conjure the gazelle. In the cave's murky light, he dipped the hollow end of a long stick into a bowl of ink, then approached the wall. He looked up and into another eye, a white human eye, painted like a religious icon, high on the wall of the cave. He began the hunt by speaking the name of the animal he was about to stalk, "Khet."

With that signal, the old man standing at the mouth of the cave sat down in the scratch gravel and began to chant. The old one, clad in animal skins and wearing a long beard, was the leader of his clan and the boy's teacher. His chanting was a slow rhythmic hunter's song spoken in the language of the gazelle, the song the tribe always murmur-sang while hunting. The boy ground the hollow stick into the empty eye socket of the animal, then put his lips to the end and blew the ink out of the stick to create the animal's eye.

Under the spell of the old one's soft chanting, the boy felt the animal slowly coming to life. Soon he and the gazelle would see one another.

The hunter could move no faster than the stone walls of the cave that surrounded him, or he risked alarming the animal and ruining that part of the hunt happening at the same moment out in the valley. The boy never felt himself move, but by continuous force of concentration, found himself advancing upon his prey. This same technique was being used by the hunters in the field. The best of them were called Those Who Walk Without Being Seen, and they formed an elite group within the tribe. Their symbol was the white disembodied eye, painted like a religious icon high above the gazelle. These elite hunters were amazed and intimidated by this ten-year-old boy's incredible patience during the hunt and his ability to control the minds of the animals. It was just one more strange thing about this remarkable child, one more reason to fear him.

On the surface, the boy appeared catatonic, asleep on his feet. There was no indication of the intense mental struggle being waged. The painted animal was constantly on the verge of flight. It felt the boy coming too close, almost close enough to grab him. The boy could feel the animal's every impulse, every thought, but he showed her nothing, remaining absolutely calm. The hunters of the tribe spent their whole lives learning how to conceal their fear and excitement from the animals at close range. When this "magic" came naturally to the boy, both in the field and up in the cave, the people said that he must have been born without a heart. In fact, the child had rarely displayed any emotion at all: no anger, no fear, no love.

When he crept within arm's reach of the gazelle, he heard the old one's chant slow even further, becoming a hallucinatory drone. Steadily, the boy inched his wiry black arms above his head. In one hand he held a chisel, in the other a heavy hammering stone. Then, without any visible signal, the old one and the boy suddenly shouted the name of the animal at the same time, "Khet!" In a lightning fast attack, the boy brought the chisel to the wall, then crushed down with the stone to cut a deep gash into the painted wall. The fresh scar ran straight into the heart of the gazelle.

A moment later, the old man stood up and entered the cave to inspect the young one's work. He could see that the hunt in the field would be successful. Pleased and excited, he looked into the boy's unique eyes, a mixture of brown and amber yellow, then raised his staff above his head in salute, speaking the boy's name—"Ra!"

At the mouth of the cave, the boy sat in the sun watching the old one pick his way down the rocky trail, then out across the desert floor to where the tribe had established its camp. An afternoon fire had been made, and he watched the plume of smoke rise into the breeze where it shredded and disappeared. Soon the hunter's horns were heard in the distance, and he watched the children of the camp sprint out to meet the returning heroes. When they came to the top of the last dune, he saw they were carrying a pair of gazelles tied at the feet to two long poles, which the men carried on their shoulders.

When the old one saw what they had brought, he raised his staff high above his head and shouted his praise. The hunters returned the gesture, and then the entire tribe turned to face the cave dug into the side of the hill. As one, they saluted the odd young hunter with the brown-amber eyes.

The boy coolly returned their signal.

That night, after their tribe had feasted, the hunters began their dance around the central fire. They wore hollowed-out wooden masks, eerie helmets, painted to resemble the animals of their world: the hippopotamus, the jackal, the bull, the hawk, the gazelle. As always, the boy kept his distance from the others. He found a large smooth rock well away from the fire and sat there observing the ritual dispassionately. He noted how frightened everyone became when confronted by one of the animal masks. Each time one of the dancers broke away from the fire and shook his head at the onlookers, everyone, not only the children, jumped backward and shrieked with real fear.

At one point, the jackal-headed dancer broke through the ring of spectators, sending them squealing in all directions. He danced out to the rock where the boy was sitting, planning to bring him into the celebration by giving him a good scare. The dancer shook his head and made a series of grunting noises, but nothing made the boy so much as flinch. Looking through the open mouth of the mask, the man looked into the boy's eyes. A moment later, it was the adult hunter and not the child who became frightened. Stumbling backward, he retreated to the fire and the ring of other dancers. Although everyone witnessed the incident, no one regarded it as particularly strange. In their turn, all the members of the tribe had gone to the boy, attempting to coax him into the group's common life. Many of them had come away from the encounter in fear.

For his part, the boy felt no particular malice toward these people. He occasionally felt something like gratitude, even though he knew they had discussed killing him more than once in order to put the mothers at ease. He regarded them as a simpler species, and although he didn't know where he would go, he knew that he was destined to become one of those rare people the tribe encountered from time to time, individuals who lived apart from any group.

While the heat and noise of their fire-dance continued, a mysterious event took place, unnoticed by any member of the tribe. The moon was full that night, turning yellow and dying into the horizon. On a quieter night in the camp, someone would have seen the large triangular shape gliding through the sky, casting a weird, straight-edged shadow across the top half of the full moon. It hung there for a moment blotting out the moonlight before sliding away into the blackened night sky. Sensing the disturbance, the boy turned to look behind him, but by then the shadow had gone.

Hours later, as the camp slept, this same silent shadow circled past the moon once more. Something was hovering over the camp, watching, waiting. Only a pack of jackals, always alert to being hunted, noticed. They bayed and turned to run. The boy's eyes opened and fixed on the swaying bird-skull fetish strung like a wind chime to the edge of his tent—an animal hide tied to a series of sticks that provided shade during the long hot hours of the afternoon. An abnormal breeze rustled through the camp, then suddenly died. Curious, the boy sat up. Soon another gust rolled through, only this one didn't die. It became a steady wind that slowly increased in strength. Within seconds, it had become a gale, waking everyone in the camp. Stronger still, first one tent and then another collapsed or was lifted away in the wind. Now the Old One was on his feet, moving through the camp and shouting above the storm, ordering a retreat to the cave on the hill.

A dazzling light appeared from above. A square beam as radiant as the sun shone down on the desert floor just north of the camp. As it slowly plowed toward them, the tribe's people scattered, terrified, away from the light. The Old One, a commanding presence, stood his ground and ushered all those he could find away from the light, toward the mountain.

The boy's first impulse was to obey the man and go with the others, but then, curiously, he calmly turned and began to walk directly toward the light. It was as though he had no will of his own. The Old One ordered him to safety, but the boy marched on, through the chaos of wind and light, out to the rim of the camp. He was inextricably drawn toward it, called by an irresistible force. He looked directly into the blinding white light glaring down from above. And as he reached a hand up into the light, something touched his hand. Soft and warm, this bright presence quickly wrapped itself around him, engulfing the boy in its brilliance, submerging into his skin, into his soul. He felt, perhaps for the first time, an emotion he could neither hide nor control. It was excitement. The excitement that comes with a sense of deliverance. The excitement it is only natural to feel when your destiny is announcing itself.

2

CAIRO, 1928

On the ramshackle outskirts of Cairo, from the minaret of the Jebba al-Sa'laam mosque, the muezzin's afternoon prayer call pealed out over the last rooftops of a city that had changed little in the last two centuries. A freshly polished 1924 Rolls Royce Imperial Touring Sedan, property of the Egyptian Ministry of Antiquities, whizzed past the last buildings and out into the long hard sand of the desert. Moving south along the highway to Giza, the car swerved around the occasional lorry full of workers or farm produce.

Taylor's message, as welcome as it was, couldn't have been delivered at a worse moment. Professor Langford was midway through a meeting with the Egyptian Interior Minister. His Excellency was going on and on about the changing political climate and how it would be a terrible personal risk for him to extend Langford's British-sponsored excavating permit. Langford, a Swede, had been in the country long enough to read between the lines of the minister's speech. He wanted cash, enough to compensate him for the "grave personal risk" he would be taking. Langford, who had become fairly adept in Arab negotiating technique, counterattacked immediately. Making certain to act angrier than he actually was, he shouted about all the money he had spent and all the jobs he and his team had created. He stood up and pounded on the minister's giant cedar desk, reminding his plump, mustachioed friend of all the snags and broken promises he had endured in this most frustrating of countries. That's when the door opened and the note was delivered to Langford. The handwritten dispatch ended the meeting.

Langford,
Sitting down? We've got something. Probably a Tomb. Too soon to tell. Excavation continuing. Very exciting. I suggest you get your aristocratic hind-end out here AT ONCE. And don't bring any of those pudding heads from the ministry. Let's keep this quiet for as long as we can.
    Taylor.

Refolding the letter, Langford cringed at his foreman's undiplomatic language. He knew that the note, which Taylor had neglected to seal, must have been read by at least ten pairs of eyes before reaching him and that the minister, at whom he was now smiling politely, would learn it's entire contents within ten minutes. He had to hurry. The way rumors spread in Cairo, if he wasn't quick, there would be a souvenir shop built at the edge of the dig site by evening. Excusing himself, he hustled downstairs and found the driver assigned to take him home. In his broken Arabic, he explained the new itinerary and that there would be a sizable tip for speedy driving. Within minutes, they had swung by the swank Sheppard's Hotel, picked up his brainy, nine-year-old daughter, Catherine, and were careening through the congested downtown toward the zoological gardens, scattering pedestrians as they went. Langford dug his fingers into the vehicle's velvet armrest, and didn't breathe normally until they were well out of town on the southbound highway.

Catherine, already a daredevil in pigtails, leaned through the sliding glass partition into the driver's compartment, practicing her Arabic with the driver and squealing at every near-collision. She had arrived in Cairo twelve weeks before, called to join her father when an important discovery had seemed imminent. A prodigious learner, she had become something of an expert on hieroglyphs in that time, visiting the Egyptian Museum almost daily, annoying and charming the staff with hundreds of questions. In her braided hair and thick glasses, she looked destined to become a matronly bookworm. Once they were cruising along the highway, she settled back and cracked opened a thick book entitled *Ancient Egypt*.

In the backseat, suppressing his excitement with all the strength of his Victorian upbringing, Professor C. P. Langford, member of The Egypt Exploration Society and The British Royal Museum, looked every inch the gentleman archaeologist dressed, as he was, in puttees, khaki jodhpurs, and field jacket. Normally, he would never dress like this for actual fieldwork, and wished he could change before meeting Taylor and the others. He had only worn this costume to impress the Egyptian officials.

Langford and Taylor met in Luxor in 1920 when both men were visiting Egypt for the first time. Langford, the aristocratic family man from posh London, and Taylor, the rough-and-tumble graduate student from the University of Pennsylvania who had dropped out of school and volunteered to fight in the World War. After the armistice, he'd wired home for money, then spent some time touring Greece and Palestine before ending up in Egypt. In Luxor, Langford had naturally stayed at the luxurious Winter Palace. Taylor, constrained to a more modest budget, came there every afternoon pretending to be a guest because the hotel had flush toilets and the *International Herald Tribune*. The two men spent several afternoons exploring Beban el Malook (the Valley of the Kings), with Taylor doing most of the talking. But it was their visit to the Temple of Ti, farther north, that cemented the partnership.

Not far from the Great Pyramids, adjacent to the famous Steps Pyramid, stands the Temple of Ti, the only monument of grand scale erected in honor of a nonroyal personage. Overseer of the pyramids, scribe of the court, chief astronomer, and special adviser to a number of pharaohs, Ti was also known as "Lord of the Secrets." They spent an entire week probing the tomb, discussing the many well-preserved reliefs and friezes that adorn the burial site. When Langford slipped the tomb's caretaker a little baksheesh, they were awarded access to a little-known collection of papyrus fragments unearthed by Mariette, the Frenchman who had excavated the tomb forty-five years earlier. From these fragments, already ancient by the time Ti took custody of them, the men developed their present theory: that something was buried halfway between the Steps Pyramid and one of the Great Pyramids of Giza, probably Khufu's. The papyri referred to a "plague" or "pestilence" or "demon" that was stolen and "ferried away." The clues were sparse, and the chances for success weren't good. If the Good Citizens of Stockholm, as enthralled as they were with the recent Tutankhamen discoveries, had realized what an incredibly long shot this excavation was, they never would have funded it.

But fund it they did. When Langford returned to Cairo the previous March, he brought with him guarantees of nearly one million Swedish krona. After only six weeks of fieldwork, they discovered a small burial chamber. Langford, supposedly the "diplomatic half" of the team, rushed into town and invited all the foreign newspaper correspondents and several government dignitaries to witness the opening of the tomb. Even Howard Carter, the world's most famous archaeologist took time off and made the trip from Luxor, where he was in his third year of cataloging the contents of Tutankhamen's small tomb. So, on a beautiful May morning, the entrance was cleared and the two men crawled through the opening. It would be very interesting to have a record of their conversation inside. When they emerged, grinning and embarrassed, they carried with them the only artifact of any interest: a mummified cat still in it's crude wooden coffin. The international press had a field day. Long, satirical articles appeared on the discovery of "The Kitty-cat Tut," etc. It was a humbling, humiliating experience for Langford, who had imagined himself on the verge of lasting fame for his contributions to science.

Cruising southbound with the green ribbon of the Nile on one side and the vast Sahara on the other, Langford couldn't help contemplating immortality once more. One never knew what one might find. But then the Great Pyramids, the only remaining wonders of the ancient world, came into view, and the gentleman archaeologist quickly regained his perspective. The overwhelming size of these structures on the

Giza Plateau, the pyramids of Mycerinus and Chefron and especially that of Khufu made Langford laugh at himself. How pitifully insignificant his little project seemed in the shadows cast by these magnificent, eternal works.

But that was before he saw what he'd found.

Before the tires stopped rolling, Langford's boots were crunching across the gravel. With Catherine fluttering behind, he climbed to the edge of a silt and stone plateau many thousands of years old. But the plateau had been transformed, hollowed out by one bucket of earth at a time by the hundreds of Arab laborers the team had employed over the past few months. Now it was a small shallow valley littered with digging equipment and divided into nicely measured parcels by surveyor's stakes. Nearly three hundred laborers, fellahin, were working that day. The great majority of them were local men dressed in haiks—long white cotton robes—and makeshift turbans.

The bulk of activity was taking place at the far end of the site. Long fingers of dust spiraled into the breeze where the fellahin were dumping the excess sand and broken rock. As soon as these men emptied their baskets, they turned and headed back to a larger than normal "hot pit." A pair of wooden hoisting cranes had been moved into place at the edge of this pit, and ropes were being strung through the pulleys. They were preparing to lift something out of the ground. Something heavy.

"Daddy, the treasure's over there," Catherine informed him in Swedish, pointing toward the cranes and the crowd of workers.

"We'll go see Ed Taylor first." Langford spotted Taylor and a group of other men bent over a worktable outside the "office tent." They seemed to be studying something.

Langford, notorious for telling unfunny jokes in several languages, had been polishing a witticism for the last several minutes. When he came within shouting distance of the group, he tried his luck.

"Ed, if we found a pet cemetery, I quit."

Just as he feared, no one laughed. In fact, no one gave him even the faintest sort of courtesy chuckle. But what really struck Langford as odd was that none of the men even noticed his ridiculous "gentleman explorer" outfit. The group's intense concentration told Langford that this was no ordinary find. Both he and Catherine were immediately caught up in the drama.

"We can't decipher his writing. Take a look."

Taylor made room for Langford to step up and look at the large sheet of paper spread across the table. It was covered with a series of strange markings, charcoal rubbings taken from an etched stone surface. It only took Langford a few seconds to understand why the group was so perplexed. But to everyone's surprise, Catherine said it first.

"Those aren't real hieroglyphics," she said in English.

"At least not the kind we're used to."

"Taylor," Langford said, suddenly edgy, "where did these symbols come from?"

"I'll show you." The foreman strode off toward the dig site. Thirty yards short of the pit, which was crowded with workers, all of them shouting instructions at one another, Taylor stopped at what appeared to be a gigantic stone tabletop. It was three feet tall and twenty feet across. The massive slab was the same chalky gray as the gravel it sat in.

"It's a cover stone," Taylor explained. "The largest one I've ever seen. When you bury something with a rock this size, you mean to keep it buried."

Langford excitedly walked around the perimeter of the stone, inspecting it's engraved surface. This was truly a world-class find. Not only was the stone striking for its sheer size, but the sculpted surface was a stellar example of the ancient Egyptian stone carver's art. The face of the monolith was organized, like a target, into a series of concentric rings. The outermost ring contained thirty-nine characters written in the strange language Taylor had showed him. Inside the next band, there were symbols that were clearly related to ancient Egyptian writing. They seemed to be an extremely early, extremely crude version of the later hierogylphs. Next was a ring of strange arched lines crossing the surface of the stone in different directions. Some of the points where these lines intersected were marked while others where not. It looked like some ancient form of geometry. But it was the engraving at the very center that defined the stone as a masterpiece.

Langford hopped up onto the stone for a better look at the centerpiece. Over a background of the precisely cut arching geometrical lines, there were symmetrical etchings of the goddess Nut. Arching her back to hold up the sky, she fed the children of Earth from her breast while they sailed beneath her in the Boat of a Million Years. Between these beautiful pictures, at the very center of the stone, was a cartouche in the classical style. Inside the oblong cartouche, a frame around a sacred name or word, were six of the strange hieroglyphs from the outermost ring. Did these characters spell the name of some prehistoric pharaoh? Was it some sort of message?

"Very queer," muttered Langford, an accomplished student of Egyptian writing. He shook his head and came back out to the periphery of the ring, where he studied the second ring for a few moments before speaking to Taylor and the others.

"This inside band is somewhat legible: this one here could be the symbol for years . . . a thousand years . . . heaven, the stars or something like that . . . lives Ra, sun god. But what in the world do you make of these outer symbols?"

As Langford bent down to study the signs, he asked himself the same question Taylor and the others had been pondering all afternoon. Have we found an undiscovered language? And if so, who were its authors?

"What are these things over here?" called Catherine, rummaging through the neatly stacked collection of "incidental finds"—each one tagged, bagged, and cataloged.

Taylor explained. "Those are little pieces of the tools and cups and things that the workmen used when they buried this stone. But look at this one," he said, holding up a gold medallion embossed with an *udjat*, a symbol that was half bird and half human eye. He handed it to Catherine. "This was wrapped in a piece of cloth and left on the center of the stone."

"At last you've found something lovely," Catherine said, dazzled.

"The Eye of Ra," Langford said, stepping down off the cover stone for a closer look at the design on the medallion. He turned it over in Catherine's hand before speaking to Taylor.

"Very, very rare to find this motif on a piece of jewelry. Perhaps it belonged to a priest."

Catherine held the find up to the light, admiring it until the men fell back into their conversation. She then unclasped her own necklace and slipped the medallion onto her chain.

"Taylor, if this is a cover stone, what did you find buried underneath?"

Just then a shout went up from the pit, and two hundred workers began to pull the dozens of thick ropes strung through the pulleys. Langford wanted to move closer, but Taylor grabbed him by the sleeve and led him to the top of a small hillock to one side of the pit.

"Trust me, we're in the best spot."

Everyone in the dusty valley, from the most highly educated scientist to the poorest of day laborers, understood they were watching a singularly remarkable event: the excavation of Earth's strangest-ever archaeological find. Responding to the foreman's rhythmic command, the fellahin slowly pulled the ropes taut, lifting a giant quartz ring, more than fifteen feet tall, up from its centuries-long sleep. Perfectly round and the lustrous color of pearls, it was an oversize, meticulously wrought jewel. The entire surface was etched and decorated in intricate detail, as complex as an electronic circuit board, as beautiful as a sultan's amulet.

"It's one of God's bracelets," Catherine said excitedly to her father.

In his decades of investigation and research, Langford had never seen anything like this. In spite of its design similarity to certain first dynasty finds, it seemed impossible that ancient Egypt could have produced anything so technically advanced. Seven fist-size quartz jewels were set into the ring at even distances, each one surrounded by a golden shroud. These shrouds were replicas of the striped pharaoh's headdress, or nemes, like the one on Tutankhamen's famous death mask. Running along the inner edge of the ring were the same indecipherable hieroglyphs found on the cover stone.

When the workmen had the ring standing at a ninety-degree angle, they began to prop it up with a series of padded wooden poles. Taylor pulled the dumbstruck Langfords a few paces to the right. As the sun passed behind the ring, they were surprised to find that the material was semitranslucent.

"What's it made of?" Langford asked.

Taylor shrugged. "Beats me. It's harder than steel, but there's no oxidation or corrosion. Some type of quartz, but not one that I can identify."

Langford turned back to the ring and stood there calmly for a moment before suddenly erupting in a giant roar of celebration. "We did it!"

Catherine watched as her father, usually so stiff and formal, wrapped his surprised American partner, Taylor, in an exhilarated bear hug. The two of them broke into a wild, shouting celebration dance. Then something went wrong in the pit.

The fellahin were shouting and pointing at something. Then they began to abandon their work before the support poles were securely in place. The huge ring tottered dangerously, threatening to fall over and crush the crowd. Taylor ran toward the pit shouting in Arabic.

Langford turned to Catherine and commanded her sternly in Swedish, "You are not to move from this spot."

She waited as long as she could, about five seconds, before chasing after him to investigate. The situation in the pit worsened to utter chaos within a matter of seconds. While scores of people were leaping in to man the ropes, scores more were fighting to get out. Everyone, it seemed, was shouting at the top of their lungs.

A moment later, Catherine could see the problem. A section of the bedrock had split open leaving a deep gash where one of the supporting poles had been anchored. She watched as Taylor and her father led the effort to resecure the beam. Whatever was at the bottom of the freshly opened hole was sending a panic through all the Arabs who looked down at it.

Catherine couldn't stand it any longer, she had to see. She hurried around to the far end of the pit and slithered down one of the walls. Her father and the other men were down in the dirt working right beside the mysterious cavity. She climbed over the ring itself and came into the crowded circle of workmen at it's center. She pushed her way between the men and peeked down into the hole.

"Fossils!"

"Catherine!"

She heard the anger in her father's voice, but couldn't take her eyes off the freakishly twisted figures the Earth had opened to reveal. Partially buried in the stone, the bones splintered as if crushed with great force, was a very human-looking hand. But next to it, flattened to sharp angles was what looked like a large exoskeletal head—definitely not human. The chilling thing was, the shiny black almond-shaped eye staring out of the head. It could have been rotten biological tissue that had petrified, or a thick sliver of onyx set into a statue. Or perhaps the fellahin were right: over and over they used an Arabic word she recognized, the word for devil.

Hypnotized by this mangled preview of hell, Catherine felt herself being lifted into the air, floating toward the edge of the pit. Her father plunked the girl down, gave her a long hard stare that meant his patience was exhausted, then ordered one of his assistants, a rotund young man from Liverpool, to keep an eye on her.

For several minutes, as the men worked to steady the ring in its upright position, she sat watching the last light of afternoon deepen into violet evening. She stared up at the ring, strange desert jewel, and came to an irreversible decision. She promised herself no matter how long it took, no matter how hard the job was, she was going to solve the mystery of where the ring had come from. She got to work immediately, running to her tubby escort and making an announcement.

"I'm going back to the car."

Sensing he had no choice in the matter, he followed her back to the limousine where she set to work thumbing through her copy of *Ancient Egypt*. Soon she found what she was looking for: a picture of the god Anubis, the jackal-headed deity responsible for shepherding the deceased down to the Land of the Dead.

"Look at this," she said, passing him the open tome. "That smashed-up thing down there is Anubis. We've got to show this to my father."

Her companion, who'd gotten only a quick glimpse at the carnage before he was conscripted into the role of baby-sitter, took the book and laid it across the hood of the car. As he was squinting at the page, another chauffeur-driven motorcar pulled up. Out stepped the Egyptian Under-Secretary of the Ministry of Antiquities himself, come to pay a "routine" visit.

As the foppishly dressed, mustachioed bureaucrat strolled past, surrounded by his entourage of flatterers, he tipped his hat to the little girl.

"Good evening, Miss Langford. Has anything interesting happened today?"

3

*LOS ANGELES,
PRESENT DAY*

Soaked from head to toe, toting an overstuffed book sack and muttering to himself, Daniel Jackson slogged north along Gower toward Sunset Boulevard. He was a clean-cut man with sandy brown hair and a fair complexion, just shy of thirty years old. He had forgotten his umbrella and didn't have enough money for the bus. His shoes looked like hand-me-downs, but the long cashmere trench coat he was wearing gave him an air of respectability. As he walked, he seemed to be lashing out at some invisible enemies.

In fact, Daniel had to ask himself whether he was really going over the edge this time. What was supposed to have been his day of renewal, his reacceptance into the academic "community," felt instead like his entombment day. Turning west on Sunset, he entered the little grocery near the corner hoping Mr. Arzumanian would let him put a bottle of wine on his tab. He figured that if it was his burial day, he might as well get embalmed.

"Mr. Dan, my friend, what's happen'?" boomed Arzumanian, burly and habitually enthusiastic.

"Amen ench shat ahavor ar. Nrank char hasskanum yes enchkar khalatse em." Daniel summarized the nightmare in fluent Armenian. "So, I was hoping to get a bottle of wine, but I don't know when I'll be able to pay you back."

"I got idea. *Yes kpokhem,"* replied the shopkeeper, offering a trade. He needed Daniel to translate a negotiation between himself and one of his suppliers who spoke only Greek. He wanted to make the call right away, but when he saw the pain on Daniel's face, he suggested they put it off until the next day instead.

With the bottle of booze completing his "look," Daniel stepped back into the rain and headed for home, wondering how he'd ended up like this. Wasn't he the boy who had won the scholarships in high school for his translations of Phoenician poetry, then had been accepted at UCLA when he was only sixteen? The young wizard with the triple major in languages, philology, and ancient history? How had he let so much promise slip through his fingers to end up a scorned, dead-broke, friendless, lonely, unemployed, and very wet ex-professor? He remembered that disturbing statistic about the percentage of boy-genius-types suffering from early insanity. Daniel knew he was in a bad way.

He splashed his way across the parking lot of Tkenchenko's Tires, a seedy garage in a crumbling brick building. He saw the owner, Vladimir Tkenchenko, shaking his balding head in disgust from under a Lexus he had up on the hydraulic lift. Daniel lived in the converted office space above the garage and, several months behind in his rent, had already been served his eviction notice. Unless his luck changed pretty soon, he would have to start calling everyone he knew, asking if he could sleep on their floor for a few nights. He walked right past Vladimir and up to the shop's grimy business counter.

"Any mail for me?"

Sitting at the desk laughing into the telephone was the prettiest girl Daniel knew, Svetlana. When she saw who was asking, all the joy went out of her expression. Without interrupting her conversation, she stood up and dropped two pieces of mail on the counter. A few months earlier, before his grant money was gone, things had been different between them. They had joked and flirted and even gone around the corner for Thai food a couple of times. But just when things were starting to warm up between them, he'd run out of funds and had turned into "the problem tenant."

He inspected that day's correspondence. A "Final Warning" from the phone company and another missing children card, which Daniel studied, just in case.

Daniel, even more deflated than he was before, walked out of the garage and sat down in the drizzling rain on a stack of spent radials, staring into space. Across the street, a filthy homeless man was lecturing a cat about not digging in the garbage only ten feet from where a tough-looking chauffeur was guarding his sleek limousine. What a messed-up city.

His mind began replaying the conference and the disastrous speech he had given that afternoon to the nation's top archaeologists. Most of them knew him by reputation and thought he was slightly demented, a victim of too many science fiction novels. Unfortunately, today's events had only reinforced their opinions. The articles he had published over the last year or so had been greeted with universal scorn by the academic "community." Even though his research methods and the depth of his information were still admired, the conclusions he was drawing from the evidence were increasingly "different." He was rocking the boat, and his colleagues attacked him savagely in the professional journals.

"Ignores long established facts," was a typical comment. Some of them went beyond criticism into personal attacks: "Jackson is either misguided and incompetent or he is engaging in substance abuse." Or, the one he had clipped out and taped to the kitchen wall, "This is the sort of archaeology we expect to find in *The National Enquirer* . . . his work has no place in the world of respectable science."

Daniel was fully aware of how unconventional his conclusions were. That's why he had hedged at first, publishing a very watered-down version of what he really believed. But he was convinced that his theories conformed to the facts better than the time-honored explanations of early Egyptian civilization.

When he had walked into the giant Scottish Rite Temple on Wilshire Boulevard that morning, he knew he would be facing a skeptical audience. But he hadn't expected them to be hostile and downright insulting.

Dr. Ajami, his department chair when he taught at Columbia, had flown out to participate in the conference. When none of the event's organizers wanted to introduce Daniel, Ajami stepped forward and gave Daniel a glowing introduction:

"He graduated with his Master's at the age of twenty, speaks eleven different languages, and I fully expect his dissertation to become the standard reference of the early development of Egyptian hieroglyphics. He has written several seminal articles on the comparative linguistics of the Afro-Asiatic language groups, and, of course, on the development of the Egyptian language from the Archaic Period to the Old Kingdom, which will be his topic today. Please welcome one of Egyptology's most promising young scholars, Daniel Jackson."

As he was making his way to the podium during the introduction, he overheard a pair of aging professors enjoying the following conversation. Daniel recognized them as two of the dinosaurs of American archaeology.

"Ah, another wunderkind," blustered the pudgy Professor Rauschenberg.

"I own socks older than this kid," chortled the lanky Dr. Tubman.

They gave Daniel a skeptical once-over as he made his way past them. When they assumed he was out of earshot, they continued:

"Not quite up to Sir Allen Gardiner," the one snickered.

"But let's hope he's not another Wallace Budge!" the other guffawed.

Although Daniel didn't think it was funny, he understood the obscure joke. Budge was a maddeningly dull lecturer, known for putting huge roomfuls of his colleagues to sleep with an avalanche of details.

Once Daniel was settled at the podium, the air in the room was thick with tension. He was an unpredictable scholar, something his profession wasn't used to. He glanced at the ceiling for a second, just long enough for everyone to wonder what he was doing, then he suddenly turned and shot a question to Professor Rauschenberg:

"Sir, what kind of car do you drive?"

Confused, the old fellow answered, "A Ford."

"A Model T?" Daniel's question got a laugh.

"I'm not quite that old. I drive an Escort."

"I see." Daniel scratched his chin. "Power steering and power brakes?" he asked.

"Don't forget power windows!" he old fellow said, trying to play along.

"So, in the unlikely event that a long-dormant volcano erupts in Santa Monica this afternoon and we're all exhumed hundreds of years later by wunderkind archaeologists, there's really no chance of them mistakenly dating you and your car to the early part of this century."

"What are you driving at?" asked Rauschenberg's companion, Dr. Tubman. Indeed, no one in the audience had the slightest idea where Daniel was leading them.

"Henry Ford starts out modestly, almost primitively, with the old Tin Lizzy, the Model A. Then he slowly develops his product into the sophisticated technology we enjoy today.

"Which leads to my central question about the ancient Egyptians: why didn't their culture 'develop?' I believe the evidence shows that their arts, sciences, mathematics, technology, techniques of warfare are all there, complete from the beginning!"

Daniel gave them a minute to mull and murmur, then went back on the attack.

"What I want to argue here today is that the Egyptians of the pre-Old Kingdom era somehow 'inherited' all of these arts and sciences. Then, after a short 'getting acquainted' period, we see the full flowering of what we call ancient Egypt."

There was an audible, clucking reaction in the audience. He pressed on.

"Their writing, for example. The hieroglyphic system of the first two dynasties is notoriously difficult to interpret. The common wisdom holds that it is a crude version of the more complex writing we find later, at the time of the Old Kingdom. *But*, what I have tried to demonstrate in a series of articles, is that this early language is already a fully developed system, a combination of phonetic and ideogrammatic elements. If this is true, they were able to move from crude cave paintings to a complicated system for describing the world and themselves in virtually no time at all, a few generations."

Daniel paused and watched quietly as the first group of scientists made their way to the exits. He wanted to argue that the old system was even more elegant than the later hieroglyphs, but since he was the only person who could read them fluently, he knew he'd be talking to the air. He changed the subject.

"Let's take another example. The theme of today's conference is Khufu's Pyramid," he began.

Dr. Ajami coughed politely to catch Daniel's attention then nodded, as if to say that is indeed the theme, please stick to it.

"The same argument applies to Khufu's Pyramid. Most scientists believe that this masterpiece of engineering must have been the result of generations of practice. According to this theory, Djoser's Step Pyramid at Saqqara, the so-called "flat pyramid" and the large tombs at Abydos are seen as warm-ups, learning exercises that lead to the infinitely more complex and precise Khufu's Pyramid.

"As many of you know, I don't subscribe to that theory. In my view, Khufu's Pyramid must have come first, to be followed by the lesser structures just mentioned. The evidence supporting the traditional sequence of construction is based on folklore and written records that were made hundreds of years after the fact. The scant evidence we do have suggests, in my view, that the people living along the Nile were slowly forgetting how to build these structures, getting worse and worse at it with each passing generation."

Another contingent of conferees stood up and walked out. Others were giggling audibly, but Daniel pressed on. He didn't have any other choice.

"Unfortunately, the many attempts to determine the construction dates of the pyramids using carbon C_{14} tests haven't given us conclusive results. Enough conflicting data exists to justify just about any theoretical position.

"But ask yourselves this question: All the lesser pyramids are heavily inscribed with the names of the pharaohs who ordered their construction. The mastabas surrounding the pyramids are blanketed with cartouches announcing the names and titles of their owners, lists of offerings, construction dates, which gods they worshiped, the musical instruments they played, etc. Typically, we find painted histories in these tombs, extolling the many godlike qualities of the person buried there. The pharaohs were the greatest egoists in the history of the world. And yet, the greatest pyramid of them all, Khufu's, has no writings whatsoever. Not a mark anywhere, inside or out. Does that make any sense?''

An imposing older gentleman, Professor Romney of U. C. Berkeley, got to his feet and interrupted.

"It's an interesting theory, Dr. Jackson, one that most of us are familiar with.''

Someone in the crowd began humming the *Twilight Zone* theme, which cracked up some people and left others confused.

Romney, a tall gaunt man, was not distracted. He stared at Daniel and continued.

"You suggest the pyramid wasn't built for a pharaoh because there wasn't a name on it. But what about Vyse's discovery of the quarryman's inscription of Khufu's name written inside the relieving chamber, sealed since its construction?''

Daniel rolled his eyes. "Oh, come on! That discovery was a joke, a big fraud perpetrated by Vyse himself.''

Not only was that the wrong thing to say in front of this conservative crowd, it was definitely the wrong way to say it. The audience erupted into angry, vehement dissent. A few of the more boisterous even began to boo. Another score of professors stood up and left.

Professor Romney made his voice heard over the shouting: "That's too easy, Dr. Jackson. If you had done your homework, you wouldn't have to defame the good reputation of dead men to support your ideas,'' he thundered.

Up to that point, Daniel had maintained a certain ironic amusement with how badly things were going. That changed to a hostile, lethal precision in the bat of an eyelash.

"Before leaving for Egypt,'' he began, "Vyse bragged that he would make an important discovery that would make him world famous. Using his father's money, he hired an elite team of experts and brought them to the Giza Pyramids. But after several very expensive months, they had nothing to show for their troubles. So Vyse fired the lot of them and imported a gang of gold miners from his father's South American mining operation. Less than three weeks later, they 'discovered' what forty centuries of explorers, grave robbers and scientists could not find—the secret room, 'sealed since construction.' In this otherwise empty room, they found the thing that made Vyse's reputation: the long-sought-after cartouche with the name of Khufu. The cartouche appears on three walls of the chamber, but, strangely, not on the wall Vyse sledgehammered into rubble to enter the room. The name is written in a red ink that appears nowhere else in ancient Egypt. It is astonishingly well preserved and, incredibly, it is misspelled.''

"Well, what can you expect from an illiterate quarry-man?" Romney asked.

By this point, Daniel had abandoned the podium and was stalking up and down the stage like a hungry circus tiger. He walked to a chalkboard and, with surprising speed, wrote out a series of hieroglyphs.

"This is the symbol Vyse claims to have found in the relieving chamber. Now we all know, if we've done our *homework*"—he stared bullets at Romney—"that Vyse carried with him the 1906 edition of Wilkenson's *Materia Hieroglyphica* published in Amsterdam by Heynis Books. Diligent students such as yourself, Professor, will not have failed to notice that in the very next edition the publishers include a loose-leaf apology listing the errata in the previous edition. This list includes the hieroglyphic for the name 'KHUFU.' They'd misprinted the first consonant of Khufu's name. It should have looked like this . . ."

Daniel drew an almost identical set of symbols vertically down the chalkboard.

"What an exceedingly strange coincidence that the cartouche Vyse discovered is misspelled in the exact same way! If a quarryman had misspelled the name of the pharaoh, especially on his burial chamber, he would have been put to death and the wall would have been torn down and rebuilt."

Daniel paused and gave the professor an ugly look, adding, "But I'm sure you knew all of this already because you look like a man who takes his homework seriously."

These last words were delivered just as Professor Romney stormed from the conference hall. Before he left, he turned for one parting shot.

"You sound like a bad television show or that *Chariots of*

the Gods book." That brought a few chuckles and scattered applause, but Daniel could feel he had won back some of the audience. A few of the important names were still in the room, and now he hoped they were ready to listen.

"Now if we could get back for a moment. Perhaps the real origins of their civilization lay buried in the wadis of the Western Sahara—"

"Professor, if I may." At the very back of the room, in a smart, expensive dress and oversize glasses, stood a woman who looked to be about sixty years of age. In fact, she was much older.

"Let me say first," she said with a faint accent, "that your command of the facts is impressive. I have just one question: Who do you think built the pyramids?"

This was the question Daniel had hoped to avoid. No matter what his answer, ridicule would surely follow. Daniel had learned over and over again that when it came to matters of Egyptian history, the academic community behaved like religious zealots. It was as though all previously accepted theories were sacrosanct, written in stone by the great Almighty. All those who challenged these findings, condemned as heretic. Daniel had hoped that he could stimulate a diatribe with his colleagues in the audience and reexamine this period with an open mind, acknowledging that there are still so many unanswered questions about the very nature of the origins of Egyptian culture. But the moment the question was asked, Daniel knew it was only a matter of time before this symposium would disintegrate into another humiliating experience. Reluctantly Daniel stammered an answer.

"That's, er, the whole point," he told her, "I have no idea who built them or why."

A collective groan of disappointment went up in the lecture hall. The stylish elderly woman nodded briskly, as if she were satisfied with that answer before she turned and left.

A heavyset bearded man in a tight shirt called out a suggestion in a mock English accent. "The lost people of Atlantis?"

Those people still in the audience laughed and then began gathering up their belongings.

"Or Martians, perhaps!"

"I didn't say that," Daniel defended himself.

"No, but you were about to," the bearded man retorted.

"You're missing the point entirely," he said into his notes. The atmosphere in the room was about as intellectual as a school cafeteria during a mass food fight. More than half the audience was gone and more were leaving. Fishing through his pile of documents, Daniel found the report he wanted and vainly attempted to continue, speaking into the microphone without looking up.

"New geological evidence dates the Sphinx back to a much earlier period. Knowing this to be true, we must begin to reevaluate everything we've come to accept about the origins of Egyptian culture. We simply have to start from scratch . . .

When the door closed behind the last laughing group of conferees, Dr. Ajami, who was still sitting patiently on the podium, approached Daniel. His mood was plain.

"I'm very, very disappointed with you, Daniel. I thought we had an understanding that you wouldn't discuss this nonsense here today. I took a risk presenting you here today, tried to do you a favor, but now I'm afraid you've killed your career. Good-bye." Then Ajami joined the others in the lobby.

Daniel, his hands beginning to tremble, his face hot with humiliation, stared out at the vacant auditorium before quietly closing his notebook and leaning to the microphone.

"Are there any questions?"

As Daniel sat in the rain watching the ink on his phone bill start to run, he thought about the old woman at the back of the auditorium again. How he'd like to chat with her over a nice cup of tea and then strangle her to death. She had breezed into the room just when he'd turned the tide, and had asked him the exact question he was trying to avoid.

At length, he stood and made his way upstairs to his apartment where he met with yet another unwelcome surprise: His front door was standing wide-open.

"Burglars," he whispered.

Normally he would have run away and let them take whatever they wanted, but not today. Sopping wet, he slipped in the door and found the umbrella he had set by the door so he wouldn't forget it. Normally a real peacenik, Daniel stalked down the entry hall, poised for a fight.

Edging around the corner, he could see one of them going through his desk. Leaping into his front room, umbrella at attack position, Daniel found himself face-to-face with the same elderly woman from the conference. She looked up for a moment, then went back about her business, nonchalantly leafing through the papers on his disorganized desk.

"Come in," she said with the trace of an accent. Her voice was calm, professional. "Your cleaning lady must be taking the year off," she said without much of a grin.

For the second time today, this woman was confusing him to the point of semi-speechlessness. Gathering his wits, and relaxing his death grip on the parasol, he formulated his question.

"Uh . . . Is there some . . . What the hell are you doing in my apartment?"

"Now this is a truly beautiful piece of art," she said, picking up the graceful sculpture of an Egyptian woman that Daniel kept above his desk. The marble bust, with traces of its original paint, showed the delicate and very beautiful face of a young woman. "I'd guess fourteenth century B.C. probably from the area around Edfu." She glanced around at the secondhand and thirdhand furniture before asking, "How did you ever manage to afford it?"

"Please be very careful with that," he said nervously. Daniel didn't want to discuss how the treasure had come into his possession. Yes, it was his only expensive possession, but it was far more valuable to him than any price it could fetch in dollars. His visitor, sensing how concerned he was, set it back carefully on the special shelf above the cluttered desk.

Daniel finally placed her accent. It was Swedish, but was now so slight that he guessed she'd been living in the States for most of her life. Everything about this woman spoke of power, privilege, and complete self-confidence. Only the inch-thick lenses of her glasses, which magnified her eyes to the size of half-dollars, disrupted the effect. She peered through them now at Daniel.

"I've come to offer you a job."

"Job?" His mind started to race. "What kind of job?"

Strolling over to a framed snapshot on the wall, she changed the subject once again. ''Your parents?''

''Foster.''

''Oh, that's right. Your parents died in that plane crash back in . . . what was it, '73?''

''Ah yes, let me think,'' Daniel broke into a savage imitation of the old woman, ''yes, I believe it was '73. An excellent year for a fiery death, wouldn't you say?''

The woman realized she'd made a hurtful mistake and apologized, but Daniel didn't let her off that easily.

''No, really, if it would amuse you, let's definitely have a chitchat about the way my parents died.''

When Daniel was finished, he walked past her into his small kitchen for something to drink. He stared into the wasteland of his refrigerator until the woman continued.

''My name is Catherine Langford. And I have some very early hieroglyphics I'd like you to work on.''

''Since when is the military interested in hieroglyphs?''

Catherine stopped talking and feigned confusion. ''Military? What makes you think this has anything to do with the military?''

Daniel was guessing. He figured she must've flashed some sort of badge or credential to get his suspicious landlord Vladimir to open the apartment. And that chauffeur across the street was sporting a military-style crew cut, an oddity on the streets of Hollywood. The way she avoided his question answered it for him.

''I think I'm too old to run off and join the Army,'' Daniel told her.

Catherine was delighted with how quick an observant he was. ''Very impressive, Doctor. Look, I wish I could explain everything to you, but there's a certain amount of secrecy involved with this project.''

''Well maybe you can divulge this much: why should I take a job I know nothing about?''

Catherine had her answer ready to go.

''You have no family or friends here in the city. Your landlord mentioned that he'd served you an eviction notice because of your rent being overdue, and there's a stack of unpaid bills on your desk. Now, it looks to me like young

Dr. Jackson needs a job. And after your speech this afternoon, I wouldn't sit home waiting for the phone to ring."

Daniel didn't know what to say. Those were pretty good reasons to take whatever job she was offering.

"But there's an even better reason you should come to work for me, Daniel."

This woman had a lot of nerve. "And what might that be?" he asked.

"To prove that your theories are right."

She unclasped her smart little handbag and took out a set of old black-and-white photos, holding them out for him to inspect. The pictures offered glimpses of the large cover stone the Langford Expedition had found near Giza. There was no indication of the large ring they'd found beneath, or the fossils. As Daniel flipped through the pictures, all the muscles in his face went slack. The expression, which Catherine had seen before, told her that she'd just hired the newest member of her team.

"Enough!" She snatched the faded exposures away from him, handing him another envelope in return.

"What's this?"

"Your travel plans," Catherine explained preparing to go.

Daniel opened the envelope, took one look at the plane ticket, and sneezed. "Denver? Look, as you can imagine, I'm not real big on flying."

"Get over it," she said deadpan. Then, with a smile, she pulled the door closed behind her.

4

YUMA, ARIZONA

The unmarked sedan coasted to a stop in front of a modestly landscaped two-bedroom house in the suburbs of Yuma, Arizona. Although it was almost winter, the noon sun made the street an oven, forcing the souls who lived there to hide in their air-conditioned interiors. Even the dogs, lolling, tongues out in the shade, were too hot to come and bark. The old joke applied that day, the one about the guy from Yuma who dies and goes to hell. When he gets there, he goes home for his blanket.

Doors clicked open and two officers from the nearby Marine Corps Air Station stepped into the heat. Their crisp uniforms announced they were both commissioned officers out on official business.

While the first officer stepped onto the porch and knocked at the door, the other, carrying a thick black folder, surveyed the garage. Evidence of happier times: a basketball rim above the open garage door, bikes parked at attention.

The front door opened, but the door chain was still latched. Through the crack an attractive woman about forty years old peered out at the men. She knew this moment would come, she'd spent the last two years fearing this moment and wishing it would come at the same time. Now they were here, and she hated them. It meant she had lost the battle for her husband's life.

"Mrs. O'Neil?" asked the first officer.

The door slammed closed. The officers looked at one another and were about to knock again, when it swung back open. Sarah O'Neil, still in her housecoat, her hair matted from sleep, scrutinized the officers coldly. Years of working as a schoolteacher had taught her how to freeze boys in their tracks no matter how old or how innocent they might be. But a moment later, her fierce expression began to melt into one of pain.

"Wipe your feet," she said, then disappeared around the corner into the kitchen. The soldiers obeyed her orders, then came into the house. The living room, decorated almost exclusively in white, was a shrine to tidiness. Unfortunately, it did not contain what the men were looking for.

"Mrs. O'Neil, is your husband at home?" asked the first officer.

From the kitchen, the sound of something being sliced on a chopping block could be heard. "Yes he is," she answered.

After another uncomfortable moment, he asked the empty room, "Ma'am, do you think we might be able to speak with him?"

"You can try. Last door, end of the hall," she said, and continued her cutting.

Moving through the living room, they passed a mantel full of carefully arranged photos, each one in a frame. The younger officer picked one of them up: a dozen people at a backyard pool party making goofy faces into the camera. The stark contrast between the explosion of life in the picture and the absence of it in the room was spooky. The soldier carefully replaced the frame and went on.

At the end of the hall, the pair found an open door leading into another orderly room. This one belonged to a teenage boy judging from the sports trophies and the big pool skating poster. Here the officers found what they were looking for. Sitting in an armchair, staring through the window at his own backyard, was a barefoot, shirtless, unshaven man wearing only a pair of blue jeans. His greasy hair was down to his collar. A few moments earlier, he had been holding a pistol, rolling it over in his hands, practicing pointing it at his head, wishing he could pull the trigger. The moment he heard their voices in the living room, he'd leaned forward and stashed the gun in the top drawer of the desk.

Walking into the room, the younger officer smirked before he could stop himself—during the drive from the base, his partner had recited a dozen or so stories about how deadly and skillful O'Neill had been before all the trouble, but then this. This long-haired, out-of-shape, watery-eyed dude who looked like he was strung out on drugs. What sort of classified military communiqué could possibly be going to this burned-out building of a man?

The officer with the folder quickly stepped forward.

"Pardon us, Colonel O'Neil. We're from General West's office."

After a long pause, the man in the chair turned his head to look at them. His eyes were so lifeless, he didn't seem to understand who had entered the room.

The older officer thought it best to repeat himself. "General West sent us here, sir."

With a slow, empty gesture he motioned for them to sit down and get on with it.

Sarah walked into the hallway and noticed that they hadn't closed the door. She took a deep breath and moved to the hall closet, pretending to look for something. She heard her husband talking.

". . . Years old so you aren't even sure if this threat still exists."

"As I told you, sir, everything we know about it is included in this briefing statement."

O'Neil was getting increasingly annoyed with these two. They were from the same office that had run him out of the service in the first place. "Aren't you guys still worried that I'm 'unstable'? Haven't you read my discharge papers?"

The older officer hesitated for a moment before deciding to put his cards on the table. He leaned forward to emphasize how serious he was. He wasn't sure how O'Neil would react to what he was going to say next. "I don't think you understand, sir. We don't want you for this project in spite of your condition. We want you because of it.''

That stopped O'Neil in his tracks. He couldn't believe the incredible arrogance it took to walk into his home, knowing the shape he was in, then inform him, almost matter-of-factly, that they wanted to take advantage of his weakness. He was stunned.

He looked up toward the doorway and saw Sarah standing there, trying to act as if she weren't listening. But she was listening, and now she was suddenly very afraid. She turned her head just enough to make eye contact with her husband. But as quickly as she did, the younger officer was on his feet and pushed the door closed with a sharp click.

As soon as she was alone in the hallway, everything came flooding in at once. She was sure the two men had come to offer Jack some sort of kamikaze mission. The more dangerous the mission, she knew, the more likely he was to accept it. And because of his skill at creating "accidents," she would never see him again. She began imagining the last horrible chapter of their marriage: her sitting at home waiting for the phone to ring so some junior officer with a soothing voice could tell her that Jack had been killed.

She closed the closet, then wandered back into the living room, pausing to straighten the picture on the mantle. She sat on the couch and looked calmly around the room, allowing herself to wonder for the first time whether it wouldn't be better if he went. She knew that's what he wanted. She'd put up a good fight to save him, but perhaps it was time to admit defeat and let go. The familiar dull ache rose up in her chest, the feeling her heart gave her when it was about to break again.

Twenty minutes later, Sarah spied out her kitchen curtains as the officers returned to their car minus the folder she'd seen them bring in. When they had driven away, she walked through the living room to the back of the house where she heard the shower running.

She opened the bedroom door and saw something that brought tears to her eyes almost instantly. Laid across the bedspread was her husband's neatly pressed uniform. Next to it was the black folder the men had delivered.

5

DECODING CREEK MOUNTAIN

Swerving along a twisting two-lane highway deep in the Colorado Rockies, Daniel, never a very good driver, felt it was necessary to check his road map every time he was headed into a turn. As if this weren't dangerous enough, he was sneezing constantly. Over his right shoulder, the backseat was awash with moist tissue paper.

Then, at long last, after four full days on the road for a trip that should have taken thirty-six hours, he saw the sign: "CREEK MOUNTAIN, U.S. GOVERNMENT SPECIAL ZONE."

He turned the oil-burning, steam-hissing muscle car, a black '68 Dodge Charger with a tape of Elvis's Greatest Hits permanently lodged in the 8-track player, off the highway and up the steep, tree-lined entrance road. When he saw the soldiers at the gate, he was so relieved he honked his horn and waved.

Pulling up to the checkpoint, he encountered a pair of not-very-amused Marines, hands on holsters. One of them stepped out of the kiosk and approached the car.

"I'm Daniel Jackson," he said, as if the men at the gate should have been expecting him. "I didn't think I was going to make it."

"Your credentials?"

Daniel made a violent grab for something on the seat, and before the Marines could draw their weapons, he sneezed into it, then tossed it over his shoulder. He handed the stack of papers Catherine had given him over to the guard, who studied them carefully. Daniel sneezed again.

"You got quite a cold there, Doctor Jackson," observed the soldier, inspecting the vehicle's littered interior.

"Uh-huh. Allergies," Daniel told him. "Always happens when I travel."

When they raised the gate and waved him through, Daniel coaxed the Dodge up one last hill and then out into the clearing where he expected to find all the Quonset huts, jeeps, and heavy artillery he associated with the words "military base." Instead, he found two dozen civilian automobiles parked near the mouth of a large cave cut into the side of the mountain. The only indication that this was indeed a military installation was a group of Marines doing calisthenics in a clearing between the pine trees. Daniel found a parking spot and turned off the key. The engine continued to chug as he got out of the car and opened the trunk. It finally died with a loud backfire.

The big soldier who had been leading the exercise drill jogged up behind Daniel as he was struggling to lift his enormous book bag out of the trunk.

"Daniel Jackson?" the sweaty soldier inquired. But before the road-weary archaeologist could answer, this muscular soldier had grabbed his hand and was shaking it eagerly.

"I'm Kawalsky. Lieutenant Colonel Adam Kawalsky. Where've you been? Dr. Langford thought you changed your mind."

"I decided to drive. Took me longer than I expected." The man was six foot, four inches, dripping with sweat and being entirely too friendly for Daniel's taste. "So, is this an army base?"

"I'm not authorized to discuss that," the soldier read him the textbook response.

Daniel had to grin. "No, seriously. Is this like a camp for army scholars, a think tank or something?"

"I don't know what kind of security clearance you have, sir, and until I do, I can't discuss that subject."

Giving the soldier a "whatever" look, Daniel returned to the project of extracting his books from the trunk, now with the additional problem of somebody watching him.

"Help you with that?" volunteered Kawalsky, stepping in.

Daniel tried to warn him: "Careful. They're books, and they're really"—Kawalsky hoisted the bag with one hand, and slammed the trunk shut with the other—"heavy."

Daniel, no wimp, was somewhat alarmed by the ease that Kawalsky was able to lift the literary load. Following the soldier toward the tunnel entrance, he thought he must be one of the strongest men in the world.

They walked through a pair of giant concrete doors and into a dark cavernous hall. When his eyes adjusted to the light, Daniel saw they were in a very large room with a polished concrete floor. Strangely, the only things in the room were a small drab shack made of corrugated tin and a guard's kiosk next to it. Kawalsky signaled to the guard without breaking stride, and the doors of the little shack swung open automatically. Daniel followed him into the small structure.

"We all call this thing the telephone booth," Kawalsky explained, "like on *Get Smart*."

Daniel had no idea what that meant, even when the room around them shuddered and then began to sink. The small room was actually an elevator. One that was descending at a brisk clip. It seemed to Daniel that it was a long way between floors. He watched the numbers go by: 5, 6, 7 . . . Kawalsky, used to it, offered his guest a stick of gum. "Equalizes your ear pressure."

Daniel took the gum and chewed nervously. 13, 14, 15 . . .

"Uh, exactly what floor are we headed for?"

Kawalsky, stone-faced, "That's classified information, sir."

This time Daniel knew it was a joke, but didn't think it was funny—21, 22, 23 . . . Daniel started to say something else, but the elevator stopped in front of the number 28. The doors opened onto a hallway as sterile as you'd find in any hospital. Daniel followed the lieutenant through the buzz of neon lightbulbs, past closed office doors, and around several corners moving deeper into the antiseptic subterranean maze until Kawalsky suddenly stopped and knocked on one of the doors.

"Dr. Meyers? Are you in there, sir?"

The door cracked open and out came the shiny head of a middle-aged man with bulging eyes. He squinted at Daniel through his bifocals before saying, "You must be the fresh meat." He came out into the hallway with a dyspeptic expression on his face. "It's Jackson, isn't it? I'm Dr. Gary Meyers, Ph.D. on loan from Harvard."

His pompous manner made it easy to dislike Dr. Meyers, and Daniel started getting the hang of it right away. Daniel had heard of him, of course—being a professor at a school like Harvard meant sitting on powerful advisory boards, having your articles published in the most respected journals, and enjoying all the benefits of being part of the academic establishment. On the one hand, Daniel could care less about Meyers. He was one of those elite ivory tower professors who hadn't done a stitch of original thinking in years. On the other hand, he knew that without their help, he would never get the grant money and support staff to move ahead with his own career. Furthermore, although he would never admit it, he longed for his approval.

"Where the hell am I?" Daniel wondered aloud.

"A goddamn nuclear missile silo," twanged a woman's voice behind them.

"Dr. Shore"—Kawalsky turned on his heels—"until Dr. Jackson gets his security classification, we are not—"

"Oh, shut up, Kawalsky, you overgrown testicle," she snapped, somehow managing to make it sound flirtatious. Coming out of her office on the other side of the hall, was a woman about forty years old. Short, stacked, and aggressively sexy, she was the kind of creature you'd least expect to find working in an underground military bunker. Prowling straight toward Daniel, she explained in a Texas drawl.

"Don't worry, darlin'. The place has been completely converted, but technically it's still a military installation, so these jarheads get to act like they own the place." Daniel smiled. He knew he liked this woman.

"Anyway, hi. I'm Barbara Shore, the token astrophysicist on the team." Her eye shadow matched the dark blue of her tight jumpsuit, making her look like a dame you might meet in a bowling alley. They shook hands and made small talk for a minute before she turned to Kawalsky.

"Lieutenant, let's show this nice man to his new office,

and you be nice to him or you can forget about that back rub I promised you." In spite of her venomous tone, it was clear she liked the big soldier.

Kawalsky, holding back a smile, turned and led the group down the hall to a door marked 28–42. He pushed the door open and said, "This is where you'll be working."

Daniel couldn't believe his eyes. The "office" was the size of a small warehouse. The walls, over twenty feet high, were covered with large charcoal rubbings and photographic enlargements of hieroglyphics. On the long worktable, a slew of computer equipment was hooked up and on-line. Two smaller tables held various artifacts, and the bookshelf was stocked with every conceivable volume on the subject of hieroglyphic interpretation (including photocopies of everything Daniel had published on the subject). There was even a portable stereo, a coffee machine, and a small refrigerator. But it was the wall directly across from the worktable that caught and held Daniel's attention. Something round and huge was fixed to the wall, floor to ceiling, and covered with a parachute-size sheet. Daniel figured it must be the stone tablet, the cover stone Catherine had showed him in the snapshots. He pulled the cloth to the floor revealing the strange treasure found at Giza all those years ago.

This was the moment he'd driven all the way from L.A. for, and it did not disappoint. Amazed and delighted, he stood there gaping at the ancient stone.

In the meantime, Catherine Langford came to the door, nodded hello to the others, and entered the room. In her own sweet time, she let Daniel know she was there.

"Glad you could join us."

Daniel turned and looked at her. His lips moved as if to speak, but nothing came out. He looked back at the giant monolith once more before asking her the obvious question.

"Where did you find this thing?"

"The Giza Plateau in 1928," she explained, coming up behind him. "You can see that there are two rings of hieroglyphs. With Dr. Meyers's help, we've been able to translate the inner track of writing, which is an extremely early form of hieroglyph. But the outer one has been giving us fits. The symbols, as you can see, are unlike any ever found.'' Catherine let him absorb the information and then dangled the bait in front of him.

"Although we've showed these signs to a number of experts, including a few of the people who walked out on your talk the other day, no one has been able to make heads or tails of them. Like Champollion with the Rosetta stone, we thought the two scripts might be parallel translations; but if they are, we can't find the similarities. It doesn't help that it's written in a circle without any discernible punctuation.''

While Dr. Meyers started into a long-winded explanation of the various decoding programs they had used, Daniel's attention wandered to a translation written on a portable blackboard near the stone. He listened with one ear for a while, but finally interrupted—

"This is all wrong.''

Moving to the blackboard, he wiped away the word "TIME" and replaced it with the word "YEARS.''

"I beg your pardon!'' puffed Meyers moving to protect his translation. He looked to Catherine for support, but she gestured for him to back off, which he reluctantly did.

Daniel was completely comfortable with the hieroglyphs. Over the last three years, he had become virtually fluent in this dead language, the precursor of the writing system used by the pharaohs. Although many of the symbols remained the same, the grammar was radically different. There were probably less than ten people in the world who could read these early symbols. Daniel mistakenly assumed that Dr. Meyers was one of them, and spoke to his eminent colleague over his shoulder as he worked.

"You used Budge, didn't you? Why do they keep reprinting his books?'' Erasing and rewriting at incredible speed, Daniel fell into a hypnotic rhythm as he tried to capture not only the literal meaning but the felling sense of the script. Then he stopped, puzzled.

"Now this is curious,'' he said to no one in particular. "The word *qebeh* is followed by an adverbial *sedjemen-ef* with a *cleft* subject.'' He turned slowly to Meyers and asked: "In his sarcophagus?'' Daniel scrunched up his face like the indelicacy of the translation was causing him physical pain.

"I don't think so," he said condescendingly. "I think 'sealed and buried' is a little more accurate."

As Daniel continued to work, the other people in the room exchanged incredulous glances. They'd all watched Meyers, whose degrees and academic awards were conspicuously framed on his office walls, labor for weeks to translate the message. Daniel's speed was incredible. Within minutes, he had finished and backed away from the board. Moving to the stones, he offered his audience a play-by-play (or glyph-by-glyph) reading of the ancient message.

"Beginning here, it reads: 'A MILLION YEARS INTO THE SKY IS RA, SUN GOD. SEALED AND BURIED FOR ALL TIME HIS . . .' " Moving back to the board, he used the eraser like the sword of Zorro to dispatch the last word of Meyers' translation. ". . . Not 'DOOR TO HEAVEN.' The proper translation is 'STARGATE.' " Then he read the message once more.

Everybody stared at Daniel, stunned by this awesome display of skill. Dr. Shore tiptoed up behind Meyers, whispered something in his ear, and patted him on the fanny.

"All right," Daniel wanted to maintain his momentum, "will somebody please tell me why the military has an astrophysicist working with an archaeologist in a nuclear missile silo studying Egyptian tablets that are five thousand years old?"

"My report says ten thousand."

In the doorway standing at attention was a split-and-polish soldier, Colonel Jack O'Neil. Clean-shaven and sporting a boot-camp–style haircut, he was a man who had undergone a complete and radical transformation. The expression in his eyes was no longer one of being controlled by his ghosts; it was an expression of self-assurance and command.

Kawalsky, spotting the silver eagle insignia on O'Neil's uniform, snapped to attention, "Sir!"

"At ease."

Opening his black folder, O'Neil removed a document and handed it over to Kawalsky for his inspection. There was nothing outwardly unusual about this man, but nonetheless he was frightening. He conveyed irreconcilable opposites to the scientists in the room. At the same time that he seemed as calm as the dead, he looked coiled and ready to strike. The mood in the office, even before Kawalsky handed back the document, had turned black, like finding a rattlesnake midway through an Easter egg hunt.

"Catherine Langford, my name is O'Neil. Colonel Jack O'Neil from General West's office. I'll be taking over from this point forward." Catherine, not sure what to make of this, turned to Kawalsky, who looked up from the document more stunned than anyone, and nodded.

Daniel hadn't heard anything after the words "ten thousand years." As Catherine and the others began to pepper O'Neil with questions, he interrupted them all.

"Wait a second. Ten Thousand Years?? I'm sorry, but that's impossible. Egyptian civilization didn't even exist until—"

"Actually"—Dr. Meyers saw his opportunity to tell Daniel something he didn't know—"the sonic and radiocarbon C_{14} tests are conclusive." Meyers pointed to the tables that held the Langford Expedition's "incidental finds," a collection of tool fragments and pottery shards. "These artifacts from associated and overlying strata have been tested to the same era. Besides"—and how he was getting downright snotty—"they're clearly Epipaleolithic or Neolithic. Probably related to the Natufian in Palestine, which makes them at least that old."

Daniel, milking them for information, tried a different approach. "These are cover stones. There must have been a tomb underneath."

"Something more interesting than a bunch of bones, darlin'," Shore began to explain before she was cut off by O'Neil, who stepped between them.

"Excuse me, Dr. Shore, but that information has become classified."

"Oh, come on, Colonel," purred the astrophysicist, "he's part of the team." O'Neil stared back at her like a thresher stares at wheat. When she saw that flirting was getting her nowhere, she appealed to her boss: "Catherine, what in the hell is going on here?"

Catherine gestured for everyone to remain calm. Over her many years on the project, she'd weathered so many storms and endured so many major setbacks that she knew how to take this one in stride. Besides, she had developed the skill of compromising her way to exactly what she wanted. All the same, she had a bad feeling about O'Neil and the way General West had sent him here without warning. She guessed it must have something to do with Daniel being brought in.

"Effective immediately," O'Neil announced, "no information is to be passed on to nonmilitary personnel without my written permission."

Daniel, nonmilitary personnel if ever there was such a creature, asked the colonel if he was kidding. "I just drove here all the way from L.A. What exactly is it you want me to do here?"

O'Neil, as smooth as a razor blade answered, "You're a translator, so translate." Then he turned to Kawalsky. "Lieutenant, I want all information not directly pertaining to these tablets to be removed from this work space and brought to my office immediately. Until that happens, you are the only individual authorized to be in this room." With that he turned and started out of the office.

Kawalsky, not quite sure, called out to him. "Your office, sir?"

O'Neil, already in the doorway, looked back over his shoulder. "And I'll need an office."

"Yes, sir!"

Before he could get out of earshot, Shore called out, "Who was that masked man?" She made sure to say it loud enough for O'Neil to hear.

Catherine was already on the move. She took off out the door chasing after O'Neil. That left Kawalsky and the rest of the scientific team staring at each other. He was hoping they would cooperate with the orders, because he was in no mood to enforce them.

Daniel still wanted to believe he had somehow misunderstood. "You guys can't be serious about restricting me from information," he said to Kawalsky. "I mean, if I'm going to have any chance of figuring out what this stone says, I'm going to need information. Otherwise, what the hell am I doing here?"

Kawalsky didn't like this situation any more than Daniel did. What more could he add? They'd all heard his orders delivered in no uncertain terms. Inwardly, he was dying. West had taken command of the project away from him after almost three years, just when they were getting close.

Adding salt to the wound, his replacement was this strange, O'Neil character, who, the documents told him, had come out of retirement to take the job.

"Your quarters are over there, directly across the hall. If there's anything you need, don't hesitate to ask."

"Didn't you hear what I just said?" Daniel was about to explode. His life was a big enough mess without this high-handed military bullshit. "How am I supposed to decipher this thing without any information?!"

Kawalsky had no use for being yelled at. He was the sort of guy who would treat you just as well as you treated him. And this was the wrong moment to jump on his case.

"I have my orders," he said in a monotone. He pointed toward the door, the expansion on his face giving Daniel and the others every incentive to use it.

Daniel couldn't believe what he was hearing. "Do you always follow orders? Always?"

"As a matter of fact, I do."

"Colonel, just a minute." Out in the hallway, Catherine caught up with O'Neil. "I think you owe me some kind of explanation. I have been personally assured by General West that I would have complete autonomy."

"Plans change." He shrugged.

"Apparently," Catherine said patiently, "but I'd appreci-ate some elaboration."

O'Neil tried to finesse her. "The way I understand it, the folks at headquarters feel things have gotten a little too loose around here. And now you've brought in another civilian."

"Colonel O'Neil"—her tone made it clear that she wasn't buying that story—"Jackson was approved."

O'Neil didn't want to lie, so he kept quiet.

Catherine sensed as much and asked him point-blank, "This doesn't have anything to do with him, does it? What's this all about? Why'd they bring you in?"

The colonel thought about all the answers he could give her. After West had read the file on Daniel, he guessed this was their best shot and decided it was time to roll in his heavy guns. Something about Catherine made O'Neil decide to tell her the truth.

"I'm here in case you succeed."

6

"BINGO!"

Kawalsky, using both hands to balance a big tray of hot cafeteria food, used his boot to reach out and turn the doorknob. It took him a couple of tries to get it open. Inside, Verdi's Egyptian opera, *Aida*, was screaming through Daniel's boom box at full volume. Without spilling a drop, he pushed backward into the room. But when the door closed, he knew he was in trouble.

The lights were out, and the room was pitch-black inside.

Over the last twelve days, Daniel had managed to make this vast office just as cluttered and messy as his apartment in L.A. had been. The more frustrated he got about not being able to translate the outer ring of hieroglyphs, the worse the room became. Kawalsky, really concentrating now on not dropping the hot food, knew better than to try stumbling around in the chaos.

"Jackson! Hey, Jackson, dinner! Turn on the lights, man."

The music went dead in mid-crescendo. A moment later, the lights clicked on. In front of where the cover stone was mounted to the wall, the Marines on the staff had built Daniel a two-story scaffold, set on wheels, so he could study the beast up close and personal. On the upper plank of the scaffold, all that was visible was Daniel's hand holding a remote control.

"Good morning, Lieutenant" came the voice.

"It's almost eight P.M." Kawalsky growled. Over the last several days, he had come to consider Daniel a royal pain in the ass. With more than a little disgust, he asked, "Why don't you clean this place up a little?"

"That information is classified."

"Ah, give it a rest, Professor." Kawalsky brushed away a pile of potato chip bags and candy bar wrappers, creating a space to set down the tray. He told Daniel that he was going into town and asked whether there was anything he needed.

Daniel flipped onto his stomach and dangled his head over the side. "Yeah. Could you pick me up a point of reference. And maybe some context. No, seriously, Kawalsky, just give me ten minutes along with the goddamn janitor. I'm sure he knows more about what was under this cover stone than I do."

Kawalsky sighed a here-we-go-again sigh. "That might be true," he said, knowing that in fact it was, "but the janitorial staff has clearance."

"Look, Lieutenant"—Daniel's tone got nasty—"you people want me to solve this puzzle for you. You want me to decipher this stone that no one else has been able to read. But you won't give me enough information to do my job."

"Have you got a problem with the food around here?" Kawalsky asked, picking up Daniel's untouched Sloppy Joe from lunch and giving it a whiff.

"How about this." Daniel had another one of his bright ideas. "What if someone anonymously slipped an unauthorized copy of a report under my door? They'd never know who it was. They'd never even know I got it! I'd just figure this thing out, and we could all go home happy."

"Jackson, do me a big favor and get off my back. You know I'm under the strictest kind of orders."

Daniel winced. He was failing, again, to make even the slightest dent in the armored plate he assumed Kawalsky had implanted in his forehead. For him, the military mind was as impenetrable a mystery as the outer ring of hieroglyphs. And both were giving him fits.

He sat up on the scaffold. "So disobey orders!"

Disobey orders? If Daniel were an enlisted man, Kawalsky would already have him on his feet marching toward the stockade for thirty days of solitary confinement. But he was a civilian, and Kawalsky had to take it. The thing that really pissed him off about Daniel wasn't a military issue, it was a human thing. Kawalsky was clear in his own mind about the fact that the two of them were not only worlds apart, but that they were working under difficult circumstances. Recognizing this, he had endeavored to conduct himself in a manner that acknowledged and respected their differences. But Daniel, less in control of himself, less grown-up, had treated Kawalsky more and more condescendingly the more frustrated he became about not being able to decipher the hieroglyphs. Kawalsky, aware of his own limitations, knew he was no brain surgeon. But neither was he an idiot, and he didn't appreciate being treated like one.

The big soldier shook his head in disgust. "It must be hard to always be the smartest guy in the room." Then, after stealing the french fries off Daniels' dinner tray, he headed for the door.

The moment the door closed, Daniel started down the scaffold. He had decided that tonight was the night. They weren't going to lock him in a room with the world's greatest decipherment toys and the most interesting archaeological problem of his generation, then deny him the crucial information he needed to solve it. He grabbed the empty coffee-pot and headed down the hallway. From his desk post the night guard, Higgens, glanced up at Daniel.

"What's up, Doc?"

"How's it hanging, Higgens?" Daniel faked a yawn and shuffled past the guard toward the water supply. But once he was around the corner, Daniel broke into a jog. He ran down the hall to Colonel O'Neil's office. From the pocket of his wrinkled blue oxford button-down, he produced a fingernail clipper and went to work on the electronic keypad guarding O'Neil's door. After he'd jimmied the housing off, he turned out the nail-file blade and laid it across the switching mechanism. Short-circuiting, the contraption exploded with a small electric pop. His heart pounding like a drum, Daniel reached for the knob, opened the door, and stepped inside. There, now he'd done it. Destruction of government property. There was not turning back now. He closed the door behind him.

The office felt about as cozy as the vice-principal's office at Daniel's junior high school. There was an unpadded steel chair behind the utilitarian steel desk. On the desk, O'Neil's computer was in screen saver, generating a lava-lamp-like psychedelic pattern. Daniel opened the tall filing cabinets in the corner, but, except for some local phone books, they were completely empty. Next to the cabinets, set into the wall, was a heavy three-foot combination safe. Daniel's nail clippers were no match, so he moved to the desk and sat down. A quick search of the desk offered next to nothing. There were neatly arranged office supplies, a picture of O'Neil with his wife and son in one of those unbreakable frames, and a Bible in the bottom drawer that probably came with the desk. Had O'Neil predicted Daniel's break-in and systematically removed all clues from the office? Or was he as uncomfortable and as empty with himself as he was with others? Down to his last hope, Daniel hit the space bar on the computer, displaying the main menu. He typed in the word "QUERY" and the computer showed him a list of options. He moved down to "PERSONNEL" and told the machine to search "O'NEIL, JACK COLONEL." The words "PLEASE WAIT" flashed up at him.

The computer in Daniel's room was a prototype 586 while O'Neil's machine was something the Flintstone's might have had around the house. Impatiently, he scanned the walls for more clues. There was a map of the United States, a chart of the stars in the Northern and Southern Hemispheres, and a poster called "The Metric System." Unfortunately for the burglar, this was the most boring office he had ever set foot inside. That's when he saw the guard, or at least his silhouette as it rippled over the corrugated pane of frosted glass. Higgens stopped at the damaged keypad, and Daniel held his breath. After a moment, the sentry continued on toward the bathrooms. Daniel estimated he had two minutes until he came back.

When he looked down, the screen was displaying the following: "O'NEIL, J. COLONEL—RETIRED, TWO YEARS— RETURNED ACTIVE DUTY, ONE MONTH."

Strange. What was important enough about the cover stones to bring O'Neil out of retirement? And why him? What was it about O'Neil that made the brain trust at

General West's office think he was especially qualified for the job?

Daniel queried the computer several more times, but each time the only response was: "CLASSIFIED—ACCESS DENIED." For a mind like Daniel's, one that thrived on the in-flow of fresh information, those were about the most frustrating words he could imagine. At last, he sunk back in the chair and gave up. Tomorrow they would come to his office and, at the very least, fire him. At worst, they'd—he didn't even want to think about all the legal trouble he might get into. But no matter what the Air Force or Marines did to him, he knew that his reputation among his peers, already in critical condition, had just been delivered to the coroner.

Sliding the door open quietly, he peered outside. The coast was clear, but Daniel didn't move. Something was wrong. He closed the door again and walked over to the wall. What was O'Neil doing with a chart of the constellations, a star map? ". . . A million years into the sky . . ." He stared at the diagram for a long minute, his mind slowly gaining speed, then racing like an overheated engine until it smashed into the idea. He literally gasped. Not knowing what else to do, he reached up and tore the chart away from its thumbtacks, then hurried out of the office. He was halfway back to his computer before the last slice of closing-door-light glinted off the empty coffeepot on the desk.

The hot white glare of the computer scanner rolled across the hastily cleared tabletop, and over the surface of O'Neil's chart, digitizing its patterns and uploading them into the computer. Chomping unconsciously on a Fifth Avenue bar, Daniel was working like a six-armed demon—he was in pure concentration mode. Leaning over the keyboard, he isolated a few of the major constellations, then went into "split screen" and began comparing them, one by one, to the mystery-glyphs he'd already put on disc. He concentrated his search on Orio because of its visibility from both the Northern and Southern Hemispheres. Two of the cover stone's symbols were close, but no cigar. Daniel leaned back and glanced up at his exquisite 1400 B.C. statuette, which he'd set atop the computer, his only witness.

"Are we on the right track?"

She said nothing audible, but Daniel bolted upright in the chair and typed in new parameters, allowing him to turn the constellations like three-dimensional objects. Almost at once, he found a strong similarity between Orion and one of the mysterious symbols from the outer ring. This same symbol also appeared inside the elliptical cartouche at the center of the stone. But the fit wasn't perfect. The lesser stars connected to the star Betelgeuse to form "the hunter's bow" were absent. And Rigel wasn't connected to Sirius in the traditional way.

Those words: "in the traditional way."

Daniel stood up, walked across the room to the bookcase, and did something he hadn't done in years. He consulted the work of Professor Budge. Opening to the Appendices at the back, he found another map of the constellations, different from the first. Grinning now, he sat back down. He looked once more at the screen, then down at the book, then into the black eyes of his Egyptian companion.

"Bingo."

7

THE SEVENTH SCHOOL

Shortly after dawn on a chilly pine tree morning, a Cadillac limousine from Lowry Air Force Base in Denver passed the checkpoint and, moments later, slid to a stop outside the gaping mouth of an entrance that the Army Corps of Engineers had cut into the mountain. Several high-ranking officers, hastily gathered from different parts of the country, stepped out of the vehicle and marched across the pavement. At the center of the group, a pace ahead of the others, was a stern soldier about fifty years old, the breast of his tight blue uniform jacket heavy with medals. It was General West. Respected and feared by all who served under him, West was famous for three things: for always making the right decisions under pressure, for erupting into superhuman fits of rage when his orders were not executed exactly as he wished, and for being the best damn poker player in any branch of the armed forces.

The group strode through the giant concrete doors, the silo's first line of defense, and into the chilly darkness of the mountain's interior; their hard shoes clicking like hooves on the concrete. They stepped onto the waiting elevator platform and made the long trip down.

When the doors opened on the 28th floor, O'Neil was waiting for them.

"Jack O'Neil, how the hell've you been, soldier?"

O'Neil shook his hand and lied, "I've been good."

West nodded, but he knew it wasn't true. After O'Neil's problems began, he'd started reading every document the Army had with O'Neil's name on it, especially the psychological status reports coming out of the veteran's hospital. For two years West had been waiting for just the right time to use him again. This was the perfect mission.

"How about Sarah?" the general asked. "My men said she acted a little nervous."

O'Neil was cagey. "Some days are better than others, but she's getting better." O'Neil, for his part, had no illusions about why the general had called him back. The words the officer had said to him back at his home still echoed in his mind. He wasn't being asked back in spite of his condition but because of it.

As the group continued their march toward the conference room, West spoke under his breath to the colonel, "I've got a few things to tell you that I couldn't put in the report."

Lieutenant Kawalsky, a reluctant chaperon, pushed open the door to the conference room. When Daniel stepped inside, charts, books, and printouts threatening to spill from his arms, he got an ugly surprise.

"Goddamn it," he said to no one in particular. He had been expecting a one-on-one chat over doughnuts and coffee with the notorious General West. That had seemed forbidding enough. This room, however, was crammed with both military personnel and members of the scientific staff, all of them dressed to the gills. Daniel was wearing the same clothes he'd woken up in thirty minutes ago. Bleary-eyed, he looked around and recognized a few faces: doctors Meyers and Shore were there, some of the technicians he wasn't allowed to talk to for security reasons, and, of course, O'Neil.

The room was unlike the others in the silo. It was simply but tastefully decorated. Most of the space was occupied by a large circular mahogany table surrounded by two dozen straight-backed chairs. Daniel wondered how they'd ever gotten the table, larger than the elevator, down here. An elegant floral arrangement had been imported from somewhere, and the kitchen staff had set up a buffet table laden with fare vastly superior to the gruel he'd been picking at for the last two weeks. The whole scene felt swank and polished, like he'd stumbled into a cocktail party being held in the Officers Club at West Point.

This was not good. If these people were anything like the archaeologists he'd faced in L.A., they were going to think his theory about the cover stones was more anti-scientific mumbo jumbo. What made it worse was that they all knew what was buried underneath the stone while he was shooting in the dark.

He spotted Catherine holding court with a cluster of uniformed soldiers. She gave Daniel a wink, then paddled across the carpet toward him with one of the men in tow.

"Daniel!" The old woman was glad to see him. "There's someone I'd like you to meet. This is General West." Daniel, still loaded down with documents, did his best to extend a hand for the older man to shake.

"Hi," said Daniel.

"Pleasure to finally meet you, Professor." West gave the appearance of always knowing what he was going to say next. "I read a few of your articles before I signed off on you participating here." He wasn't above using flattery.

"Oh yeah?" Daniel was both surprised and suspicious. "What did you think?"

There was an edge of challenge in his question, as if Daniel wanted West to prove he'd understood. The last thing Catherine wanted was any sort of conflict between these two, so she tried to change the subject. But West gestured to her that he wanted to field the question. He looked Daniel dead in the eyes for a few seconds, a poker game habit, and then he bluffed.

"I've only got one criticism. Let me put it to you in military terms," West began. "You are so damned concerned with protecting your flanks that you fail to push hard enough to take your objective. The whole time you're writing, you're looking over your shoulder, wondering what other academics are gonna think of you."

"Well, the scientific method of my—"

"Screw scientific method, son. There's only two explanations: you either haven't got the balls to buck conventional wisdom. Or"—and he paused for drama—"the conventional wisdom is right, and you're just plain old fucking crazy. Let's find out which one it is."

The general turned to Catherine and apologized for his language, then he yelled to the crowd.

"All right everybody, we've come a long way to hear this. Let's get down to it and see what this young man has for us."

Daniel went to the front of the room and stood with his back to a wall-size chalkboard. He looked around the room, smiling at everyone as if this were the first morning of a new semester.

"Anytime you're ready," West said sourly.

"Oh, right. Okay, I brought some stuff, some handouts. I didn't know there were going to be so many people here, so you'll have to share." West took one of the rolled photocopies without taking his eyes off Daniel.

When the room was quiet, his explanation began. "Okay, obviously what we're looking at is a picture of the cover stones. On the outer track are the symbols which we assumed were words to be translated. Uh, could you move that stuff?" Daniel unfurled the same large star map he had "procured" two nights earlier, spreading it out across the table. While he was doing so, he stole a glance at O'Neil, but received no reaction. Circling one of the constellations, he went on with his lecture.

"This is the star constellation Orion," he announced, "and although drawn slightly differently, it matches this symbol on the tablets, the cover stone. These symbols weren't fragments of an unknown language. They are, instead, a catalog of the constellations."

"Excuse me, Professor," began the irksome Dr. Meyers, "but couldn't that symbol just as well stand for the constellation Bootes?"

"Or Cepheus or even Puppis?" asked Dr. Shore. "They're all more or less the same shape."

Daniel smiled. Their questions gave him a chance to show off a little. Rummaging through his pile of documents, he found Budge's thick book, and as he flipped through it, he explained.

"Of course the map I've put up shows the Greco-Roman

system of organizing the stars into constellations. But the tablets we want to understand were written much earlier, employing the ancient Egyptians' astronomy.'' Holding the book open for everyone to see, he answered his questioners. ''In the older system, the stars are connected in a slightly simpler way. Look at Betelgeuse, the brightest star in Orion as it appears on this older map,'' he said pointing to the book. ''As you can see, it is identical to the symbol from the tablets.'' Everyone sitting close enough to see the smaller map had to agree, the two shapes were a perfect match.

''Now, if I am right,'' Daniel went on, ''the cartouche that runs down the middle of the central cover stone organizes these constellation symbols into a unique sequential order, forming an address.''

''An address?'' Catherine asked. ''You mean coordinates?''

''Exactly. The centerpiece of the tablets holds the key.'' Taking a black marking pen out of his pocket, he drew the symbols from the cartouche vertically down the board. When he turned again, he was pleased to see that even Colonel O'Neil was leaning forward, hanging on Daniel's next word.

''The cartouche is actually a map. What it gives us are the seven points necessary to chart the course to a given destination.''

''Seven points?'' Dr. Shore asked.

Daniel drew a three-dimensinal cube on the board, then marked each wall of the cube with a dot.

''Yes, to find a destination in any three-dimensional space, we need to find two points in order to determine the exact height: two points for the width, and two for the depth.'' Each time, he drew a line between the dots on the opposing faces of the cube, leaving him with three intersecting lines. ''The cartouche gives us those points of reference.''

General West asked the obvious question. ''You've got six dots, but you said we need seven.''

''Yeah, these six symbols pinpoint a destination, but in order to chart a course to a position, we've got to have a point of origin.''

"I hate to bring this up," sniggered the ever-obnoxious Dr. Meyers, obviously delighted to do just that, "but there are only six symbols in the cartouche. Where's the seventh one?" Daniel couldn't believe that Meyers, of all people, didn't recognize the seventh sign. It would have been simple work to humiliate the vermicular pedant. Instead, Daniel made a game of it.

"What my esteemed colleague is saying is that to the layman it appears that there are only six symbols. It takes trained Egyptologists like ourselves to recognize the seventh symbol. Because the point of origin is not inside the cartouche as we might expect, but down here, below it." Daniel completed his sketch by drawing in the ellipse that surrounded the constellation symbols, and then, with two downward strokes, the "upside-down *Y*" shape coming off the bottom of the cartouche. The finished drawing looked like a tall oval mirror standing on two legs.

"This symbol at the bottom is the point of origin. It's a picture of the place the tablet was found." Daniel began to draw the glyph on the board. "You see, it's two, uh, two of these funny little guys on either side of the pyramid with a sunbeam directly above it. This is also an ancient hieroglyph for 'EARTH.' The sunbeam represents the god Ra."

Daniel waited for a comment, a question, anything. Was another audience going to walk out on him in disgust? Everyone stared at the drawing trying to comprehend the consequences of what he had told them. Since all of them knew what was buried under the cover stone, they knew what the next logical move would be. Predictably, it was Catherine who spoke up first.

"He did it," she proclaimed, and banged her fists down on the table.

"Did what?" Daniel asked.

Dr. Meyers still had his doubts. "There's no symbol like that on the device," he reminded everyone.

"Perhaps there's a hieroglyphic equivalent, or some other kind of representation."

What had Daniel just heard? "Device?" he asked nobody in particular. "What device?"

Dr. Shore winced. She'd just violated the order about passing information to Daniel. She glanced over to Kawalsky, who was giving her a dirty look, one that said: loose lips sink ships.

Catherine got to her feet. She looked first to Colonel O'Neil and then to General West. "I imagine you'll have to show him. He's the only one who can identify it for us."

West looked at O'Neil and pretended to think it over. Actually, he'd made the decision during his chat with Daniel a few minutes before.

"Show him."

O'Neil nodded to Kawalsky, who walked over to the back wall and, folding back a panel, revealed a switch box. He pushed a button, and the entire wall began to slide away, revealing an enormous bay window that looked down and out into a much larger room below. Even before he came to the window to see the contents of the room, Daniel suddenly understood how monstrously large a nuclear missile silo is, converted or not. The whole maze of offices, complete with cafeteria, that had seemed so extensive was only a small fraction of the total space.

The floor of the silo was jammed with sophisticated machinery of various sorts, an extremely high-tech operation. And at the center of this steel landscape of computers and wiring and sensors and steel plank-ways sat the giant ring itself. The same mysterious contraption that Catherine had seen resurrected over sixty years ago from a dusty grave in the middle of nowhere. Now it seemed to be the central component of a single endless glistening machine.

"What the hell is it?" was Daniel's only question.

"It's your StarGate," Catherine told him.

Daniel felt his mind go white, like this rush of strange information was triggering a mental seizure. The thick ring, more than three times his height, had been mounted on a raised steel platform. A wide ramp ran from the floor up to the platform and the mouth of the ring. Now that it was cleaned and polished, there was no mistaking the material for metal. It looked closer to opal, semitransparent but gently bending the light around it into several colors at the same time.

"You found this thing in Egypt?" Daniel couldn't believe it. He wanted to ask more questions, but he heard General West barking an order.

"Take him downstairs and see if he can identify the 'seventh symbol.'" When O'Neil moved for the door, West added, "Not you, Colonel. We have to talk."

Catherine lead Daniel and a dozen curious spectators down a tightly winding circular staircase and into the "Booth," where the handful of technicians who maintained an around-the-clock surveillance, became visibly confused by the sudden intrusion of this large tour group into their tranquil work space.

The darkened room struck Daniel as a miniature version of the Mission Control room in Houston that he'd seen during space launches. It started to dawn on him what this whole project was leading toward. Most of the onlookers crowded around the thick Plexiglas observation window. Daniel went to follow them, but Catherine pulled him over to a video screen that showed him a close-up shot of the ring. The camera out in the silo was fixed on that section of the ring where the symbol for Scorpio was engraved into the crystalline surface.

The camera brought Daniel close enough to appreciate the incredibly detailed ornamental carving work that had gone into the ring's construction. He could also see one of the seven triangular shrouds anchored to the rings outer edge. Made of pounded gold, each of them housed a large chunk of sculpted quartz.

In the greenish cast of the monitor, Catherine suddenly looked small and gnarled. They both took seats in front of the screen as she explained.

"Even though we didn't realize the symbols on the cover stones were constellations, we knew they matched those symbols you see etched into the device, the StarGate. Our problem was that we never knew about the seventh symbol. Now let's see if you can find it."

"Mitch!" Catherine called one of the technicians over, a sleepy-eyed guy about Daniel's age. His nameplate said he was Special Operator Technician, M. Storey. Catherine explained what she wanted.

"No problem, let's give the wheel a spin," said the technician, who typed a long series of commands into the computer. A few seconds later, Scorpio slid off the screen and was replaced by Norma and then Serpens Caput.

Looking through the Plexiglas, Daniel could see the inner part of the StarGate turning like a wheel inside the larger, stationary ring. At the base of the device, a special apparatus had been fitted like a clump around the inner half of the ring. It's motorized rubber wheels were responsible for turning the ring. One by one, the symbols moved across the screen: Libra, Bootes, Virgo, Crater.

Slowly, the visitors in the booth gravitated toward the monitor to see what was happening. Daniel startled them all by suddenly yelling, "Hold it!"

He learned forward and scrutinized the image on the screen for several seconds. A triangle with a circle perched on top. Slowly, he lifted his black marking pen, to Special Operator Technician Storey's dismay, drew the symbol from the cartouche directly over the symbol isolated on the monitor. Clearly, they were the same symbol, just different enough to miss the similarities if you didn't know what you are looking for.

"It's Earth!" exclaimed Dr. Shore.

"Thalassa!" said Meyers.

"Eureka," Daniel translated.

"It's been here under our noses the whole time."

Storey arched an eyebrow at the visitors, thoroughly confused.

For Catherine, however, everything was suddenly very clear. She charged to the back of the room, picked up the intercom phone, and spoke in hushed tones to General West one floor above. When she returned to the group, she issued the order she'd waited her entire life to give.

"Let's run a test."

Like a magic incantation, those simple words transformed the booth into a madhouse of noisy activity. A uniformed soldier with a clipboard shouted out role assignments; technicians scrambled to their stations yelling across the room for up-to-the-minute readings; a bank of large printers spasmed to life and with much staccato squealing, began spitting out data.

"Okay, Mitch, let's take it for a test-drive," said Catherine, pulling up a chair next to technician Storey's. She nodded to Dr. Shore, who called out the first set of numerical coordinates.

Storey pecked at the keyboard with his two index fingers, somehow able to keep the numbers straight in his head, and then his "ENTER." The very next second, the sliding inner wheel of the StarGate turned until the constellation "TAURUS" was at the top. Like an overgrown combination lock, the ring registered the motion with an audible click. Immediately the large shroud surrounding the topmost quartz jewel separated. Like the jaws of a clamp, its two halves slid apart. How the fist-size brick of quartz had a clear path to the center of the ring.

"Chevron One locked on," Storey called out.

The wheel reversed direction until the second figure on the cartouche, "SERPENS CAPUT," was at the top. But this time, one of the clamp-like chevrons near the bottom of the StarGate clicked open. As it did, a low frequently hum began to fill the room, growing with intensity as the unlocking procedure continued. Slowly, everything in the room began to tremble slightly.

"Chevron Three locked on," Storey alerted the room. Then he said to Daniel, "Do me a favor and grab that coffeecup," continuing to hunt and peck, without lifting his eyes from the keyboard. Daniel reached over and snagged the mug that was vibrating its way off the table.

"*Gracias.*"

"*De nada.*"

"Chevron Five is locked on."

As each piece of the "address" was steered up to the top of the StarGate and the whining hum from the machine rose in pitch, the mood in the room grew tense. Daniel silently called the names of the constellations: Serpens Caput, Capricornus, Monocerus, Sagittarius, Orion," and soon, the seventh symbol, "Earth."

As the sixth symbol, Orion, locked into place, Catherine turned to Daniel and whispered to him, "This is as far as we've ever been able to get." By the thick tension in the room, Daniel could feel she was telling the truth. Everyone in the room held their collective breath awaiting the locking in of the seventh symbol.

"How did you know what it could do?" Daniel asked.

"The ring itself. It's made out of a quartz-like substance

unlike any found on Earth. It has remarkable qualities."
Before Catherine could go on, Storey yelled out to the room.
"Chevron Seven is locked on!"

As soon as the seventh sign was in place, the shaking in
the room dropped away and became instead a rich deep
tone. It sounded almost like the lowest possible note on an
old pipe organ. Daniel looked at Catherine, his eyes asking
if that was supposed to happen.

Before she had a chance to answer, a second "note,"
higher than the first came pealing through the safety window, filling the booth. The sound had a disturbing effect on
Daniel, but he wanted to ask Catherine a question.

"Shhhhh." Her finger to her lip, she closed her eyes,
saying, "listen to it."

Daniel listened as a third note sounded and a fourth, each
one at a slightly higher frequency. The strange thing was
that each note was so distinct from the others even though
they blended together. Then he understood. And by the
time the seventh and final tone sounded, he was smiling.
The ring had built a single, self-harmonizing note far more
complex than Daniel, a classical music aficionado, had ever
imagined possible. It wasn't music, but it was beautiful.

Then something much stranger began to happen. Like
watery snakes drawn into the air by a charmer's song, seven
streams of light came out of the quartz gems stationed
around the front of the StarGate. Akin to lasers but obviously obeying different laws of physics, the light came
pouring toward the center of the ring. Literally pouring, as
if someone had turned on a series of garden hoses and liquid
light came spouting out of them. The light pouring upward
from the bottom gems behaved no differently than the ones
coming from the sides or the top. Somewhat like bright
liquid ropes, they all dangled toward the center in a random,
twisting dance before dissipating into thin air."

"*Tres* cool," Story gasped. Catherine and Daniel both
looked at him in agreement, then at each other, speechless.

As the tendrils of light grew in length, they grabbed onto
each other and quickly began to spread until they formed a
thin pool, a solid shimmering surface, like a thin sheet of
mercury stretched over the empty center of the ring.

The gentle beauty of the image along with the strange

harmony of the tone sent a wave of euphoria through the men and women in the booth. Everyone was turning to confirm the feeling, smiling at the others.

But a second later, the mood changed dramatically. The mirage gained mass and started sloshing back and forth like a thick slab of turbulent water. Then it exploded out into the room like a giant wind sock suddenly clawing for their faces. Involuntarily, everyone jerked backward, some tumbling to the floor. Someone started screaming to turn it off, turn it off, but before anyone had time to react, the energy was violently sucked back through the ring and shot out the other side with astonishing, ungodly speed to create the illusion of a tunnel of rushing light or a roaring circular waterfall pouring straight down to hell at two million miles an hour. Only this one wasn't pouring down. It was on its side, pointed at the far wall of the silo, and it was plummeting to a place much farther away than hell.

By now every computer in the booth was screaming its own version of bloody murder, lights pulsing, printouts sputtering, and the technicians attached to each machine were fighting to keep up with the inputs.

Catherine yelled at the people nearest the observation window, asking whether the soldiers surrounding the Star-Gate were okay. Fortunately, they were. "It's guiding itself!" shouted a technician at the far end of the room. Dr. Shore, leaping over stray cable, ran back to see what he had. The man showed her a detailed schematic of the universe with a blue dot pulsing on the screen to represent Earth. A small red *X*, a laser crosshair, began to trek across the monitor, leaving Earth and traveling through the galaxy until it stopped at the far end of the screen. Shore, eyes wide, shouted to Catherine.

"It's locked onto a point in the Cirrian galaxy. It's got mass. Could be a moon or something, maybe a large asteroid."

"Did you say Cirrian galaxy?" Daniel was scratching his head. "Isn't that . . . ?"

"On the other side of the known universe? Yes, it is." Catherine was nervous, but obviously enjoying the moment.

The phone rang, and Storey snapped it up quickly without missing a beat on his keyboard. It was General West calling

down from the room directly above them. As the technician
listened, the expression on his face slowly became one of
disbelief. "You what??" he asked incredulously, but the
next moment his tone of voice had changed. "Yes, sir. Yes,
sir, right away, sir."

"What is it?" Catherine asked over the noise.

"They want to send a probe through," Storey explained,
his eyes wide with skepticism.

"A probe?" Catherine had no idea what West was asking
for. She was about to get back on the phone when through
the observation window, she saw a pair of soldiers wheel in
a refrigerator-size device with a long mechanical arm, a
Mobile Analytical Laboratory Probe. The M.A.L.P., or
Maple Unit as it was called, was pushed to the base of the
ramp leading to the StarGate. It was a giant, awkward, one-
armed steel monster designed by Cal Tech in Los Angeles
that looked like Santa's sleigh redesigned for the twenty-
third century: miniature video cams, atmospheric testing
devices, an automated chemistry lab, paper-thin radar
dishes to scan for broadcast waves. The clumsy contraption
had taken three years to build and was worth several million dollars.

While the probe was being readied, a squad of eight or
nine heavily armed Marines jogged in and took up defensive
positions around the StarGate. Daniel scoffed. Who in the
world were they expecting to break in and disrupt their
little test? One more glaring instance of military paranoia,
he thought.

The phone rang again. This time, Meyers was ready to
pounce. "This is Dr. Gary Meyers. Yes, General. Yes, sir,
we are prepared to monitor any and all activity sent through
the Gate. Yes, sir, it should be able to record that type of
transmission, yes."

As soon as he hung up, Meyers immediately made his
way to one of the computer banks and began explaining
something to the technicians. Most eyes in the room were
still on Catherine, waiting for her instructions. Although she
resented being kept in the dark about the probe, she looked
around the room then yelled enthusiastically, "Let's send it
through and see what happens."

The technicians in the silo hooked the probe to a tow

chain like the ones used to pull roller coaster cars to the top of that first steep hill. When they were finished, they turned and looked up to the conference room above the booth. General West nodded, approving the release of the probe.

The technicians rushed away from the ramp just as the towing chain lurched into action. While the probe trundled tanklike up the ramp toward the turbulent light storm, Daniel asked Catherine an urgent question.

"Isn't it just going to smash into the wall?"

"It shouldn't."

Daniel moved several steps toward the back of the booth just in case she was wrong. When the probe came to the top of the ramp and nosed into the energy field, there was an audible power surge. Just as the first atoms of the machine were being visibly sucked into the tunnel, the body of the machine was swallowed up by the energy field and a blinding white light flared out into every corner of the room.

When they were able to turn and look again, the probe was gone.

The high-ranking military personnel visiting the booth erupted into cheers for a second until they realized the test wasn't over. Daniel, dumbstruck, astonished, dazzled, turned to Catherine for an explanation.

The old woman wiggled her eyebrows and said, "It's starting to get exciting, isn't it?"

"What's happening now?" Daniel noticed the technicians were still glued to their monitors.

"We're waiting to see if it can send data back through the Gate," Meyers told him. They waited for a minute, but nothing happened. Daniel whispered a question to Catherine.

"How long have you guys been working on this?"

"My father found it near Giza when I was a child. But the Egyptian government didn't release it until '74. Then we had to get it from the British, and it took forever to get our financing."

"From the Pentagon." Daniel's distaste was plain.

That hit a nerve. Catherine snapped back, "I've been involved with this project since I was nine years old. It took me more than fifty years to find the money, and without it the whole project would have been scraped. What would you have done?''

Just then Dr. Shore shouted, "Something's coming in!" Now it was the technicians' turn to raise a shout. All eyes turned to Dr. Shore, who was monitoring the inflow of data through the Gate. After a few seconds, the signal started to die. "We're losing it. We're down to thirty percent. Down to five." When Shore pronounced the signal dead, the inner ring of the StarGate turned on its own and shut down.

Catherine joined most of the other technicians crowded around Shore's workstation. Daniel leaned over to Storey and asked what was happening.

"The probe," he explained, "was sending us data, but it's all digitally encrypted and compressed. It's gonna take a couple of minutes to unpack and decode the transmission and see if we got anything worth sneezing at."

While a cluster of technicians led by Meyers crowded around a bank of computers at the back of the room, the mood of anticipation in the room was so thick, the collective blood pressure of the room rose precipitously.

Seconds later, Dr. Meyers made the announcement. "We got it!"

Now the room went crazy. Everyone began cheering and shaking their fists in the air. The entire science staff started hugging each other. Suddenly, they were in control of significant, detailed data about a piece on the far side of the universe. After months of sweating it out in these remote underground tunnels, the really exciting part—from a scientific point of view—was must about to begin. Complete strangers exchanged high fives. Meyers approached Daniel and in his excitement went to give him a hug, but at the last minute settled for a handshake.

"Congratulations, really. You did amazing work." And a moment later, Dr. Shore planted half a dozen kisses on his cheek, saying, "You're a goddamn genius is what you are."

Daniel smiled and returned all the compliments. He couldn't remember a time when he'd seen a group of Ph.Ds anywhere near this happy. As the celebration continued, he found Catherine and pulled her aside.

"You're planning to go through that thing, aren't you?"

"Yes. That's exactly what this is all about." As she was

speaking these words, a group of soldiers entered the booth and took up positions around the mainframe computer. Two of the soldiers, obviously familiar with the room, walked through pulling out removable hard disks and gathering up notebooks. They took all the information recently downloaded from the Maple Unit.

At first, many of the celebrants didn't notice what was happening, and those who did had no idea what the men were doing. But the soldiers' attitudes made it clear that they weren't sent to open champagne bottles. Dr. Meyers walked over and got right in their faces, "What's going on here? What's the meaning of this?"

Just then the intercom phone rang again, and as the impromptu party changed into a series of fierce arguments, Catherine dashed to pick it up. After a moment, she yelled at the top of her lungs:

"*Quiet!* Everyone!" Then she went back to her conversation with General West looking just as eager as a sixteen-year-old girl talking to her prom date. She must have said "I understand" ten times in twenty seconds, her expression darkening each time she spoke the words. Now everyone was quiet, concerned. She hung up and faced the room. "The general says that he's very pleased and that we should all be proud of the work we've done here. He also said that we're all fired. They'll be taking over from here."

8

MILITARY INTELLIGENCE

Daniel didn't stay to hear the screaming. In a flash, he was upstairs hunting the clean white corridors for General West. Instead, he caught O'Neil coming out of the conference room.

"Just what in the hell do you think you're doing?!" Daniel was ready for a fight. "Is that the Army's idea of loyalty? You pen these people up in the ground for months, and then just when it gets exciting, you fire them?"

O'Neil hardly heard what Daniel had said. He had too much on his mind after his meeting with General West, and besides, he didn't particularly care one way or the other about the science staff. All he wanted to do right now was get back to his office and think about tomorrow.

"Doctor Jackson," O'Neil said, trying to calm him down, "thank you for your contribution to the mission. When there is more to report, we'll be in touch."

"You said 'mission.' When are you going through?"

O'Neil fired a look at Daniel that said "back off" and growled, "All pertinent information will be released at the appropriate time."

"And who's going to make that decision, the Pentagon?"

"Military intelligence," O'Neil said.

"Now there's a contradiction in terms."

"You don't know how right you are." And O'Neil continued down the hall.

"Do you really think you'll be able to keep this thing quiet? I'll bet the scientific community would want to know about this."

That wasn't something O'Neil could ignore. He wheeled around and moved carefully back toward Daniel. There was something incredibly menacing about the man. Daniel's throat was suddenly dry. He gulped.

"Well, Professor, who's going to tell them? Everyone else on the staff has signed a secrecy oath except for you." Coming toe-to-toe with Daniel, O'Neil asked with mock courtesy, "Are you going to tell them, Professor Jackson?"

Inwardly, Daniel was on the verge of wetting his pants. But he struggled to remain calm and dry on the outside. Something about O'Neil told you that he could kill you eight different ways with his eyebrows. Not only that he could, but in the right circumstances that he definitely would. Refusing to be intimidated, Daniel came right back at him.

"If I have to, yes, of course."

"Go ahead." O'Neil's words were full of contempt. "But do yourself a favor. When you're on that bus back home tomorrow and you stop off to pick up some of that crap junk food you're always eating, grab the latest edition of *The National Enquirer* and read the story about the space alien baby born with the head of a frog and the body of a man. And when you're done reading, ask yourself if you believe it."

Daniel thought for a moment about how he could prove to the world that the U.S. military had an ancient Egyptian space-travel device buried deep inside a Colorado mountain. But even before O'Neil had gotten to the point of his story, Daniel knew how hopeless it would be for him. No one would believe him. Especially coming from him.

"Is there anything else, Professor?"

Daniel thought a moment and realized he better try another tact. "Please keep me on this mission. I've spent the better part of my life studying languages, ancient Egypt, archaeology, exactly the things this project is all about."

"I appreciate that," O'Neill replied. "But the decision has been made."

Well, if pleading wouldn't work, Daniel decided to get pissed. "I've gambled my reputation and dedicated my life to this. What have you dedicated *your* life to, Colonel?!"

O'Neil started to answer, but then caught himself. He gave Daniel a cold, dismembering stare and said, "Pack your bags and get off this base."

"Hold on, Jack. I think we're going to need him."

Both O'Neil and Daniel spun to see General West leaning out the door of the conference room. He waved both men down the hall and into the room.

When Kawalsky hit the lights two minutes later, Daniel and O'Neil were sitting next to each other in the dark watching television. West had ordered them to sit down and study the decoded imagery the probe had beamed back through the Gate. The probe's camera panned across the surface of a large interior stone wall and kept moving until it showed a brightly illuminated circular form, another StarGate.

"Freeze and enhance," General West commanded.

The general's assistant, Lieutenant Anderman, was stationed at the disk player. A communications technology specialist, he digitally corrected the image and then zoomed in on the details of the ring. Fascinated, Daniel stood and walked to the screen.

"These markings . . . they're different."

"That's why I wanted you to see this," said the general.

Lieutenant Anderman narrated over the image. "The readouts tell us it's an atmospheric match. Barometric pressure, temperature, and most importantly, oxygen."

West walked over and stood in front of the screen. He spoke directly to Daniel.

"We're planning a short reconnaissance mission. Nothing fancy. Survey the area inside a quarter-mile perimeter, gather as much information as possible, and bring it back."

Anderman amplified, "Once you're on the other side, you'll have to decipher the signs on that Gate and, in essence, dial back home. Like a fax machine."

"But here's the thing"—West squatted down, eye to eye with Daniel—"I'm not going to send our men over there unless I'm sure I can bring them back. The question is, can you do it?"

Daniel had another idea. "Why not try reestablishing the contact from this side?"

"Because," O'Neil explained, "once our team goes through, the entire silo will be evacuated and sealed. We don't know what might come through from the other side."

Now Daniel understood not only why the soldiers had surrounded the StarGate as the probe was going through, but why this whole operation was located in such an unlikely spot.

Daniel looked up at the ceiling. Every fiber of his body was urging him to say yes, to promise the general anything he wanted to hear in exchange for being able to visit the place he had seen through the static on the video screen. It suddenly seemed to him that his whole life had been a preparation for exactly this moment, when he would embark upon a dangerous voyage to an unknown and forgotten land. If he didn't go, the story of his life wouldn't make any sense. But what about the others? He looked at O'Neil, and especially at the good-natured Kawalsky. He couldn't put their lives at risk just to satisfy his curiosity. His moment had finally arrived, but now the stakes were too real, too high.

He looked once more at General West, who raised his eyebrows in question.

"Yes, I can do it," Daniel said with resolve.

"Are you sure?"

"Positive."

West nodded, then looked at each of the soldiers in the room one by one. When they had all signaled their agreement, West decided, "Fine. You're on the team. You leave tomorrow at 06 hundred hours."

O'Neil, deep in concentration, sat motionless on a folding metal chair, a dim forty-watt bulb dangling overhead. He was studying the nine-foot long section of earth taken from directly below the StarGate by the Langford Expedition. The pair of fossilized human bodies had been fused directly into the rock over ten thousand years ago, turned instantly into gnarled stone sculpture. The muscular corpses were almost perfectly preserved. The only damage came where the long scepters they carried had been chipped lose and taken away for testing, and several perforations in the bodies where genetic scientists had extracted DNA samples. But the twisted metallic skulls drew and held O'Neil's attention hour after hour.

Since he'd arrived at the silo and taken over the project, O'Neil had spent many hours in the darkened room, contemplating the ghoulish artifact. It was the only way he had to prepare for what might still be on the other side of the StarGate. It seemed to him like a strange mirror, reflecting his own fate, they way he would die. Every bone in his body told him they would still be there, that he would face these warriors, at once so advanced and so primitive. Less than twenty-four hours remained before he would lead his team through to the other side and find out.

It was not a good mission. The probe had made it through, but there was no evidence that humans could survive the trip. Even if they encountered no enemy forces, the chances of coming back from a thing like this were remote at best. And O'Neil's chances were slimmer still. Not only had West given him what amounted to a suicide mission, but O'Neil had no plans to come back. Before General West's men had left his home in Yuma, he knew this would be his last assignment.

For the previous twenty-two months, O'Neil had wanted nothing more than to die. He had become a living zombie: exhausted, broken, empty in every way. More than once, he'd loaded a pistol and wedged his thumb backward across the trigger. But he refused to do it. Not only would it probably kill Sarah, but his religious convictions wouldn't allow for suicide.

Coming from a man who had been responsible for so much violence in his life, this refusal was truly ironic. The black sheep of a fine family, O'Neil was born with chaos and wildness in his heart. By the time he was eighteen years old, O'Neil was brought before the court for the third time. A lenient judge gave him a choice: he could enlist himself in the Army or spend a year in the Washington State Correctional System.

He chose the Marine Corps and from his very first day, he proved himself to be an exceptionally disciplined and gifted soldier. After only twenty weeks, he applied for and won a transfer to the Marine Corps. Combat Development Training Facility at Quantic, Virginia. There he was taught the finer points of infiltrating enemy territory, wilderness survival, political assassination, the manufacture and detonation of explosives, how to blend chemical weapons from common materials. He rose quickly, being promoted to the elite Jump Two Company. Everything was going fine until he started going out on "house calls"—usually political killings that never made the newspapers. That's when O'Neil realized two important things about himself: he was a talented assassin who hated himself deeply for killing, especially when he knew they were innocent. He never complained, never flinched. He buried his conscience and learned to drink scotch. He stopped feeling altogether, earning himself the nickname "Voodoo" because he seemed only to come to life when Jump Two went into action. For seven years, everything that was ever alive in him sunk deeper and deeper to the bottom. On the outside, he was the fearsome warrior who let actions speak instead of words. Inside, he was vacant. And that's when he met Sarah.

She'd just graduated from a small Jesuit college in the area and found a job teaching school on the base. Mutual friends introduced them, and one thing led to another, although no one really understood what a fresh flower like her saw in the withdrawn, taciturn young corporal. She found him fascinating, and she made him laugh. They started seeing each other every day, and two years later, Sarah told him she was pregnant. O'Neil went ballistic, accusing her of doing it on purpose, trying to trap him into marrying her.

Sarah responded by packing a suitcase and driving up to her parents' house in Boston. Only ten minutes after she'd gone, O'Neil made a disturbing discovery: he'd fallen too far in love with Sarah to back out now.

Three days later, in the middle of a blizzard, he showed up at her parents' house and waited all day in the car until she would come out and talk to him. For six hours they steamed up the Ford's windows, fighting like a pair of wet cats until, at four-thirty in the morning, they went into the house and woke her parents. O'Neil introduced himself and then asked for their daughter's hand. In the thirteen years since their marriage, O'Neil had never broken the promises he made to her that freezing night.

Even that last day in Yuma, O'Ncil remembered the commitments he had made. Standing in the doorway as Sarah wept hysterically, trying one last time to reach out and make human contact with him, O'Neil recalled that he had promised to love and cherish her only so long as he should live. As far as he was concerned, those days were gone.

He stood there for a minute, trying to speak, wanting to say good-bye to her. Each time he tried, the words clogged themselves in his throat. Finally, he just turned and started walking away.

By the time West found him sitting in the dimly lit, refrigerated room, O'Neil had already been there for half an hour staring at the crushed figures. O'Neil theorized that when the Gate was buried in stone, these two creatures must have tried to beam through.

He didn't look up when he heard the security door slide open. He didn't need to, he knew West would come looking for him.

"Our people tell me those things used to be alive," West said, walking over to the limestone slab.

"I thought I was doing this alone," O'Neil said at last.

"And you will," West assured him, "as soon as the team completes their survey and returns, you'll be on your own."

O'Neil was resigned to his orders, but he offered his opinion to West. "The more people we send through, the greater the chances something's gonna go wrong. And Jackson could be a problem. He's smart. He won't go along with this plan if he figures it out."

"Then it's your job to make sure he doesn't."

They both stared at the twisted shapes a moment before O'Neil said, "General, you've opened up a doorway to a world we know nothing about."

All afternoon and well into the evening, the antiseptic corridors of the silo's office complex resembled a college dormitory on the day after final exams. All the doors stood open. Crates of books and trunks of personal belongings littered the hallways where the departing residents said their good-byes. A few were angrily discussing ways to get back on to the project, but most were simply sad to be leaving and uncertain about what the future would hold. Because he was such a wild card to begin with, no one thought it strange that Daniel wasn't packing fast enough to make the last shuttle down to the Denver airport. Then, after Shore and Meyers had stopped by to say their good-byes, Daniel shut his door and started to get ready.

Kawalsky had issued him a set of olive green combat fatigues. He was doing up the last button when the door opened.

It was Catherine. She looked tired. "I thought you didn't like to travel," she said with a weary smile.

"I got over it." It was good to see her. Daniel had worried about what Catherine would think when she heard he was part of the mission. He hadn't known her long, but he liked and respected her a great deal and wouldn't have betrayed her for the world.

She found the nearest available chair and sunk into it, relieved to be off her feet. "Listen," she began in her pleasant British accent, "we think the trip through the ring shattered some of the instrument glass on the probe. Just as a precaution, I've got some poor bloke down the hill at the Air Force Academy's metal shop building you a special case for your glasses. Making it out of lead. It should be here 'round about six."

The idea of going anywhere without his glasses disturbed Daniel. He suddenly saw himself groping around blindly on a strange planet, and it wasn't a pretty picture.

"Thanks, that was really . . . uh, thoughtful."

"Right. And I'm going to box you up a lunch." Catherine was poking fun at herself.

Daniel smiled, then said: "I've been thinking about what I said down in the booth. You know, about taking money from the military? Look, I'm sorry if it—"

"That's not important now," Catherine interrupted him. "This is." She stood up, came across the room, and looked him seriously in the eyes. "The first time I saw that ring being dragged out of the dust in Egypt, I knew something like this would happen—that there would be some incredible journey to be taken. And, naturally, I thought it would be I who would take it. But, now I've turned into an old woman, so it's going to be you instead of me.''

Daniel started to say something, but Catherine cut him off. ''I'm glad. If it can't be me, I want it to be you.''

She reached up behind her neck and unfastened the medallion Daniel had always seen her wear. ''This was found with the StarGate,'' she told him. ''It always brought me luck.''

Daniel took the ancient bronze disk and turned it over in his hands, inspecting the engraving work. ''This is the Eye of Ra—an extremely rare and valuable piece. I can't accept this.'' Catherine reached out and put a hand on his cheek.

''Bring it back to me,'' she said before gathering herself to leave.

''Wait a second.'' Daniel hurried over to his computer and picked up the ancient figurine of the Egyptian woman. ''You were right, this piece is from the fourteenth century B.C. Take care of her for me.''

Catherine smiled and accepted the bronze statuette, then, on her way out the door, she called back to him.

''Bon voyage!''

Daniel sneezed as she walked out the door.

9

THE EVACUATION

The away-team was scheduled to rendezvous outside the silo at 5:45 A.M. Kawalsky, responsible for the final equipment check and issuing last-minute instructions arrived early and found, to his surprise, Daniel sitting in the hallway reading a book. Too nervous to sleep, he'd spent most of the night pouring over the most ancient hieroglyphs he could find, pre–First Dynasty stuff, memorizing as much as he could. Scattered around him on the floor was an hour's worth of the mess Daniel generated wherever he went.

"Jackson, where do you think we're going, to a library? Get this stuff cleaned up."

Kawalsky, keyed-up and combat-ready expected Daniel to jump when he gave an order. Daniel, on the other hand, had no intention of taking orders from some testosterone-swollen army-educated grunt who couldn't possibly understand how crucially important these hieroglyphs might turn out to be.

He looked up at the lieutenant with eyes puffy from a long night of hodophobia, commonly known as "travel allergy," and calmly blew his nose. Kawalsky, pissed off, decided not to argue. He tossed Daniel a big envelope and went on to his next task.

The envelope contained the thin lead sheathe to protect his glasses from the ring's vibrations. There was also a note from Catherine that read: "Didn't I promise to pack you a lunch?" At the bottom of the envelope, he found five jumbo Fifth Avenue bars.

Two more soldiers reported to Kawalsky. They were Feretti and Brown, faces Daniel remembered from the morning he drove onto the base. Feretti, living up to his name, was a restless man with bushy eyebrows who couldn't seem to keep still. He was perpetually hyper, always digging through his pockets, looking around in all directions, investigating everything. He seemed to be the best of friends with Brown even though they couldn't have been more dissimilar. A calm, slow-moving kid with a Mississippi accent who chuckled at every stupid wisecrack Feretti made, he didn't seem to be cut out for the mission. Daniel couldn't have guessed from looking at him that he was an accomplished atmospheric physicist, a dynamite blues guitarist and, like Daniel, an alumnus of Berkeley. In fact, Daniel would never learn much of anything about either of them, largely because they had closed ranks and were determined to give him the cold shoulder. The rumor circulating around the base was that Jackson was an uppity civilian with political connections who had somehow gone over the heads of West and O'Neil, forcing his way onto the squad. No self-respecting military man was going to fraternize with him. The unspoken plan was for everybody to make life as hard as possible for him.

Daniel took the clue and returned to his reading. At 5:44 and 45 seconds, O'Neil turned the corner. He drew extra attention because he was wearing a black beret. Six soldiers snapped into an inspection line offering the colonel a precision salute. Daniel, the seventh, shuffled into place at the end of the line, vaguely trying to fit in.

O'Neil, as serious as a corpse, asked the assembly a single question.

"Does anybody want to say something before we go?"

There was no reply. The colonel stepped down the line looking into each of the soldiers faces, deep into their eyes when—

"Aaachoo!"

Everyone present turned down the line to look at Daniel,

who was wiping his nose with some of the toilet paper he'd stolen from the latrine.

"All right, then. Let's move out." And O'Neil pushed through the doors leading into the Booth.

Unlike the day before, when the Booth had a technician for every monitor, this morning there were only two men inside, technician Storey and one other. The rest of the science team had either been evacuated or were in the process of going. General West wasn't kidding; he wanted the silo completely sealed before the away-team stepped through the StarGate.

With a nod, O'Neil signaled that they were ready. Speaking into a microphone so the remaining workers out in the silo could hear, Storey made the announcement.

"Initiating the commencement sequence."

As the "Away Squad" trooped past him, Storey eyed the last man in line, Daniel. The technician felt, as did most of the scientific staff, that while he was glad at least one of them was going along, he wished to hell it didn't have to be Daniel, a Johnny-Come-Lately to the project who most of them considered an annoying, arrogant little crap. Thus, it was with mixed emotions that Storey offered Daniel the thumbs-up signal as he marched past.

The squad entered the silo and gathered at the base of the ramp that led to the center of the ring.

"Permanent Cameras On," called a voice over the loud speakers.

Daniel licked his lips and tried to swallow, realizing that his mouth had gone completely dry. Was he really going to go through with this? He knew the probe had arrived intact, but he wasn't made of metal. What if something went wrong? What if the StarGate couldn't reassemble personalities?

From this angle, the ring looked even bigger and much, much more dangerous. The entire group stood petrified and silent as the technicians made some final adjustments to their computers. Then Storey's voice came over the speakers, booming through the room, calling out the coordinates. "Left 11.329," and then after the ring had spun up to the section showing Taurus, "Right 148.002," spinning Serpens Caput up to the "register clamp." Daniel felt his stomach rise to his throat as the eerie harmonics started to issue from the ring. The individual light beams trickled out of the quartz jewels and slowly blended into the delicate, shimmering energy field. As the seventh symbol was wheeled to the top, and the rumbling sound coming from the ring shook everything in the silo, the group stepped well away from the ring. A moment later, the thin force field thickened and started to boil until it sloshed over the edges of the ring and then splashed violently out into the room. It hovered there for a split second, defying all laws of gravity, before being vacuumed savagely back through the ring and out the other side to create the ghostly tunnel of light, the circular waterfall, speeding away through the wall of the silo. Now the deafening roar quieted as the StarGate began cycling through its harmonic progression.

The technicians rolled a pushcart loaded with equipment into place at the bottom of the ramp. O'Neil pointed to Kawalsky and one other soldier. The two men went to the cart and steered it to the top of the ramp, putting them only a few feet from the gaping mouth of the ring. When the ring's harmonic progression reached it's twelfth stage, everything was ready.

One of the technicians approached O'Neil and pointed toward the cart saying something to him that Daniel couldn't hear. O'Neil nodded and shook the man's hand. Then both technicians jogged for the security doors, which locked down behind them.

"Initiating the final sequence." It was Storey's voice over the loudspeakers. "Godspeed," he added before he, too, made for the final elevator.

O'Neil turned to look up into the big observation window of the conference room. Daniel followed his glance up and saw General West pick up a telephone hookup that ran to speakers in all parts of the silo.

"Final Evacuation," he said, and approached the bay window. Looking down on the men, he offered them a simple salute, then turned for the exit as the window's shielding wall slowly slid closed.

The men at the top of the ramp had their eyes locked onto O'Neil, who gave the order with one finger, "Go." Using the handheld remote control, Science Officer Brown sent the equipment cart rolling into the energy field. As soon as the front tip of the cart came into contact with the energy field, it evaporated into a forward shriek of light. The violent speed at which the heavy vehicle was sucked through the ring sent a shock wave of fear through the men who were about to attempt the trip.

All except one. After a brief glance backward at his soldiers, O'Neil walked at a casual, even pace into the white teeth of the turbulent, sloshing pool. For a moment he seemed suspended in mid-stride until his forward momentum was magnified a million fold. He was gone.

Kawalsky ordered the next soldier, Rogalla, across the last ten feet of ramp. The soldier, nervous, tried to edge into the force field. Daniel winced, imagining half of the man being transported across the galaxy while the other part of him stayed here in the silo. Fortunately, the ring's energy quickly reached out, surrounded him, and took him whole.

One by one, Kawalsky commanded the soldiers up the ramp. Ferretti disappeared into a blur, and then Brown. Now only Daniel and Kawalsky were left. The lieutenant signaled that he would go last, but Daniel froze.

"No hesitation," Kawalsky shouted. Then he put his money where his mouth was and jogged up the ramp, leaping into the center of the ring. He hung there for a split second, pinned to the shimmering surface of the energy before he was sucked through.

Daniel walked tentatively up the ramp until he was inches away from the turbulent light.

A deep hollow clapping sound filled the room, the sound of the giant concrete doors closing high above him, the echo bouncing down the silo walls. Like a young pharaoh sealed inside his pyramid, Daniel was now the only soul left in this huge structure. He shut his eyes tight and inched forward.

10

THE OTHER SIDE OF THE GATE

Shortly after his twelfth birthday, Daniel was persuaded by his foster father to try out for the Pop Warner football team, one of the man's worst ideas ever. Daniel quit an hour into the first practice, immediately after going through "the Gauntlet." He could see it was a bad situation right from the start. He was supposed to run a straight line between two rows of bigger boys who all got to cream him with big pads. When the coach blew the whistle, Daniel stood up and asked, "Why would I do a thing like that?" But the coach, a big red screaming face, quickly convinced Daniel that he did indeed want to participate in the self-torturing drill. His teammates came through and did their part. They whacked him silly. The incident is noteworthy now because it was probably the only physical experience that in any way prepared him for the trip he was about to take, the much rougher ride through the StarGate.

As soon as his eyes touched the bright surface of the threshold, he saw the silo wall speeding toward him like a falling house. Much too fast for him to react. By the time he flinched, he was well out of the Earth's atmosphere, accelerating through pitch silent black twisting out of control, smashing blind through speeding interstellar darkness. He felt himself glide for a second until a wrinkle in the energy field threw him end over end. No gravity, no control, no sense of up or down, only the sudden bruising glances off what felt like the walls of a tunnel.

Shooting past a cluster of what appeared to be new stars, there was a long flesh of light, enough time to see his legs elongated, stretched miles out in front of him, until they snagged and his head came whipping past, as he sailed toward a face-first collision with a gigantic planet. His scream wouldn't sound. He hit the surface and zoomed out the other side, crashing again into the electric burn of the walls, spinning through a vacuum of light and sound. Then arriving.

Daniel came through in pieces. The toe of his right boot came first. Then his left hand materialized. The tip of his nose spread out to become his still wincing face. For a split second the pieces dangled in the light at the bottom edge of the StarGate until more molecules came to fill the gaps.

When Daniel was whole once more, the ring spat him out onto the hard floor like unwanted luggage, covered in frost. Later, he surmised that the frost was a by-product of his molecular reconstruction. Just as microwaves can heat objects by increasing the rate of molecular movement, the StarGate chilled its cargo by packing the molecules tightly at the moment of reconstitution. For less than 1/100th of a second, the atoms of Daniel's body were squeezed together at a rate of zero movement, long enough for him to be coated in a thin layer of ice.

Freezing and completely disoriented, he was unable to control his fall. He fell out of the ring and hit the floor hard, but not as hard as he would've if he'd gone through first. The entire team lay in a pile on the stairs at the base of the StarGate, spilling off the top of the equipment cart. It was several seconds before the first of them, Kawalsky the ox, was able to shake off the dizziness and sit up. When he could focus again, he glanced around the room at what looked like a massacre. Right next to him, curled up like an icy newborn, was Daniel, a pond of vomit near his head.

When Daniel found he couldn't breathe, his first impulse was to claw his way back into the beam and get back to Earth's oxygen before he suffocated. That's when he felt a pair of powerful hands close around his arms. Panicked, he tried to fight back.

"Jackson, you all right?" It was Kawalsky hoisting Daniel up into a sitting position and then pulling his arms above his head. He started breathing again. When the first cool breath of the new atmosphere hit his lungs, the sting opened his eyes and he began to cough.

The passage through the ring had knocked the wind out of him. When Kawalsky was satisfied that Daniel was okay, he went to check the next soldier. The chill from the frost deepened into Daniel's skin. He shuddered and felt like needles were stabbing him everywhere.

Remembering who and where he was, he squinted away from the bright light pouring out of this second StarGate, nearly identical to the first, and saw the luminous outlines of the others, scattered around him in various states of recovery.

The trip through hadn't been what he'd expected. Not that he assumed it would be some rhapsodic, beam-me-up-Scotty experience, but neither had he expected to have the crap beat out of him.

"Everyone all right?" Kawalsky asked.

The soldiers, dazed, disoriented, grumbled in the affirmative until the group's wiseacre, Lieutenant Feretti, joked sarcastically, "That was a rush, let's do that again!"

It was painful to laugh. One by one they sat up or, if they could, got to their feet. Still coughing and shivering from the cold, they gathered at the equipment cart. As O'Neil started issuing instructions, the inner ring of the StarGate began to spin. Then suddenly it stopped with a click, shutting itself off and plunging the room into absolute darkness.

O'Neil's voice cut through the darkness, "All right, ladies, let's go to work. Phase One. Just the essentials."

With a sharp crack, O'Neil cracked open a flare that sputtered to life, hissing an orange-white light into the room. With choreographed precision, the team began to off-load only the equipment they needed for their first reconnaissance expedition. Kawalsky broke open a second flare and held it aloft. Daniel watched as Freeman expertly assembled a specially built video camera and Brown mounted a miniature radar dish to the top of a backpack-size unit for the collection of technical data. While the soldiers continued to prepare, Daniel waded beyond the murky pool of light to the nearest wall in search of clues.

The room was a tall black marble box. Daniel inched forward until he found the wall, then ran his hands over the polished surface. Although the large stones were beautifully cut and set, there was no trace of writing anywhere. Daniel moved deeper into the shadows, reading the empty walls by Braille.

The team was strapping into their equipment, ready to roll. Feretti, Porro, and Reilly switched on powerful flashlights, the beams intersecting in the dark air as they scanned the room. The men gathered at the large doorway, the only way into or out of the room. O'Neil thrust his flare around the corner peering into the next room. It was a short stone hallway.

Everything seemed clear, so he gave Freeman the sign to switch on the intense light at the head of his camera. Then he turned and pointed.

"Feretti, you take point. First team, move."

Swinging his rifle up to patrol position, Feretti stepped through the threshold into the dark corridor followed by Brown and another soldier.

"Kawalsky, you and Freeman cover the rear. Reilly, you and me. Let's go." They, too, bolted into the hallway.

Kawalsky looked around like he'd lost something. With a muted growl, he said, "Jackson, let's go." Daniel snapped away from his investigation of the wall and trotted through the doorway.

After a few yards, the hallway widened into a larger area that resembled the apse of a cathedral. By that time, Daniel had caught up to Freeman. Noticing something, he reached out and grabbed the nose of the camera directing it's light down to the floor. He and Freeman were standing at the edge of a circle twelve feet in diameter. It appeared to be a metallic disk, probably made of copper, that had been carefully set into the surface of the floor. Freeman looked at Daniel and shrugged. Two steps later, Daniel had another idea and grabbed the camera once more, this time directing its light straight up. Sure enough, an identical disk was cut into the ceiling directly above the first. Daniel stood gazing at the ceiling until Freeman, annoyed and not wanting to fall behind, shook lose and moved forward. By that point, Daniel was pretty certain these opposing disks weren't made of copper.

Picking their way carefully through the dark hallway, alert to any sign of danger, the team came to the Grand Gallery. This vast chamber was designed in a monumental architectural style and finished with polished facing stones. For some reason, it began to feel vaguely familiar to Daniel. Along the walls, towering ornamental columns rose up to support the stone roof. They were moving uphill now. The floor of the immense gallery was built at a gently rising angle. Even O'Neil was impressed with the chamber, but not enough to distract him from the task of finding an exit. The team moved up the floor of the Grand Gallery, dwarfed by its size.

The team's flashlights revealed the dim outline of a steep ramp at the end of the Grand Gallery that climbed up to yet another chamber. With no responsibility other than to look around, Daniel was doing just that. While the soldiers, armed to their teeth, were anticipating combat, Daniel felt like he'd been transported to an archaeological nirvana. At the same time, he couldn't shake the eerie feeling that he knew this place. It wasn't déjà vu. He just couldn't quite put his finger on it.

When Feretti was alone at the top of the steep ramp, he suddenly squatted down. The movement set off a chain reaction as each member of the team hit the deck. Before Daniel knew what had happened, Freeman had cut the light on his camera and dropped to the floor. All eyes were glued to Feretti, who lifted up just high enough to study the contents of the next room. Without turning around, he gave the come ahead signal. Daniel started to go until Freeman reached out and grabbed him by the ankle.

"Not you, bonehead. Stay down."

O'Neil sprinted silently to the base of the ramp then crabbed up the incline to Feretti's position. After conferring for a moment, O'Neil signaled the team to approach. Daniel checked with Freeman and got the go-ahead. By the time the team gathered on the ramp, they could see that Feretti was already deep into the next room. It was some sort of Entrance Hall. There was light at the end of this room, sunlight. The hall, another large boxy room, was punctuated every few yards by huge stone pillars.

The team watched Feretti dart from one of these pillars to the next until he was in position to see where the light was coming from. He turned and gave the group a thumbs-up. O'Neil responded by sending two more soldiers into the hallway to meet Feretti. When he was convinced the area was secure, the rest of the squad came forward.

When the team converged in the Entrance Hall, O'Neil conferred with Brown, who had already taken atmospheric readings.

"Conditions are similar to inside. Radiation, electromagnetic and other exposures indicate normal." O'Neil listened to the report before poking his head around the corner and studying the last hallway. Satisfied with what he saw, he turned back to the squad and pointed again to Feretti and Brown, who immediately turned and went. Moving one pillar at a time, the team advanced toward the huge square doorway and the sharp daylight beyond. A few strides before the threshold, O'Neil lifted a hand in the air, stopping the troops progress. Without turning back, he signaled a soldier to either side of the doorway, twenty feet wide. When they'd peered outside and given the all clear, O'Neil took the last steps forward and leaned out to check the area above the doorway. Then and only then did he lead the way out into the sun for their first look at this new world.

The team came out onto a long stone pier that extended into an ocean of sand. They could barely believe their eyes as they saw nothing but lifeless brown sand dunes stretching away in every direction under an intensely blue sky. Down at the end of the stone platform, forty yards away, stood a pair of obelisks half buried in the loose sand. The team gazed around at this arid brown world, each man lost in his own thoughts. Except for a hot breeze there was no movement, no sound. No indication of any life on this sandy twin of Earth.

Before Daniel was outside, he had a theory about what this massive structure was going to look like. He walked into the sunlight and while the others stood mesmerized by the barren vistas of this new world, Daniel turned and craned his neck for a view of the structure he had just exited. It wasn't what he expected. The door was only a small proportion of the structure's exterior. On either side of the door were massive stone pylons, thick walls that towered above the entrance. Into the pylon walls were built narrow slits, windows that allowed air in, and, in case of attack could allow weapon fire to the outside. These pylons were very much in the style of those to be found at the ancient temples of Luxor and Karnak. Everything was starting to make sense.

While the others were stupefied, O'Neil was on the move. "Hold and secure positions around this entrance. I want a better look at where we are."

"Hold on, I'll go with you," said Daniel.

O'Neil didn't respond. Daniel trailed after the three soldiers as they jogged down the gently sloping ramp. As the dunes grew higher around them, so did the temperature. Daniel guessed it was 90 degrees in the air, 110 on the sand.

Kawalsky, well over six feet, and Feretti, well under it, made it to the base of the ramp first and took up defensive positions at the base of the obelisks. When Daniel approached, he saw that these marble pillars, forty feet tall and tapering to sharp pyramidions at the top, were different from any he'd seen on Earth; they were not covered with hieroglyphs. Astonished, Daniel couldn't believe that his theories were being proven right before his eyes.

After examining the twin spires, Daniel ran past the soldiers and up the side of the first dune where O'Neil was already standing, looking back. When he reached the top he turned and looked back, hoping he would see the structure more clearly and, also, hoping that it would further support his hypothesis.

What he saw knocked the wind out of him. It was much more than he had hoped for in his wildest dreams. Not only was the enormous structure completely Egyptian in design but from this distance he could see the structure was merely an entrance to a much larger structure. A structure more famous than any other in human history: a pyramid. But it was a pyramid so monstrously, phenomenally large that it seemed to be hovering directly above Daniel, ready to come down and crush him. It had to be twice or three times as large as the Great Pyramid of Giza. Unlike the dilapidated pyramids at Giza, this one showed no signs of decay. Its smooth facing stones were all perfectly in place and seemed to glitter in the hot suns. Hanging up in the electric blue sky behind the pyramid were not one, not two, but three suns.

Now Daniel understood why the interior of the building had seemed familiar. It was a far more advanced version of Khufu's Pyramid. Perhaps this was the very same structure the ancient Egyptians had once tried to reproduce. In a moment of triumphant exhilaration, he realized that he had been right all along. He leaped to his feet and shouted to the dunes. "I knew it!"

O'Neil had no idea what Daniel was talking about. He watched coldly as Daniel gyrated through an impromptu victory party in the sand, laughing, punching the air, and yelling, "I knew it," about twenty-five times. Ignoring Daniel, O'Neil went on with his calculations. He decided on a plan, stood and marched back up the ramp to deliver his orders.

11

A LITTLE WHITE LIE

He sat in a slice of shadow between two dunes watching Science Officer Brown hammer rod after galvonically calibrated rod deep into the ground, collecting soil and mineral samples. Brown transferred the specimens into numbered glass beakers, murmuring an endless blur of facts and numbers into a tape recorder. He and Daniel were five hundred yards away from the obelisks, but even at this distance, the pyramid, that most primitive and mysterious of constructions, seemed to loom directly above them.

Daniel had been back inside the pyramid to search for information, particularly the writing he had expected to find. The constellations cut into the spinning inner wheel of the StarGate were the only glyphs of any kind. This absence of markings had scared and confused Daniel. While he stared at Brown executing his careful procedures, he was thinking hard about what the team would have to do next.

Nearby, O'Neil had found a natural stone ledge and was using a pair of binoculars to scrutinize the endless roll of pale brown dunescape. Kawalsky and Porro labored up the sandy hill to the top of bluff where O'Neil was standing. Both of the men were drenched with sweat.

"Colonel, we've surveyed the quarter-mile perimeter. Nothing to report. It's just a bunch of sand." Daniel could hear them clearly.

"All right, good work," O'Neil said. "Let's wrap it up and move everyone back inside. I want you people back through within the hour. I'll mark the equipment I want left behind."

O'Neil looked over at Daniel and started toward him.

Kawalsky wasn't sure what he'd heard. He called after the colonel, "What do you mean, 'you people?' Are you planning to stay for a while?" He was only kidding, but suddenly realized it wasn't a joke. O'Neil continued his march through the sand toward Daniel. "Sir, you're going back with us, aren't you?" There was no reply.

When O'Neil reached Daniel, he stopped and shouted to his men scattered in the surrounding dunes. "Let's pack it up! It's time to head back."

"Head back?" Daniel knew that was impossible. He didn't have enough information yet. He looked across the dunes, pretending to study the pyramid. He knew O'Neil was about to give him the order he couldn't execute.

"Get ready to move, we've got to get you back inside so you can get to work on the StarGate."

Kawalsky, Reilly, and Feretti came in earshot just in time to hear Daniel telling O'Neil:

"I need more time. We've got to scout around. There's bound to be other structures here, other signs of civilization. If I can find—"

"That would be nice, Jackson, but not on this trip. What we need from you is to get back inside and reestablish contact with the StarGate on Earth."

The soldiers came to the top of his dune, surrounding O'Neil intent on understanding his plan. Daniel was in the tricky position of announcing the bad news in front of them.

"You're not getting it," he let it fly. "This structure is an almost-exact replica of the Khufu's Pyramid." There! Now they had the whole ugly truth.

"What the hell are you talking about?" Feretti asked with a pained expression. Obviously, Daniel had overestimated the group's grasp of Egyptology.

"What I'm talking about is that we're not going to find any hieroglyphics or constellation displays inside this pyramid. No writing of any kind. I've checked everywhere."

"Spit it out, Jackson." Kawalsky was suddenly very interested in what Daniel had to say.

"Look, the coordinates were marked on big elaborate tablets back on Earth, right?" He tried to sound encouraging. "So, there must be something like that here. All we have to do is expand our search and find it."

Kawalsky spontaneously combusted. He jumped into Daniel's face. "Your only assignment was to spin that friggin' ring around and get us back home. Now, can you do it or not?"

Daniel gulped. "No, I can't."

O'Neil put a restraining hand in the middle of Kawalsky's chest and stepped between him and Daniel, as calm as ever. "Can't or won't?" he asked.

"You told us you could do it," Kawalsky roared.

"I assumed I would have inform—"

"You assumed?" O'Neil's disgust was plain.

Then Kawalsky lost it. He reached past the colonel and grabbed a fistful of Daniel's shirt, pulling him forward. "That wasn't the deal, Jackson!!"

"Lieutenant." O'Neil's calm voice froze Kawalsky, but didn't convince him to release his grip on the front of Daniel's uniform.

"Oh, this is beautiful, this is very pleasant," Feretti started yammering. "This means, correct me if I'm wrong, that we're stuck out here. Oh, that's spectacular."

Kawalsky was holding Daniel forehead to sweaty forehead, his eyes beaming pure hatred. "Listen to me, you lying son of a bitch." He lifted Daniel off the ground. "You make that thing work, or I'll break your neck." Kawalsky felt himself on the verge of doing just that, so he pushed Daniel away, knocking him backward into the sand.

"That's enough," O'Neil announced very evenly. "We'll establish our base camp right here. Kawalsky, organize a detail to haul the supplies out here."

"Establish a base camp?" Kawalsky was incredulous. "The mission objective is to recon the quarter-mile perimeter, then get back through the device. What good is it gonna do to—"

O'Neil was finished talking. "That's enough, Lieutenant! You are not in command of this mission."

It seemed like the wrong way to say the wrong thing to the wrong guy at the wrong time. Kawalsky took a sudden, threatening step closer to O'Neil. For an instant, everyone was certain there would be a fight.

No one needed to remind Kawalsky of who was in charge. It had been an extremely sore spot with him ever since O'Neil had suddenly arrived and relieved him of his command. Until this moment, he had been able to suppress his anger, burying it deep within his professionalism. But it was clear to him that the whole project had started to going to hell the minute O'Neil took over. And now here they were. They were marooned in this Saharan inferno with, at best, three days worth of water. The success of the mission had never seemed particularly important to O'Neil, and that led Kawalsky to suspect he might be prosecuting some secret agenda, something cooked up between him and General West. He had every reason to hate O'Neil.

When Kawalsky stepped toward him, O'Neil made no move to defend himself, practically daring the bigger man to attack. But the next second, Kawalsky did what O'Neil knew he would. He followed orders.

After a tense, threatening moment, Kawalsky chose the supply detail. "Feretti! Freeman! Reilly! Porro! Back inside." He turned at once and began slogging down the side of the dune, the first steps of the long trip back to the pyramid.

O'Neil returned his attention to Daniel, looking at him for a minute before saying, "Now you've endangered everyone's life except mine. Now follow the men and help them off-load the equipment and bring it back."

Daniel didn't think following Kawalsky into the darkness of the pyramid was the safest course of action at the moment, but it didn't seem as scary as staying out there in the desert with O'Neil, so he started down the dune after the soldiers.

An hour later, the soldiers were already well into the process of establishing the base camp, pounding long tent spikes into the ground, unpacking additional communications paraphernalia, stacking the supply crates to erect a shade wall. None of the soldiers discussed the limited supply of rations and water, but everyone was thinking about it.

Daniel was positive Kawalsky had assigned him the heaviest single item on the cart. It was slow, hot work tugging the small crate across the rolling desert and then up the steep side of the last dune. About halfway up, he took a break and listened to the enlisted men argue.

"I don't believe this! We're stuck out here!" Feretti was still having a fit.

"Knock it off, Mr. Doomsayer. Quit being so negative," Freeman said.

"He's right," agreed Reilly, looking up from hammering the tent spike. "If we're not back soon, they'll just turn the Gate on from Earth."

"Look, dimwit," Feretti began to lecture Reilly, "ask yourself how you got here. Was it a two-lane highway? No. You got blasted through this weird energy cannon at about fifty billion miles an hour, turning you into a friggin' zero-mass, interstellar Gumby, okay? Now think: how many directions were you going at once? One! One direction. Now, not only is the silo emptier than a church on payday, but even if those science boys do go back inside and even if they do turn that goddamn galactic garbage disposal back on, what are you gonna do? Swim against the current?"

Science Officer Brown was listening. He looked up from assembling the dish scanner and said, "Feretti's right. The beam moves one direction at a time. This is deep shit we're in."

Inside the StarGate room, O'Neil lifted the last crate off the equipment cart and walked toward the doorway. He looked down the long hallway, pitch-black except for a series of flares. He didn't see anyone coming. He immediately set the box down and returned to the equipment cart, kneeling over its floorboards. He reached into his pocket and brought out an oddly shaped tool, then bent down to work. A moment later Kawalsky's voice was in the doorway.

"Sir! Base camp is operational, sir."

Coolly palming the tool, O'Neil eased around to face the intruder, his expression as impassive as ever. He nodded in vague approval.

"I want to apologize for losing my cool out there," Kawalsky began. O'Neil's hand slid into his pocket then out again, unnoticed. "Part of it," Kawalsky went on, "is that it seems like more is going on here than meets the eye."

"So what?" O'Neil asked, implying that it wasn't Kawalsky's job to know everything.

"For instance," the soldier persevered, "what was that you said about not coming back with us. What was that all about?"

"Apology accepted," O'Neil said flatly. "This crate goes to base camp." Kawalsky stood his ground, waiting for a more human, more rational response. But O'Neil wouldn't budge: "You're dismissed, soldier."

Furious and disgusted but unwilling to show it, Kawalsky leaned over and picked up the last crate. He made sure O'Neil saw how easily he lifted it, using his strength to send the colonel a veiled threat: if I wanted to, I could break you open with my bare hands. When he'd made his point, Kawalsky set the crate on his shoulder and walked out.

The moment he was gone, O'Neil went back to work on the equipment cart. Working the oddly shaped tool into a gap between the floorboards then giving it a strong twist, he revealed a hidden compartment. A hatch door popped open. O'Neil reached inside and brought out a pair of heavy steel cylinders. The gleaming canisters were obviously the two interlocking halves of a technologically sophisticated device. He lined up the guide marks on the thick tubes and pushed them together until they locked with a sharp click. As soon as the device was assembled, a small door, no more than two square inches, slid open at the end of the canister. It held a small square orange key. O'Neil took the key, then closed the panel. Very gingerly, he layed the log-size mechanism back into the hidden compartment and locked it.

He stood up and, when he was satisfied no one was watching, he forced the key into a slit cut into the waistband of his fatigues. Then he headed out to rejoin his men.

Daniel pulled the trunk up the last sand hill and onto the rock shelf O'Neil had chosen as a base. Exhausted and hurting, he collapsed chest-first into the sand with a huge grunt of relief.

The soldiers showed how impressed they were by ignoring him completely and returning to their assigned tasks. When Daniel pushed himself up, a layer of the sand came with him. He was dripping with perspiration, and the sand clung to the moisture. Just what he needed: his uniform and face were both covered in a mask of fine grit. But that was the least of his problems. His lower back felt like the bull's eye at a hatchet tossing competition, and he could feel the first pain of sunburn rising on his neck and arms. He wondered what sunstroke felt like and whether he'd know when he had it. Then he remembered he was on another planet, and his travel allergy kicked in. He sneezed eleven times in rapid succession.

He tipped the crate onto its tall side and sat in the sliver of shade it created. He started going through the supply kit he'd been issued. Toothpicks, water purification tablets, a two-ounce mylar blanket, a sewing kit, compass, processed fruit rolls, sunglasses, breath mints, two knives, signal flares, cyanide capsules, a hammock, string, tape, bandages, first-aid materials, but not the thing he was looking for. "I can't believe the Army. There is every useless thing inside this pack except sunblock."

None of the soldiers so much as looked in his direction. Daniel tried again. "Feretti, Porro, didn't any of you guys bring any sunblock? I'm burning up out here."

"Jackson, we need that crate over here," Feretti told him matter-of-factly. Daniel wiped as much sand off his face as he could, then hunkered down into his box-pulling stance. As soon as he bent over, his back felt like the proverbial poodle in the microwave, so he decided to make two trips. He unlatched the lid and opened the box. When he saw what he'd been schlepping across the desert, he jumped back with a shout.

"Jesus. You guys plan on flighting a war here?" Two dozen semiautomatic assault rifles were strapped into the crate.

"Thanks to you we've got the time to fight one," Feretti hissed. He had just about reached the boiling point, and the sight of Daniel staring dumbly at the rifles was making him hotter still. "Why don't you do something useful, Jackson, like maybe a little reading!"

With one hand, he whipped Daniel's forty-pound back-pack in a straight line through the air. It flew straight into Daniel's chest, sending him into an ungraceful back flip off the crest of the dune. He landed thirty feet down the hill in a spectacular shower of sand and spinning books. By the time he'd sat up and spit a couple of times, his half-empty bag was rolling to a stop at the base of the slope. Obviously, getting along with the soldiers was going to take a bit of work.

Feretti walked to the edge of the dune and watched Daniel stagger to his feet. He made sure no one had been hurt before going back to his work. By the time Daniel looked up, the top of the cliff was empty. It was only him, his books, and a lot of sand in between. Reluctantly, painfully, Daniel started the long, hot walk to the bottom of the steep hill.

He reached down stiffly for the last of the books, trying to grab it without bending his back. He got it, but as he was stuffing it into the sack, he suddenly let everything tumble to the ground.

Something had been there.

Pressed into the sand a few feet away were what appeared to be hoofprints. Daniel edged closer. The prints were so deeply indented into the arid soil that only a very heavy animal could have left them. The tracks, obviously fresh, headed off around the next dune. His first impulse was to call the others and show them what he'd found, but he was certain they'd only use the occasion to give him more grief. He looked up the slope, but the soldiers were out of sight. After a brief hesitation, he decided to see what was around that next dune. Lacing his fingers behind his back, trying to look absolutely harmless, Daniel followed the trail around one dune and then another. The prints led him deeper and deeper into a maze of tall moguls, then to the base of a steep, twenty-foot wall of soft sand. It took Daniel several tries before he was able to scramble to the top and take a look around.

That's when he saw it. He froze, gripped by fear, and stared at the grotesque sight before him. Less than a stone's throw away, a huge bizarre-looking animal raised its head and studied Daniel through the blur of heat lifting off the sand. About the size of an elephant, it was a long-haired giant, a horrible hybrid of mastodon, camel, and water buffalo. Extremely top-heavy, the animal had absurdly thin legs to support its huge weight.

The two mammals stood in the hot sun staring at one blankly for a long time before the larger one turned away with a loud snort. It dropped its head back to the ground where it was rooting in the sand, probably for food. Using its meager forelegs, it began to dig. Daniel watched the powerful animal kick up big sprays of sand as it burrowed.

"Where's Jackson?" Kawalsky asked before he'd come to the top of the base camp hill. The entire contingent of soldiers started snickering. All eyes went to Feretti.

"Professor Jackson dropped his books over the side," Feretti explained, pointing to the edge of the stone outcropping. The way Feretti said it brought a bigger laugh from the men, but Kawalsky wasn't amused in the least. He hurried to the edge of the bluff and looked over the side. Jackson's backpack lay at the bottom of the long incline, abandoned.

Grimly serious, Kawalsky turned back to Feretti and got a straight answer out of him. The next moment he was barking out a crisp series of commands. He put the base on alert and mustered a search party. He ordered Brown and Porro to grab rifles, canteens, and field phones. The three of them were just about to leave when O'Neil arrived.

When the situation was explained to him, he repeated, almost word for word, each of Kawalsky's commands with one exception. He would join the search party instead of Porro.

As Daniel watched the beast dig, something in the animal's fur glinted over and over again in the sun. The reflection was coming from the area around the animal's jaw.

Daniel didn't notice it at first, because it seemed such a natural part of watching an animal graze, even an animal as weird-looking as this one. But as soon as the sight registered with him, he immediately started marching in a straight line toward the creature, reaching into his pocket as he went. He brought out a Fifth Avenue candy bar and ripped the wrapper open with his teeth, taking a big bite. The animal quit digging when it sensed the human coming closer. It looked up, potentially menacing.

Daniel hesitated long enough to question whether he was sunstroked or actually knew what he was doing. No, he was sure the metallic reflection could only mean one thing. He came close enough to see that the animal was fitted with a harness, stirrups, and a set of reins that hung down to the sand.

The earthling took a deep breath. Here was an unmistakable sign that they were not alone. It meant there was intelligent life here, a species capable of making tools and domesticating other animals to help them do their work. His heart rate surged, but he continued to move forward.

The closer he came, the slower Daniel felt like walking. The animal seemed much bigger than it did a minute before, seven feet tall at the shoulder. And much uglier. At first glance, it had appeared to be a much larger cousin of *Ovibos moschatus*, the horned musk ox native to the North American tundra. Upon closer inspection, however, the beast looked like nothing so much as an early, not-completely-successful experiment in crossbreeding. It could have been descended from the mammoths of the Pleistocene Epoch, or the horselike *Hippotraginae* antelope, or possibly from the extinct woolly rhinoceros. Or maybe all three. It had a high, humped back and long stringy hair that hung in dirty matted locks. The blistered, oily skin on its face held a pair of bulging, watery eyes set on either side of its stump-like head. Pointing straight ahead, the nostrils were glistening, moist, and unusually large. It grunted toward the human, saliva dripping off it's beard. It seemed to be friendly.

Simultaneously disgusted and fascinated, Daniel crept forward. Even with his sore back, he didn't feel like he was in any great danger. The harness, made from some type of leather and vines, told him the animal was probably tame. And besides, it looked much too slow and awkward to give him much of a race if it came to that. A real city boy, Daniel had no idea how dangerous the situation was. He had had no experience handling livestock, and didn't know that even a withered old milking cow can kick a full-grown man to death. Like most people, Daniel wanted to believe he shared a special sympathetic bond with all animals and babies. It was only humans over the age of nine that found him so obnoxious.

Holding the candy bar at arm's length, swallowing nervously, he crept closer. When he was within a few feet, he stopped short and his eyes widened dramatically. There was a red X moving across the side of the animal's sweaty face. It took him a minute to realize that the X was a laser, a targeting device. He looked wildly around the desert and spotted Kawalsky aiming down at him from a far-off dune. O'Neil and Brown came to the top and stood on either side of him.

Daniel put his hands in the air, surrendering. "Don't shoot!" he yelled to the soldiers. "This is a perfectly tame animal."

The moment Daniel's arms shot into the sky, the beast began the ungraceful process of getting down on its knees. Obviously, both hands in the air was a command it had been taught by its masters. From the soldiers' vantage point, it seemed that Daniel knew what he was talking about. The animal looked about as threatening as a cow on roller skates as it folded its legs under and settled down into the dirt, the red X of the sighting laser still trained on its brain pan.

"Don't feed it," O'Neil warned from the top of a high mound, spotting the Fifth Avenue.

"It's wearing a harness," Daniel yelled back. "Just don't shoot!" Although Kawalsky had no intention of firing until the animal attacked, Daniel felt sure the shot would ring out any second. He had to prove the thing was tame before his companions butchered it. Smiling nervously, he called to them, "Just watch. No reason to worry."

Extremely worried, Daniel came the last couple of steps toward the kneeling monster and held the candy bar at arm's length. Slowly, he leaned forward until two thick slabs of lip flesh closed heavily around his hand. Daniel closed his eyes and held on. The animal's breath was overpoweringly foul. When the powerful tongue, the size of a cave eel, slid forward across his hand, the sensation of hot spittle was too much. Daniel yanked his hand free with a yelp, but immediately turned and faked another big smile for the soldiers. By that time, they were moving closer, only their helmets visible as they dipped between the first set of moguls. The creature grunted around in the sand, found the Fifth Avenue, and chewed it up, paper and all.

Daniel reached out and petted his furry new friend. Although it was emitting a sharp, punishing body odor, the animal seemed sweet enough in disposition.

"You're a good old boy, aren't you?" Daniel asked the lubricious ogre in a high, singsong voice he used exclusively for friendly animals. Patting and scratching the brute's filthy fur, Daniel examined the reins and saddle that were made of animal skin and a poorly refined iron. Whoever made them had better skill than equipment.

"Who do you belong to, mister?" Daniel asked, reaching under the animal's fleshy wet ear to give him a nice scratching.

It was the wrong place to touch. Faster than a scared rabbit, this tow-truck-on-legs stumbled up and broke into a headlong sprint. Daniel had just enough time to get out of the way, but unfortunately, he stepped directly into a loop in the reins. Half a second later, the slack in the reins disappeared, snagging Daniel's foot and yanking him violently into motion. The next thing he knew, he was sand surfing at breakneck speed across the uneven desert floor, being towed along by this yak from hell.

Kawalsky took aim, but it was too late. The beast was darting between four-foot dunes, bouncing Daniel around like a tin can tied to the bumper of a car. The soldiers gave chase, but the beast's incredible speed quickly increased the distance between them.

Daniel was being pulled ankle first at forty-five m.p.h. across an endless skin-scratching washboard. Bumping and twisting, he glanced off the side of one dune only to crash with a spectacular spray of sand onto the face of the next.

When the terrain flattened out, and his trousers filled like a balloon full of heavy sand, he was able to control the ride somewhat by holding both hands out to the sides. He looked like a human catamaran. Despite the constant gale of sand kicked into his face by the pumping hooves, Daniel sat up and tried to reach for his snagged boot. He almost had it when the medallion Catherine had given him bounced up and out of his shirt. They were headed straight for a giant wall of sand. At the last second, the animal jagged away, but not soon enough for his passenger who rode to the top of the natural ramp, then went airborne just as the medallion bounced past his nose and over hs head. He tried a desperate backward lunge just as the slack in the reins ran out, yanking him violently in a new direction. He scraped across the hot ground, face-first, his nose scooping up a fistful of sand.

Eventually the beast trotted to a stop. Daniel, his sand-stuffed uniform making him look like a circus fat man, was sneezing like a kitten who'd just inhaled a pepper shaker. Miraculously, nothing seemed to be broken. He looked at his hand and discovered he'd snagged the chain with one finger. Painfully, he rolled over, sat up, unstrapped his boot, and started getting the sand out of his mouth, eyes, ears, and nose.

Soon he could see O'Neil, Brown, and Kawalsky coming past the last dune, jogging toward him with their rifles sighted on the animal. As the team came closer, the beast turned around and started licking Daniel in the face.

"Get your stinking breath away from me," he screamed, trying to slap the repulsive face away. The beast ignored him, continuing to nuzzle and lick. O'Neil got there first.

"Colonel, get this thing off me."

Strangely, O'Neil lowered his gun and walked right past Daniel to the lip of the nearby ledge. Brown and Kawalsky did the same thing. Seeing that he would get no help from his supposed teammates, Daniel pushed the nauseating animal away and came to see what the soldiers were gawking at.

"What's so interesting?" he asked, coming up the slope.

They were looking down into a deep ravine that ended in a spectacular set of white cliffs. Crawling by the thousands across the faces of the cliffs, marching in lines across the valley's flat bottom, and climbing up a series of gigantic ladders were thousands upon thousands of human beings.

12

"SO MUCH FOR COMMUNICATION"

Thousands upon thousands of ragged, dirty men were laboring in organized large groups, into battalions of two hundred or more, some of them working on the narrow shelves cut into the bright white cliffs, others out on the muddy floor of this colossal mining pit. It was a scene of horrible human misery. In the stifling afternoon heat, the miners were scrambling everywhere, edging out on thin ledges cut into the chalky cliffs. At the bottom of the valley, where the groundwater prevented them from going deeper, they worked in milk-colored mud. At several points around the perimeter of the stadium-shaped bowl, there had been major cave-ins, places where the soft walls had given way and crashed toward the muddy bottom, burying everything in their way.

O'Neil surveyed the scene through his binoculars. Young children, no older than seven or eight worked alongside the men. Their main task appeared to be carrying satchels of ore or coal-like substance up the network of thin trails that snaked like veins to the top of the ravine. But the most dramatic way in or out of this man-made canyon were the rope ladders. There were hundreds of these handwoven ladders hanging everywhere between levels, but half a mile from the team, two dozen of them reached spectacular lengths, connecting the very bottom of the pit with a rock outcropping three hundred feet above. Uneven in thickness and stitched with broken rungs, they looked perilously slipshod. Nonetheless, each of them wagged back and forth with the weight and motion of between forty and fifty boys at once, some climbing with their loads, others passing them on the way down.

They were dark-skinned people, some working shirtless, but most of them wearing thick robes that covered them shoulders to ankles. It seemed like bizarre wardrobe given the intense heat. Worse, their heads were covered by hoods or scarves, wrapped in a fashion similar to the bedouins of the Syria and Jordan.

The mining enterprise extended into the valley for two and a half miles. From the team's angle, the workers looked like ants moving everywhere across the surface of the valley. One work group, at least a hundred men strong, was working a long stone's throw beneath the soldiers. Their work was kicking up clouds of white dust so thick it looked impossible to breathe. They were covered with the powdery soot, giving them the eerie appearance of dusty ghosts.

The away-team was astonished, blown away. They thought they were prepared for anything. Ten-foot-tall aliens with swollen pink heads wouldn't have surprised them half as much as what they had found: humans. It sent a shock-wave of recognition through the team, a sudden awareness of being related to these people. Even O'Neil did something completely out of character. Once he'd established the workers were not armed, he handed the binoculars to Brown, who was clearly eager for a look.

Daniel's mind raced. Human beings, here, on the other side of the known universe? What was the connection? Could these people be descendants of people from Earth? Or, more disturbingly, could we be descended from them? For every answer Daniel could find, a thousand questions would arise.

Everything changed the moment the first worker looked up and made eye contact with Daniel. His shout caused a hundred heads to turn toward the top of the dune. Then, in a long chain reaction back across the busy valley, work stopped and all the thousands looked to see what was happening. Those who were close enough saw the four men in green clothing isolated against the giant wall of white sand.

Kawalsky and Feretti instinctively readied their guns and wanted to retreat up the hill to better positions. O'Neil signaled them "guns down" and watched the curious miners watch him. There was no malice in the growing crowd, but neither was there any sign of welcome. Neither side knew how to move.

"Fall back," Kawalsky decided. Then he corrected himself, "Should we fall back, sir?"

"What would that accomplish?" O'Neil asked after thinking it over. "We might as well meet the neighbors." He started off down the slope.

"What the hell is he doing now?" Brown knew exactly what he was doing.

"Let's trail him," Kawalsky said, getting up to follow. Now twenty thousand eyes were fixed on the strange visitors as they piled their way down one of the spillways into the ravine. Some watched frozen from the cliffs, laying their tools on the ground. Across the uneven valley floor, they continued to come, crowding around to gawk up at the first unknown travelers in their history. As Daniel walked down into the gorge, he felt like something was swallowing him.

O'Neil lead the way, watching the crowd gather mass. Fortunately, he saw no sign of hostility. The people seemed peaceful and curious. But there was something strange in the way they were milling about. O'Neil couldn't quite put his finger on what was odd in their behavior. He gave the crowd his iciest stare, intentionally intimidating them. But when he saw that wasn't necessary, the next step was to talk.

"Jackson, come down here." He motioned his Egyptologist forward. "Talk to them."

"What? How?"

"You're the language expert. Try and communicate."

Daniel hesitated, but then plunged in. With the entire population of the mining colony scrutinizing him, he slowly walked past O'Neil to the base of the cliff. He approached one of the miners, a skinny bucktoothed man, and spoke the historic first words between the two disparate cultures:

"Um . . . hello?"

The man turned and laughed nervously to no one in particular. He was more than a little tense about being singled out like this.

"I am *Dan*-iel. Daniel," he said again, gesturing broadly to himself. "And you?"

Blank stares.

Daniel tried a formal Japanese-style bow. This time he met with more success. Several of the men in front awkwardly returned the gesture. It was a beginning.

"Essalat imana," Daniel said very formally, bowing once again. The miners raised their eyebrows and looked at one another. Obviously, they didn't speak Aramaic. Switching gears, Daniel tried speaking ancient Egyptian, a language that hadn't been heard on Earth for the past seventeen hundred years. Since no one knew exactly how to pronounce the verbal equivalents of the hieroglyphs, all Daniel could do was take a stab at it.

"Neket sennefer ado ni," he announced. *We come in peace.* The miners stared back at him, politely curious but obviously not understanding him. He tried several slight variations of the sentence's vowel structure, but nothing seemed to work. Either they didn't understand ancient Egyptian, or he couldn't speak it.

He went through several less likely possibilities. He greeted the crowd in Berber, Omotic, ancient Hebrew, and Chadic. But nothing worked. It was an intensely frustrating moment for Daniel. He had spent his life studying these languages, achieving levels of fluency that were far beyond the merely useful. Now, he was given the incredible opportunity to actually use them, and found that they were good for nothing.

Daniel looked up at the hot suns contemplating his next move and began absentmindedly fiddling with the medallion around his neck when a man standing nearby came absolutely unglued and started screaming wildly. He was screaming something to the rest of the miners, a look of sheer brick-shitting terror on his face.

"Naturru ya ya!! Naturru ya ya!!" he cried over and over while he backed away, cringing in fear as if Daniel were going to start whipping him at any second. Everyone started

dropping to their knees as quickly as they could and "assumed the position," putting their faces to the sand in a posture of abject servitude and submission. In a few seconds, the words *"naturru ya ya"* had been repeated in every corner of the mining pit, causing the many thousands of miners to prostrate themselves facedown in the white sand. Daniel stumbled backward.

"What the hell did you say to them?" O'Neil demanded.

"Nothing. All I said was hello."

"Damnit, I told you to communicate with them."

"How?" Daniel pointed at the groveling masses.

"Oh ferchrissakes, Jackson, just communicate." Exasperated, O'Neil studied the crowd for a moment, then approached one, a teenage boy, at random. He tugged the kid to his feet with one hand and offered a handshake with the other. When the boy didn't understand, O'Neil seized his hand and shook it vigorously, saying "Hello, United States of America. Colonel Jack O'Neil."

The boy looked like he had developed rigor mortis. He was so alarmed and confused, he was about to cry. When O'Neil saw this, he relaxed his grip and let the terrified youngster take off running, scared out of his wits.

"So much for communication," Daniel commented dryly.

"Colonel, eleven o'clock." Kawalsky drew attention to something moving toward them across the floor of the valley. It was another one of the mammoth-like animals, but this one was finely groomed, with silver ornaments and carefully braided hair. On it's humped back it carried a decorated howdah whose passenger was hidden behind veils draped over the windows. As the animal ambled forward, it parted the silent crowd like a royal rowboat bobbing through water lilies.

Walking beside the animal, speaking excitedly up to the closed litter, was the same boy who shook O'Neil's hand. The window cover was pulled back, and the rider shouted angrily at the boy who immediately backed away.

The animal arrived, escorted by a small entourage that included some females. The soldiers assumed they were about to meet one of the overseers of this miserable operation and poised themselves for a showdown. But when the small door swung open, it was a thin old man who climbed down the side of the animal with surprising agility. He wore a deep red robe that was unlike those worn by the others. He had on a headdress similar to the ones worn by the bedouins of the Middle East. His gray beard was carefully shaped.

His mood was very serious, concentrated as he walked over to the group. He walked right up to Daniel. Without warning, he fell to his knees and started racing through some sort of catechism or prayer. He was talking fast, inches from Daniel's feet. Daniel looked back at his companions and asked, "What's he doing?"

"We do not know, O Holy Master," Kawalsky said with a smirk and a mock bow. It was obvious these people thought Daniel was something he wasn't.

Daniel bent and listened to the small man as he recited the long invocation. The words sounded like they could be Omotic or Berber. Possibly even Chadic. Whatever it was, Daniel didn't recognize it. Then, as suddenly as it had begun, the prayer was over. The old man pushed himself back onto his feet and was imitated by everyone on the valley. He signaled for the women to come forward. Two of them did, bringing water in big earthen cups.

The younger woman came to Daniel handing him a piece of very soft cloth. Then she raised her pitcher to pour the water. Did she want to wet the towel? He held it out to her cupped in his hand. She held out her finger and shook it "no, take that away." By the time Daniel understood what he was expected to do, it was too late. He'd looked into the girl's eyes and been electrocuted by her beauty, her impossibly magnetic eyes. His mind went into an immediate tailspin, and he started experiencing déjà vu. But how you can have a déjà vu about someone you're absolutely positive you've never seen before? Maybe it was the first sign of sunstroke. He must have looked strange because the girl reached up with the washcloth and wiped him across the brow. Daniel was surprised by the open tenderness of her gesture, the caring way she wiped the cool towel across his forehead.

She held out the pitcher again, and this time Daniel, looking into her eyes, knew what to do. He cupped his hands and caught the drink she poured him, then swallowed it while giving her a meaningful look.

The girl, twenty years old and painfully shy, then moved on to Kawalsky. Daniel noted with disappointment that she wiped his forehead in the same way. It was just part of the ceremony. The old man was speaking to him again. He tried to concentrate. Then an idea hit him.

Daniel unwrapped a half melted Fifth Avenue bar and held it out, offering the man a taste. The man understood what Daniel was doing, but was clearly apprehensive about eating the exotic brown substance. To him, as for humans everywhere, the sight of an unfamiliar food looked ugly and potentially poisonous. After some hesitation, he reached out, accepted the bar, and took a small bite. His worried eyes grew wide with concentration as he chewed. Then suddenly, his whole face lit up in a smile.

"Bonniwae," he said.

"Bonniwae," Daniel repeated the word, thrilled to be communicating with him.

"Bonniwae," he said again, giving the new taste an enthusiastic endorsement.

"What the hell does that mean?" interrupted Kawalsky.

"I have no idea," replied a thrilled Daniel.

Pointing and beckoning, the man in the red robe used sign language to invite his visitors to go somewhere beyond the high walls of the pit.

"They're inviting us to go somewhere."

"Where?"

"How should I know? Somewhere in that direction."

The squad turned to O'Neil for a decision. But he hadn't made one yet. He was watching the old man like a hawk, scanning him for any clue of deception. He didn't want to walk into a trap. The old one seemed puzzled by the silence. He repeated the invitation with clearer, broader gestures.

Daniel tried to persuade O'Neil. "Aren't we looking for signs of civilization? Okay, now we've obviously hit a bull's eye. If we want to find the StarGate symbols and get back home, we've gotta go with them. This is my best shot."

O'Neil just stood there, as expressive as a brick wall. Although it was a pretty convincing argument, he knew Daniel was more excited about playing the role of amateur archaeologist than anything else. He wasn't convinced until Brown added additional new evidence.

"He's probably right, sir. I've been taking some readings on this stuff they're mining. It's the same quartz-like material that the StarGate is made of."

"All right. There's no alternative," O'Neil concluded. "Radio back to base camp. Tell them to keep the area secure until we return."

They came out of the pit along a wide switchback trail, the old man leading a caravan ten thousand strong. At the top of the road, there were two more tall obelisks marking the entrance. Daniel broke out of line and jogged up to walk beside the old man to study his manner and dress.

His name was Kasuf, and although ceremony called for him to walk alone, he wanted to know more about these visitors so he allowed Daniel to walk alongside him. He wasn't sure whether they were gods, but with production slowing in the quartz mines lately, he didn't want to take any risks. He could see that their weapons were very advanced and their manner was not entirely friendly. They were dangerous in more than one way. Whether they were gods or not, Kasuf didn't want to take any chances, so he decided it best to treat them as though they were.

The one walking next to him, the one with glasses who sneezed so often, seemed friendly and peace loving enough. And very talkative. Kasuf listened patiently to the young man's gibberish but could make no sense of it.

Daniel had never had so much trouble communicating in all his life. He felt himself on the verge of losing his temper, so he took a deep breath and marched along with the old man for several minutes in silence. About the only thing he learned before rejoining the soldiers was that these giant pack animals were called *mastadges*.

Each of the stump-headed animals was tended to by a distinctive-looking teenager. Cleaner and younger than the miners, the shepherd boys wore striking haircuts, long dreadlocks dangling from mostly clean-shaven scalps. Marching next to Kasuf was the boy who seemed to be the de facto leader of the shepherds, the same boy who had unwillingly shaken hands with O'Neil a few minutes before.

His name was Skaara. He was a handsome skinny kid who walked with his shoulders back and his chin in the air. He was angry with himself for having run away from O'Neil before, and was determined to be fearless from now on.

The caravan snaked out into the desert. It was a full mile later before the whitish quartz-dust surrounding the mining pit gave way to the planet's natural topsoil, the same brown silica the soldiers found around the pyramid. How many centuries of chiseling pieces of quartz out of the pit's giant walls, then hauling them up the ladders a bag at a time, had it taken to create these eerie white dunes?

Daniel kept trying. Back in line, he pestered the miners on all sides of him, asking question after incomprehensible question. He wanted to learn the names of things, hoping he might stumble across some linguistic clue that could teach him to speak their language. He was practically bouncing down the trail, intensely interested in everything around him, but there were two things distracting him: his hodophobia was acting up, making him sneeze every other minute; and, of course, the girl.

She was only a few strides behind him, and Daniel kept inventing reasons to turn around. Each time their eyes met, both looked nervously away. He was in the middle of asking the confused miner next to him about their agriculture when he felt someone touch him in a rather private place. Goosed, he spun around to find the same disgusting monster that had dragged him across the desert. Now the beast was trying to nuzzle up to him affectionately.

"Get away," Daniel swatted at the animal.

The animal cried out, bleating like a ten-ton goat. Everyone close enough to witness the scene thought it was pretty funny. They were cracking up, but no one laughed harder than a strange-looking shepherd boy. He was shorter than the others, and his skull was oddly shaped. Above his Cro-Magnon eyebrows, his head swelled like something were trying to get out of the top. His big horsey teeth were so crooked, they looked like white tomahawks tossed at a red target. His name was Nabeh.

"*Mastadge,*" the boy grinned wildly.

Both the animal at the front of the caravan next to

Kasuf and this one trying to cuddle with Daniel were called *Mastadge*. However, there was a vast difference between the stately beast parading up ahead and the slobbering, malodorous monstrosity molesting Daniel.

The caravan turned and headed down a long valley with a steep line of rocky cliffs on the right. Twenty minutes later, they'd come to a break in the cliffs. Daniel looked behind him and saw the thousands of people marching in line, still coming over the last crest and down into this valley. Kasuf turned them up the slope toward the gap in the hills. When he came to the top, he stopped and called Daniel to the front, pointing across a long plain.

In the distance, Daniel saw the high walls of a huge fortress, a city. It was the ancient settlement of these people rising like an island from the endless ocean of sand. Awed, Daniel turned and shouted to the soldiers.

"It's a city."

While O'Neil trotted forward to recon the scene, Daniel had time to pick the maiden out of the crowd again. They looked directly at each other for a heartbeat until both pretended to notice something else. This exchange did not go unnoticed by Kasuf.

"Put your tongue back in your mouth," O'Neil snapped, arriving at the top of the hill. He surveyed the scene, then came down the slope to find his men. He explained that they would enter the enclosed city one at a time, at intervals of ten paces: Brown, then Kawalsky, then Jackson, then himself. Kawalsky knew that was the other in which O'Neil would choose to sacrifice his men if it turned out to be an ambush.

When O'Neil left to explain the sequence to Daniel, Kawalsky turned to Brown.

"As soon as you're inside, check above and behind, I'll be two paces behind you."

When they came within two hundred yards of the city, the old one, Kasuf, signaled for something. One of the women brought forward a long animal horn. The old man put it to his lips and trumpeted a message to the city. A set of tall doors swung open between the two main towers. These towers, eighty feet tall, were made of the same material as the rest of the city—solid stone the color of straw. The perimeter wall, which ran off unevenly in both directions for several hundred yards was only slightly lower than the towers, about the height of a six-story building. Kasuf had sent a few of the boys running ahead before O'Neil could stop them, so by the time Brown was at the gate, a throng of curious onlookers were swarming the entrance.

Before he was through the doors, Brown knew there was no possibility of avoiding an ambush if that is what these people had planned. Inside the city, there were more tall buildings crowding around narrow streets. The air itself was thick with people. A matrix of footbridges connected the upper floors of the buildings, all of them were jammed with spectators who could be concealing weapons beneath their long robes.

For the last few minutes, Daniel had been suffering another sneezing attack, drawing strange looks from his fellow marchers and, now from the people observing from the slate gray rooftops. Adding to his discomfort, his filthy friend, the *mastadge*, had been bumping him with it's oily nose looking for more candy. As he came to the doors, wide enough for ten people to walk abreast, the distance between him and the girl closed. Now they were walking practically side by side, and Daniel felt a rush of heat come to his face. He ransacked his mind for something suitable to say to her, and was about to speak when the *mastadge* nuzzled him again in a sensitive area. Daniel quickly pulled the last Fifth Avenue bar out of his pocket. Before he unwrapped it, he shook it in the animal's face.

"A little bit," he explained to the animal before he unwrapped the treat. But the big fleshy lips reached out and snatched the bar away.

"A little bit, I said!" But the animal was already chewing happily. "Now stop bugging me."

Behind him, Daniel heard O'Neil's voice saying, "I told you not to feed it."

The miners walking nearby picked up on the words "little bit," repeating them over and over. The foul-smelling *mastadge* had a new name.

Daniel's torment ended when one of the boys pulled the animal away by the reins toward a holding area just inside the gate. The animal moaned in protest about being separated from its new provider.

When Daniel looked up, he was both amazed and very uneasy. This was not a city for a claustrophobe. The rough walls towered above them as they walked along this central street. On both sides, narrow twisting alleyways cut between the buildings. At every angle, from windows and bridges, pressed into doorways and leaning over ledges, the population of this city surged forward to stare at him with intense curiosity. The team was now completely at the mercy of this people, about whom they knew almost nothing.

When they were a hundred yards deep into the citadel, they came into a large open square, where Kasuf had turned to wait for them. While people filled the square, Daniel studied the buildings around him. The primary building material was stone, large slabs skillfully quarried. But the most surprising element was wood. The rickety staircases that staggered up the sides of buildings, the gangplanks bridging the upper floors and the doors to the many apartments were all made of a gnarled rose-colored wood. Around the windows and across the cornices of the buildings, elaborate geometrical designs had been chiseled into the stone. But nowhere could Daniel spot anything that looked like a written inscription.

Kasuf stepped onto a small platform and raised his staff into the air signaling for the crowd to be silent. When they were, he turned to the visitors and started rambling through what sounded like another prayer. When he was finished, he used his long staff to point to a covered object hanging high between two buildings. As he did so, a man on a scaffolding pulled away a large piece of cloth. As the curtain fluttered to the ground, Daniel looked up in total astonishment.

Suspended under the archway by a tangle of bulky ropes, he saw an enormous gold disk, easily ten feet across. Emblazoned across its surface was an exact replica of the design on Daniel's medallion, the one Catherine found in Egypt. As soon as the giant disk was revealed, the entire city fell, its knees in one massive human wave, bowing toward the visitors. It was an awesome sight.

"I think they think we're gods," Daniel stammered.

"What do you think could have given them that idea?" He looked up at the giant disk, then down at the smaller version hanging on Daniel's chest. He reached out and took hold of the antique treasure, pulling Daniel half a step closer. The colonel looked at him, suspicious, menacing.

"Exactly what does this symbol mean?" he asked, threateningly. He was sure Daniel knew a lot more than he was letting on.

"It's the sign of Ra, the Egyptian sun god." As Daniel explained this, he felt a sour sinking feeling in the pit of his stomach. "It looks like they worship him. They must think he sent us here."

Satisfied Daniel was telling the truth, O'Neil released his grip on the medallion.

From his platform, Kasuf was making some sort of speech, gesturing frequently toward the team. Somewhere in the middle of it, Brown's radio squelched to life. The signal was so dim, Brown plugged in an earphone and cranked the volume up. Through the crackling of electrostatic interference, he heard what sounded like Feretti's voice.

It had come on so quickly, there was almost no warning. At first, Feretti had ordered the team off the crest of the bluff toward shelter. He quickly realized his mistake, struggled up the hill, and got on the shortwave radio. Down on his knees with his jacket pulled over his head, he was screaming as loud as possible into the handset. He was trying to warn the away-team. The roaring noise around him, a high-pitched shrieking howl, made it difficult for him to hear his own voice.

"Must abandon base camp!! Repeat: must abandon base camp!!" he yelled.

As he knelt, he felt something crash down on top of him. It was Porro, staggering blindly across the top of the bluff.

"Let's go!" he yelled to Feretti. "Let's get the hell out of here."

Feretti nodded. They had to get back to the pyramid or they were dead men.

* * *

"Come again, base camp. We do not copy," Brown said urgently into the handset. "Say again, base camp!" By that point, everyone's attention was riveted to the drama of Brown shouting into his radio. Whatever ceremony the old man was trying to observe had been completely interrupted.

Frustrated, Brown gave up trying. He looked to O'Neil and said, "It's no use. Something's interfering with the signal."

A deep horn blast sounded from the top of the perimeter wall near the main gate. A moment later, a second horn moaned to life, and the pair of them sent a low rumbling blast through the city. Every head in the square turned and looked as one. Something was wrong.

O'Neil made a snap decision.

"We're heading back right now. Let's move."

Kawalsky and Brown were on their feet and moving before Daniel could say, "Why?"

O'Neil's first impulse was to leave Daniel behind, maroon him, pay him back in kind. But at the last minute, he came back and grabbed Daniel by the sleeve of his uniform and started pulling him down the narrow street. The path back to the gate was choked with at least a thousand people. As the soldiers pushed forward, hands reached out to stop them, and mouths, frantically speaking, tried to explain something urgent. They were telling the soldiers not to go.

At first, O'Neil pushed them aside politely but firmly. But when he saw a handful of men pushing the main gates closed, he broke into a dead sprint, clearing the way with a series of brutal forearm shivers to the head or throat of anyone who stood in his way.

The men closing the gate ignored O'Neil's howling. They had just finished reinforcing the door with the first of three heavy cross beams when O'Neil arrived at the entrance flanked by his two soldiers.

"Open the door!" he thundered at them, showing them what he wanted with a gesture.

All of them started talking at once, waving their hands and pointing over the wall, out into the desert. It was clear they weren't going to cooperate, so O'Neil called Kawalsky over.

"You think we can lift that beam by ourselves?"

Kawalsky shot him a look that said, "easily." Standing shoulder to shoulder, they were a formidable sight, both of them taller and more muscular than these mostly thin, mostly haggard people. No one in their right minds would tangle with these two. Nevertheless, as they moved toward the gate, one of the gatekeepers reached out and grabbed O'Neil's wrist.

With a speed that surprised even his men, the colonel corkscrewed the man's arm behind his back and slammed him face-first against the door. As the man slid half-conscious and whimpering to the ground, O'Neil took his pistol from its holster and pointed it into the crowd.

"Don't do it!" Daniel screamed.

O'Neil raised the gun above his head and fired three times into the air.

Each explosion jolted the crowd. They had never heard gunfire before, and they were instinctively terrified. Everyone froze in their tracks, stunned and afraid. Kasuf, trailed by two of the city's Elders, caught up to the team and nervously came forward out of the crowd to see what was happening. *"Sha shay ti yu,"* the old man yelled.

"Brown, help Kawalsky open this door." O'Neil was going eye to eye with the crowd, daring the next person to make a move.

Daniel was sure O'Neil would start mowing people down any second. He had no idea why the colonel had gone berserk, ruining all the goodwill they had established with these strange desert people. Leaving before they had explored the city, he thought, would be a suicidal mistake. They still needed the signs for the StarGate.

"Sha shay ti yu. Sha shay ti yu." Skaara, the shepherd boy who had unwillingly shaken O'Neil's hand at the mining pit, came out of the crowd moving very slowly. O'Neil lifted his pistol, aiming for the space between the boy's eyes.

"Sha shay ti yu," he kept saying softly. He held his hands open and in front of him as he approached the man in the black beret, careful neither to threaten nor show fear. Accustomed to handling the powerful *mastadges,* Skaara knew how to approach a frightened animal. O'Neil cocked the firing pin, but the boy kept coming closer, repeating the words and pointing to the ramparts at the top of the wall.

O'Neil glanced up to the walkway at the top of the thick walls. A dozen or so people were spectating from up there, and some of them waved for him to come up. The boy pointed to the colonel, then up at the wall and used his fingers like eyes looking around.

"He wants you to look over the wall," Daniel interpreted for O'Neil.

"I know what he wants."

O'Neil turned to Kawalsky before following the boy up the ladder.

"If they try anything, drop 'em."

With one last check around, O'Neil followed Skaara into one of the towers that stood at either side of the gate. Inside, they wound their way up a circular staircase built for people shorter than the American soldier. They came out onto the stone walkway between the city's double wall. Standing where his team could see him, O'Neil looked out over the wall for what seemed like a long time.

"What is it, Colonel?" Kawalsky didn't appreciate being left hanging when he was holding a thousand people at gunpoint.

A giant low-flying brown cloud, as wide as the horizon, was rolling across the desert floor toward the city like a flash flood. O'Neil could feel the breeze turning to wind at the top of the parapet.

"A sandstorm. Coming this way," he yelled back.

Skaara pointed beyond the wall and taught O'Neil the word for sandstorm, *"Sha shay ti yu."*

"Excellent!" Daniel said sarcastically, "that would have been an excellent reason to shoot everyone!" Not content to let tempers cool by themselves, and suddenly sure he had the moral high ground, Daniel marched over to the soldiers and forced the nose of Kawalsky's rifle toward the hard-packed ground.

"Don't push me, Jackson," the lieutenant warned him.

O'Neil leaned over the parapet and called down. "We'll have to stay here until the storm is over."

Feretti realized it was probably too late, but he had to try. Lugging the thirty-pound stationary radio unit, he fought his way through the storm, staggering up the long ramp toward the shelter of the pyramid. The gusts, sweeping up ton after ton of sand, were strong enough to knock him off the ramp and out into the dunes if he lost his balance. As the dust thickened, he pulled his T-shirt up over his nose to filter the air. Squinting hard to protect his eyes, he moved more and more slowly, afraid of stepping off the side of the ramp.

He came through the tall open entrance and turned the corner, wiping the fine sand away from his face. As soon as his scratched and watery eyes were clear enough to see, he switched the radio on.

"Mayday. Mayday. Brown, do you read me?"

As the last members of Feretti's Base Squad came stumbling in out of the storm, he was already edging his way back toward the dust storm, trying to get his radio signal around the stone walls.

After a minute of trying, he thought he heard Brown's voice responding through the crackle of interference, but he couldn't be sure. The storm was too loud. Just in case Brown could hear him, Feretti screamed into the transmitter, trying to alert them to the disaster headed their way. After several minutes, he retreated deeper into the cavernous shelter. Positioning the radio set as close to the door as possible, he turned the volume up full blast and set his helmet over the top of it to help protect against the dust. With sand crunching between his teeth, Feretti moved back inside to join the rest of the team.

They had no idea whether the Away Squad was safely under the protection of the "thousands of people" Brown had told them about over the radio, or whether they were choking to death somewhere out in the desert. But all of them could sense their chances of surviving this mission quickly slipping away. Without anyone saying a word, they sat down in a semicircle facing the entrance and watched the dark wind whip sand past the doorway.

After a minute, Freeman got up and went to the radio, switching it off and pulling it several feet further from the dust.

"You're wasting the batteries," he said to Feretti. "We're not gonna get any kinda signal during this storm. We should try again when this thing passes."

"This is bad, man, this is very very bad," Feretti shook his head. "I was in Saudi Arabia for two years, and I *never* saw anything like this. Not even close."

He wanted to kick himself. If he hadn't thrown that bag of books at Daniel, if he'd exercised a little more self-control, he wouldn't have to sit there helplessly imagining O'Neil's search party being suffocated. He also knew that without Daniel, the statistical probability of them getting home was a big fat zero. They were trapped in a nightmare, and he had nailed the coffin shut.

"I don't get it. Why don't we just try and turn the StarGate on ourselves. I mean, how hard could it be?" Reilly suggested, a pragmatist.

"Hey, there's an idea," Feretti rolled his eyes, then explained why that wouldn't work. "If you spin that thing in the wrong order, we rematerialize somewhere out in the vast vacuum of outer space. Have you got any freakin' idea how many millions upon millions of possible combinations there are on that wheel!?"

"No. How many?" Freeman asked wryly.

Feretti started chalking the problem up on his mental blackboard, but then caught Freeman grinning over at him. "Shut up, Freeman."

The soldiers fell silent again, staring at the grand rectangle of the entrance. They could have been part of an ancient, surrealist drama: an audience waiting in a giant stone chamber for the actors to make their entrances.

Several miles from this peculiar stage, beyond the roaring hiss of the wind, an oblong asteroid tumbled upward over the horizon growing in brilliance as the sky darkened to evening around it. It was the misshapen pearl that was this planet's moon, and it was suddenly blotted out by a triangular shadow moving across the sky. A few seconds later, the shadow slid away and was gone.

The last light of the last sun was quickly faltering behind the impenetrable curtain of airborne sand. As it did, the light on the scene in the entrance hall dimmed until the clean edges of the radio began to decompose, dwindling into the approaching night.

The soldiers heard something coming from the direction of the entrance. Rifles snapped to the ready. It was the unmistakable sound of metal clattering on metal. It was Feretti's helmet vibrating atop the radio. The next moment, all the equipment and then the entire floor of the pyramid began to tremble.

"Earthquake! Just what we need, a goddamn earthquake."

"It's not," Freeman shouted over the rumbling, moving to a sheltered position between the pillars lining the hall. The shaking and the noise got more and more intense.

Hovering above the storm, slowly lowering itself through the storm was a pyramid-shaped aircraft. Bright beams of light knifed from its sides into the night sky. This floating pyramid was descending to a landing atop the larger pyramid on the ground.

Long mechanical arms unfolded themselves, dropping into the sky like an eagle's talons as the triangular ship lowered itself directly onto the tip of the great stone structure below. The landing arms found their targets and locked down tight. This was the explanation that had eluded generations of researchers, the answer to the riddle of the great pyramid called Khufu. It had been built as a landing station for precisely this kind of craft.

Once the landing was successful, parts of the giant spaceship's armored exterior began to move. Huge sections of the outer walls started to open and unfold. Like a high-tech origami construction, it began converting itself from spaceship to pyramid palace penthouse.

Before the long and complicated transformation was complete, a new presence was entering the pyramid. Deep inside the edifice, where the matching medallions had been set into both floor and ceiling, a rod of blue light shot between the two disks, connecting them. The beam spread sideways along both medallions, slowly shaping itself into a closed tube on light.

The soldiers, jittery, guns trained in every direction, were whispering among themselves about what to do. At the same time, a presence was moving swiftly down the dark corridors, coming closer. Feretti lit a flare and was about to toss it toward the entrance when he heard something behind him.

He turned just in time to see a jackal-headed creature towering above him. It was too late to do anything but gasp.

13

THE CEREMONY

"I don't think we should be eating anything," Kawalsky whispered over the music. The truth was, he was starving and wanted to know if the others were planning to risk the food.

Daniel, playing with a piece of the rubbery, too-spicy "bread" leaned down the table and said ominously, "They might take that as an insult."

The feast was an hour old, and still no food had been delivered. While torchlight played on the ominous disk that seemed to watch them from above, the visitors sat cross-legged behind the long low tables that had been carried into the courtyard and placed on colorful woven carpets.

In the open space between the tables, a group of elderly musicians had been sawing and plucking at their stringed instruments, playing what sounded like the same song over and over again. Earlier, Corporal Brown, a decent guitarist, had delighted the crowd by improvising on one of their instruments. The hundreds of people crammed into the courtyard cheered when he picked up the three-stringed zither-like instrument and plucked out a few simple blues riffs. Taking their clues from Daniel and Kawalsky, the onlookers had snapped their fingers and tapped their toes, even though Brown's song was as foreign to them as the present melody was to the newcomers. Only Daniel seemed

to enjoy the group's minimalist, whining music, which reminded him of the hand-clapping "Balee" chants he'd heard
performed at Nubian weddings during his visits to Upper
Egypt.

The table was set for twenty-two, all of them men. As far
as Daniel could tell, the women of this society were expected to serve quietly, then make themselves scarce. Kasuf
was among the eighteen locals, all of whom were older,
bearded, and, despite the evening heat, were attired in itchy-
looking gray robes with heavy hoods. They were obviously
the city's ruling Elders, its political leaders. They seemed
to be having a good time.

Into the circle of torchlight came a procession of serving
women dressed in dazzling silken costumes carrying all
manner of tableware: terra-cotta dishes and platters piled
high with vegetables, rough iron goblets, appetizer plates,
spatulas, napkins and knives, soupspoons and saucepans,
punch bowls of wine with thistles floating on the surface,
and, finally, a pair of four-foot-long tureens that had to be
carried in on poles. Everything was set down on the ill-
constructed tables that sagged in their middles, threatening
to collapse. Kawalsky lifted the cloth draped over the top of
the heavy tureen in front of him. When he saw what was
inside, he jumped back in horror.

Laying on its back in a shallow pool of broth was a giant
grinning lizard that had been cooked whole—skin, eyes,
tail, and all. It had the same ash gray scaly skin as a desert
snake. The animal's lips had pulled tight during the cooking
process to expose its bright yellow gums. Its feet and head
poked out of the steaming soup as if it had died peacefully
while taking a bath.

"Well, Jackson, you don't want to offend them now, do
you?" Kawalsky offered sarcastically.

"Permission to vomit, sir?" Brown asked, only half-
joking.

"They can't seriously expect us to eat this, can they?"

In one movement, the team turned to look down the table.
The Elders were enthusiastically motioning for them to dig
in. The four travelers smiled as they looked again at their
disgusting Reptile du jour. Still wearing a big smile, Kawalsky turned to Daniel.

"Jackson, how about a nice big juicy drumstick?"

"It can't be any worse than the food in the silo," Daniel replied. He knew that if it was food and it was within Kawalsky's reach, it would soon disappear.

"It could be poisonous," Brown pointed out. "None of us should eat it."

"He's right. Kawalsky," O'Neil's voice was commanding. "We can't afford to lose Jackson. Taste it."

Kawalsky was too hungry to grumble about the implications of O'Neil's decision. He picked up one of the long knives and, after checking with the Elders who gave him the go-ahead, sliced off one of the reptiles thick hind legs. Nervous, he dropped it into the broth with a big splash, which caused laughter in the courtyard. Kawalsky looked up and saw that everyone in town was watching him. He managed a smile as he fished the big drumstick out of the tureen and dropped it on his plate. He cut off a thin piece and brought it to his lips. With a deep breath, he plunged the alien flesh into his mouth and let it sit on his tongue. The townspeople started laughing, this time because of the expression on the big man's face. He bit down once into the meat, and when nothing bad happened, he chewed and swallowed.

"Tastes like chicken."

"Does it seem safe?"

"How should I know?"—slicing off another bite—"Ask 'em if they've got any salt."

Kasuf was looking down the table, watching with intense concern as Kawalsky chewed the food. For him, the acceptability of the meal was a matter of life and death. Daniel saw how concerned Kasuf was and decided to reassure him using the word he had heard the old man use after eating the candy.

"Tastes good, uh, you know, it's . . . *Bonniwae!*" he said, reassuringly.

"Bonniwae?" The old man looked horrified. In his language, that meant sweet.

Daniel cursed under his breath, frustrated. After all his travels and years of language classes, he couldn't even communicate the simple idea of "delicious." Kasuf was now speaking angrily to some of the serving people. Daniel jumped in.

"Not *bonniwae*. Tastes like chicken. Chic-ken," he said slowly. Kasuf had never seen a chicken, so he didn't understand. Daniel, thinking quick, tucked his thumbs under his armpits and did his impression of the animal, *"bock bock, bock bock."*

No one had any idea what he was doing. They stared down the table, expressionless. Then Kasuf, deeply afraid of being rude to his guests, replied. Smiling politely, he tried to imitate Daniel's imitation. Wiggling his arms as he had seen his guest do a moment earlier, the dignified leader of this people gobbled back at Daniel.

"Quit while you're ahead, Jackson," Kawalsky said between mouthfuls.

But Daniel's strongest need in life was to communicate his ideas. He didn't give up. Although it took him several more tries, he finally got the idea across that the meal was just fine.

As the elaborate dinner party wore on, both Kawalsky and Brown became bolder about sampling the many exotic dishes brought before them. They joked and laughed with the elders at the table, learning the names of the foods and then twisting them into comic English. For example, the light brown chunky sauce that tasted like pork teriyaki was called *mba hinjwui*. After a while they laughingly called it "my behind juicy."

Only O'Neil remained stone sober throughout the dinner, thinking and waiting as usual. He ate nothing but a few pieces of blackened bread and drank the water only after treating it with chlorine tablets.

Daniel had moved down the table and was trying to powwow with Kasuf, but their languages were so different that only the most primitive concepts could be communicated. He had thousands of questions but no words, not even a common vocabulary of hand gestures, to ask them. Using pantomime, he was several minutes into a question about the mining operation when he saw her again.

She was serving bread to the Elders at the far end of the table from a large basket. Daniel completely lost track of the conversation. Kasuf turned to see what the young man was looking at.

She was radiant. Her black hair was loose now and spilling over her shoulders. She wore a length of blue cloth tied around her waist as a skirt and a sheer blouse the color of burned apricots. As she moved closer, Daniel couldn't help noticing how very transparent the blouse was. He looked away, embarrassed, but then quickly looked back trying to keep his eyes above her shoulders. He followed her every move as she made her way down the line of diners. He realized how absurd he was being, allowing himself to be so smitten with this girl he did not and probably could not know. But there was something so perfect about her, something beyond her outward beauty that called him to her. He watched her hands. Her dark eyes, the timing of her smiles. She was elegant beyond her years, and there was an intelligence to each of her gestures. Something about her was so familiar, so right.

The first time he saw her, she had seemed timid and demure, but he had since realized that acting shy was merely the way these people expressed politeness in public—and they were unfalteringly polite. Each man she served seemed eager to engage her in conversation, as they would a favorite niece. The strength of her concentration as she listened, and the flash in her eyes as she responded told Daniel many things: that she was completely comfortable around the city's ruling class; that she was confident; and that she had a good sense of humor. Several times, she said things that made her guests laugh. She seemed smart enough to "work the crowd" but warmhearted enough to take authentic joy in doing so.

If and when he ever got back to Earth, he hoped to someday find a woman half as enticing as this one. He tried to shake it off and return to his conversation, but Kasuf was now busy with someone else.

"Here she comes, Romeo," Brown said with a smirk on his face. Everyone who wasn't blind or brain-dead new Daniel was infatuated.

"I don't know what you're talking about," Daniel shot back defensively, trying to save face.

"Wouldn't be so bad, would it? You two could honeymoon back at the pyramid. Rent a little apartment here in town. Find yourself a job in the mining pit. Maybe teach Greek and Latin to pick up money on the side. Start a little family.''

Daniel leveled a murderous glare at the science officer, who was obviously amusing himself to no end. Feeling chastised and suddenly self-conscious, Daniel turned away and pretended to listen to the musicians, still scraping and wheezing through their performance.

Brown's joke felt like a dagger in his heart. Here Daniel was in another part of the universe, exploring an unknown world, feasting with its exotic inhabitants, but he couldn't run away from a painful truth about himself. He was an unrealistic, romantic dork when it came to the opposite sex.

The next thing he knew she was kneeling beside him, extending the basket. Her eyes were lowered, and she seemed to be smiling just a little. He reached into the basket and selected a treat that looked like a strawberry with hair. With the others, she had been animated and warm, but now she kept her eyes trained steadily on the floor. Saddened, Daniel signaled that he was finished, allowing her to move on.

With his mind on other things, Daniel started to put the berry into his mouth when something stopped him. It was her hand. She reached up to his lips and took the food in her hand. Then, kneeling very close, she showed him that he must first peel the fruit. She stripped away the small roots and the papery skin to expose the soft green fruit beneath.

Outwardly, Daniel was calm. He seemed to be watching with appropriate interest as she showed him this simple operation. But inside, he was a crowded theater going up in flames. Utter, mind-numbing panic. The girl waited for him to reach out and take the fruit from her. When he didn't, she did something that surprised her as much as it did him. She raised the berry to his lips and, very gently, fed it to him.

There was more tenderness in it, more intimacy, than either Daniel or the young woman felt comfortable with. This awkwardness was compounded by the several people who broke into a chorus of oohs and aahs. Daniel turned and looked at the crowd. A hundred or so nosy people were watching, smiling back at him. In a flash, the girl was gone. All Daniel could do was watch her go.

Kasuf looked toward a group of elderly women. The women conferred among themselves, then nodded back at him. Some decision had been made.

"Looks like your girlfriend's got a headache," Kawalsky called down the table, a remark that seemed to be understood even by those who spoke no English.

"Just shut up and eat your lizard, Lieutenant," which is exactly what Kawalsky did.

"Jackson," O'Neil called from the end of the table, "come over here." Daniel got up and went to where the colonel was sitting half in shadow, lighting up a cigarette. "You said that thing was an Egyptian symbol, right?"

"The *udjat*, commonly known as the Eye of Ra," explained Daniel. "There are several variations of the motif, but the early tombs at Hierakonpolis and Abydos show the—"

"Yeah, yeah whatever." O'Neil didn't care. "Look, it only stands to reason that if they know one Egyptian symbol . . ."

". . . They'll know others! We can write to one another. Let me try." Excited, he got to his feet, and with the attention of the entire courtyard focused on him, made his way in front of the Elders' table. He got down to his knees and stared at the packed earth, trying to think of an appropriate symbol word. He scribbled the first thing that came into his head: "FEAST." When he looked up, the Elders all looked like they were choking on their food. Kasuf stood up, shouting at Daniel as he did so. Daniel was panic-stricken. That particular glyph, he reasoned, probably meant something nasty in their language. Quickly, he rubbed the symbol out and began writing the first sentence in hieroglyphics he had ever learned, the first exercise in Gardiner's Grammar:

"He says: the one who has come in peace, and traversed the heavens, is Ra."

Daniel wasn't halfway through the sentence's twenty-three signs when Kasuf's sandal came down on top of his work. The old man averted his eyes as he rubbed the message out with his foot. As he did this, he began shouting instructions for the crowd to disperse, flashing a nervous smile at Daniel every few seconds. Kasuf was in a difficult position. On the one hand, the gods had strictly forbidden writing in all its forms. He, as shepherd of his people, was responsible for enforcing this rule. On the other hand, these strange visitors had probably been sent by Ra. Did the prohibition against writing extend to the gods themselves? Was this a test? Kasuf didn't know. He chose to stop Daniel from writing the way he made most of his decisions, out of habit.

As the hundreds of people began milling reluctantly toward the courtyard's exits, Daniel came back to his comrades.

"Why is it, Jackson, that every time I tell you to communicate with these folks, you cause some sort of explosion. What the hell did you write?"

"Nothing, they're totally overreacting. I wrote 'banquet.'"

"That's a pretty strong reaction," Kawalsky said.

"I know, it's almost like they're afraid of writing."

"More likely, they're not allowed to write," O'Neil theorized. "I don't know what it is, but these people are scared shitless of something."

When he'd obliterated the last of Daniel's chicken scratchings, Kasuf hurried over to where Daniel was standing and fell to his knees, talking a mile a minute. He seemed to be apologizing. During his speech, a group of young men came to whisk the dinner table away. Kawalsky reached out and snagged one last piece of lizard meat before they took it. A moment later, Kasuf had summoned the group of elderly women. They surrounded Daniel, speaking their language, giggling at their own jokes, and playing with Daniel's clothes and hair.

Several more women arrived and began leading the soldiers to their sleeping quarters, while others pulled Daniel toward his.

"Should I go with them?" he asked O'Neil, really wanting to go. In spite of the responsibility still resting on his shoulders, the job of getting the team back through the StarGate, he had only one thing on his mind. The women were taking him toward the same exit he'd seen the young woman go through.

"Go ahead," O'Neil said. As soon as the colonel discovered that these people had no writing, nothing that could help them open the StarGate, Daniel became useless to him. O'Neil rearranged his mental list of who was most expendable, putting Daniel on top.

Feretti was dragged across the marble floor. Barely conscious, he felt like he'd been hit by a subway train. He was fighting to open his eyes, to stay alive, keep awake. Whoever was dragging him suddenly stopped and let him crash onto the floor. He concentrated on his breathing. He could taste the blood in his mouth, felt the marble floor cooling the side of his face. When he finally got his eyes open and focused, he saw where they'd brought him—to a sarcophagus. Standing in the middle of the room was a coffin-shaped stone box four feet high. He'd never seen a sarcophagus before but as soon as his eyes focused on it, he knew very clearly what it was. He assumed it was for him. But a moment later, the thing began to move. Section by section, the granite walls of the casket peeled away like the petals of a smooth mechanical lotus blossom. At the same time, a platform, like a narrow bed lifted upward into view. Atop this platform was a human body wrapped in dark wet cloth. To Feretti's horror, the shape came to life. Very slowly, it sat up, then pushed away the damp shroud. When the cloth fell away from the figure's face, Feretti heard himself wail. Before him was a glowing golden face, a living version of the Tutankhamen death mask. Part humanoid, part otherworldly. The black eye sockets stared at him for an unendurable moment until the mask turned away. The terrified soldier heard something move up behind him, and a moment later, the butt end of a rifle-like weapon smashed into the back of his skull.

When the women were gone, Daniel flopped down on the big lumpy bed in the center of the room and let out a great sigh of relaxation.

"I smell like a yak," he said to the walls.

For the last half hour, he had been lathered, shaved,

undressed, bathed, powdered, groomed, manicured, massaged, perfumed, and dressed in a long white robe by the enthusiastic matrons. The mattress felt lumpy, like it was stuffed with balls of string. He didn't care. It was just so good to lay down and relax. His entire body was sore, scratched, sunburned, and ready for sleep.

He told himself that he ought to spend an hour or so making notes on all the things he'd seen. But instead contented himself with replaying the sequence of events mentally. It seemed incredible to him that he had seen the StarGate for the first time only forty-eight hours before. And now here he was bedding down in the guest quarters of this town that could have existed in ancient Egypt.

He still wasn't quite sure whether he'd stumbled into an archaeologists dream or nightmare. These people's dress, customs, architecture, economy—every detail fascinated him, reshaping his notions of what life along the Nile must have been from 800–200 B.C. But nothing he had seen or learned helped him with the all-important task at hand: finding the code that would activate the StarGate in the pyramid. He remembered the conference-room discussion he'd had with General West and the promise he'd made to bring the soldiers back through the device. Ever since he'd arrived in this strange new place and had seen the great deserted pyramid in the dunes, he'd forgotten that promise. Tomorrow, he decided, he would refocus his concentration. To do that, he would have to leave Nagada.

Although these gentle people had been generous and welcoming beyond measure, they were unwilling to help him find the hieroglyphs he needed. They obviously knew what writing was, otherwise they wouldn't have reacted as quickly and as strongly as they did. After the party-ending episode with Kasuf in the central square, Daniel had tried again with the women who had lead him to this room. One of them had a highly polished piece of silver that she used as a mirror. Across the surface of this, Daniel had sprinkled some white powder and then drew a couple of symbols. The women met these attempts to communicate with the same aggressive refusal Kasuf had shown. They took the mirror away and wagged their fingers at him. O'Neil's theory made sense: it was as if writing was forbidden to them. The question of who had done the forbidding wasn't Daniel's problem. Not yet.

He made up his mind that first thing in the morning, he must somehow convince these people to lead him to another city where the people could speak, write, and think for themselves.

Daniel felt himself drifting off. He could hear a procession of musicians in the street below making their way toward his apartment. They played their instruments at a mercifully low volume. A moment later, there was unmistakable whispering outside his door. He bolted up, thinking there might be danger. A hand reached through the curtains and parted them, allowing someone to step into the room.

It was her. The girl he'd been so interested in. Now she was moving toward him, eyes cast on the ground, wrapped in a long white robe exactly like the one he was wearing. Daniel's heart pole vaulted into his throat. He got to his feet wondering what was going on. The girl looked nervous, unsure of herself as she walked toward him. When she was halfway across the room, she stopped and loosened the knot in her sash, letting the robe fall to the floor, exposing her beautiful naked body.

Daniel gulped.

14

THE DISCOVERY

Everything in this primitive city was rugged, dilapidated and scarred. The rocky plaster of Daniel's sleeping chamber looked jagged in the uneven candle light. This background made the girl's smooth cream brown skin seem all the more miraculous. She stood there with her robe at her ankles, trembling ever so slightly, looking at Daniel. Neither of them knew exactly what to do next.

By the time the shock wore off, Daniel was blushing hotter than a red pepper. He quickly realized what was going on.

"You don't have to do that," he said, and bent down to retrieve the girl's robe. He could see that this delicate creature was frightened. Obviously, the Elders had seen him eyeing her and had decided to give him a gift. Suddenly he was terribly embarrassed. He had been very indiscreet, and now his infatuation had lead to this traumatic episode for this innocent girl. He picked up the robe and went to drape it over her shoulders, but to his surprise, she resisted getting dressed. Although she couldn't understand his words, Daniel tried to explain.

"I'm so sorry. I'm really sorry. Don't worry, you don't have to go through with this. I mean, I like you, believe me. You're really beautiful, but . . . do you understand?"

Eventually, she allowed herself to be wrapped up in the

robe. Daniel put an arm around her and tenderly escorted her to the door. He pulled back the curtain and, just to make sure she understood how much he liked her, he put his hand on her cheek and smiled tenderly.

About a hundred people, the town Elders among them, had gathered on the footbridge just outside waiting for the outcome of the girl's visit. Another crowd of people were gawking from the balcony of the building across the narrow street.

"Kha shi ma nelay?" Kasuf barked at Sha'uri. *"Kha shi?"*

The girl tried explaining something to the old man, but he flew off the handle, angrily shaking his finger and yelling at her. The girl gave up trying to explain, hung her head, and started sobbing. Kasuf turned to Daniel, suddenly humble and pleasant. He started apologizing rapidly in his language, afraid the girl had done something to displease their esteemed guest. Groveling theatrically, he came forward until he grabbed the girl by the wrist, intending to drag her off. In a flash, Daniel had her free hand and was pulling her back toward him. He wrapped an arm around her shoulder and smiled his biggest, brightest smile.

"Just wanted to say"—he fumbled for words—"er, to say . . . Thanks! Yes, that's it: thank you so much. I couldn't be more pleased. It's a really weird thing for you to do, but the point I'm trying to make here is thank you, thank you, thank you." He knew these people couldn't understand his words, but perhaps he would understand his tone of voice.

The crowd stared back at him uncomprehendingly as he pushed the girl back inside.

"Good night now!"

He pulled the curtains closed and breathed a sigh of relief. The last thing he wanted was to get this girl in trouble. He turned and looked at her.

"Sorry about that."

A look of surprise flashed across her face. A moment later she was untying her robe once more.

"No, no, that's okay." Daniel motioned for her to stop, and, completely confused, she did. He signaled for her to sit down on the bed, which she did. He crossed the room until he was a comfortable distance away and sat down with his back against the wall. They looked at each other. Daniel smiled. The girl smiled. They looked at each other some more.

Since the moment Daniel had laid eyes on her, he'd wanted nothing more than to be close to her, to spend some quiet time learning to overcome their linguistic and cultural differences. Now that opportunity was here, he didn't know what to say.

Kawalsky, Brown, and O'Neil had been taken to quarters on the far side of the same building. Each was given a separate room radiating off a common parlor. They had gathered in the parlor, the only room with windows. For thirty minutes, Brown had been working the radio equipment, trying every trick he knew to raise Feretti and the others.

O'Neil stood at one of the windows where he could see the storm beating against the huge walls that circled the city. With his back turned to the others, O'Neil was absently rolling something around between his fingers. It was the orange key he had taken from the device hidden in the bowels of the equipment cart. When the curtains covering the main entryway opened, O'Neil quickly pocketed the key. Kawalsky unholstered his pistol.

They had a visitor. It was Skaara, who was starting to make it his business to go everywhere O'Neil went. His desire to stick close to the colonel put him in a minority of one. The people of Nagada, like O'Neil's own soldiers, sensed dangerous unpredictability oozing from the man in the black beret and had tried to keep their distance. Everyone, that is, except this kid, the first person O'Neil had frightened. Now he was following him everywhere, studying his every move. As soon as he was in the room, Skaara hurried to a corner and sat down against the wall, showing he wouldn't be any trouble. Kawalsky looked at O'Neil, who nodded that it was okay for the boy to stay.

During the banquet, O'Neil had noticed the teenager sitting in the shadows, watching. And that's what he was doing right now.

O'Neil left Brown and Kawalsky, walking into his private chamber where he sat down in one of the uncomfortable chairs. The boy, afraid but determined to act fearlessly, came into the room and sat down a few feet away.

O'Neil, ignoring the kid, took a cigarette out of his pack and lit it. When the flame shot out of the lighter, the boy nearly jumped out of his skin. Nevertheless, when he'd caught his breath, he reached over and pulled a cigarette out of O'Neil's pack, mimicking the colonel's movements, pretending to smoke.

"Lighter," O'Neil pronounced the word carefully, then tossed the Zippo to Skaara. The boy lit the thing several times, fascinated, before clumsily lighting the end of his cigarette. Casting a sidelong glance at the boy, O'Neil flicked the ash from his cigarette. Skaara did the same.

The two of them sat there for a moment. Skaara was starting to feel pretty damn confident. He was, after all, the only one hanging out with these remarkable visitors. O'Neil saw the boy's cockiness and couldn't resist. He took a long drag on his cigarette then inhaled deeply. With a wise-guy smirk on his face, Skaara went through the same motion, but the split second the hot smoke reached his lungs, his eyes bulged wide-open. He came up gagging. He doubled over and staggered across the room until he crashed into the bed, the fire in his throat and nose getting worse as he coughed.

Brown and Kawalsky could hear the kid coughing, but decided not to go investigate.

When he could, Skaara propped himself against the bed and threw the foul little thing on the floor, never to smoke again.

"Good idea," said the colonel, extinguishing his own smoke then coming across the room to ground out the one the boy had thrown. When he looked up, he got an ugly surprise. The boy, his eyes still full of water, was reaching for the pistol he'd seen O'Neil fire that afternoon near the city's main gate. Just as the curious young man's fingers touched the barrel of the gun, he heard O'Neil boom.

"No! Dangerous!" O'Neil pinned the boy's hand on the bed, knocking the gun away. Then he deliberately slapped Skaara's hand, slapped it hard. Kawalsky and Brown came around the corner in time to see O'Neil, the pistol in one hand, shaking the kid with the other, saying, "No, no, no, no, no."

The moment O'Neil turned him loose, Skaara darted for the door and escaped. The colonel followed him across the room, pulled the curtains open, and watched him flee.

When the boy was gone, O'Neil sat down on the rock-hard bed they'd given him and concentrated on cleaning his pistol. His encounter with Skaara had surprised him—they had actually played together—something O'Neil hadn't done in quite some time. And just as he expected, his thoughts began drifting back to Earth and his own son.

Even before Jack Junior was born, O'Neil began to change. Not only did he start feeling happier and more alive, but for the first time that he could remember, he actually began looking forward to coming home. The birth was the most rewarding thing he'd ever been a part of. At the same time, his enthusiasm for Jump Two slowly began to die. He was losing his taste for bloodshed and violence.

The afternoon of his son's sixth birthday party had been a crucial day. Standing behind his son at the head of the table, excitedly helping the boy rip into his presents, O'Neil looked up and caught Sarah smiling at him. An intense feeling of gratitude flooded into him out of nowhere. He realized that he was no longer the angry, empty kid he had been while growing up, the boy that would hurt people and things because he didn't know any other way to be. Sarah had done this for him, and even though they'd already been married for a long time, he suddenly understood that he owed this woman his life.

The next morning, he walked into the staff sergeant's office and told them he wanted out of Jump Two. At first, his superiors refused. O'Neil was the team's go-to guy, the best soldier in this elite fighting squad. But he was adamant and, eventually, rather than drive him from the armed services all together, they gave him an instructor's position at the Marine Corps training facility at Yuma. They warned him, however, that Special Forces personnel of his caliber never really retired. Someday, he would be called upon for another mission. Of course, he hadn't imagined it would lead him to anything like his present assignment, especially after he'd been tossed out of the service.

By the time the boy, J.J., was twelve, he and his dad were best friends. As a player-coach combo, they became the perennial team to beat at the local little league. The only disturbing thing was that somehow, despite his father's transformation, the boy had inherited the same wildness of heart O'Neil had. He started getting into more and more trouble at school, crossing the line between "rowdy" and "violent." Sarah was concerned about it, but when she tried to bring the subject up, the two men closed ranks. They would exchange smirking smiles, members of the house's "Boys Only" club.

Remembering how he'd indulged the boy's recklessness, O'Neil sighed loudly enough to attract the attention of Kawalsky and Brown. O'Neil banged his head backward against the wall. He didn't do this violently, but it was more than enough to draw stares from the two soldiers at the window.

Brown turned to Kawalsky and, trying to keep the question as light as possible, asked, "Is it just me, or is there something real wrong with that guy?"

"Just follow his orders," Kawalsky said. "He must have been put in charge for a good reason."

Brown stared back at him for a minute before asking, "you really believe that?"

They had been sitting there staring at each for an awfully long time before Daniel felt the need to try talking. He cleared his throat like he was about to call a meeting to order, then introduced himself to the angel sitting stiffly on his bed.

"I'm Daniel. Daniel."

"Dan-durr?" she asked.

"No, Dan-yur. Me Daniel," he enunciated carefully, pointing to himself. She smiled tentatively and nodded.

"Dan-yur," she repeated before pointing to herself and saying, "Sha'uri."

"Sha'uri? Ok, Sha'uri. Hi."

After another awkward pause, Daniel went on.

"We came from the pyramid." He looked at her. "You know, pyramid? Four equal sides converging to a single apex. Um, you're probably not going to like this, but I'm going to draw you a picture." He raced his forefinger through the sand on the floor, outlining the shape, then looked up at her expectantly. Sha'uri turned her head and averted her eyes.

"I know, I know. You're not allowed." Frustrated, he stood up and walked to the far side of the room, put his forehead against the wall, and went on talking.

"What is it with you people? I mean, I've heard of graphophobia, but this is ridiculous. Anyway, you're obviously not going to be able to help us find what we need, so I should just give it a rest, right?" Sha'uri sensed how frustrated he was. She took a deep breath and a huge risk. When Daniel turned around, she was leaning over the drawing he had made, augmenting it.

Daniel came back across the room to see what she was doing. Across the peak of the pyramid, she drew a line and above that, a circle. It was the same sign Daniel had found on the cover stones, the seventh symbol that had cracked the code to the StarGate.

"That's the sign for Earth! Do you know this symbol?"

Sha'uri looked up at Daniel suddenly very nervous. She had broken one of her people's fundamental laws, a violation that could have lead to her immediate execution. Since she wasn't dead already, she calculated that Daniel wasn't an agent sent by the gods to test the city. But now she had another problem. She had to communicate the extreme danger of the situation to him. She knew he'd want to know more, but she couldn't help him any further until he understood how dangerous reading and writing were.

With Sha'uri holding a torch and showing him the way, Daniel pulled the hood of the robe she'd found for him low over his face. As they stole furtively through the winding streets, Daniel realized that Nagada was built on a slope. They were nearing the corrals where the hundred or so *mastadges* were kept penned up at night. They were "perfuming the evening" with the pungent aroma of fresh dung. The back perimeter wall of the compound loomed in the distance. Then Sha'uri stopped at a tall stone building with a doorway defined by a graceful lancet arch. She pulled him by the sleeve into the pitch-black atrium where the torch's flickering threw just enough light into the recesses of the abandoned structure for Daniel to see that it was probably once a covered marketplace, but now, judging from the intense smell of manure, acted as a commodious compost heap. Daniel's eyes began to tear up under the assault of the biting acrid stench.

Taking him deeper into the squalid darkness, Sha'uri showed him a stone staircase that lead down to a dead end. Whatever door might have once stood at the bottom of these stairs had long since been blocked over with large stones. Nevertheless, they descended. About halfway down, Sha'uri passed the torch to Daniel and reached into the gap between the stairs and the wall. She loosened a hidden retaining pin, then pushed one of the stone slabs out of the way, revealing a narrow opening—just enough space for them to slide through.

Once they were inside, they found themselves in the basement of the building in a thick forest of beams that rose up to support the wooden floor above them. Low corridors ran off in several directions. Sha'uri took the torch from Daniel and led him into one of these dank passages. She hadn't been down there since she was a girl, but after only a couple of wrong turns, she brought them to the top of another narrow staircase. This one was very ancient, and carved from a single large stone that had begun to crumble in several places. At the bottom of these stairs, they found themselves in a square earthen cell. More tunnels twisted away into the darkness, but Sha'uri brought the torch close to the wall, filthy with years of dust and grime, and illuminated the symbol for Earth: sun-over-pyramid.

Astonished, Daniel came to the wall and reached out to touch it. It had been carefully carved an inch deep into a smooth section of the stone wall. It was the only writing in the room. Daniel thought for a minute and then noticed that all the walls were made of roughly cut stone. All except the area around the symbol. On a hunch, he began brushing the centuries of dirt away from the lone hieroglyph until he found what he was looking for—a crevice.

The sign was cut into the middle of a door. He scraped away as much dirt as he could from between the door and jamb, he wedged his fingers into the space. Prying at it with all he was worth, he managed to budge it open about half an inch. Sha'uri propped the torch against the wall and lent her fingers, as strong as Daniel's, to the effort. Finally, the door swung open.

Daniel pushed the torch through the doorway.

"Oh, my, God." Daniel couldn't believe what he was looking at. There was a narrow hallway five feet tall and approximately fifty feet long. Every inch of it was jammed with Egyptian hieroglyphic writing, the long dead language he could read and write fluently. There were portraits, painted scenes, etchings, and carved reliefs in the classic "frontalism" style. But mainly there was text, long strips of hieroglyphic writing chiseled into the walls.

Daniel thought he must have died and gone to Egyptologist heaven. Sha'uri had led him into a lush forest of mysterious signs, probably the most densely written and rewritten palimpsest ever. An intense, convoluted puzzle that, despite its jumbled, Talmudic format, was executed with religious care, giving the room a shrine quality. Daniel licked his lips and waded deeper into the room.

Sha'uri couldn't believe it, either. Like everyone in Nagada, she vaguely knew what writing was even though she couldn't do it. As a child, she and her friends had invented several symbols and written each other notes in the sand. But when they were discovered, they were punished very severely.

In her world, there was no need for writing. There were no books, street signs, or spelling bees. They had stories of course, but only ones that were spoken. Once a song or a story was forgotten, it was lost forever. Before stepping into this small corridor, she had absolutely no idea that this galaxy of symbols existed. She couldn't comprehend how utterly complex the rules for understanding them must be. She looked at Daniel with new eyes: was he a wizard that he could interpret and make these marks?

Obviously he was. Holding the torch to the wall, he'd already been able to discern that every entry told a story. The earliest were large historical tableaux. Generations of historians who came later found whatever space was left and shaped their stories to fit the empty spots. Most of the writing moved right to left, but some of it went in the opposite direction. Where necessary, the script ran top to bottom while in other places it was written in the style called boustrophedon the back-and-forth format that meant, literally, "an ox travels back and forth when plowing the fields." This riot of writing, this colorful cacophony of characters, taken together, was a semiotic treasure chest, a cave full of archaeological loot. It was the ancient history of the people of this world.

Daniel isolated the cave's original story. Told in relatively large pictures sculpted directly onto the wall, then painted over, it was not an uplifting tale. The first panel depicted several of the tutelary gods, the same anthropomorphized animal deities worshiped in ancient Egypt. They were tearing children from the grasps of their screaming mothers, herding them away across the desert. Anubis, the jackal-headed god of the dead, seemed to be supervising the work of the other gods. Horus, the hawk, was present as was Thoth, the baboon-headed deity of words and magic, the one who recorded the names of the dead in the underworld.

The scene shifted to some kind of battle or civil uprising, and then the people were shown in chains floating over the desert, as if in a collective dream. When they woke, they fell to the ground where the gods and their warriors brutalized the people, forcing them through a StarGate.

Daniel studied the hieroglyphic writing surrounding the pictures. The grammatical elements were definitely related to the writing he'd found on the cover stones, but the symbols before him were even more rudimentary. No one on Earth had spoken the language of the ancient Egyptians since the last temples were ordered closed by the Christian Emperor Theodosius I in A.D. 391. Since the hieroglyphs left behind on temple walls and papyrus scrolls was written in consonants only, linguistic researchers could only speculate about the vowel structure. Several top-notch Egyptologists, Daniel included, had developed pronunciation schemes, but they were all largely guesswork. Daniel, never afraid to venture a guess, started reading the signs aloud.

Holding the torch, he moved close to a section of the glyph-cluttered wall and began. *"Naadas yan tu yeewah. Suma'ehmay ra ma yedat."* It was a story about moving across a desert, a population migrating not out of choice, but by force.

Sha'uri watched and listened carefully. As Daniel read the signs on the wall, she tried to see the connection between the painted symbols and the sounds he was making.

"*Nandas sikma ti yu na'nay ashay,*" Daniel continued.

"*Seekhma?*" Sha'uri asked, the word had caught her attention.

Daniel whipped his head around and looked at her. Was she trying to communicate? Had he stumbled across a word she understood?

In her language, *seekhma* was the word meaning "children." Over Daniel's shoulder, she could see a picture carved into the wall, a scene of many people being herded like animals. Many of the figures were clearly intended to represent children. "*Seekhma,*" she said again.

"*Sikma?*" Daniel asked urgently, pointing to the hieroglyph for children. Sha'uri looked at the symbol, which held no meaning for her.

"*Seekhma,*" she said, pointing to the illustration on the wall, singling out the children.

"Yes!" he yelled. "Yes, *sikma,* children! Of course!"

Daniel's suspicion had been right all along. Sha'uri and her people spoke a dialect of ancient Egyptian. And, by a stroke of sheer luck, they had stumbled across this word, *seekhma,* which had changed little over the centuries.

Excited, Daniel immediately found another symbol, the one for "god."

"*Nefer?*" This time the written symbol was more abstract. The glyph consisted of an eye over two feathers. Sha'uri looked at the symbol, but couldn't immediately guess its meaning.

"*Nef-ear? Naifar?*" Daniel asked, then showed her the picture of Anubis and several other animal deities who were herding the humans across the desert.

Neyoum ifar!" Sha'uri yelled, as if she had just won a round of charades.

"*Nay-youm-ee-far?*" Daniel asked, realizing how radically different their pronunciations were. He practiced saying the word several times, quickly bringing his accent in line with hers. He was doing it, he was speaking the dead language of the pharaohs, a language he had been looking at for many years.

Sha'uri said the word several times, carefully enunciating each syllable, teaching Daniel to say it the way she did.

"Yes." He was agog. "Teach me to speak. Uh, teach— *takera? Tekira?* Sha'uri *takera* Daniel, okay?"

"Sha'uri tahki-yeer Dan-yur."

It was the first time in her life that a man had openly asked her to teach him. Sha'uri swelled with pride. This man with all his exotic skills was asking her for instruction. It was the first moment of her transformation.

For his part, Daniel was smiling like he had died and gone to heaven with this beautiful woman assigned to be his guide. And it wasn't even midnight yet.

According to the watch on O'Neil's wrist, it was 8:21 P.M., Rocky Mountain Time. But beyond the city's fortress walls, the first of the day's three suns was dawning on the horizon. The storm was over, and the dark sky looked utterly clear.

O'Neil stood at one of the parlor room's windows next to Brown, who had set the radio on the sill and was trying to reestablish contact with Feretti in total disregard of whether the neighbors might still be sleeping. He had a big strong voice to begin with, and now that he was frustrated and starting to fear for the base-camp team, it became even stronger. Finally, he turned to O'Neil.

"No use, I can't raise 'em."

"What are you getting, more interference?"

"No," he replied, "nothing but dead air. There should at least be a tracking signal, but I'm not getting anything."

"Colonel!" The shout came from outside.

O'Neil crossed the room and stepped out onto one of the many rope and lumber footbridges suspended between the buildings. In the shadowy street below, he could make out the vague outline of his lieutenant.

"Jackson's not in his room," Kawalsky called up. "I've been looking everywhere, but I can't find him."

"What is that you're holding?"

"His jacket," Kawalsky answered, obviously peeved about having to carry it around for His Royal Professorship.

O'Neil looked out at the horizon where the night sky was melting to purple morning. They could feasibly leave now for the pyramid, but O'Neil decided to wait for full daylight. He estimated it would be another half an hour before they had full visibility.

The colonel figured Daniel was most likely out collecting wildflowers and writing poetry, but there was the odd chance something very good or very bad had happened. If that was the case, he wanted to know about it. They could afford thirty minutes of looking for him, no more.

Two minutes later, O'Neil was downstairs. He and Kawalsky were following their noses toward the sharp smell coming off from the *mastadge* corral. They spotted Skaara sitting on the fence surrounded by a handful of other kids.

Skaara still had O'Neil's lighter. He felt he had earned the right to brag about his encounter with the aliens, and that's exactly what he was doing, firing up the lighter and retelling the story of how he'd gotten it. Nabeh, the crazy-looking shepherd with the big head and wild teeth kept trying to touch the flame even though Skaara warned him not to. Nabeh, older and slower than the other boys, was Skaara's sidekick and devoted pal.

The boys scattered when they saw the two soldiers walking toward them. All except Skaara, even though he was as frightened as any of them. He knew firsthand how unpredictable and violent the man in the black beret could be. Skaara sat on the fence without flinching.

"Wait here," O'Neil told Kawalsky. He walked over to the boy by himself. He leaned against the corral fence and watched the big woolly *mastadges* work out some of their morning energy by racing around the corral. He wanted to tell the kid that he was sorry about slapping him the night before, that he'd done it strictly out of concern for the boy's safety. And if he'd overreacted, he at least had plenty of reason to do so because of everything he'd been going through for the past couple of years. But O'Neil, even if he spoke the boy's language wouldn't have been able to dive that far into his own feelings without starting to drown. Instead, he stood there quietly watching the *mastadges* sprint through the cold morning air. When he looked over at the boy, Skaara lit up an imaginary cigarette, took a deep drag, and then exhaled visibly into the frosty morning air. The kid was letting him off the hook, showing him there were no hard feelings.

"I'm looking for Jackson," O'Neil said to the boy, who, of course, didn't understand. "See? Jackson," he held up the jacket, but still got no glimmer. The other boys began edging their way closer. How could the colonel get his message across to them? Speaking slowly and too loudly, he explained, "We're . . . looking for . . . Jackson." O'Neil made circles with his hands and held them over his eyes, imitating a pair of glasses. The boys copied his movement, cupping their hands over their eyes and laughing.

"No. I mean . . ." O'Neil pretended to sneeze.

"Ohh!" Skaara suddenly understood and pointed to O'Neil, *"Bock bock, bock bock?"* in a fairly good imitation of Daniel's chicken sounds. They all understood at once. All the boys quickly joined in like a choir of chickens.

"Yeah, that's right. Chicken man. Where's chicken man?" O'Neil said, happy to have finally made some connection with these kids.

Skaara took Daniel's jacket from O'Neil then yelled some type of command to the animals. A moment later, the mangiest member of the herd, "Little Bit," came trotting over to the fence, neighing like a truck motor badly in need of oil.

Skaara held the jacket up to the *mastadge's* nose. When Daniel's smell penetrated the beast's giant nostrils, it suddenly reared up on it's thin but powerful hind legs and let out a roar that woke up half the city.

Skaara shouted for Nabeh to let her out. As soon as the gate was open, the big ox came barreling out of the corral at a furious clip. She was half a block away before Skaara led the boys in pursuit of the animal.

"Smart boy," O'Neil said.

A cracked and faded pyramid hovered in the sky, rays of light as bright as the sun's shooting from its underside. Below, the deteriorating image of a boy-king, attired in full pharaonic regalia, extending his arms to bathe in the light. At his feet, several of ancient Egypt's animal-headed gods were kneeling, their heads bowed in supplication.

Daniel scratched his chin, thinking. He was sure now that this sequence of paintings had come first. Whoever the original historian to come down into these catacombs had begun with this story, the strange coronation of this boy-king. Sha'uri was leaning against the opposite wall doing her best to stay awake and help Daniel with the work. She'd never seen anything like the incredible concentration he brought to this task.

"Barei bidi peesh," he asked her, *"shana? sha'ana?"*

"Chan'ada," she gave him the pronunciation.

"Chan'ada sedma miznah, no: miz- mir- mirnaz. Chan-'ada sedma mirnaz, min?"

"Min," she said with a smile.

"Looks like you found what you were looking for." A voice came from the darkness.

Sha'uri gasped, and Daniel, caught completely by surprise, thrust the torch wildly in the direction of the voice. It was O'Neil stooping to walk under the narrow chamber's low ceiling with Kawalsky right behind him.

"You scared the hell out of me," Daniel yelled, his heart thumping like mad. "How'd you get down here?"

"I thought you didn't speak their language," O'Neil said hotly, coming deeper into the chaotically painted passageway.

"It's ancient Egyptian," Daniel said, "but like the rest of their culture, it's evolved independently. But, once you know the vowels, take into account the neutralization of aspiration, the loss of apical and final consonants—"

"Give it to me in English, Jackson."

"I just had to learn how to pronounce it. It hasn't been a living spoken language in more than a thousand years?"

"This place is a damn trip," said Brown, coming around the corner with a powerful flashlight. "It looks like King Tut's tomb got turned into a subway station full of graffiti."

O'Neil was interested in only one thing. "What does it say in here, Jackson?"

Exhilarated, eager to explain what he had learned, Daniel moved across the riot of hieroglyphs like a kid in a candy store.

"It's . . . well, it's simply unbelievable. These walls tell the story of the original settlers of this planet. These people came through the StarGate some ten thousand years ago. It says . . ." Daniel walked up to a long series of drawings and hieroglyphs, tracing his finger quickly over the etchings.

"A traveler, from distant stars, escaped from a dying world looking for a way to extend his own life. His body was decaying and weak, yet with all his powers and knowledge he could not prevent his own demise," Daniel paraphrased. "Apparently, his whole species was becoming extinct, so he searched the galaxies looking for a way to cheat death. Look here . . ."

Again Daniel rushed over to another series of drawings. As O'Neil listened to Daniel, he became lost in the story. It was as though O'Neil could completely visualize every word Daniel said. The visions did not so much surprise O'Neil, but confirm something deep within his darkest worries. He listened intently as Daniel continued.

"It says he came to 'a world, rich with life.' Where he encountered a 'primitive race, perfect for his needs.' Humans! A species he could repair and maintain indefinitely. He realized, within a human body, he had a chance for a new life. That's when he found the boy!"

Daniel moved over to a series of strange drawings. Etched crudely was a flying pyramid hovering over a human, shielding his eyes from the bright light. Around the drawing, several other people running away. Daniel pointed to the figure beneath the pyramid.

"He came to some kind of village. It says that the villagers ran, frightened as 'the night became day.' But one young boy walked toward the light. 'Curious and without fear,' he walked into a trap. Ra took this boy and possessed him. It's like some kind of parasite looking for a host.

"Transposed into this human form, he appointed himself ruler of all mankind. The original pharaoh, Ra the sun god!"

This was the part O'Neil had been waiting to hear. Slowly he moved closer, examining the drawings as Daniel went on.

"Using the StarGate, Ra, or Reayew as they pronounced it, brought thousands of people here to this planet as workers for the quartz mines. Just like the one we saw. Clearly, this quartz-mine mineral found here is the building block of all his technology. Only with this could he sustain eternal life.

"But something happened back on Earth, a rebellion or uprising. After hundreds of years of oppression, the people waited until Ra was here, on this side of the Gate, then they revolted, overtaking Ra's guardian war gods, and they buried the StarGate so Ra could not return. Fearful that a rebellion could happen here on this world, Ra outlawed reading and writing. He didn't want the people here to remember the truth. These drawings here are the only record they have, and none of them can read it! It's amazing."

When Daniel was finished, he waited for O'Neil to respond, but he didn't say anything, didn't move. He only stared at the wall, a faraway look of concentration on his face.

"Jackson, I think you better come over here." Kawalsky had taken the flashlight and was exploring farther down the shaft. "Tell me if this is . . . Just get over here." The guy sounded so excited about whatever it was, Sha'uri automatically got up to see what it was.

Kawalsky was only about ten yards away from the group, but with the low ceiling, the darkness, and the torches, it was tough getting to him. It wasn't a place for claustrophobics.

Kawalsky had gone around a corner and found the corridor's dead end. Enshrined in sacred writing on all sides, stood a single thin stone pillar with a vertical cartouche. Even though it was partially buried in the sand, Kawalsky could see how similar it was to the one that ran down the center of the cover stones. Daniel could too. As soon as he turned the corner and saw the shrine, he knew they'd found what they needed to operate the StarGate.

"They must have kept this here hoping that one day the Gate on Earth could be reopened," Daniel said, then poked the torch close to the tablet and tried to read the cartouche. He didn't understand a single character, which was encouraging. That probably meant they were constellations as seen from wherever this place was in the universe.

"Damn"—he suddenly remembered something—"My notebook is back there in my room. I made a list of all the signs on the—"

"Your jacket, sire," Kawalsky unceremoniously shoved the

jacket at Daniel, then went to work on digging out the lowest couple of symbols from the moist sand. Daniel consulted his notes. Sure enough, the top symbol on the cartouche matched one of those on his list.

"We've got it," Daniel proclaimed. "The symbols match."

"Problem. Big problem." Kawalsky was grave. Flash and torchlight converged on the big soldier, then moved down to the bottom of the cartouche. The last symbol was gone, broken off.

"Where's the seventh sign?"

Kawalsky got frustrated and started scooping up rough handfuls of dank soil, throwing them aside. Daniel stopped him quickly and took control of the excavation process. He dug carefully along the base of the wall until he found the fragmented remains of the seventh symbol, one piece at a time.

They spent a long time trying to fit the pieces together. All they needed was enough of the symbol to distinguish it from the others on the StarGate's wheel. After twenty minutes, they realized it was useless. Either the tablet had been intentionally broken or it had simply been eroded by too many years in the sand. There was no trace of the last symbol.

Daniel and the soldiers were stunned. There was a feeling that their incredible string of good luck had finally ended. It seemed appropriate that they were gathered around the tunnel's dead end. Now the team had two chances of ever getting home: slim and none. It was a long time before anyone spoke.

"This seventh sign is supposed to be the point of origin, right?" O'Neil asked. "Ask the girl. Maybe she knows the sign for this planet."

Sha'uri, watching the scene unfold, guessed what the colonel must be asking and shook her head.

Daniel put the question to her anyway, then turned to O'Neil. "No good, she can't write anything except the name of Ra."

"In that case, we're heading back to the pyramid." O'Neil stood up and took the torch from Sha'uri. When

none of the others got to their feet, he made himself clear:
"We leave immediately."

"Don't you understand? I can't make it work without the last symbol," Daniel shouted at him. But O'Neil didn't even look back.

15

THE GOLDEN FLYING MACHINE

A wall of sand spilled into the city as the main gates were pulled open. O'Neil unceremoniously walked out of the city, leading his soldiers. He was now absolutely determined to return to the pyramid, as if he knew exactly what he was going to do when he got there. Daniel, much less eager to go, dillydallied at the gate saying good-bye to Sha'uri, trying to explain to her that he was going to come back.

Kawalsky turned back and shouted at him.

"On the double, Jackson."

"Forget him. He's useless to us now."

Kawalsky did a double take. He didn't understand O'Neil's attitude. He glanced over at Brown, both of them thinking the same thing: the U.S. Marine Corps does not leave its people behind. Cardinal rule. Even when the squad considered them annoying jerks.

Eventually, Daniel tore himself away and jogged after the squad trying to catch up. "Hey, wait up," he yelled, feeling mistakenly that his discovery of the cartouche had carned him full membership to the team.

Kawalsky turned to watch Daniel coming toward them, spotting something else in the dunes behind him.

"Colonel O'Neil, it looks like we've made some friends." Skaara and his gang of shepherd boys came riding up behind Daniel, clinging to the sides of Little Bit, ready to enlist.

"Jackson," O'Neil barked, "get rid of those kids."

O'Neil pressed on with his march as Daniel stood and yelled at the boys in their language. They understood him well enough and shuffled their feet in the sand for a minute, neither following nor turning back. A few minutes later, when O'Neil turned to check, the kids were still there, trailing the soldiers by about one hundred yards.

"Damnit, Jackson, I told you to get rid of those kids!"

"I tried!" Daniel barked right back at him.

"Sir"—Kawalsky stepped in to make a suggestion—"we could get there a lot faster if they gave us a ride."

O'Neil was somewhere else. He didn't hear a single word of what his lieutenant had said. Still staring at the boys, he unholstered his pistol, took aim, and fired three quick shots.

"What are you *doing!*? Stop!" Daniel demanded, but he was too far away to do anything.

O'Neil fired three more times, his bullets ripping up the ground right in front of the *mastadge*, scaring her into a sudden awkward dance. The boys jumped off in all directions, hiding behind the dunes.

When the shooting was done, everyone looked in angry horror at O'Neil.

"What are you doing shooting at children? What's the matter with you?" Daniel went into a paroxysm, ballistic. "What if you hit one of them!?" Kawalsky and Brown kept quiet, but they were asking themselves the same questions. None of it made any dent on O'Ncil, who immediately turned and continued the march, reloading as he went.

Skaara poked his head over the dune and watched as the team slowly disappeared deeper into the desert. His heart felt like galloping hooves inside his slender frame. His new friend, the man in the black beret, had betrayed him. When Nabeh flopped down next to him wondering what they would do next, Skaara turned his head away even though it was obvious he was crushed.

O'Neil put Brown in charge of counting out the pace. Pressing for time, he ordered them to march as the armies of Rome had two thousand years ago: sprinting for fifty paces, then walking for fifty, then sprinting again. In this way, they covered the two-hour trek to the pit in about thirty-five minutes. Twenty minutes later, O'Neil looked up and saw something that froze him in his tracks.

"What in the . . ."

There were now two pyramids, one perched directly on top of the other. The golden walls of the upper pyramid, full of hieroglyph-like symbols, had opened into horizontal sections, revealing the complex machinery lying just below their surface. The golden flying machine that had stacked itself atop the pyramid seemed very ancient and very modern at the same time. It was obviously hollow on the inside, conically shaped, because it fit over the top of the lower structure like a golden shell. Only the bottom third of the first pyramid remained visible.

"Looks like somebody was home after all," Brown said.

"It's a spaceship," Daniel blurted out, drawing skeptical looks from his colleagues. "Well, maybe not a spaceship," he backpedaled, "but some sort of flying machine. It was on the wall of the catacomb."

In fact, he was right the first time. The ship, fully self-contained, allowed Ra to fly between the far-flung mining operations he maintained in this corner of the universe. Although he hadn't been to this small planet for many years, he had come immediately to find out why the quartz shipment had not been made on time.

O'Neil took off his small backpack and took out a pair of high-powered binoculars. The walls of the golden spacecraft were not built in one piece, but in movable sections. Soon after landing, the ship had unfolded and opened to its present size. Large sections split away from the main body and extended mechanically downward. In doing so, it revealed long strips of the complex machinery lying just below the golden surface.

The colonel scanned the surrounding area for signs of life, but could detect none. On the ridge where the base camp had been, he spotted some half-buried equipment scattered in the sand. A shred of canvas waved from an abandoned tent pole.

Without telling anyone what he was planning, O'Neil grabbed a handful of flares from his pack and started tucking them into his waistband.

"Sir?" was all Kawalsky said.

"I'm going inside," he informed them, checking the action on his automatic rifle.

That didn't make any sense. Why waltz into a potential ambush before you'd gathered as much information as possible? It was obvious to Kawalsky they should first try establishing radio contact with Feretti's team. He tried to propose the idea to O'Neil, but he was already gone, moving toward the pyramid like a human torpedo. He seemed completely oblivious to his soldiers supposedly under his command.

Kawalsky watched him go, then surprised Daniel by saying, "What are we supposed to do, stand here and hold our privates? I've had just about enough of that guy."

The big soldier unscrewed the cap of his canteen and slugged a long drink while Brown and Daniel looked at each other, not quite sure what was going on. "I guess we should go after him, back him up. What do you think?" Kawalsky looked at Brown for his opinion.

"Well, I'm not staying out here by myself," said the technology officer.

Kawalsky realized that leaving Brown here with Daniel was tantamount to leaving him by himself. Kawalsky held up his rifle and turned to Daniel.

"You know how to pull a trigger?" he asked.

Daniel forced a smile. "I don't really understand what's happening here," he said.

"Welcome to the armed forces, pal," Kawalsky said before dumping himself over the edge of the dune and chugging after the colonel.

A few minutes later, O'Neil was at the base of the ramp. He took up a position behind one of the obelisks and took a minute to assess the situation. Everything outside the pyramid was still. He peered up at the strange triangular structure perched like a Louisiana bayou pole-house atop the great pyramid. What Daniel said about it being a spacecraft seemed ludicrous, but it was better than any explanation he could come up with himself.

"Colonel O'Neil, slow down a minute." Kawalsky came running up to the obelisk. "This is all screwed up. We want to back you up, but you gotta tell us what's up. It's our job to follow orders, but you've got a responsibility to keep us informed." Kawalsky tried to maintain a tone of voice somewhere between obedient and threatening, loyal and mutinous.

"You don't want to go in, that's fine with me. But do me a favor and stay down so you don't give me away," he said glancing toward the upper pyramid. He was getting ready to go when Kawalsky reached out and caught him by the arm.

"You're not going in there alone. Just like we're not leaving Jackson behind anywhere. Marines take care of their own."

O'Neil was totally focused: reach the equipment cart, retrieve the canisters from their hidden compartment, and initiate the detonation sequence. For the sake of everyone on Earth, nothing must interfere with that goal. He had hoped to leave the men well out in the dunes, hopefully sparing their lives. But now it was too late. He couldn't risk explaining the mission to them—they might try to interfere. They would have to be sacrificed.

O'Neil looked blankly back at his lieutenant, and said as much as he could afford to. "I've got to get to the StarGate room," he said. "I wouldn't mind the help, but I'm going one way or the other."

"Two teams?" Kawalsky asked, apparently satisfied.

"Two teams," O'Neil announced. "Lieutenant, you and Brown take the rear." O'Neil took several quick breaths to oxygenate his blood, then, without warning, took off like a shot, running up the ramp at full speed. Daniel stayed in his crouched position, watching O'Neil go.

"Will you move!?" Kawalsky looked at Daniel like he was crazy. "Go!"

Daniel went. But a second later, he started asking himself what in the hell he was doing, sprinting headlong into this recently reinhabited pyramid right behind the psychotic colonel. Wouldn't the smart Daniel, he asked himself, be running in the opposite direction? The rifle Kawalsky had given him felt like a live eel in his hands. It was a struggle to keep a hold of the heavy, alien object.

He felt worse when he followed O'Neil into the shadows of the tall entryway and saw Feretti's helmet laying next to the radio. He stopped and looked down for a minute, gulped, then took off chasing O'Neil. He caught up to where the colonel was crouched against a pillar.

"Listen," O'Neil said.

Daniel was gasping for air, but fear instantly taught him how to do so in complete silence. He was too scared to listen, so he watched O'Neil listening instead.

"Good," he said, then spun around the corner and advanced six more columns in as many seconds. If Daniel had waited another second to follow him, he would have seen the shadow fall across the spot where they had been. Someone was just outside the pyramid, looking in through one of the square windows that ran the length of the entrance hall.

It was Skaara, standing on Nabeh's shoulders. He caught a glimpse of the two figures, Kawalsky and Brown, as they darted past the window. When they were gone, he jumped into the sand and led the charge for the next window.

Inside, O'Neil was standing stock-still in the shadow between two pillars, checking forward, deciding on the best path to the StarGate. Daniel was only a few feet away, his back against the opposite pillar, facing back toward the entrance. As he waited for the colonel's instructions, he noticed something moving through the shadows of the cavernous hall. Just as he tried to say something, O'Neil sprinted away around the corner.

Daniel flattened himself against the column and watched the huge figure step into the light. Daniel recognized him at once. It was Horus, the Egyptian god of the sky, the deity who sat at the side of Ra and helped to judge the worth of human souls in the land of the dead. He was just as the ancient Egyptians had depicted him—the athletic body of a man and the enormous head of a hawk. He wore armor on his shoulders, forearms, and shins. In his metal gloves, he carried a five-foot-long weapon. Daniel kept perfectly still until the shape disappeared again into the shadows.

Farther back, Brown watched Kawalsky head off around one of the pillars. Two counts later, he started to follow when *thwack!* Something heavy came down on his head with a horrible cracking sound. Brown staggered, then went to his knees. He fought desperately to recover, tried to get up and run, but a powerful blast of white light spit from the end of a five-foot rifle, shearing off the top of his shoulder.

The force of it smashed him hard into one of the pillars, where he collapsed, bleeding and dazed.

"Brown, report!"Kawalsky called out. "Where are you, man?"

Brown heard him but was too dazed, in too much pain to respond. He pushed himself across the floor toward the pillars, crawling toward the light streaking in through the small square windows.

He managed to get himself under the very window Skaara was peering in through. The boy, standing once more on Nabeh's shoulders, got a ghoulishly good view as a second Horus guard turned the corner and bore down on the defenseless soldier. He carried a pole-like weapon, a scepter that flared out at one end like a cobra's hood surrounding a large amethyst jewel set in the middle. The warrior raised the weapon, a rifle, and brought the butt end of it down on Brown's neck.

As soon as he had heard the shrill whine of the first shot, O'Neil hit the deck, belly-sliding for cover. He was near the end of the Entrance Hall, about to enter the sloping Grand Gallery, crouched and silently waiting for word to come from behind. He had no intention of giving away his position by calling to his soldiers.

He couldn't wait any longer. Silently, he headed for the doorway leading into the Grand Gallery when a grenade-size ball of light came fishtailing through the darkness, heading straight for him. He leapt out of the way, and the shot exploded against the wall behind him with concussive force, raining scraps of granite on the floor.

Kawalsky ducked out from his hiding place and fired blindly toward the area where he'd seen the power burst originate. Then, from the side, he felt his assault rifle clubbed from his hands by a single heavy blow. He turned and came face-to-face with his attacker. It was another one of the Horus soldiers. The creature's large head, a stylized image of a hawk, seemed to be made from the same metallic substance as his body armor. The parts of him that weren't covered were intensely muscular.

Standing too close to fire the long rifle, the warrior brought it up with both hands into Kawalsky's chin, snapping the man's head back violently. But Kawalsky reached out and grabbed onto the weapon before his opponent could step back and fire. The two of them began to grapple at close quarters, which built Kawalsky's confidence. Hand-to-hand combat was his specialty, and this opponent, although skillful, seemed no match for him.

The hawk had a unique weapon that kept Kawalsky off balance. As the two men battled for control of the weapon, he used his sharp beak to poke and slash. Kawalsky countered by forcing the rifle upward, then attacking the man's unarmored midsection. Using the staff for extra leverage, he landed a vicious kick to the other man's stomach, doubling him over. He twisted the weapon free and was about to attack again, when he was hit from behind, a sledgehammer blow nailing him right on the crown of his head. In the liquid, woozy moment before he blacked out, Kawalsky turned around and looked into another pair of expressionless bird eyes staring down at him. He realized too late that the enemy was working in pairs.

Daniel had watched the whole thing. He was standing a few strides away, petrified by fear. The fight was over so quickly, and now, Kawalsky, the strongest man he'd ever met, had succumbed to these impossible yet utterly familiar creatures. In all the time he'd studied Egyptology, it had never once occurred to him that ancient gods might in fact be real.

Inching backward deeper into the shadows, he listened to his own deafening pulse pounding against his eardrums. As soon as Kawalsky had fallen, the twin Horus warriors had separated, retreating into darkness. His mind started scattering in a thousand directions, adrenaline racing through his bloodstream. Daniel took a deep breath and tried to focus. When the thing comes back, he told himself, use the rifle. Concentrate: point the rifle at the head—no, at the stomach, Kawalsky kicked him in the stomach—and then pull the trigger.

Then there was something behind him. He felt it coming around the corner of the pillar, but it was moving fast and before he could react, it took him. A powerful hand clapped down over his mouth and pulled his head back to expose his throat. Daniel's eyes bugged to silver-dollar size, sure he was a goner, waiting to feel the ice-hot knife blade slit open his throat.

Then came a whisper. "I need your help." O'Neil's lips were practically inside his ear. "We're going to StarGate, and you're going to cover me, understand?"

The colonel waited until he felt Daniel nod yes, then, still cradling the head under his arm like a football, he leaned around the pillar to check the hallway. When the coast looked clear, he stood Daniel up and pushed him up against the wall just hard enough to capture his full attention.

He could see that Daniel was on the verge of freaking out, so he spoke to him in a deliberately calm, almost relaxed way.

"This is how it's going to go. You follow me forward, but keep looking back and shoot at anything that follows us. Now, let's move. Fast." He reached down and clicked the safety switch on Daniel's rifle to the off position. A second later, they were running at top speed deeper into the pyramid.

What was O'Neil making him do? a voice screeched inside his head. This was only the Entrance Hall! They weren't even close to the StarGate room, and the rest of the way would be in the pitch-black. Daniel's stride began to falter until he realized that the alternative to sticking with O'Neil was facing the Horuses by himself. He increased his speed and raced beyond the reach of the last light coming in the square windows.

O'Neil broke open a flare as he ran, and began waving it erratically over his head to make himself a more difficult target. As soon as he had his bearings, he tomahawked the flare far out ahead of them. When they ran past, Daniel sped up to get out of the light, then turned to run backward watching for anyone who might try to follow.

They took the rest of the Grand Gallery at full speed. O'Neil used another flare when he guessed they were coming to the hallway with the medallions embedded in the floor and ceiling. He held the flare until they came to the doorway, then lobbed it through the medallion hall into the StarGate room. Before the flare had stopped rolling, O'Neil was inside, rifle-first, looking everywhere for the enemy. No one else was in the room. There was still time.

O'Neil ran to the equipment cart, fishing the claw tool out of a pocket in his fatigues. Daniel entered the room a second later, trying to stay close, trying to stay alive.

"Get back to the door!" O'Neil hissed, hardly turning to look.

"Colonel, I saw the thing that got Kawal—"

The next thing Daniel knew, O'Neil had a pistol pointing right into his face. "Do it or you're a dead man."

Daniel practically fell backward. He was sure O'Neil meant it. He retreated until he was at the edge of the flare's light, then squatted down near the tall doorway. He pointed his rifle uncertainly toward the shadows of the Grand Gallery and waited for the Horuses to attack. He glanced over his shoulder at O'Neil.

"What are you doing over there?" Daniel could see that O'Neil was working something into the floorboards of the off-loaded equipment cart. "Come on, O'Neil, let's get out of here."

Ignoring him, the colonel continued working until he got the hatch door to pop open, revealing the secret compartment built into the vehicle. He pulled it open, fully prepared to insert the orange key.

The compartment was empty. The canisters had been taken out without tripping the fail-safe system: the detonator. O'Neil stared in disbelief at the empty space. Then and there he realized he was facing a superior enemy. A moment later, Daniel saw the feet.

Stepping into the doorway were two of the huge falcon men, their helmets glistening in the chemical light of the flair. They held their ground as a third figure, taller by a foot, advanced slowly out of the darkness and stepped between them, his weapon aimed. Both Daniel and O'Neil recognized him at once. It was Anubis, jackal-headed god of the dead.

"Put the gun down. It's over, Jackson."

Daniel nervously complied with the order. As Anubis approached, Daniel got his first face-to-face look at one of these ghoulish, horrific, impressive creatures. The jackal-headed warrior strode into the light with a pompous, ceremonial style. As he walked past, Daniel studied this flesh and iron incarnation of what he had always assumed to be a myth. The warrior's head was especially disconcerting. It appeared to be both inorganic, sculpted from some metallic or quartzose material, and, at the same time, alive. Daniel thought it might be some kind of helmet constructed from biomorphic metal. Could they be cyborgs?

Anubis continued across the room until he was a pace from O'Neil, then slid the palm of his hand along the underside of the long, ancient-looking rifle. As he did so, a group of flanges, the ribs of the narrow gun barrel, flared open, making the weapon ready to fire. O'Neil didn't flinch. The two of them stared at each other for a long beat, almost as if they recognized one another until the strange warrior gave a signal to the pair of Horuses.

It was eerily similar to the pictures Daniel had studied the night before in the catacombs: Anubis was the leader of the other gods. They seemed to work for him.

The two Horus guards stepped forward, each grabbing one of the intruders roughly by the collar with their powerful hands. Holding their hands low to the ground, they forced their captives to walk stooped low to the ground. If they tripped, which both of them did, the Horuses dragged them effortlessly across the floor.

They moved away from the StarGate and into the next room, the hallway with medallions set into the floor and ceiling. The guards pulled the Americans onto the large round plate. O'Neil, alert, cooperating to buy time, noticed the jackal making an adjustment to his armored cuff.

On the back of the wristband, a mounting shaped like a scarab beetle held a large clear jewel in place. The jackal pressed down on the gem. The next second, a needle of blue light jabbed through the dark hallway, rising from the edge of the medallion to its twin on the ceiling high above.

The beam traced around the circumference of the medallions, leaving a razor thin curtain of wavering blue light in its wake, surrounding the five men standing on the medallion.

As soon as the light completed its circuit and closed into a cylinder, there was an upward rush of bright white light that seemed to lift them off the ground. Daniel and O'Neil both felt a familiar, tingling burn and a sudden escape from the prison of gravity. The same disorienting experience they'd undergone during their trip to this planet, the sensation of StarGating. Clearly, the medallions were based on the same technologies that governed the huge quartz rings.

When the rising flare of white light was above their heads, they found themselves in a different room, standing on an identical medallion.

In the near-complete darkness, Daniel adjusted his glasses and noticed they were surrounded on three sides by the outstretched wings of a statue. The menacing form looming over them stood at least eight feet tall and was wrought from a single block of lustrous black stone. Daniel recognized the unpleasant receptionist as the Egyptian deity Khnum, the ram-headed god.

Daniel correctly guessed he was directly above the medallion hall, inside the strange craft that had perched itself atop the pyramid. The Horus guards tightened his grip on Daniel's collar, twisting the fatigue green shirt closed around his throat like a choke leash. Once more he and O'Neil were stumbling forward with their heads lower than their hips.

They moved across a polished floor, their captors' armor clanking softly in the darkness. The echoing acoustics told Daniel that the room around them was large enough to make their sounds seem very small.

The clang of a large handbell pealed out of the darkness ahead of them. A moment later the entire chamber filled with a low-pitched growl, a rumbling mechanical timpani roar. Glaring light scissored into the room from several directions at once as giant panels, eighty-foot-long plates of the pyramid's thick exterior walls, began sliding open as daintily as twelve small earthquakes.

They were in a long rectangular room with a very high ceiling, like a primitive cathedral. Giant faces looked down at them from the walls, sculpted delicately into the slender pillars supporting the ceiling down one end of the room. The tiled floor was an elaborate symmetrical mosaic.

As the overhead panels continued sliding open, Daniel could see a golden throne, elaborately sculpted and embedded with precious stones. The throne sat on a platform at the top of a flight of stairs. Directly above hung a giant sun disk embossed with an *udjat*, the Eye of Ra. It was identical to the one that hung above the main square in Nagada, except this one appeared to be fashioned of solid gold. When they were halfway to the throne, Horus yanked back on Daniel's collar and forced him to the floor. O'Neil scuffled briefly with his keeper until Daniel urged him in a sharp whisper.

"Just kneel!" he counseled.

Reluctantly, O'Neil turned and let himself slowly drop to his knees, looking defiantly at Anubis the whole while, carefully shaping the misperception that he would offer only symbolic, ego-salving resistance.

By now, sunlight was pouring in from all directions, bathing the room in a warm yellow glow. Two shafts of light climbed the walls on either side of the throne eventually reaching the sun disk. A pair of doors behind the throne pulled open to reveal another, smaller room behind.

Children, ranging in age from seven to nineteen years old, moved through the door and out onto the throne platform in a tight cluster. Wearing very little, the children were dressed in the fashion of ancient Egyptian courtiers. They were barefooted, with very short skirts around their hips and jeweled yoke collars hanging from their shoulders. They were protectively surrounding something at their center.

When the children peeled away, they showed the visitors what they'd been fawning over, a chillingly accurate statue of the supreme pharaoh, Ra, the god of the sun.

It was a breathtaking piece of work made entirely of gold, inlaid everywhere with precious jewels. Every detail—the long braided beard, the two snakes writhing from the head-dress, the painted eyes—had been rendered with obsessive craftsmanship. Its perfectly proportioned arms lay folded across the chest holding the traditional symbols of governance, the crook and flail. The shepherd's crook signifying Industry, and the flail representing Domination, especially over slaves.

The eerily expressionless face bore a vague resemblance to the one on Tutankhamen's famous death mask. But a single glimpse at this startlingly lifelike sculpture made the Tut mask seem amateurish by comparison. This far more threatening image made the greatest artifact of the Egyptians seem like a hopelessly sentimental cartoon.

Daniel was wondering whether the guards would give him

the opportunity to move closer and examine the lustrous idol when it suddenly moved. Cautiously and deliberately, the thing took a step. A mile deep in concentration, Daniel surfaced with a gasp.

The figure moved with austere grace to the throne, clad in the style of the ancient pharaohs. Draped over the shoulders was a yoke dripping with ingots of red jasper and bright black onyx. Wrapped around the waist was a skirt, the stiff brocaded kilt that extended down to the knees.

"Pharaoh King Ra," Daniel whispered, somewhere between terror and delight.

He and O'Neil looked at each other, then back to the bizarre creature still marching throne-ward at a tediously slow speed. It's skin, like Anubis's helmet, seemed to glow ever so slightly, emitting a ghostly pall. Daniel wondered whether he might be made of the same unidentifiable substance as the StarGate.

When he arrived at the beautiful chair, twenty paces from his guests, the shape suddenly sat down at normal human speed, then leaned forward studying them. A minute passed before Ra languidly lifted a hand and flicked a finger toward Anubis. His soldier obeyed the command, reaching up to his throat, and rolling a small tumbler tab with his index finger.

Immediately his large jackal head began to retract beginning at the snout and moving backward. The frightening helmet was built from some type of "smart metal," an alloy capable of remembering and executing complex sequences of commands. The headpiece peeled away in a section-by-section folding action until it revealed the human face beneath.

It was the handsome, humorless face of a large youth. The mask continued to retract section by section until it was gone, receding back into the thin metallic yoke around the young man's neck.

Neither of the Americans could believe it. They'd never seen technology even remotely similar to this. Daniel nervously looked up at the pharaoh, and after a long beat, Ra gave a lazy nod in the direction of the children. His minimal command was translated into a flurry of urgent whispers that soon led to two young children, no more than ten years old, carrying out either side of a large tray. On the tray, dismantled into its constituent parts was the device O'Neil had expected to find in the hidden compartment of the equipment cart.

The nervous boys set the tray as close to the doomed visitors as they dared, before scampering back to the safety of their group. Daniel scrutinized the electronic fragments, uncertain what they were. He spoke out the side of his mouth to O'Neil, who was locked in a stare down with the man of gold.

"What is this stuff?" he asked, neither expecting nor receiving an answer. "Look, there are words." He leaned forward to inspect it. "They look like instructions." The next moment, Daniel realized the printed words were from a scrap of a warning label, the international symbol for nuclear danger. It didn't take long for him to figure out what the wreckage on the tray was.

"That's a bomb, isn't it? That's what you were looking for? What were you thinking?"

Daniel's first reaction was anger. A bomb? How could O'Neil have done such a violent and stupid thing? But that emotion was quickly overwhelmed by the cold stab of fear running from his throat down to his belly. It suddenly occurred to him that both he and O'Neil were about to die.

Daniel spent the next few moments looking for a way out of the situation. He decided that if he got the chance, he would explain that he'd had nothing to do with bringing the explosive. Also, he realized that no matter what happened, he'd gotten everything he'd come for. He'd answered the ancient riddle of the pyramids and proven, at least to himself, that his theories about ancient Egypt had been valid. He had overcome hyper-astronomical odds and bested many enemies to arrive at this very spot—the spot he was always meant to stand in. Whatever happened next, he was at peace with himself. Of course, he still wanted to get the hell out of there alive.

Suddenly, the golden figure sat forward on his chair. A moment later, his entire shape began to mutate, his skin lost its golden veneer and his helmet-mask began to fold in upon itself, retracting behind his head. When the strange transformation was complete, there stood before them a darkly beautiful young man-child with long braided hair. He appeared to be barely twenty years old and perfectly formed. His face was the picture of innocence.

When the delicate face became visible, the soldiers, who considered this youth their god, put their faces to the floor exactly as the miners had done when they saw Daniel's medallion. With all eyes toward the floor, O'Neil saw his chance and attacked instantly. He leapt toward Anubis, jamming his shoulder viciously into the young man's side and seizing his weapon at the same time. Before he could recover, O'Neil chopped into the side of Anubis's neck with the butt of the rifle, collapsing him to the floor. In one swift motion, he duplicated the way Anubis slid his hand down the underside of the gun, snapping it open, then firing at the Horus next to Daniel. The blast caught the guard's shoulder, pinwheeling him across the smooth floor.

At the first sign of trouble, Ra ordered the children to surround him. Quickly, they formed a human shield around their leader. By the time O'Neil whirled around to fire, his weapon was pointed at a curtain of terrified children. O'Neil hesitated. He knew he should fire through the children, but he couldn't bring himself to do it. He turned instead to fire at the second Horus, who was just swinging his weapon into position.

Daniel, horrified, saw that this second Horus had the jump on O'Neil. He stepped into the no-man's-land between the combatants and screamed in the soldier's language not to do it. Too late, the second Horus figure discharged his weapon, and the shot ripped into Daniel's gut, killing him immediately. As his body fell to the floor, O'Neil had a clean shot and took it, blasting the guard backward. Then O'Neil made a second ruinous mistake, he took an instinctive step toward his fallen comrade, even though it was clearly too late to help him. This tiny moment of wavering inaction was all Anubis needed to come from behind. As O'Neil turned to hunt down Ra, he was greeted by a bone-crunching kick to the chest that sent him flying backward.

O'Neil was able to push himself up to his hands and knees, and looked ready to continue to fight. Anubis was approaching now, his helmet reactivated. Behind him, the falcon-headed warrior trained his firearm at the colonel.

O'Neil struggled to regain his footing, but then suddenly collapsed like a sack of steak knives.

Ra came out from behind the children and lifted a subtle gesture to Anubis, who went to O'Neil and looked him over. Just in case the man was feigning unconsciousness, Anubis reared back, then crushed into his head with the blunt end of his rifle. They watched him for a minute, waiting for a movement, a sign that he was still alive. Using his boot, Anubis rolled O'Neil over onto his back, then cautiously knelt down beside him. He reached out and, with one hand, pinched O'Neil's nostrils closed, then clapped down over his mouth, preventing all breathing. Then he waited.

O'Neil didn't know what to do. Even after the crushing blow to the head, he was indeed only pretending to be unconscious. As soon as they had regrouped, he ended the fight because he knew he couldn't win. Now Anubis was preventing him from breathing, and it took all his willpower not to make a grab for the jackal's weapon. He relaxed for a minute until his body began to convulse involuntarily, searching for oxygen.

As soon as they knew he was still breathing, Anubis took his hand away. Now the best O'Neil could hope for was that they'd keep him alive in order to torture him. At least that would preserve the possibility of completing his mission.

A minute later, O'Neil felt Anubis's strong hand seize his collar and begin dragging him across the floor of the chamber. As a precaution, a second soldier accompanied him, a few paces behind. It meant that O'Neil couldn't try to ambush his enemy, but it also meant they were afraid of him, vulnerable.

Ra, still surrounded by his juvenile entourage, came across the floor to inspect Daniel's body. The shot had blasted a hole right through his chest. As Ra leaned over, he noticed something that made him intensely angry. He squatted down almost on top of the mangled corpse and stared at the medallion hanging around Daniel's neck. The *udjat*, the Eye of Ra.

16

THE WRATH

Feretti was wearing out the metal on his belt buckle. He'd been trying for half an hour to dig a scratch, even a small one, into the hard stone wall. He wanted to leave it as a sign to anyone unfortunate enough to get themselves thrown in there after he was gone, one way or another.

Abruptly, the thick crisscrossing bars in the ceiling, the only way in or out of the watery tomb, slid open. Those who could still stand rose to their feet, resigned to whatever might happen next. But nothing happened. Feretti looked up at the opening, anticipating the worst. He'd already figured out that they'd need to be Chinese acrobats to get out of here; four men balancing on each other's shoulders might be able to reach the bars. Unlocking them would be a whole different can of beans. No, there was only one way out of this hellhole, someone upstairs tossing you a rope ladder.

Just then, they dumped O'Neil roughly through the opening. Knocked unconscious, his body plummeted down and hit bottom with a loud splash. The cell was filled with just enough water to make it impossible to lay down. The captives had to sit or stand, making restful sleep impossible.

The cold water revived the colonel immediately. He came up swinging until a pair of strong arms locked him up from behind.

"Sir! It's me, Kawalsky! Are you all right?"

O'Neil stopped fighting and looked around, his eyes adjusting to the darkness of the cell. Brown lay facedown in the water. Porro was dead as well, floating nearby.

"What about them?" he asked, but no one answered.

"What about Jackson?" Freeman and Feretti asked at the same time.

O'Neil sat down, looking at the ceiling for several moments, wondering how they were going to climb out.

"Jackson's dead," he said finally.

Standing by herself at the top of a dune, Little Bit, the *mastadge* that had fallen in love with Daniel, howled at the midday suns. The shepherd boys, startled, looked in all directions for signs of danger. When he saw they were safe, Skaara faced up the slope and yelled at the filthy bellowing beast to keep quiet before returning to his treasure hunt. The four kids had stumbled across the abandoned base camp and were busy digging as much of the equipment as they could out of the sand. They'd already found the box of rifles, the shooting tools they'd seen O'Neil use. They knew what to do with these, but other discoveries proved somewhat more puzzling—the crate of Spam, for example.

A moment earlier Nabeh, no Einstein, had exhumed a green bowl with a strange leather ring suspended around the bottom of the dish. He didn't understand until Skaara yanked it out of his hands and set it on the bigger boy's head. Nabeh squealed with delight, his crooked teeth poking out of his mouth as he broke into a beaming smile.

A loud sound coming from the direction of the pyramid got their attention. All heads turned to see a large section of the exterior wall rolling back to reveal a large cavity within the structure. Two *udajeet*, one-man gliders, rocketed out of the port and hovered in place as a larger craft, a chariot glider, floated out to meet the others. Skaara didn't need to see any more.

"*Udajeet! Aba na wali, yalla!*" he commanded. Rabhi and Aksah, the other two boys, didn't hesitate. They sprang airborne over the side of the bluff, plummeting down the same steep embankment Daniel had traveled the previous day. Skaara was about to bail over the side himself when he noticed Nabeh still standing atop the dune, frozen like a deer staring into the headlights of the doom. He ran back and tugged his older friend over the side of the bluff. When they finished tumbling, there wasn't quite enough time to cover themselves in sand before the three aircraft were overhead. Fortunately, the pilots didn't notice the boys laying stiffly frozen in the sand. The penalty for trespassing into this forbidden territory surrounding the pyramid was public execution. Unfortunately, the boys could see that the ships were flying straight toward Nagada. The boys sensed there would be trouble.

It took more than an hour for them to load the *mastadge* with everything they were able to salvage and make it back to the city. Long before they entered the main gates, they could see that Ra's messengers had brought a ruinous message to the city. A dozen columns of black smoke rose in the windless sky, spreading out to form a dark cloud above the town. When they were only a few hundred yards from the gate, one of the gliders lifted straight up above the perimeter wall, then trolled slowly out across the desert. It was joined by the other glider and then by the chariot. One of the Horus guard pilots spotted the boys and swooped over to take a look. The boys were clinging to the sides of the *mastadge*, staring back at Horus in the cockpit of his small airship. Just like the mythical creatures he had heard about and even seen drawn on the catacomb walls, here he was, Horus flying above him. Without emotion, the soldier returned their gaze. When he was satisfied that the children were returning from the mining pit, he flew on.

Skaara jumped off the animal and led it by the reins through the main gate, which was standing wide-open. It was even worse than the boys had feared. There was pandemonium in the wide street leading to the central square. Some fires had been extinguished, but several were still out of control, and the disorganized effort to fight them was causing as many problems as it solved. People were trampled underfoot. There was screaming, tears, panic. There were wounded people lying everywhere.

Rabhi and Aksah lead Daniel's *mastadge* the long way around the city to the corral, while Nabeh and Skaara waded into the anarchy. Keeping to the wall so they didn't get knocked over by the men wildly trying to put out the fires, the two boys slowly advanced down the town's main artery.

Nabeh's building was one of those still on fire. The boys ducked into a doorway directly across the street to watch the chaotic fire-fighting effort. Skaara looked down, and noticed they were standing in blood. Behind them, curled up against the wall was a boy two or three years older than Skaara. He'd been shot in the hip, and his leg had been badly scorched from flame. They turned the boy over. He was unconscious, having passed out trying to hold his leg in place. Nabeh shook the boy, trying to wake him up, but it was no use. Without any discussion, they decided they would carry the boy to help. Nabeh lifted him off the ground and, with Skaara's help, draped the boy over his back. Dodging men barreling toward the fire with loads of water, stepping over the fallen, they fought their way toward the central square, to the place children were supposed to go when they got sick or injured.

The situation in the central square was even worse. Both boys had seen dead bodies before when there had been accidents at the mining pit, but never anything like this. Apparently, Ra's soldiers had rampaged through the town on an indiscriminate killing spree, and here is where they'd done their most ghoulish work. Blood was spilled everywhere across the paving stones. The broken bodies of the victims had fallen in unnaturally twisted positions. One old man, working alone, was gathering the dead, one at a time, dragging them across the square and piling them against the wall that served as a goal for a soccer-like game children played there.

When they came to the children's clinic, they saw that it had already burned and was now completely empty. Skaara looked around the courtyard for help. It felt like the end of the world. Screaming, crying women seemed to be running in every direction, each one responding to some private emergency, rushing to find those dearest to her, her children, parents, a lover, convinced that all had been lost in this senseless attack.

Finally someone stopped to help them. It was Sha'uri, Skaara's half sister. She came running up to the boys holding the side of her face, blood everywhere.

"Sha'uri, har an'dona?" he asked her. But she waved off his concern, moving to the boy on Nabeh's back. As she inspected the boy, Skaara watched the blood seep out of the gash above her right eye. It would leave a nasty scar.

After a moment, she turned and began leading Nabeh toward the wall and the stack of dead bodies. When Skaara saw where she was headed, he became hysterically angry. He and Nabeh had found the boy and, whatever it took, they were going to save him. He yanked hard on her arm to stop her progress. As gently as she could, she told him.

"He's already dead. Put him with the others, then come with me," she said in their language. Skaara could not believe what he was seeing all around him. He found comfort in how his people were working together to help one another. How Sha'uri was able to be so strong, organizing the relief effort. Whether she knew it or not, Sha'uri was a natural leader. But suddenly her tough veneer weakened as she turned back to Skaara, her voice cracking. "Where is Dan-yer? Tell me what happened to Dan-yer?"

Skaara didn't know how to answer her. He couldn't answer her. There was already too much sadness here. He couldn't add to it. He turned away from her distractedly, pretending he hadn't heard her questions.

His feigned distraction became painfully real as he looked to the far side of the big square, up to the giant disk suspended between the buildings at the far end of the square. Crucified across the front of the medallion, bound at the wrists, was Kasuf. Skaara felt his stomach nearly fall out of his mouth. Even before Nabeh turned back to see what was going on, Skaara was running as fast as he could across the uneven ground. A crowd had gathered trying to figure out how to get the old man, beaten and bloody, safely down.

The men of Nagada prided themselves on their endurance and toughness. They aspired to be like the sand: stoic, hard to hold, and able to absorb all the rain—tears—the gods could send. Skaara was already fifteen and thought he'd made the passage to manhood, but seeing his father bludgeoned and humiliated brought him to tears in a single moment. The wide-open crying of an infant.

And the longer he cried, the angrier he became. He knew

the people of the city had done nothing wrong. "Why? Why did this happen to us?" he asked.

One of the town Elders standing near said, "The visitors. They brought this upon us. False gods. They seduce our praise and angered the almighty Ra."

"No, it's not true," argued Skaara.

"It is. Ra has returned to us. We have angered him with our false worship. We must repent and serve him obediently."

Skaara was angry and confused. He refused to believe they could have been party to this, even inadvertently. He wanted Kasuf to explain it to him. Perhaps Kasuf could make it all clear.

Why were they taking so long to cut him down? All the windows and balconies surrounding the disk were crowded with people trying to help, but no one was actually doing anything. A network of thick ropes supported the stone disk, which weighed slightly less than one ton. Two men had tried to shimmy out along the bottom rope, one from each side. But their weight caused the ropes, spun from vines and animal sinew, to sag dramatically. Everyone screamed at once, from the windows, balconies, the footbridge, and below that they were too heavy, that they would kill themselves along with the old man. As one of the Elders explained a rescue plan involving long planks, others shouted their criticism. It was a mob trying to save their patriarch by committee.

By the time Skaara came back from the corrals, two useless ladders had been moved into place, and a group of citizens had stretched a piece of canvas into a trampoline below. In other words, no progress had been made.

Laden with *mastadge* gear, he entered the building and took the stairs at a workmanlike pace up to the roof. He stepped out onto the sloped roof carrying a training saddle and a length of rope, moving carefully to where the topmost of the ropes supporting the medallion was tied to the eaves. He slid the last few feet and was lucky to break the slide when his feet found the rope. Someone had lost a shoe, Skaara wondered whether it was someone who fell. He decided to take the shoe with him. Balancing the saddle in one hand, the rope and shoe in the other, he stood up and slid his barefoot out onto the rope, then left the building behind with the next step. He braced himself for what he knew would come next.

When the assembled rescuers saw Skaara's tightrope walk, everyone screamed bloody murder. People in the window just below him were reaching up trying to grab him by the ankle, but Skaara obeyed the rule: don't look down. He knew it was dangerous, but he was angry in a way he never had been before. He was not concerned at the moment with his personal safety. The howling of the crowd made no dent in Skaara's concentration. It actually started to feel quiet, the more focused he became on his task. One foot and then the next. The fence of the *mastadge* corral was much harder to walk than this wide rope, and Skaara couldn't remember the last time he hadn't made it all the way around. Stay relaxed, stay balanced, you're almost there.

On the ground, Sha'uri ran to the people forming the trampoline to help. Skaara was two-thirds of the way to the medallion where many ropes came together, forming a web for the boy to move through.

He anchored his leg between the rope and the disk. When he knew he could hold on, he flipped himself over the edge so that he was hanging chin to chin with his father.

"Are you all right?" the boy asked.

"Humiliation is worse than death," replied the old man, who averted his eyes, unable to look at Skaara.

Skaara had never heard Kasuf speak like that. Nor had he ever seen tears in his eyes. Overwhelmed at seeing this man he admired so broken, Skaara focused on his next task, getting the harness secured around the old man's middle.

"Arch your back," he said, and the old man did his best to comply. Although he'd never worked upside down, Skaara was quite an expert with these harnesses, and a minute later was cinching it tight around the old man's middle. He then tied the rope to the shoe and tossed it to the crowd on one of the footbridges.

"I'm gonna cut him down, be ready."

All capable hands quickly took possession of the rope as Skaara unsheathed a long cleaning knife, showing it to the people on the footbridge. When the front man nodded,

Skaara leaned over and informed Kasuf, "You're gonna swing around for a second until I can get to the second rope."

He cut the first rope, sending Kasuf swinging sideways by one wrist. A moment later, the second rope was cut, and Kasuf, the Chief Elder of the city swung through the air in a sixty-foot arch before gravity took him back the other way. The footbridge crowd lifted the old man to safety, then rushed him into a nearby apartment to doctor his wounds.

Though the people were thrilled to see their leader was safe, they avoided looking at him, attempting to save him the embarrassment. The foreman of the footbridge crew retrieved the rope, and after several throws, Skaara had a hold of it. He tied a toe loop for himself, then shouted for them to lower him down.

When he was still thirty feet off the ground, he surprised everyone again.

"Catch me," he shouted. Then, without warning, he jumped out of the sling, and plummeted downward, secure in the knowledge that Sha'uri, Nabeh, and the others would catch him in the safety net.

17

"THERE CAN BE ONLY ONE RA"

Silent and still, the sarcophagus sat at the back of the room. Slowly the sides of the ancient polished box began to retract, lowering into the floor. As the side wall pulled back, the narrow table at the center lifted up. On the table was a human figure covered with a wet cloth, a death shroud, laying motionless on the table. A minute later, the body on the slab suddenly began to spasm, gasping for air. It sat up and tore away the cloth.

It was Daniel, reborn. It took a few minutes for him to breathe normally again, feeling as though his diaphragm and lungs, after their short vacation, had forgotten their work. He fell back on the table, dizzy, and looked around to see where he was. As best he could, he scanned the eerie, empty room. He was startled to see a small boy, seven years old, waiting patiently for him to wake.

Daniel struggled to sit up, the semicircular canals in his ears slowly adjusting to give him back his sense of balance. Coughing and blinking, he got to his feet and looked at the child who beckoned him to follow as he turned and walked out of the room. Daniel was unsure whether he should follow.

The boy led the way into the throne room, site of his ill-fated interview with the boy-king Ra. Daniel thought he must have slept for a long time. He felt alert and physically strong. Stronger than he'd felt for a long time. Even though the light was dim and his glasses were missing, he found he was able to focus sharply on everything around him. Like the other children, the boy ahead of him nearly naked. He wore a very short skirt, an Egyptian kilt, and a heavy gold chain around his neck.

A cat strolled across the floor in front of them. A moment later, Daniel spotted another cat curled up on the stairs leading up to the throne. He turned to look at the cat, which seemed in no way different from the house pets he'd grown up with. It blinked at him lazily and turned away. When Daniel turned back to the boy, he had vanished. Daniel moved down the hallway until he came to a broad doorway.

He peered inside and found another marvelous surprise. Wide sheets of pure white silk hung in the darkness, suspended from the low ceiling to within inches of the floor. Billowing through the gaps between the sheets were rolling clouds of steam. The air was hot and moist, like a sauna.

Too curious to be truly afraid, Daniel walked into the fog, pushed the fabric aside, and waded deeper into the mist.

He inched forward until he found the source of the steam, a shallow, perfectly round pool. Then the vapors parted allowing him to see the object of all this decadent luxury.

Appearing then disappearing behind the lifting steam, Ra lay motionless, submerged to his shoulders in the scalding water, surrounded by his young attendants. Although he in no way acknowledged his resuscitated visitor's entrance, Daniel intuitively knew his presence was felt. Silently, he came closer still, until he was poised at the very lip of the bathing pool, the size of a tiny lake.

Ra opened his eyes, staring straight at Daniel. The two of them studied each other for a long time before a hand rose dripping out of the water. With a relaxed gesture, he called for his robe. Two of the children carried the robe to a spot near where Daniel was standing.

Very slowly, Ra lifted himself up and marched through the thigh-deep water with feline grace. His skin was no longer gold, but had somehow returned to it's natural color, a burnt almond tone common among the people of North Africa.

If the story told on the walls of the catacomb were

true, the naked youth slithering toward him was in the neighborhood of ten thousand years old, the creature within even older than that! Only forty-eight hours earlier, Daniel, famous for the "recklessness creativity" of his academic ideas, would have dismissed the idea. But now, even with the evidence of Ra's lithe body displayed before him, he was ready to believe it. Fascinated, Daniel watched the enigmatic creature prowl toward him through the mist.

"I was dead, wasn't I?" Daniel spoke in the language Sha'uri had taught him.

Ra stepped into his robe allowing the children to wrap him inside. When he heard Daniel's mispronounced words, something like a smile moved across his lips.

"That is why I chose your race. Your bodies, so easily repaired." Ignoring his visitor, Ra turned and walked at a leisurely pace out of the room.

With Daniel and the children trailing behind, Ra led the strange procession down the length of the throne room, up the stairs, and past the throne itself into his private chamber.

The room was cluttered with fantastic works of art, beautiful furniture and trinkets of all sizes. As he moved past a long marble table, Ra casually drew Daniel's attention to the spot by dragging his fingers across its surface.

Arranged on the table like a museum display, were the team's captured belongings. Rifles, pistols, field radios, spare ammunition, and Daniel's books, one of which was laying open as if someone had been studying. The eeriest artifact on exhibit was one of the men's camouflage army uniforms, complete from chin strap to boot strings. At the end of the table, still on the long tray was the disassembled bomb. When Daniel looked up, Ra was peering at him amused.

He spoke to Daniel in a soft voice, velvet and croaking at the same time.

"Your people have advanced much since I left," the strange boy monarch said. "Your world has become dangerous"—he stressed the last word. His dialect seemed slightly different from Sha'uri's, perhaps the "high" pre-Egyptian language of palace life. Daniel didn't understand every word, but he gathered Ra's meaning.

"You have harnessed the power of the atom," Ra said,

gesturing toward the dismantled bomb. "But you still do not fully understand my power. The power within the quartz."

"What do you plan to do?" Daniel asked, starting to understand the ugly implications of the statement.

"You should not have reopened the gateway," he rasped. "Soon, I will send your weapon back to your world. I will encase it within a shipment of the precious mineral of this planet. It shall increase your weapon's destructive power, a hundredfold." A wry smile crossed his lips.

"Why would you do such a thing?" Daniel asked.

"I created your culture, your language, your arts, your government. I created your entire civilization," declared Ra, who moved uncomfortably close to Daniel before he said, "And now, I will destroy it."

The blood drained out of Daniel's face. His expression of thinly veiled dread seemed to please Ra, who smiled once more before slinking over to a dressing area surrounded by tall mirrors. Daniel followed him, trying to invent some convincing argument about how they had come in peace. The tray full of bomb parts staring at him from the table made that difficult to do.

"Why did you give me back my life?" Daniel wondered if there was still a way out.

"I need you. You will restore faith, the faith of these people in the power of their one supreme god."

"Faith?" Daniel had no idea what the ominous words meant.

"An early discovery I made about your race," he whispered almost secretively. "Myth, faith, habit. Control of these gives more power than any weapons." Ra lifted his arms to allow the convey of children to slip a tunic over his head. "Myth, faith, habit," he reiterated. "A scribe like yourself should remember those words."

He sat on a gorgeous folding stool, every inch painted with cryptic heraldic symbols, as the children laced him into a pair of sandals.

"You will obey me before my people. They will witness your obedience as you kill your companions. The ceremony will begin tomorrow in the late sun."

Daniel tried to laugh at the idea, but a single strangled

blurt is what came out instead. He looked at the arrogant man-child like he was mad, asking, "And if I refuse?"

Calmly, Ra explained the alternative. "Then I shall have to destroy you and all who have seen you."

The children were still busy adorning Ra in his jewels, but he interrupted their work and prowled down the steps toward Daniel. He kept coming until he was dangerously close, until they could feel one another's breath. Daniel cringed reflexively when Ra brought his hand up between their faces. A mule at heart, Daniel decided irrevocably that he wouldn't flinch again. And he didn't, even when Ra put a finger against Daniel's lips and then started to trace a path down his chin and throat, then continuing down his chest. The hand stopped on the medallion Daniel still wore around his neck. Ra looked down, turning his disk bearing his name gently over in his hand, and then he pointed his amber yellow eyes back into Daniel's. For one brief moment, a strange light glowed deep within Ra's eyes, inhuman, a glimpse at the creature residing deep within the shell of this eternally young child.

"There can be only one Ra," he purred before jerking down with enough force to split the chain, liberating his seal from the neck of the detestable usurper.

Even though Skaara hadn't told her what the boys had seen at the pyramid that afternoon, Sha'uri sensed something must have happened to Daniel. He would have returned to her if he could have. Although he had rejected her on the night she was escorted to his chambers, she knew there was a bond between them, a connection neither of them could have planned or controlled or resisted. They'd found the secret museum together, the forgotten ancient history of her people. That cluttered, jumbled record of events many millennia hence had immediately changed everything about the present. Suddenly, everything needed to be reevaluated. And none of it would have been possible without him. His coming here had changed her in ways she knew she would always cherish.

She brought a candle across the city and lit it when she was alone in the catacombs. Recalling Daniel's explanation of the hieroglyphs, she read and reread the forgotten history of her people. Now she knew why letters had been made taboo, they were so powerful. Of course Ra had wanted to hide the truth of his beginnings, they were not divine. He had not been born in the sun, and had not conquered Tuat. He was just a creature that wanted to survive, at whatever cost. A cost Sha'uri was no longer willing to pay.

18

IN THE BEGINNING . . .

His species was so entirely different from this human host body he had discovered. His people had nothing within their own nature akin to empathy, sympathy, love, or kindness. This was a race that existed only to survive and acquire. After thousands of years of this existence, their knowledge seemed unending, yet they still lacked wisdom. Their unending pursuit of acquisitions, knowledge, art, science, and possessions had eventually led to the extinction of their race.

As the last breaths escaped the people of his world, he was millions of light-years away from home, searching desperately for a host. He was determined not to follow the fate of his own kind. He had mastered the technology to transfer himself into another being but had to choose carefully. Along with inhabiting the host's body, he knew he would absorb certain personality traits that were exaggerated within the host's psyche. Perhaps had he known the intimate details of the life of this young boy named Ra, he might have chosen another. Or perhaps not.

Ra's childhood proved to be an excellent preparation for the life he was to lead. It made it easy for him to walk directly toward the blinding light and ferocious wind tearing unexpectedly across the desert that night one hundred centuries ago. Although both his parents were alive, for all practical purposes he had grown up an orphan. His mother was a lunatic, barely able to care for herself. His father was worse—a violent, aggressive outcast who spent weeks at a time wandering the desert by himself. From infancy, the boy had been reared by the entire tribe at once, belonging partly to everyone but to no one in particular. Because he was not an especially lovable child, no one took care to nurture and touch the boy. While other children slept huddled between their parents, Ra was the only child his age with a private tent. Under these circumstances, he grew into an almost feral child: aloof, unresponsive, slow to trust, and quick to attack. The situation only worsened as Ra got older and began to develop his skills under the unwelcome tutelage of the Old One, the leader of the tribe. He despised being segregated from the hunting crew and forced to spend his days practicing magic in the caves. He felt alone in every possible way, and developed a caustic resentment for all those around him. When the frightening lights came across the midnight sky, he had no idea what might lay on the other side, but he was prepared to embrace any fate other than his own.

His hatred for his own people proved useful, as there were no inner conflicts when the boy became the pharaoh king. There would be no feelings of guilt or remorse as Ra's people were put to hard labor. In fact, a strange new sense of pleasure became the most powerful trait he absorbed from this strange young boy. Ra was now a part of himself, and together they became the sun god, to be feared and worshiped by this primitive human race.

The pharaoh king learned quickly the ways to govern this species. There were two main aspects of his education. The first was learning how to gain and then maintain a monopoly on violence. If not a monopoly, then at least an overwhelming ability to destroy his opponents. His retinue of soldiers and elite guards understood that if he ordered them to cut their own throats they would obey, but Ra rarely tested them.

In brief skirmishes with some of the slave populations, Ra taught himself to wage war and to strike back with devastating, unmerciful strength. At this he became remarkably adept.

The second aspect concerned the psychology of governing. After teaching himself to wield an iron fist, he learned
how to wrap it in a velvet glove. While force brought
immediate results, myth, faith and belief were stronger
weapons at his disposal. Through what he absorbed from
the young boy, the pharaoh king understood the fears and
weakness of these people and played upon them, ruthlessly.
He re-created his own likeness into the now-famous Tut
mask, which became his only public image. Only his own
elite entourage would have the privilege to see the true face
of Ra.

His guards, as well, had to be redeveloped. If they were
to serve him successfully, they, too, would have to call upon
the fears of the people. Through the mythology of these
primitive people, the pharaoh king learned that the jackal
held a special place with their nightmares. His best guard,
the king's champion, he decided would only be seen publicly
with the head of a jackal and be known as Anubis, the
jackal-headed boatman who takes men's souls to hell.

The rest of his guards would also take on these kinds of
illusions, such as his many Horus guards, with their hawk-
like heads, along with his Thoth guards and Ramses guards.
All to take on mythology all their own. An intricate mytho-
logical web, weaved by the master himself, Ra, sun god.

He knew of the power of mythology because it now
existed somewhere within himself, in the part of Ra that he
absorbed. For the first time in his existence, he now had
dreams. Sometimes disturbing dreams, sometime pleasant
and comforting ones. It was a strange new sensation. One
he liked, very much.

A vision came to him of a vast underground chamber with
magnificently painted walls. Unseen musicians played an
intoxicatingly lovely song. In the middle of the room stood
an enormous balance scale. He saw himself sitting in one of
its dishes. Suddenly thousands of people were in the room
with him, lining up to test their weight against his. It was
implicitly understood that the scales measured not the
weight of a physical body, but the worth of a person's soul,
or "Ka." One by one, they climbed into the dish. Ra found
he could manipulate the device at will, tipping it in his favor.
The people in the hallway realized this and began to pile

onto the other side of the scale en masse. No matter how many people jumped into the dish on the other side, the scale indicated that the slender boy was heavier.

Ra had not only now created his own mythology, slowly he began to believe it.

In the first several months after his arrival on Earth, the desert people were afflicted with powerful and disturbing dreams. In these dreams, the sun itself split open to deliver a living god onto the land. Night after night, this awesome event repeated itself on a rocky plateau not far from the banks of a great river. A site that would later come to be known as Heliopolis.

Far to the south, the mountain people of the Nubians and the herders of the Sudan, inspired by the overwhelming beauty of their shared vision, headed north along the banks of the Nile searching for the landscape of the dream. Others came from the west, out of the Sahara. From as far north as Syria and Palestine, they gathered their belongings and set out. On the backs of camels or behind herds of goats, they came carrying spices and spears and children. They converged toward the spot speaking no common language, sharing nothing in common except the scorching dreams and the craving it had left in their hearts. Scratching pictures in the dirt and speaking with their hands, they exchanged tales along the way of the lengths they had come and the dangers they had faced. Wave upon wave, they wandered to the base of the plateau, none of them knowing exactly why they had come. As each new group arrived and communicated their experience, the miracle was reaffirmed.

They organized themselves into a teeming anarchic squalid camp, that spread along the banks of the river for miles. This wretched rejoicing rabble packed themselves together to create the planet's first metropolis, or better yet: theopolis, for this was a city of god.

As powerful as the blazing dreams had been, they didn't prepare the people for the stunning majesty of what actually happened. As the city slept, the opulent and unwashed curled up together on the ground, a shadow blotted out the moon. Soon the winds came, and a harsh flood of light poured down on the makeshift city. They followed the light west from the city, running at top speed fighting one another for position, yearning to welcome their god to Earth.

They ran headlong into the light, shielding their eyes. Then, at the center of the radiance, standing in a light so intense it should have washed out all trace of color, they found him. The sun god Ra, his entire body composed of incorruptible gold, blazing with a feverish golden hue. He was surrounded by a company of kneeling servants. When these obeisant figures stood up, they pounded deep spikes of fear into the hearts of the people. Each had the body of a human but the enormous head of an animal. The menagerie of animal spirits these people would soon know all too well: Khnum, the ram; Sebak, the crocodile; Horus, the hawk; Apis, the bull; Anubis, the jackal; Hathor, the cat; and Ammit, a strange beast known as "the devourer." They formed an impressive and unnerving retinue. Spontaneously, the people laid themselves facedown in the sand and wet grass, weeping, overwhelmed by the miracle. The power of the moment stamped itself so deeply and so indelibly into these people's imaginations that hundreds of generations later, long after this scene had been intentionally erased from memory, human beings would continue to ache for a repeat of the scene, for the advent of a dreamt-of messiah.

This was not the only legacy Ra would bequeath to the subsequent history of Earth.

His worshipers called him Ra-hotep-kan, sun god, because he had come from the light as bright as the sun. Ra allowed it, since it did not conflict with the myth he had prepared for them to live by. He told them that he had been to a place called Tuat, the land of the dead. Conquering that land, he made servants out of the animal-gods that lived there. He called upon the people of the wretched city to dedicate both their love and their labor to him and his works. When they died, he told them, they would be escorted to Tuat by his servant Anubis where their spirits, their Ka, would be weighed on a scale. If the deceased person had lived in pious service to Ra, they would dwell forever in the land of the dead. If not, Ammit, the devourer would be waiting nearby.

Construction of the great pyramid began almost at once.

The people did it willingly, gratefully, for Ra. They studied and learned and labored under the supervision of the animal-headed gods, most notably Thoth, the ibis, the god of scribes, dreams, and magic. The pyramid project was by far the largest and most complex ever undertaken on the planet, and it was a transforming experience for the people who built it.

Ra could see that they were motivated by a mixture of love and fear. This illiterate, barely civilized workforce learned to cooperate, think together, quarry and cut stone, haul the heavy loads across the sand, and raise the pyramid in less than half the time it would take to build much smaller structures thousands of years later.

When the structure was nearly complete, Ra brought out from his spacecraft a giant ring of quartz, The StarGate. The StarGate was installed inside the pyramid, in the room built especially for it. By that time, the majority of Ra's workers had been born in the squalid city, the sons and daughters of those who had come to the place as holy pilgrims. For this second generation, the building started to feel less like sacred labor and more like toil. They were less blind in their submission to Ra, being more likely to visit the places their parents had suddenly abandoned years before, the speak with those who decided not to follow the dreams. They could not be joyful in their work when their nights were spent in hunger and the unsanitary conditions of the sprawling shanty town. Daily witnesses to the fabulous luxury that surrounded their king, they began to want more for themselves. And what was their reward upon finishing this giant masterpiece? A small group of people kept a hidden journal, detailing the truth about Ra and his origins. Someone within Ra's elite entourage had leaked out this information to these young rebels who were not about to let this knowledge be forgotten.

On the night that the pyramid was declared finished, Ra moved through the jubilant, celebrating city with his corps of bodyguards, selecting hundreds of people for a "special honor." They were taken into the pyramid and sent through the StarGate, never to be heard from again.

These roundups continued for months. At first, the zealots of the city lined the streets begging to be chosen. Many of these volunteers were older people who were passed over in favor of stronger, younger bodies. Those who worked inside the pyramid relayed what they had heard; that the chosen people were being forced through the giant ring and sent to faraway deserts to build other pyramids. Forgetting his own rules of mythology, Ra moved with too much haste. In the weeks and months that followed, Ra's frequent trips through the city came to be feared. Young people were covertly slipped out of the city. Despite their devotion to him, the recurring scene of children being torn away from their families began to breed resentment against Ra. Then the persistent rumors of a rebellion on another planet came back through the Gate and spread through the city. It was said that Hathor, the cat, had slaughtered the entire colony in a sea of blood.

Ra began to spend weeks at a time away from the city, busily establishing new settlements, his need for more of the quartz mineral intensified. He not only needed it to fuel his sarcophagus in order for him to attain eternal life, but as his power became more widespread, his minions needed power for his technology. So more and more mining settlements had to be established. But in his absence from Earth, he left the increasingly thorny problem of discipline to his guards. Whenever he returned, hundreds more of his healthiest subjects were chosen to accompany him into the pyramid, where they disappeared forever. As disaffection grew, resistance began to organize.

One particular plot involved several hundred people, enough to ensure that word got back to Ra through his network of spies. But the arrogant despot elected to ignore the threat. Convinced of his invincibility, he personally wandered through the mud and stench of the city pointing out those he wanted. When the citizens hid behind their shelters, Ra ordered his guards to break in and drag them outside. Behind the walls of a small mud-brick building, the conspirators were laying their plans. Ra's henchmen, however, paid no attention to the hand-scrawled map of the pyramid's interior. They dragged the men, a dozen of the plot's chief conspirators outside and lined them up. At least one of the men was chosen, and taken through the Gate to the place where Nagada would be founded.

When the signal came from the palace servants that Ra was gone, the plotters rushed inside the pyramid, killed the last few of the animal guards, and tore the StarGate down. They spent hours trying to break it with hammers, but were unable to leave even a scratch. Instead they dragged it out into the desert and buried it under the first heavy stones they could find. Months later the cover stones were carved and put into place. When they brought the giant cover stones out to bury the Gate once and for all, Anubis's smashed body was already in place.

Since that time, Ra had not been seen on Earth. The once cohesive society that had spontaneously appeared in the desert disintegrated like a mirage. Those who had buried the StarGate fought pitched, deadly battles with those who remained faithful until there was only chaos in the place.

Children, they say, rarely listen to their parents but never fail to imitate them. The same was true of the rulers that came after Ra. Although he was fiercely hated and soundly defeated, the rulers who came after Ra duplicated almost every aspect of his reign, bequeathing a sadistic and painful paradigm of political rule to the generations to follow.

19

KNOWLEDGE IS POWER

Sha'uri had been gone for several hours when Skaara, Nabeh, Rabhi, and Aksah came into the catacombs looking for her. She was sitting in the small painted chamber, the secret museum, mourning quietly to herself.

She heard the boys coming and was going to order them to leave her alone, but as soon as they stepped into the narrow tunnel room, she knew what she had to do. She told them to gather around her. The boys, still frightened of being discovered in this unholy place, reluctantly approached. Once she had them all in place, she began to recite to them the long-forgotten history of their people, doing her best to remember all that Daniel had taught her about the secret story written on the walls.

As she read the words and explained the pictures, her voice grew steadily stronger, more confident. Even though she had heard the story before, when Daniel had read it to her, this time, as the words left her own lips, she became resolute. Telling the story was cathartic. She told them she would not allow herself to live like this anymore. Something had to be done!

And in that single hour, the children grew to be men. Knowledge is power and, as the story unfolded, these youths became strong.

For Skaara, the story affirmed what he had somehow

instinctively known all along. This validated all his suspicions, answered the questions he'd been asking since he was small, erased all the doubts that had plagued him. And he got angry. Angry about all the people he'd seen killed by Ra's soldiers. Angry about all the lies. The generations of lives lived, not in spiritual service to god, but as dupes and slaves.

He swore to himself that even if it took the rest of his life, he would do something about it.

Preparations had been underway all night. Those responsible for organizing the event had arrived shortly after dawn, the earliest allowable hour. Kasuf was among the first to make the trip, riding to the pyramid on the back of a *mastadge*, then supervising the prearrangements for the ceremony from his chair next to the ensemble of drummers.

As the third sun surged into the sky marking the official arrival of morning, several thousand of Nagada's citizens had already reached the pyramid, the feared and seldom seen palace of their living god. They gathered into a human sea around the long sloping ramp, the same ramp by which the quartz was delivered to the pyramid. A steady stream of latecomers continued to feed the crowd's numbers, coming over the dunes in a ragged procession that stretched as far as the eye could see.

The top of the pyramid's Entrance Hall had been festooned with lengths of silk bunting, wide burgundy ribbons that cascaded the forty feet to the floor of the platform, effectively screening the view into the structure.

The crowd suddenly fell into a hush as a section of the fluttering fabric was pulled back. A moment later, the soldiers were forced into the bright sunlight by a pair of Ra's Horus-helmeted henchmen. Each of the warriors carried one of the long weapons, the pulse rifles. The soldiers were herded down the wide sloping ramp, halfway to the obelisks.

Only four members of the team were still alive: O'Neil, Kawalsky, Feretti, and Freeman. Under normal circumstances, the soldiers would have taken advantage of being led out into the open like this. They would have counterattacked and tried to escape in the time it takes to blink. But the beatings, followed by so many hours sitting upright in the watery pit, had taken most of the life out of them. Besides, there was nowhere to run, no physical space to escape into. They were surrounded on all sides by the tightly packed crowd from Nagada. They stood on the ramp looking like an assembly of zombies. O'Neil, powered by sheer meanness and single-minded determination, still had a good deal of his energy. But, in addition to the pair of armed guards standing behind him, a group of four more stepped into the light and took up positions at the top of the ramp. The colonel seemed to have lost fifteen pounds overnight, trading them for fifteen years added to his face.

One of the Horus guards stepped up behind the haggard troops and, swinging the thick end of his weapon, hit Freeman behind his already wobbly knees, buckling him to the ground.

"Everybody kneel down," O'Neil shouted, leading by example. The Horus seemed almost disappointed when the entire team followed O'Neil's command. He brought his helmet close to O'Neil and stared at him oddly, more intimidating than any drill sergeant but still not enough to scare the colonel.

Like most of those in attendance, Sha'uri wore a long colorless robe with a hood pulled low over her eyes. She slipped through the crowd until she made eye contact with Skaara and Nabeh standing on the opposite side of the ramp.

Skaara, ever so casually, glanced up at the two Horuses standing guard over the soldiers. When he was sure the gods were not looking, he pantomimed a silent sneeze. He was asking, with some urgency, where Daniel was. Sha'uri's facial expression told Skaara not to worry, but inside her heart was in a tailspin, afraid his absence could only mean one thing.

All attention suddenly shifted to a remarkable sight at the entrance. One of Ra's child attendants, a girl about nine years old, came padding barefoot from beneath the bolts of burgundy fabric. The Nagadans had never seen anything like this little girl. In contrast to their coarse garments, which covered them head to toe, the girl seemed to be practically naked. What little there was of her clothing was unimaginably fine. The colorful short skirt, and the yoke collar dripping with jewels. Her long straight hair was pulled back into a tight clean braid.

The child made her way down the ramp keeping her eyes glued to the floor, concentrating single-mindedly on her errand. It was her job to tell the drummers from Nagada to begin. Having come to the pyramid palace as a very young child, she could not remember seeing people who did not live within its confines. Nor had she ever wanted to. She had been taught that the miners were filthy, disease-carrying slaves, inferior in every way to those like herself who lived beside Ra. The striking contrast between her own beauty and the worn-down look of the people in the crowd only reinforced the stereotypes she had been taught.

She located the leader of the drumming ensemble, and recited the order for him to begin. At the last minute, she looked into his eyes and gasped at what she saw. Not only was the man brutishly ugly by palace standards, but he was amazingly old. He must have been well into his forties!

Although she and her companions knew what it was to grow older, none of them had ever met someone older than Ra, who was eternally twenty. When the palace children reached the age of twenty, a select few of them were kept on as Horus guards, and the best fighters among them had the chance to become Ra's champion, Anubis. There was only one, extremely difficult, way to gain this valuable position: killing the current Anubis. The children who were not made into guards were taken away, but none of them knew exactly where.

The girl backed away from the horrible man with the sun-withered skin. Twice before, she had seen the quartz caravans delivering their loads, but always from the great height of the spacecraft. From that angle, the miners were mere dark specks scurrying in the sand, anonymous worker ants. In one great flash of recognition, she realized what it meant to get old. She turned and hurried back to the top of the ramp, where another dozen or so of the palace children had just come squinting into the daylight.

The drums began, drowning out the sounds of the crowd, focusing everyone's attention on the entrance. What followed was a pathetic scene, a painfully obvious, self-aggrandizing religious ceremony-cum-political manipulation. Ra celebrating Ra. Worse: Ra coercing others to celebrate him in a ceremony as subtle as the half-time entertainment at a college football game. The Americans found the flamboyant, overly dramatic entrance disgusting. The long skeins of burgundy silk were pulled aside to reveal a beautiful throne sitting on two long bars. The four Horus guards at the top of the ramp lifted the throne and carried it into the sunlight.

A moment later, the frightening jackal-headed warrior, Anubis, came through the doorway clutching Daniel by the arm. The American soldiers, still on their knees fifty yards away, looked at one another in confusion. O'Neil looked like he'd seen a ghost. And, in a sense, he had.

"You told us he was dead," Kawalsky snarled at his superior officer, trusting him less than ever.

O'Neil didn't know how to respond. Something was very wrong with this picture. He had seen Daniel's chest and stomach turned into minced meat with his own two eyes. No human body could suffer that kind of devastation and come out of it alive. Not even close. But there was something else. If anything, Daniel now seemed stronger, more alive. His glasses were gone, but he wasn't fumbling around like a squinting worm. The idea crossed O'Neil's mind that the Daniel Jackson standing next to Anubis, the one who looked relatively relaxed and revitalized, could very well be an imposter. His suspicions were fueled by the fact that Daniel wasn't making eye contact.

When he came into the open, Sha'uri fought the impulse to call out to him over the rhythm of the drums. Instead she looked eagerly across the ramp once more to her brother and gave him a nod. At once, Skaara and Nabeh squeezed their way through the crowd, moving to their positions. Sha'uri was already where she was supposed to be.

Anubis stepped out into the middle of the platform at the top of the ramp and stretched his powerful arms into the air, silencing the drums and the crowds. It was Kasuf's cue.

Assisted by a pair of Nagada's Elders, Kasuf mounted the platform not far from where the soldiers were kneeling like sacrificial heifers. The old priest was in obvious pain, his visibly bruised face telling only a small part of the internal injuries he had suffered. He had been afraid to come that day, knowing that another thrashing would end his life.

But he had been more afraid still that a similar beating might be meted out to one of his people instead.

The crowd waited in nearly perfect silence until Kasuf suddenly began. At the top of his lungs, he shouted the name of Ra. When they heard the name of their dreaded king, the thousands fell to their knees and prostrated themselves facedown in the sand.

Daniel, usually so curious and alert, seemed to be lost in thought. He stood looking out into the desert over the heads of the crowd until a swift kick from Anubis took his feet out from under him. All must bow before the omnipotent Ra.

From memory, Kasuf sang a short liturgical paeon to their king-god. At the end of the song, he stood and called a question to the prostrate thousands. They shouted back their answer in one deafening voice.

"Ra, sa' adam y'emallah nhet!"

Kasuf called another question, projecting his voice as far into the desert air as he could. Again, the answer came.

"Ra, sa' adam y'emallah nhet!"

Several times more, his call met with this response. As if spontaneously submitting to popular demand, a brilliant gold figure emerged slowly from the deep shadows inside the pyramid. It was Ra, disguised in his golden facade. He moved slowly, fluidly into the sunlight, floating over the ground like a figure walking through a dream. At length, he arrived at his throne and, as his servant children clustered themselves around him, he delicately sat down. One at a time, the cheerless crowd began to stand. Everyone knew what would happen next, and although it made them angry, not a single person dared to express their feelings.

Anubis left Daniel's side and went to Ra's throne. Dropping to one knee, he extended his weapon in both hands, offering it to his lord with a ceremonial gesture, his head deeply bowed. Ra nodded once very broadly, then, milking every ounce of drama the moment would yield, he extended his arm, pointing theatrically toward Daniel. Anubis bowed once more before standing up and walking back to Daniel.

While this charade was transpiring, Skaara was doing everything he could to catch Daniel's attention. He couldn't simply call out. Anubis was too close, and the other Horus guards were scrutinizing the crowd carefully. Skaara coughed, he scratched his head, he pretended to sneeze. Nothing worked, and there wasn't much time left.

The whole time, Daniel was staring at his feet, lost in a confused tangle of thoughts. There certainly wasn't any love lost between himself and the Marines he'd come with, but he couldn't imagine killing them. And yet, that seemed like the only reasonable course of action under the circumstances. Daniel realized no matter what he did, the kneeling soldiers were as good as dead—himself included. On the other hand, he could refuse to pull the trigger. But in that case, he believed Ra would make good on his promise to kill "all who had seen him."

The dilemma was doubly painful because Daniel had brought it upon himself. He hadn't told the whole truth when General West had asked him whether he could bring the men back through. The digital pictures of the second StarGate sent back to Earth by the Maple Unit were clear enough: there was no cartouche in the room, no reliable way of establishing the new coordinates for the trip back home. He guessed that West was going to send the team through whether or not Daniel went with them. He was willing to risk himself to satisfy his curiosity, and, as he had done so often in his life, he had failed to consider the consequences of his actions on other people. Now, millions of people would have to pay dearly for his selfishness and overweening curiosity. If he did as Ra asked, he could at least spare the few here who he had "contaminated" by allowing them to think he was a messenger of Ra. Sha'uri being one of them.

He lifted his eyes and looked at the soldiers, all of them staring straight back at him. O'Neil figured Daniel couldn't look at them because he'd decided to accept whatever false promises Ra had made him.

Skaara, still fidgeting nearby, interpreted Daniel's demeanor as one of despair, just at the moment when he was trying to offer some hope. But Daniel was actually trying to summon the strength to do this horrible thing, the power to embrace the lesser of two evils.

With an exaggerated gesture, large enough to be seen far back into the crowd, Anubis trust the pulse rifle into Daniel's hands, then yanked him roughly down the ramp toward the soldiers. Daniel felt dazed as he was marched past the stone-silent crowd feeling the first heat of the morning, the giant's hand strangling the blood in his arm, and the sun continuously glinting into his eyes from all directions. He thought there must still be a way out, some compromise to be struck, some alternative he could present to the sadistic boy-tyrant that would save the lives of his companions, the wretched slaves in the sand around him, and the people back on Earth who would be next. Then Anubis stopped him. He was now face-to-face with the soldiers. He could see their lips moving, speaking urgent words, threats, ideas or please, he couldn't hear them. He felt Anubis's hands on his hands, arranging them on the rifle, pointing it at the soldiers, then reaching down and sliding his hand along the underside of the gun causing it to click open, ready to fire. The harsh glare of three guns poured in from every angle, the beams jabbing like fingernails into his eyes.

He realized something was reflecting the sunlight from below, someone's jewelry or perhaps a shiny button. It was very distracting. How ironic that such a paltry annoyance could catch his attention when people's lives, thousands of them, were hanging in the balance. Nevertheless, Daniel stirred from his catatonic musings long enough to deal with this bothersome detail. As Anubis made his way back up the ramp, leaving Daniel guarded by the two Horus guards tending the soldiers, he glanced down into the crowd and saw Skaara using O'Neil's lighter to reflect the sun up into his eyes.

When Skaara had his attention, he opened his long coat just enough to show Daniel that he was concealing one of the rifles from the base camp. Then, with a slight tilt of his head, he directed Daniel to look on the other side of the ramp. Daniel followed the boy's eyes to where Sha'uri was standing. She smiled up at him eagerly as the boys surrounding her showed him that they, too, were armed.

Daniel nodded once to show he understood, then suddenly broke out of his torpor. He took a deep breath, then let his instincts carry him the rest of the way. He shouted to the crowd in broken but passionate Egyptian.

"There is only one Ra. He tells me to kill these men, my friends, my brothers. I will obey him unto death."

Really getting into his act, Daniel pointed a finger at the soldiers, thundering about how evil they had been to challenge the god of the sun. Slowly he raised the rifle to his shoulder and leveled it at the other Americans.

Suddenly, Daniel whipped around to face the pyramid entrance. He closed his eyes and squeezed the trigger. The deadly pulse of energy exploded out of his rifle, careening toward Ra's throne with a terrifying whine. Before it hit, O'Neil was already on his feet and in the process of disarming the nearest Horus guard. The shot exploded into the ramp less than five feet from Ra and his entourage, sending chunks of paving stone and dust flying into the air.

At the same time, Skaara took out his rifle, pointed at the sky, and held the trigger in the fire position. The other shepherd boys did the same thing. The result was predictable: all hell broke loose. The terrified crowd scattered in 360 directions, everyone crashing into everyone else.

O'Neil snapped open the pulse rifle he had just taken from one Horus, and used it to kill the other. Freeman hoisted Feretti onto his shoulder and lugged him to the edge of the ramp, tossing him over the side before jumping himself. He never made it to the ground. While he was still in the air, Anubis fired from behind the smoke at the top of the ramp. The shot went through Freeman's head like a soft watermelon, raining pieces of him onto the screaming crowd.

Daniel and O'Neil, the last ones off the ramp, saw Freeman get hit. They both turned and sprinted for the opposite embankment, leaping with reckless abandon toward the dunes below. They heard the shots whiz past them but never realized how very close they had come. Before they were on the ground, Anubis was running toward them, glad that he would be the one to kill O'Neil. But when he came to where they had jumped, they were gone. He jogged farther down the ramp, sure of spotting them somewhere in the stampede. Anubis unsheathed a wickedly long knife and jumped down into the sand. He scanned the area for several seconds before he correctly guessed what must have happened.

The moment the soldiers were on the ground, they had been wrapped in the thick, hooded robes, making them impossible to distinguish from the thousands of others who were now beating a disorganized retreat into the dunes.

Anubis looked into the sky and signaled the *udajeet*, the gliders, to come closer. As the two small planes swooped down, the jackal-headed god reached out and grabbed one of the terrified Nagadans. He plunged the long blade into the man's heart, then quickly ripped his victim's long cloak off. He tossed the body aside and draped the hooded robe over himself, showing the glider pilots what they were looking for.

The glider pilots understood. They skimmed low over the melee, scrutinizing as many individuals as possible. But there were thousands of them, and they were running without pattern in every direction.

Kawalsky, still wearing his waterlogged boots, should have been an easy target. Not only was he much taller than anyone who lived in Nagada, he was carrying the wounded Feretti on his hip. Nabeh, Rabhi, and Aksah hustled the soldiers across the sand and into the middle of a thick herd of *mastadges*. Daniel and O'Neil were already there, waiting to mount Little Bit. There were twelve of the animals; two to carry the soldiers to safety and ten to act as decoys if the *udajeet* gave chase.

Rabhi and Aksah helped load Feretti into the sling saddle hanging off the side of another *mastadge*, and, as soon as everyone was aboard, Skaara reached his hand into the hypersensitive area behind Little Bit's ears. He gave her a quick scratch, then got out of the way. The dozen animals suddenly took off in all different directions.

The glider pilots swooped down overhead. The rear glider nearly collided with the one in front as they veered to follow different *mastadges*. By the time two gliders returned to formation, the animals had dispersed in every direction. Scanning the horizon, the two glider pilots could not see them anywhere.

20

NOWHERE TO RUN

Ra sat in his private chamber seething like a basketful of vipers. Barely in control of his temper, he waited for the pilots to return with the clever vermin who had come through the StarGate. He was rehearsing the exact manner in which he would make them pay for their crimes against him, when he felt a tug at his sleeve. One of his servants, a ten-year-old boy, had come to notify him that the *udajeet* pilots had returned. For no reason, Ra slapped the child hard across the face, knocking him down. As soon as he had done so, he felt much better, relieved. Then, the eternally young king stepped out of his chamber and mounted his throne, composing himself for his visitors.

The pilots, a pair of Horus guards, marched quickly into the room, deactivating their helmets. They came to the base of the stairs leading up to Ra's throne and knelt down. Anubis, his armor still stained with blood, came into the room and stood at Ra's side, looking down at the two empty-handed warriors.

Ra fixed his eyes on the soldiers and very calmly, he hissed the question. "Where are they?"

"They vanished."

Furious, Anubis came down the steps and kicked the soldier who had answered the question. "What do you mean, vanished?"

The other soldier spoke up. "They are still in the sand. Surely the sandstorm will kill them." Losing control of their small planes in the wind, the Horuses had searched as long as they dared. Waiting any longer to turn back would have meant certain death, so they decided to head back and take their chances with Ra.

As angry as he had ever been, Ra stood and walked across the room to his jewel box. The box opened automatically as he approached, revealing its contents: a coin-size quartz jewel connected to looping, ornamental strands of black wire. The wiring fit around the boy-king's hand like an elegant, fingerless glove, hiding the quartz jewel in the palm of his hand. Calmly, he turned and came back toward the anxious pilots. He motioned for the man who had spoken first to stand up.

Nervously, the soldier complied. He wanted to explain why he had cut off the chase, but Ra signaled that everything was all right now and to be quiet. He came face-to-face with the soldier and showed him a reassuring smile.

"You tried," he said, slowly reaching up to stroke the man's cheek, "I know you tried." He studied the pilot's face for some time, regarding him, it seemed, tenderly. But his hand suddenly flew open only inches from the pilot's face. When he saw the medallion in Ra's palm, the loyal Horus guard had a fraction of a second to contemplate how his life was going to end. The dark glove's jewel came to life and slammed the man backward against a pillar like a wrecking ball. Slowly, Ra moved in for the kill. He reached out and brought his hand down toward the dazed man's skull. The Horus knew that if the jewel touched his head, he would die. But he was only half-conscious, unable to do anything but watch his death happen to him.

Ra's hand came gently to rest on the head. Immediately the man's legs shot out stiff, and his whole body began to spasm violently, as if he were receiving an electroshock lobotomy. The head itself began to vibrate at an unnatural rate of speed, then suddenly went still. Over the next few seconds, the man's facial features began to distort radically. The skull lost the integrity of its shape, swelling and constricting like a thin bag of water.

The ring's jewel worked on the same principles as the

StarGates. But here, the quartz was put to much more sinister purposes. As Ra held the jewel down tight on the crown of the man's head, he was actually rearranging his molecules, liquifying him from the inside.

As serenely as if he were watering flowers in the garden, Ra stood over the man, distracted from his own pain by this hypnotic display of gruesome magic. When his victim was dead, he closed his hand around the deadly gem and sighed.

Calmer now, he walked to the other terrified soldier and ran a finger down the curve of his nose. "Let this serve notice. I will not accept failure." He turned and walked back into his chamber.

Hurricane force gusts came streaking through the desert with enough force to play the dunes like a giant wind instrument. Fighting their way through the blasting sand, O'Neil and Daniel held tight to Little Bit's hairy flanks. The hoods of their robes were pulled down past their chins. The air was so thick with dust, their eyes were useless anyway.

Fatigued, Daniel stumbled and fell into the sand. The *mastadge* halted its progress, turning back and howling even louder than the wind. O'Neil pulled his mask away from his eyes and fumbled around the dune until he found Daniel already half buried in the sand.

The *mastadge* continued screaming into the storm as O'Neil walked Daniel back up the dune, but then suddenly trotted away, disappearing into the abrasive night. O'Neil, thinking fast, tried to have Daniel call to the animal before it got out of range, but it didn't work. He couldn't understand why this *mastadge* would suddenly jilt her beloved, stranding them both in the storm. In spite of their screams, the animal was gone.

O'Neil hauled Daniel to the top of the dune where they both sat down. They were about as far up Shit Creek as anyone could get and their paddle had just jogged off into the desert. O'Neil pulled his hood tighter over his head and felt the sand gathering around him, slowly burying him alive.

Half an hour later, Little Bit came trundling back, howling over the wind as she approached. When the beast was close enough, the marooned men were able to pick out the shapes of several helmeted figures closing in on them. The one in

front scrambled to the top of the dune, pulling off his helmet
and ski mask, grinning wildly. It was Nabeh, the slightly
demented shepherd boy.

Standing behind him, decked out in the uniform of a
United States Marine, was Skaara. He squinted at O'Neil
through the flying sand and gave him a "thumbs-up."

Propped up by the boys, his eyes swollen closed, Daniel
felt his way up the rocky hillside to the entrance of the cave.
When Kawalsky saw who it was, he lowered his rifle and
came to the entrance to help. O'Neil walked into the shelter
under his own power and surveyed the scene.

A dozen or so of the boys, none of them old enough in
O'Neil's view to wear a military uniform, were buttoned
into the oversize camouflage togs they'd rescued from the
base camp. Stacked against the walls were two dozen rifles
and several crates of ammunition. Halfway back in the
cavern, a makeshift hospital had been set up. Brown, his
arm in a sling, was doctoring Feretti.

"You made it!" Kawalsky greeted O'Neil with a roar.
Now all the surviving members of the team were present
and accounted for. O'Neil reached up and clapped the big
man on the shoulder, a soldierly greeting, before continuing
deeper into the cave for an inspection. He noticed that
Skaara and Nabeh were moving with him, a step behind, as
if they were now his personal bodyguards. O'Neil turned
and studied them with a disappointed look.

"What do you think, Colonel?" Kawalsky asked.
"They're not exactly Special Forces but they're real eager
to enlist." Obviously Kawalsky was as proud of the job the
boys had done that day as they were of themselves.

"Take the guns away from them, Lieutenant, before they
hurt themselves."

"Come again, sir?"

"You heard me. Collect the guns and send them home."

Kawalsky came within inches of exploding. He was fed
up with O'Neil coming into situations he didn't understand,
situations Kawalsky had completely under control, and
screwing everything up.

"There isn't anywhere for them to go," Kawalsky stayed
cool, informative. "If they showed up in the city, they'll be

executed for helping us. Besides, we could sure use the help, sir.'' His tone left no doubt who he was ready to stand behind if it came to a choice.

"For what!?" O'Neil got in his face, suddenly furious. "To do what, Lieutenant!?"

O'Neil's outburst caught everyone by surprise. Stunned, no one knew what to say. To Kawalsky, the answer was obvious. The team needed to help to getting back through the StarGate and safely home. He was bewildered that his superior officer had apparently forgotten the goal of their mission.

Daniel, who understood the source of the confusion, propped himself onto an elbow and called out to O'Neil. "Why don't you just tell them the truth? Tell them about the bomb."

Kawalsky stared at O'Neil like he might be the new commanding officer and asked him, "What's he talking about, Colonel O'Neil?"

"My orders were simple. I was to stay behind and look for any signs of possible danger to Earth. If I found any, I was supposed to blow up the StarGate. Well guess what, I found some.'' O'Neil turned away not wanting to continue this confession.

Indignant, Kawalsky snapped at O'Neil, "Why wasn't I told!"

"It was strictly need to know." O'Neil was matter-of-fact.

"Need to know? Don't you think this is something I would damn well need to know?"

"You weren't even supposed to be here. None of you were. You were all supposed to go back through the Gate with Jackson."

Even though Kawalsky knew O'Neil was right, he didn't like it. He had been the commander of this operation long before O'Neil came along, and this option had never been discussed with him. He had always understood that the military often moved in strange, mysterious, and often stupid ways, but this was too much for Kawalsky to comprehend. There was nothing he could say.

Frustrated with the everlasting stupidity of the military mind, Daniel interjected.

"And this great plan of yours would leave you here with

a nuclear weapon? Well, it's his now, and tomorrow he's going to send it back through the Gate along with a shipment of the quartz mineral they mine here. Apparently, when the bomb goes off, this shipment will detonate and cause an explosion a hundred times more powerful than that bomb alone is capable of."

"He told you all this?" O'Neil asked skeptically.

"Yes."

"All right then," O'Neil stepped forward, reassuming command of the situation. "I'll intercept the bomb before he can send it through."

"Colonel, listen to me," Daniel pressed. "It's the other Gate, the one on Earth that poses the threat. Think about it. As long as that one is up and functional, he'll always have access. That's the one we have to shut down!"

O'Neil hissed back, "You're absolutely right, but thanks to you, we don't have that option, do we?" He stood up, walked as far toward the mouth of the cave as the sandstorm would allow, and sat down.

"I knew it all along," Feretti broke the silence, "this was a friggin' suicide mission."

It took more than an hour for everyone to calm down and remember that they were on the same side. Daniel was kept busy the whole time explaining what he'd learned inside the pyramid, then translating everything for Sha'uri and the new recruits.

When everything was quiet, Daniel approached O'Neil, who was still sitting at the mouth of the cave blankly watching the sandstorm.

"So, you've accepted the fact that you'll never go home?"

O'Neil felt as hollow as he had the day General West's men arrived at his house. All he did was stare straight ahead. Daniel tried again.

"Don't you have people who care about you? Don't you have a family?"

"I had a family," O'Neil said in a quiet monotone. "No one should ever outlive their own child."

Daniel didn't know how to respond. Although he'd known plenty of pain in his life, he still didn't know how to respond to the pain of others. It was a brute fact. It was there, beyond the power of words. When his parents died, he'd had to put up with a long line of fools coming up to him saying, "they're happy now" and "it's probably all for the best." He wouldn't try to cheat O'Neil of his pain with any sugarcoated platitudes.

At the same time, he had to do something. O'Neil was sinking fast, deep into some hopeless place within himself, and the team couldn't afford that right now.

"Colonel, listen"—Daniel was quiet but urgent—"I don't want to die." That caught O'Neil's attention. "Your soldiers don't want to die. And these kids helping us don't want to die. It's a shame you're in such a hurry to."

The words punched O'Neil in the gut. He was about to respond, to say or do whatever it took to get Jackson out of his face. But when he looked up Daniel was already walking away, and Skaara was coming toward him balancing a full bowl of food for his commanding officer.

O'Neil watched him spill a few drops of broth over the rim of the dish, his tongue poking between his teeth to help him concentrate. During the altercation with Kawalsky, Skaara had backed him up, telling the bigger soldier in Egyptian that he'd better back off or else.

"Anasaar?" he asked, offering the bowl to O'Neil.

Still thinking about what Daniel had said, O'Neil turned and focused on the storm. Skaara was confused. He sniffed at the bowl of stew and decided it was pretty decent for cave cooking. Completing his journey, he arrived at O'Neil's side and set the bowl down in front of him.

When the man in the black beret ignored him, Skaara playfully slid the plate closer. Then a little closer. Then once more. Then several more times, he invited the colonel to eat. It was the goofiest thing O'Neil had seen for a long time, and he waved the boy off to make him quit. But Skaara could see he was winning the battle and wouldn't let up.

When O'Neil turned his glum face to show the kid he was serious, to just leave him alone, Skaara clucked like a chicken and flapped his wings. Something Feretti taught him a few minutes earlier.

O'Neil caved in. It was too ridiculous, he had to smile. "Chicken, right?"

"Shickan!" the boy repeated with so much exuberance, O'Neil couldn't help but laugh. He reached out and used his fingers to mess up Skaara's hair in a spontaneous show of affection. Then he leaned forward and picked up the bowl, accepting the gift the boy had brought him.

Twenty minutes later, the bowl was empty and the colonel was gazing out at the storm, his mind on the other side of the universe. He was thinking back to a particular afternoon in Yuma. A clear day in late spring two years ago when he'd pulled into the driveway, honked to say he was home, then got the equipment bag out of the garage and threw it in the back of the station wagon. He got back in the car and leaned on the horn, to no avail. He didn't know what was taking the kid so long, but whatever it was, it couldn't be worth showing up late for the very first game of the season. He slammed the car door and went to the front door, which was locked. He had left the keys in the ignition. By the time he was back and unlocking the front door, he sensed that something must be very wrong. The moment he swung the door open, he knew it for sure.

He scanned the living room. It was messy but normal.

"Son, you in here? J.J.?"

He walked into the living room, but by the time he was in the hallway, he was running. He burst into the boy's room. His uniform jersey was hanging on the back of a chair. He went into his own room. The nightstand on Sarah's side of the bed was opened. It was supposed to be locked at all times. That's when he heard the siren and figured it all out.

For a minute he stood there like a statue staring at the open drawer where Sarah kept the pistol. He knew it was loaded, and knew if he reached for the key taped to the underside of the bed it wouldn't be there. He kept hoping he was wrong, that the sound of the siren would veer away to some other part of the neighborhood. But it kept coming.

He checked Sarah's bathroom. Nothing, clean. He came back in to the hallway and started toward the kitchen, but then turned and ran to the back porch. The siren was almost to their door when he looked outside and saw two of the neighbor kids standing in the yard, leaning over his son. There was a long fan of blood spattered across the wall of the garage. The gun was laying nearby in the grass.

He hardly recalled opening the door and coming outside, nor hearing the two friends try to explain what had happened. But he remembered the image of the boy's crumpled body, half-dressed for the baseball game, lying bloody and disfigured in the grass. Before the paramedics arrived to tell him what he already knew, he got down in the grass and did something he hadn't done for years. He cradled the boy in his arms, rocking him back and forth.

One bullet right through the head. After that, Jack O'Neil, Sr. didn't want to move anymore, didn't want to speak, didn't want to go through the motions of grieving for the boy. All he wanted to do was lay down next to his child and die. That's how the paramedic team found him when they came through the gate a few minutes later, the same state Sarah had to nurse him through while she struggled to deal with her own loss. It was the same state of self-loathing and anguish O'Neil was in two years later when General West's men came to visit.

He just wanted it to be over.

When O'Neil reemerged into the present, Skaara was sitting next to him, drawing in the sand on the cave floor and watching O'Neil think. He'd never met a soldier before, but he knew O'Neil was a good one. He had already made up his mind to be like this man, to become someone with the skills and determination to protect his people.

As Daniel made his way to the remote area of the grotto where Sha'uri had set up her camp kitchen beneath a natural ventilation shaft, he saw something he took as a bad sign. Feretti and Kawalsky were huddled in a conspiratorial conference. When Daniel came close to them, they turned and glared at him until he was gone.

Still looking back at the clutch of soldiers, Daniel came to the makeshift "kitchen." Sitting around the fire, the shepherd boys were holding their bowls, obviously ready to eat.

"Is it ready?" he asked Sha'uri, who was busy stroking the fire below the small pot. She indicated that indeed it was, so Daniel took one of the bowls and scooped out a measure of both broth and meat before returning it to the amazed child. All the boys stared at him like he'd just pulled his tongue out of his nose.

"What?" he said in English.

One of the kids said something and all of them, Sha'uri included, started cracking up.

"What?!"

While the boys continued making jokes too fast and too colloquial for Daniel to catch, each one apparently more sidesplittingly funny than the last, Sha'uri took two servings of food out to the soldiers. Daniel, fed up, tackled Nabeh to the ground, pinning him.

"Why do you laugh?" he demanded in ancient Egyptian.

But by that point, everything was funny, and Daniel's question only succeeded in knocking the boys over backward, laughing even harder. Finally, Nabeh regained control of his breathing and explained.

"Bani ne-ateru ani, hee na'a ani-ben." Literally: The ones who are husbands do not do this, this kind of work.

"Husband?" The short hairs on Daniel's neck stood up. He rolled off Nabeh just as Sha'uri returned to the room. "Sha'uri"—he switched back to Egyptian—"crazy boy here just called me your husband."

Daniel had meant it to be lighthearted even though he wanted an answer. The boys busted their collective gut repeating the words "crazy boy" and pointing at Nabeh. Nabeh got the joke; he punched Daniel in the arm. But to everyone's surprise, the young woman fled the area, retreating into a dimly lit region of the cave. Like men of all galaxies, they looked at each other understanding they'd done something wrong, without knowing exactly what.

Daniel stood up and, after a suitable pause, followed Sha'uri around the corner. He found her sitting by herself at the very back of the cave.

"What is it?" he asked. He realized that she wasn't angry, but somehow ashamed.

Nearby the boys had snuck up to spy on them. Sha'uri could hear her brother shooing them away. Only when they were gone did she speak.

"I'm so sorry. Please don't be angry with me, but I didn't tell them."

"Tell them what?" Daniel asked.

"That you did not want me."

Daniel was puzzled until he realized she meant the night

she came to his room in Nagada, the night the townspeople had offered her to him. Now she was turned away from him, this fragile creature he understood so poorly, feeling ashamed and rejected. He reached out and took her shoulders awkwardly into his hands. His pulse quickened and his mouth started going dry, sitting there in the dark with this woman he desired so badly, wanting to comfort and assure her. Desiring nothing more than to kiss her, but painfully aware of the many great distances that separated them, how imperfectly they knew each other and knowing that he would soon have to leave this place or die trying. In spite of all that, he pulled her closer, and when she turned her face to his, began to trace her features with his fingertips. He started having that same sensation of déjà vu he'd experienced the first time he'd seen her, but this time he understood why. This upturned face he held in his hands was the same face he'd loved on Earth, the same face he'd taken with him to Colorado. Sha'uri could have been the model for the fourteenth-century statuette that had been his greatest treasure on Earth. Daniel felt like he should tell her, explain the whole amazing coincidence. But by that point their lips were too close for words, too close to do anything but kiss.

The first thing Daniel saw when he woke up the next morning was Sha'uri's face. It was still peacefully sleeping only inches away from his. He thought about everything that had been said and done the night before, and he couldn't help it—he bust out grinning. He rolled on his back, put his hands under his head, and grinned at the ceiling. That's when he noticed Nabeh was sleeping only inches behind him. Still wearing his helmet, his mouth hung open in a way that changed Daniel's expression immediately. Suddenly, sitting up seemed like an irresistible idea. When he did, Daniel realized that all the shepherd boys had snuggled into a limb-tangled circle around him and Sha'uri. Obviously these folks had a slightly different sense of privacy than he did.

He could see Skaara working on something at the mouth of the cave, white smoke from one of the dying fires of wafting everywhere around him. Stepping carefully over the ring of dreaming boys, Daniel tiptoed through the cave to see what Skaara was up to. Inspired by the visual history he'd seen in the catacombs, Skaara had decided to tell a story of his own. He was sitting on a stone-block stool, furiously sketching a scene onto the wall.

Kawalsky, the first one awake, had posted himself to lookout duty, just beyond the mouth of the cave. He nodded a "morning" in at Daniel, who sat down near the artist to watch him work.

Skaara was no Rembrandt. He was using a soft red stone to mark down the story of the rescue he had helped to plan. The wobbly pyramid, drawn small, was surrounded by gigantic stick-figure boys shooting dots into the air. Hovering above the pyramid, the planet's three suns hung just below the pair of gliders maliciously spying on the whole scene. A set of confused squiggles represented the soldiers kneeling on the ramp, and Ra, a big frown plastered across his face, sat facing them. Daniel, spiked hair and three long toes on each foot, was shown holding his gun, blasting backward toward the pyramid. Nabeh was visible, smiling maniacally, his head shaped like a half dome.

As Daniel settled in to watch, Skaara was working on the image of himself. Drawn from his perspective, he became the largest figure on the rough canvas. With one hand, he held the long reins trailing across the desert toward a trio of *mastadges*. In the other, his airborne rifle was shooting right through one of the suns. The way he drew his own face changed the meaning of everything else in the picture. His mouth was opened in a ferocious war cry. Daniel watched, fascinated, as Skaara repeatedly twisted his own face into an angry mask, then tried to transfer the image onto the rock.

Next it was Daniel's face that twisted. He suddenly realized what he was watching and how important it was. Skaara was writing, recording the first history of these people done in many centuries. Daniel, the boyish historian could not help but love that. For Daniel, wherever there was writing, culture, and a serious attempt to understand the lessons of history, there was hope. The grin came back. Daniel had lucked out and was sitting here in a cave on a different planet watching the dawn of a new "ancient Egyptian" culture.

It was one of those perfect moments, but one that brought with it a sense of responsibility. Whether Skaara's talents as an historian would be allowed to flourish and infect the rest of his people was still in question. They still had to face Ra.

As Daniel sat there in the rising sunlight, his mind went blank. He had been staring at Skaara's large drawing for several minutes when it fell out of his mouth.

"The point of origin." His first words of the morning caught in his throat. Kawalsky turned around in time to see Daniel digging through the fire for a half-burnt stick.

"Jackson, what're you doing?"

"The point of origin!" This time his voice rang out clearly, tearing through the cave like a wake-up bell. Daniel fished a twig out of the fire and using the charcoal end of it, traced over the top angle of the pyramid. Then, with another, he drew a line connecting the three suns. The angles were parallel and congruent, like the stripes of a chevron. It was a symbol Daniel remembered from the StarGate. It had to be the seventh symbol, the point of origin, the thing he needed to make good on his promise to get them all home. Neither Kawalsky nor Skaara understood why Daniel was messing up the boy's artwork.

"I found it! That's it, three suns above the pyramid."

Now everybody was waking up looking at Daniel.

"Here it is, the seventh sign. We're going home!"

21

THE TROJAN HORSE

Standard procedure on shipment days called for every able-bodied person in Nagada to come to the pit. They worked for two or three easy hours, no one climbing the eleven-story ladder more than twice. When the carts were loaded, a small contingent brought the ore to the pyramid and sent it through the StarGate. By the early evening when they returned, the city was ready to celebrate the feast of Tekfaalit, marking the end of the forty-day work cycle.

Prayers and songs thanking Ra for all he provided were followed by an outdoor feast. Celebrants moved from house to house, offering and receiving food and drink. This was the only day of the month to drink the delicious Tabaa, a sweet liquor brewed from fermented desert shurbs that when ingested in sufficient quantities produced states of intoxication. The Nagadans made sure to ingest the necessary quantities. By midnight half the two was ripped to the gills, and the party in the streets routinely lasted into the next morning.

But today, was no ordinary Tekfaalit. Ra had been anticipating the moves of his human subjects for thousands of years. Although he could be rash, he also knew how to be careful. Less than a thousand workers had been permitted to enter, and they were being driven zealously up and down the ladder by Ra's most sadistic henchmen. But it wasn't physical fear of the guard that made the workers obey, it was because they believed the myths they had been told since birth. That was why Ra needed so few guards to shepherd so many workers.

Strapped to his back was the tall staff weapon, but his tool of choice was the leather whip. He lashed at the fellahin almost continuously, eager to bring the shipment to his master as quickly as possible. A few of the older workers had already collapsed under the strain, but they had done so well away from the sharp eyes of the hawk-helmeted guard.

High above on the cliffs, ready to march in the direction of the pyramid, four stately *mastadges* stood tethered to four-wheeled cargo carts. Each of the hairy animals had been painstakingly washed and groomed, decorated with ornate prayer shawls, small bells, and long braided garlands of dried desert flowers. The rickety wooden carts behind them each carried about a ton of quartz, and, with the workers dumping the ore by the sackful, were nearly full and ready to move. By tradition, the first cart was filled only with the largest nuggets, normally no larger than walnuts. The last cart, the heaviest, was filled with quartz powder.

Spread around the dusty floor of the pit were half a dozen processing pavilions. These workstations were marked by a small obelisk rising through the canvas roof of a large tent. This is where the raw quartz was sifted, sorted according to size and purity, the cleaned. Everything was saved, down to the last granulated shavings, which were blended with other materials to produce valuable alloys.

Loading their sacks full with the mineral, the fellahin carried them across the hot sand to the base of the giant ladders running like a scar up the side of the cliff. Climbing these ladders was no easy feat. Climbing them with one hundred pounds of deadweight on your back in one hundred-degree heat was not only tiring, it was dangerous. Since the great majority of the Nagadans had been forced to turn around and march home, those who were working had to make many trips up the wall.

Eventually, one of the laborers wilted and collapsed near where the Horus guard had stationed himself. He had been waiting his turn at the base of the ladder when he apparently succumbed to heat exhaustion. Several nearby workers tried to help him regain his feet, but before they could do so, Horus was jogging toward them screaming for the man to get up and work.

When he came within striking distance, the powerfully built young man used his whip to put a stripe across the back of the fallen worker, cutting right through the thick material of his robe. The man tried to stand but slumped once more into the sand, sending Horus into a rage. The hawk-headed god unsheathed a serrated dagger, ready to teach the others a gruesome lesson.

But at the last second, the miner flipped nimbly onto his back, showing Horus the business end of a pulse rifle, the very weapon Ra had handed to Daniel. Horus, frozen, stared at the exhausted worker, Colonel Jack O'Neil of the U.S.M.C. Staring right back, O'Neil methodically cocked the weapon open and hopped to his feet. At the same time, several of the surrounding "miners" pulled rifles from beneath their robes and trained them on Horus.

Slowly his fingers loosened around the whip handle, and he let it drop to the ground. Kawalsky moved behind him and took the pulse rifle off his back.

Kasuf's voice came piercing down from the top of the cliff towering above them. Horrified, he came running along the lip of the ravine toward the scene of the confrontation. When he understood what was happening, he flew into an absolute panic, pointing and screaming. Hundreds of surprised miners began slowly surrounding the ragtag commando squad and their prisoner, obviously confused about what to do.

Whatever the old man was saying, it was working. O'Neil saw Sha'uri, Skaara, and the other amateurs in the group looking up toward the man, listening. He knew the old man was trying to scare everyone back into obedience. Something had to be done quickly.

"Jackson," O'Neil yelled, "what's he saying?"

Daniel listened for a minute, then tried to interpret Kasuf's apoplectic rantings. "He's saying we're going to bring misery to his people . . . uh, massacre—that Ra will slaughter everyone who disobeys. And . . . now he's telling them not to cooperate with us . . . not to anger the gods."

"Don't anger the gods, huh?" O'Neil looked at Horus with contempt. Casually, he paced off the short distance between them, and peered into the golden screen at the throat of the large hawk mask. He was standing face-to-face with the dreaded, invincible deity and wasn't at all impressed. All attention was once again riveted on him.

Then, just as nonchalantly as he had approached, O'Neil turned his back on the hawk-headed soldier, standing well within his reach. He knew his men would take the man out if he tried anything cute. O'Neil shook his head in a display of noncomprehension.

"This guy ain't no god!"

He turned, pointed his rifle at Horus's chest, and pulled the trigger. The blast hit the warrior square on his armored chest plate, knocking him backward like he'd collided with a truck. He landed in a heap several feet away.

"Nghaaaaaah!"

Kasuf screamed out like he was the one who had been shot. The scream modulated into a long plaintive wail spilling into the long human-made valley. Kawalsky, O'Neil, and Brown, not knowing what to expect next, concentrated on covering the crowd with their rifles. No one on the floor of the pit could believe what O'Neil had just done. Only a few days before, they had felt the consequences of Ra's anger, cowered helplessly as their city was hacked apart and burned for a crime much less severe than this. And now, this violent miracle, this impossible, unimaginable crime had taken place without warning right before their eyes. A few of the miners immediately fell to their knees and, following Kasuf's example, broke into ardent prayer. But most were too stunned, too confused by what they had witnessed, to react at all.

O'Neil was on the warpath now. He turned to his troops and boomed out his command. "Okay, let's get to the carts. Now!" The very next moment he was leading the way, crashing through the crowd toward the base of the cliffs.

Daniel knew something wasn't right. Lagging behind the others, he looked into the faces of the astonished populace. Frightened and utterly confused, they avoided his glance. He could see that they didn't understand what had happened. Without quite knowing why, he knew it was imperative for them to understand that the killing was an act of tyrannicide.

"Wait a second!" he called forward. He ran over to the helmeted villain's limp body, and twisted the connecting tabs at the base of the helmet. The elaborately decorated metallic plates silently retracted, folding themselves back into the golden collar at the top of his breastplate.

Beneath the mask was the unremarkable face of Ra's darkest-skinned warrior, the bald-headed young man who supervised the slaughter of Nagada. Except for his armor and the *udjat*, the Eye of Ra design, tattoed on his shoulder, he looked like he could have belonged to any family in the ancient city.

Daniel hoisted him up to a sitting position, displaying him to the assembled miners.

"Take a look at your gods!" he shouted in Egyptian loud enough to be heard over Kasuf's song. "He is a man like any other."

Soon both Kasuf and Daniel were drowned out by the excited chatter spreading like a brushfire through the ranks of the workers. It was an amazing moment. Daniel watched as the veils of illusion fell away from the eyes of these downtrodden people. With a certain amount of showmanship, Daniel shoved the slack body forward into the dirt. He picked up the pulse rifle Kawalsky had given him, and moved to rejoin the squad.

Most of the Nagadans were now firmly on his side. As he passed, many offered words of congratulation or encouragement. Buoyed, Daniel sauntered with an extra bounce in his step. He felt he'd handled the situation pretty damn well.

He spotted his beautiful Sha'uri beaming down at him proudly. Her expression quickly changed to one of horror as she looked again in the direction of Horus. Sudden cries from the crowd alerted him to an approaching danger.

O'Neil's shot had hit nothing but armor. It had knocked the man unconscious, but now he had come around and woozily grabbed one of the mining tools, a pickax from the ground. By the time Daniel wheeled around, the warrior was rearing back with the ax, ready to chop.

Without time to think, Daniel pointed his weapon and fired. It was only the second time in his life he'd pulled a trigger, but his shot hit exactly where it needed to—beneath the armored breastplate—and ripped into the soldier's unprotected stomach. The pulse sent him pinwheeling backward through the air. The gruesome flight ended with his head finding the corner of a retaining wall. Even the professional soldiers grimaced at the moment of impact. If the crowd was stunned before, now they were positively stupefied. But none more so than Daniel, who stood with the gun quaking in his hands.

"Not so easy, is it?"

O'Neil had scrambled down the ladder and was easing the rifle out of the shaken scholar's hands.

It was Nabeh's idea to replace the lead animal in the delivery train with the filthy slobbering beast that saved Daniel and O'Neil from the sandstorm—an act of heroism that had earned her a place on the team. Using the bangles and garlands from the lead animal, the boys did what they could to improve the looks of their decidedly uglier friend before harnessing him to the front cart.

As soon as O'Neil made the top of the ladder, he shouted the order for the caravan to head out. Skaara relayed the order to the other shepherd boys. With whoops and shouts, they spurred the *mastadges* into action. Although the carts were piled high with the heavy ore, the powerful beasts pulled them with surprising ease. O'Neil had been expecting a slow trudge across the sand, but found he had to jog along behind the last cart to keep up.

In the shadow of the obelisks, Daniel saw an irate Kasuf holding Sha'uri by the sleeve of her thick gray robe. He was obviously berating her for taking part in what he considered an act of suicidal madness.

Kawalsky raced ahead to join the caravan, but Daniel lingered, watching the scene with mixed emotions. Sha'uri was an integral part of the plan she had helped to design; the team needed her. On the other hand, it was incredibly dangerous. Chances were that they would all be killed, a fact the shepherd boys seemed not to understand. Daniel was willing to take the risk because he wanted to protect the Earth from Ra. But why should Sha'uri risk her life for the good of a planet she hadn't even imagined a month before.

As Kasuf continued to shout, the girl was visibly torn. Trained to be blindly obedient, especially to this man who was not only her father, but the Chief Elder and patriarch of her people, she felt immobilized, her feet frozen to the spot. When she looked up and saw Daniel, she gained the courage to try and explain why she had to go to the pyramid, but this only incensed the old one further.

Since before Sha'uri was born, Kasuf had preached unquestioning servility to Ra, shepherding his flock away from conflicts they were bound to lose. He was among the very few who knew the whole secret history of Nagadas ancient rebellions and he knew how painfully each of the uprisings had ended. His people thought they had tasted Ra's full vengeance when the Horuses came to punish the city, but the old man knew better. He understood how venomously cold-blooded the sun god could be. To Kasuf, it felt like the end of the world, the sky shattering and crashing down around him. And at that moment, Sha'uri seemed like the only part of the world he could control. He wouldn't allow this ignorant young woman to tell him how to behave toward his unforgiving god.

"Sha'uri."

When she heard Daniel call her name, the decision was made once and for all. Slowly and deliberately, she twisted her arm free of Kasuf's grip. After all, she was physically stronger than he. Kasuf stepped back, aghast at this act of insubordination.

Without rancor, Sha'uri said it was better to die on your feet than live on your knees. It was a hard thing to say to the old man she loved so much, and then ran to catch up with Daniel.

As she came toward him, Daniel suddenly remembered the formula for power Ra had blithely explained to him: Myth, Faith, Habit.

The people in the mining pit who had witnessed the confrontation and then the execution had seen a crucial part of Ra's false governing Myth—the immortality of the gods—exposed as a sham. This new evidence had severely undermined their Faith. But, looking back at Kasuf, Daniel realized that Habit, once it was established, would always be the last of the three to die.

* * *

Ra sat draped sideways across a chair staring blankly out the great window of his pyramid craft at the endless empty desert. He was idly stroking the black cat lying across his arm. He called the cat Hathor in honor of the female god who had once saved his fiefdom by drowning it in the blood of the rebels. Conflicting versions of the story reached Earth a few years before the StarGate was "sealed and buried for all time." Recorded by scribes on papyrus and carved into stone by masons, Daniel knew the bloody story well, but had always considered it merely another episode in Egyptian "mythology."

The boy-king, bare-headed and his skin showing its natural brown color, spotted the caravan crawling across the barren sea of sand. He stood and watched for a few moments. Nothing distinguished this caravan from the countless others he'd observed. Still, something about the scene brought the barest smile to his lips. He realized that he was glad the fair-skinned one with the glasses had escaped. It made everything more interesting. There was even the possibility that he was part of the delivery team, disguised no doubt as one of the fellahin.

Swaying back and forth ever so slightly, Ra fell into a daydream. When he emerged from it several minutes later, his mood was completely different. He shouted a command, and a moment later, two of his Horus guards were kneeling before him awaiting their orders with heads hung low.

He told the nearly identical soldiers to transport the tray with the captured American weapon to the StarGate room before going to meet the shipment. When the shipment was sent through, the bomb would be set to go off and sent along with it. Like a pair of waiters at an unappetizing banquet, they marched the length of the throne room balancing the large platter, laden with the disassembled nuclear explosive.

They marched the length of the throne room and stepped onto the medallion, wrapped in the black arms of Khnum. Ra looked at Anubis and raised his eyebrows ever so slightly, obviously expecting something. It was a sadistic game Ra played with his servants when he was angry or bored—forcing them to guess what he wanted. Guessing wrong could, and often did, lead to brutal, painful punishment. In this case, Anubis had enough information.

Anubis pressed the jewel mounted in the scarab on the back of his thick quartz and iron wristband, activating the medallion. When the circular wall of cloudy blue light closed the Horuses and their cargo, they were gently ferried down to the medallion below.

Young Skaara was in charge of the operation now. During the long march through the arid desert, O'Neil and the boy rode atop the piles of quartz locked in an intense discussion of strategy that went well beyond the skill of their interpreter, Daniel. After teaching them some basic vocabulary, Daniel could only stand by and listen as the two of them sped through one idea after the next. With gestures, pantomime and twenty-five words in common, the man and the boy pored over every detail of the plan, occasionally breaking out of their huddle to explain a new wrinkle to the others.

Long before they reached the pyramid's entrance ramp, they assumed they were being watched. There was a strict protocol to be observed before the delivery could be brought into the pyramid. The religious people of Nagada, were, of course, scrupulous about practicing these rites even when the pyramid was empty. Skaara had participated in many deliveries, and, as Kasuf's youngest son, had even led the ceremony before. But this he would be doing so under Ra's scrutiny while accompanied by the four uninitiated visitors. Anything wrong or unusual would arouse suspicion.

When they were assembled at the base of the long ramp, Skaara knelt down between the obelisks and sang in a strong clear voice.

"Atema en-Re. Hallam a'ana t'yon shaknom, assar Atem Re." (Ra who comes from the sun, we now submit gratefully the results of our labor, Holy Sun God Ra.)

When he was finished, he stood and looked at Nabeh for an opinion. His eccentric friend shrugged in return as if to say the song had been good enough.

"What is that?" Skaara noticed something under Nabeh's haik.

"What is what?" he tried to act innocent.

"Under your haik. It's the green hat, isn't it?"

Nabeh didn't know what to say, so he grinned nervously. Everyone had told him he couldn't bring the helmet, but he didn't want to leave it back in the cave. He could tell from the way Skaara was talking to him, that he'd made a big mistake.

The next moment, Nabeh's lunatic eyes filled with dread as he looked past Skaara's shoulder to the pyramid entrance. Three Horus warriors stepped onto the platform at the top of the ramp, each of them holding one of the deadly staffs.

Paralyzed, Skaara spent a moment visualizing what would happen to them all if these guards discovered Nabeh's beloved polyurethane treasure. Not knowing exactly what to do next, Skaara ordered the delivery crew, all of them wearing their hoods pulled low over their faces, to kneel in respect to the gods.

After what seemed to him an appropriate amount of time, Skaara stood and unharnessed Daniel's *mastadge,* Little Bit, pulling her aside and handing the reins to Nabeh, speaking angrily under his breath.

"If they find the hat, they will kill us."

Nabeh, the simpleton, didn't quite realize that the helmet would implicate him in the wild escape Sha'uri and the boys had engineered.

Heavy rope handles hung from the sides of the carts. At Skaara's signal, the hooded workers assigned to the first cart came forward, grabbed onto the ropes, and slowly began to drag the vehicle up the incline.

As it moved away, an unexpected problem reared its ugly, oleaginous head. Daniel's *mastadge,* jealous, began to moan and then to bellow. Nabeh spoke to the dressed-up beast, trying desperately to quiet him down. But no matter what the boy threatened, the animal refused to stop blubbering. Frightened, fearful of being discovered, none of the hooded workers turned to look back at the animal—a curious bit of behavior.

"Fa'al!" shouted the lead Horus, carefully eyeing the workers at the lead cart.

"*Hassim ni kha'an souf!*" Without hesitation, all the workers held their hands straight out in front of them.

Still suspicious, the hawk-headed warrior came several steps down the ramp, staring straight at Nabeh, who was engaged in a nose-to-nose discussion with the unruly *mastadge*. He had calmed the animal and was facing away from the ramp, but was still attracting too much attention to himself. Skaara felt sure the Horus was about to order his subnormal friend to turn around, and then all would be lost.

The Horus came a few yards down the ramp, suspicious, but eventually returned his attention to the first cart, where the six workers stood stiffly looking forward, their heads bowed. He toured the cart for a moment before waving it through, past the other helmeted guards.

When the armored soldier turned and marched back up the ramp, everyone breathed a huge sigh of relief. Skaara stole a swift glance at Kawalsky and Feretti, standing barefoot alongside the hindmost vehicle. They peered back from beneath the hoods of their itchy woolen haiks and nodded.

As the first cart disappeared into the shadows of the Entrance Hall, the mastadge made one last attempt to communicate with Daniel. He erupted in an earsplitting howl.

The chief Horus shot another look back at the animal and thought for a minute before hissing an order to the other two guards. They immediately turned and trotted inside while their apparent leader studied the reaction of those standing at the obelisks. Again, no one showed him any reaction. A moment later, he too followed the cart into the darkness.

"I knew this Trojan Horse plan was no damn good," Feretti whispered to Kawaksky, as anxious and fidgety as ever. "Should we go in?"

"It still might work," Kawalsky replied.

Inside, all three Horus figures surrounded the cart. The one in charge shouted an order, but no one moved. He stepped up to one of the laborers and yanked the hood back, revealing the terrified face of a redheaded young shepherd. He threw the boy to the floor and moved to the next person in line. He grabbed on to the hood and pulled it back. Sha'uri screamed as the man's powerful hand tore out a clump of hair. Taken off guard by the sight of a woman, the three hawks looked at one another.

But that surprise was nothing compared to the one that came a split second later. Erupting out of the quartz pile, Daniel and O'Neil lifted their weapons, took aim, and began firing. At the same time, conventional guns flashed out from beneath the shepherds' haiks, and a wild volley of bullets sprayed into the vast hallway, ricocheting everywhere. Unfortunately, both Daniel and O'Neil had chosen the lead Horus as a target. The combined power of their shots had shredded the unarmored parts of the man's body, but left time for the other two to retreat into the shadows.

The redheaded boy made a dash for the doorway. A fist-size meteor from one of the pulse rifles flashed across the room and caught him squarely in the back of the head, killing him instantly. Daniel jumped into the no-man's-land between the cart and the pillars, successfully pulling a pair of trigger-happy shepherds to safety behind the heavy tub of quartz.

"Go, everybody, inside." Kawalsky led the charge up the ramp, moving at top speed. However, a door, a giant stone slab, started to drop down from above. Kawalsky was fast, but not fast enough to make it inside before the monolith sealed the entrance. When he realized he'd never make it, he slowed to a trot and glanced over his shoulder. Nabeh, legs churning like rubber bands, holding his helmet on his head with one hand, was trundling along at a surprising clip. Kawalsky hesitated long enough for the boy to pull even with him. He reached up and snagged the helmet off Nabeh's head, then flung it like a Frisbee, skittering up the ramp just as the door was closing.

Strike!

The helmet wedged itself under the heavy stone block at precisely the right moment. Though slightly crushed, it held the door open, a few inches off the ground.

"Break off some wood from the carts. We'll lever the door back open!" Kawalsky must have been dreaming. The slab must have weighed at least three or four tons. But Feretti didn't hesitate to sprint-limp back down the ramp and join him in smashing five-foot planks of wood free from the sides of the transports.

O'Neil was gone. He had been there one moment before firing at the Horuses, but when Daniel looked back, he had disappeared. Everything had gone dark and eerily quiet inside the Entrance Hall. A murky light sifted between the pillars turning the chamber into a chessboard of light and dark. Daniel, clueless in the ways of warfare, felt momentarily safe. No bullets were flying, and he had Sha'uri by his side. He thought Ra's soldiers, outnumbered if not outgunned, might have fled the scene.

Eventually, it occurred to him that the guards might be using this lull in the action to move to new positions. Suddenly realizing how exposed and vulnerable they were out in the middle of the wide hallway, he silently gathered the attention of his pathetic little battalion and signaled a retreat to the pillars behind them. Precisely the mistake Ra's soldiers were expecting them to make.

They reassembled in the darkest spot they could find in the space between the pillars. But with the safety of the wall came the danger of the light from the windows. They were no longer invisible. Whispering her instructions, Sha'uri positioned the boys between the pillars, giving each of them responsibility for covering a different angle of approach. When they were in place, everyone held their breath and waited.

Just as Daniel had imagined, the helmeted soldiers were on the move. A bright blade of sunlight was slicing through the gap kept open by Nabeh's helmet. Stealthily, one of the Horus guards found the narrow ledge running along the bottom of the great door and stepped onto it. Shuffling his feet carefully along the narrow outcropping, he moved toward the center of the room only inches above the light. Although the raiding party was watching the area around the door carefully, the soldier, working with the home-field advantage, had correctly calculated that the sliver of blinding light would make him invisible to anyone looking in that direction.

He came to the end of the ledge and stepped off, silently making his way through the inky shadows to the first pillar, then advancing up the hallway.

He leaned into the space between the pillars and the exterior wall, catching sight of the team. One of the young shepherds was staring straight toward him, but the darkness kept him hidden. From his angle, Daniel's back was a wide-open target barely twenty yards away.

Very slowly, he lifted his staff up to the firing position and took aim. Sha'uri, sensing something, checked behind them once more. The barest glimmer reflected off the beveled quartz jewel set into the rifle. Her scream startled everyone, including the Horus. He pulled back on the weapon just enough to send the shot six inches over Daniel's head. He fired once more, but this time only to clear a path for his charge. He advanced all the way up to the pillar behind which the team was cowering.

An arm's reach around the corner, Daniel thought he could taste the end of his life. Sha'uri had already pulled the last of the boys behind the next pillar. Keeping his back pressed to the stone pillar, eyes forward, every nerve in his body at full alert, he waited for the first sign of movement to come around one of the corners.

Knowing his armor protected him even from the powerful pulse rifle in the fair-skinned one's hands, the Horus slid forward headfirst. The second before he came around the corner, a shot rang out, striking him in the back of his helmet, throwing him across the floor like an empty garbage can into the shadows.

By that point, Daniel was so wired, so pumped with adrenaline, he was having trouble breathing. One of the kids poked his head around the corner and asked if Daniel was all right. Daniel didn't answer, didn't even look at the boy. He knew there was at least one more of the armored killers lurking in the dark. Perhaps there were many more, riding the medallion down from the pyramid-shaped craft above.

"**O**kay, on three." Kawalsky looked at the boys. "One, two, three, lift!"

Feretti and Kawalsky jammed their shoulders against their planks of wood as the shepherds, working in pairs, did the same. The eight of them, hoisting together, were slowly lifting the door back up an inch at a time. When it was six inches above the top of the helmet, Kawalsky felt his share of the weight suddenly increase. Skaara had abandoned the lever he and Nabeh were working, and was attempting to shimmy his way under the door.

"No! Not yet!" The Herculean Kawalsky, veins bulging in his forehead, looked down and saw Skaara's head and shoulders disappear under the door. "Get him out of there, damn it!" Kawalsky barked.

As though he understood the command, Nabeh dropped to his knees and reached under the door, returning a moment later with his battered treasure, the helmet. He shared the good news, showing the helmet to Kawalsky.

"Put it back! We need that under there!" Kawalsky gestured with his chin. "Put it back!"

Nabeh either didn't understand what Kawalsky wanted him to do, or pretended not to. He put the helmet back on his head, picked up his plank, and rejoined the effort to lift the door.

Squinting into the darkness, Skaara looked for his companions. He spotted a figure moving through the shadows. Skaara let out a sharp hollow whistle, a private signal they had used since childhood. Quickly Sha'uri rushed over to the remaining shepherd boys, telling them to make a run for the doorway. When the boys turned to see what Sha'uri was talking about, they found an anxious Skaara waving frantically for them.

Nervously, the boys looked at each other deciding who should go first. Finally the first boy swallowed hard and jumped into the open, running as fast as he could for the door. As soon as he took off, the others were right behind him, bounding toward the exit like scared jackrabbits. Before Sha'uri could even entertain the idea of trying to join them, she felt Daniel tug urgently on her arm. He had seen one of the sinister silhouettes hurry past on its way to the door. But before he could reach them, the last of the children escaped. Daniel and Sha'uri pressed flat against the pillar as the Horus guard turned back into the hall, his armor's soft rustling barely audible.

The weight of the immense door seemed to be growing as Kawalsky and Feretti started to feel the fatigue. Although they and the boys were still lifting with the same amount of determination, the door began to sink, sliding down an inch at a time. Skaara helped the last of the shepherds wriggle under the door just as the lifting crew was running out of gas. Kawalsky was about to give the order to let the door down, when Skaara crawled back under the door.

"Get back here!" growled Kawalsky, but Skaara might as well have been miles away.

"I can't hold it any longer," Feretti grunted.

"Keep holding."

"No, I can't. It's too friggin' heavy."

"Keep holding." Kawalsky's voice was steady, playing for time.

Daniel and Sha'uri held their breath as the Horus guard slowly marched past them, then continued into the darkness of the room. Momentarily safe, DAniel sighed and put his arm around Sha'uri.

Unbeknownst to either of them, a second Horus was creeping up from behind. Unlike the other attackers, this soldier was moving with a great deal of patience, careful to remain absolutely silent. He was close enough to get a good shot, but wanted to get right up behind them, certain of killing them before he fired.

Slowly he lifted the weapon and aimed for Daniel's blond disheveled hair. With a swift movement of his hand along the bottom of the rifle, he clicked it open. Daniel spun at the sound, but before he could react there was a tremendous explosion from a pulse weapon. Unfortunately for the guard, it was not his weapon that had discharged. The explosion hit him from behind rocketing him off his feet, twisting and turning him into the shadows.

As the smoke dissipated, the image of O'Neil holding the pulse weapon appeared. It was the first time Daniel had ever been happy to see the soldier in the black beret. O'Neil put a finger up to his lips, telling them to keep quiet. As O'Neil stepped forward to confer with Daniel and Sha'uri, a scream came from the direction of the door. It was Skaara shouting at the top of his lungs.

O'Neil hit the ground before anyone could blink and before the perfectly aimed projectile flashed out of the darkness, nearly taking his head with it. Skaara had spotted the Horus lying in ambush near the cart, just in time. He had been guessing O'Neil, the dangerous one, would come to their rescue.

Daniel and Sha'uri pulled off to one side as O'Neil rolled

to another. And while the shots had missed O'Neil, they sailed past him and hit into the large stone door above Skaara. A second later, the door slammed closed with a thunderclap.

Thinking Skaara had been killed, a world of rage swelled through O'Neil, all the anger he'd never been able to vent when his own son had died in such a pitiful, useless way. Now he would make the Horus pay for the deaths of both boys. Firing madly, he went on the offensive—a kill or be killed stratagem.

The Horus, calm as swamp water, waited for his best shot. Twenty yards before O'Neil was on him, he took it.

Whether by intuition or pure luck, O'Neil knew when the shot was coming and initiated his dive just before the weapon's sizzling white payload ripped toward him. The shot never got close. But it pinpointed his enemy's position, and as he rolled out of his controlled tumble, he blasted the hawk right between the eyes. His helmet slammed backward pulling the rest of him along in a long clattering skid into the shadows.

"Colonel, let's go." Daniel ran into the light. Sha'uri, holding a pistol Feretti had kicked under the door, was a step behind him.

The sight of them instantly reminded O'Neil where he was. Avenging Skaara's death wasn't part of his mission. He tried to swallow his feelings and head for the StarGate, but he didn't get far. He turned back and waded into the shadows searching for the fallen Horus. When he found him, he knelt down, took a pistol out of his waistband, and pumped five slugs into the man's unarmored middle.

"All right," he said, coming back into the light, "let's roll."

Outside, Kawalsky looked like the sweatiest, angriest pediatrician in history. Holding the recently delivered Skaara by one ankle, he lifted the spindly fourteen-year-old as high as he could, until they were face-to-upside-down-face.

"Don't do that again." Each word snapped at the kid like a verbal firecracker.

The pulse blast had shattered the wooden plank Kawalsky was using as a lever. Without his strength, the door came down in a hurry. But not before he'd grabbed Skaara and yanked him outside in the nick of time.

Still hanging by his heels, Skaara pointed into the air and shouted, *"Udajeet"*—gliders.

Like a pair of swooping condors but several times more fleet, the twin aircraft shot away from the upper part of the pyramid before banking back toward the vulnerably positioned squad.

"Scatter! Scatter!" Kawalsky realized there were going to be casualties. While the brigade scrambled for cover, Kawalsky put his back against the huge door and waved his arms to give the planes a better target. He was hoping to draw enough firepower to open a breach into the pyramid. The silent fighter jets each sent a spray of power bursts rocketing down at the platform, exploding close enough to shower Kawalsky with stone shrapnel, but far enough to protect the integrity of the door. They knew what he wanted them to do.

As the gliders banked away and began looping around for their next approach, Kawalsky broke into a dead run for the obelisks.

"Two more! Take cover!" Feretti hollered the warning from a ditch he'd found along the edge of the ramp.

Kawalsky, hustling down the stone incline, looked over his shoulder. Sure enough, a third and fourth glider were scorching down from the opposite side of the mountainous structure. Capturing him in their sights, both pilots fired at once. As the twin power balls screamed a long trail through the sky, Kawalsky veered and performed a full-speed swan dive into the dunes a second before a large section of the ramp was blown to smithereens.

22

"WAIT FOR ME!"

When it amused him, Ra was a masterful player of games. He had often won, not only with his skill, but with something more important to them: his tenacious will to control and dominate. Ra was a very bad loser.

While the raid on the pyramid unfolded far below, the eternally young Ra entertained himself by playing two games at once, both of which he was assured of winning. With his menagerie of children arranged around him in his sitting chamber to bear witness, he distracted himself by playing an ancient board game while simultaneously directing the destruction of the renegade earthlings.

Sitting bolt upright on a hard wooden chair, an extraordinarily detailed hunting scene chiseled into the arms, he seemed completely absorbed in a round of Senet. The game, once called the chess of the pharaohs and still played along the Nile today, required intense concentration. His opponent was a handsome thirteen-year-old boy who, like all of the children brought to the ship, had been personally chosen by Ra because of his outstanding physical beauty. Ra admired this child above the others not only for the purity of his skin and the lithe outline of his body, but for his intelligence. He showed promise of becoming the friend and companion Ra had never been able to find.

The vastly superior player, Ra set himself the handicap of

glancing down at the pieces, pyramids and obelisks, only every other move. This added a psychological dimension to the game that Ra enjoyed: he had to know his opponent's mind in order to anticipate what he would do next.

But the elaborate handicap he'd given himself in his contest with the Americans was the one that tickled him. Deliberately selecting a shy, stammering child, Ra ordered her to sit on the window ledge and give him a running account of the scene at the base of the pyramid. If she failed to mention anything of importance, he promised her, she would be pushed outside. Terrified, the girl's speech became even more labored than usual. Like a stuttering parrot, she fought against the words and her fear, squawking her gibberish report from her perch to her master's ear.

As far as Ra was concerned, these disadvantages turned a grubby chore of police work into an artful mental challenge. Not content merely to kill the trespassers, he wanted to orchestrate their slaughter like a piece of music. And he was going to do it blindfolded with one arm tied behind his back.

When the invaders announced their arrival by starting the gun battle in the Entrance Hall, Ra didn't wait for the girl to spit out her choppy description. Everyone in the room could hear the shots echoing through the desert's silence as distinctly as if someone nearby were slowly clapping their hands. He called for Anubis to seal the pyramid's entrance.

Next he summoned the remainder of his security force, the last four of his Horus soldiers and ordered all of them into the sky. The pilots were to smash the uncouth rabble gathered at the obelisks, destroying them with all the fire-power the gliders had. Two of the *udajeet* would have been enough, but as always, Ra sought to strike with all available force. Without a word, the soldiers turned and hurried to the glider bays, activating their helmets as they went, transforming themselves into a squadron of menacing hawks.

Absolutely delighted with himself, Ra leaned forward to take the boy's pyramid with his obelisk, a move that would put the game squarely in his control. But, to his extreme annoyance, neither his opponent nor any of the other children were watching him win. Lured by the girl's report, they had crowded to the window to see for themselves what was happening below.

"Is this how you serve me?!" Ra shrieked, raking his arm across the board, knocking the game pieces everywhere. He got to his feet as if he would hurt the child closest to him, the eleven-year-old boy, but turned to Anubis instead.

"Set the bomb and send it through, now!" Ra ordered.

"I will make it happen," Anubis said, bowing as he moved toward the door. Turning back he added, "Or I will die in the attempt."

O'Neil, carrying his last flare, led the advance toward the StarGate. Arriving at the short hallway with the pair of quartz medallions set into the floor and ceiling, he stopped short, alarmed. Torches had been lit and set into braces along the walls. Near the StarGate, on a table that hadn't been there before, the dismantled bomb was in plain view, still neatly arranged on the silver tray O'Neil recognized from his visit upstairs.

Daniel tried to march into the room, anxious to get to the Gate, but O'Neil straight-armed him to an abrupt halt. After the many obstacles they'd faced to arrive at the spot, O'Neil couldn't believe Ra would leave the finish line unguarded.

He slid toward the door concealing the sputtering flare behind his back. After lobbing the stick to the far end of the room, he flashed in behind it, ready for snipers.

The room was empty.

"Okay, Jackson, fire it up."

Daniel, wanting to get the hell out of there, was only too eager to oblige. He released the grip he had on Sha'uri's hand, laid his rifle down at the base of the huge quartz ring, and got down to work.

Sha'uri had heard about the StarGate all her life, but this was the first time she had seen it, and she was just as surprised by its stern beauty as everyone on Earth who had seen its twin. More than her companions, she felt like a trespasser, that she was violating sacred ground. She reminded herself of all she had learned in the catacombs about Ra and this place, but she couldn't completely quell her feelings of guilt for what they were doing. As if this weren't confusing enough, she knew that when the ring was called to life, she would either have to dump herself into another world like a load of stones, or face whatever fate Ra's soldiers had in store for her.

Daniel reached into his pocket and pulled out the notebook with the six symbols he'd copied from the cartouche in the catacombs. He tore off the appropriate page, then put a hand on the sliding inner ring of the device, which turned with a minimum of resistance. He spun the first symbol into place. The ring gave off a sharp click, and a second later the top clamp split open to reveal the quartz jewel at its center. As he was wheeling the second constellation to the top, he felt Sha'uri tugging on his sleeve.

"Nani?" he asked.

"*Koner onio,*" she said. When Daniel didn't understand her, she pointed toward the table where the colonel was putting the bomb back together. Daniel couldn't believe it. They were on the verge of getting it all done, and O'Neil was going to blow them up.

"Hey, what are you doing?" Daniel demanded. "I thought we agreed that it's the StarGate on Earth we have to shut down."

O'Neil looked up, but didn't stop working. Racing against time, he wiped the sweat off his forehead and continued to reassemble the ghastly device. "Jackson, that's exactly what I'm counting on you to do: get back to the silo and destroy the Gate."

"But I thought we agreed to go back together and—"

"Change of plans, Jackson!" His tone of voice made it clear he wasn't going to negotiate. "I'm staying here."

"You're staying what? Why?! What are you talking about?"

"I have to make sure this thing goes off okay. I'm completing my mission." With that, O'Neil plunged the orange key into the slot between the bomb's two canisters. He then pecked additional instructions into the device's miniaturized keypad. As soon as he hit enter, blinking red numbers popped up on the display panel: 12:00, 12:00, 12:00.

"What about Kawalsky and Feretti!? What about her!?" he said pointing at Sha'uri.

"Take her with you if you want, but get moving." He pressed the "ENTER" key once more and the countdown began: 11:59. 11:58. 11:57. Daniel was flabbergasted. He stood there not understanding why O'Neil was doing this. "You're running out of time, Jackson."

Daniel looked at Sha'uri then back at O'Neil. He was about to say something else when a sharp click from the next room froze them all in place. The next second a sizzling white projectile rocketed into the room and hit Sha'uri square between the shoulders.

Daniel grabbed his rifle, wheeled, and fired in a blind fury. Three successive shots exploded into the soldier's stomach, ripping him almost completely in half.

Daniel raced over to where Sha'uri had fallen near the door and cradled her in his arms. She was bleeding pretty badly and had lost consciousness. He pressed his lips against her forehead and begged the girl to hold on, to be strong enough to survive until he could get her through the StarGate to medical help.

O'Neil came over to see if Sha'uri's wounds were treatable. He tried to find a pulse but couldn't. She was already dead.

10:45. 10:44. 10:43.

"They've got us, man, we're screwed. They caught us out here with our pants around our ankles, and now we're totally goddamn screwed."

"Keep it together, soldier," Kawalsky barked.

They'd jumped into a space between the sand and the side of the ramp, too shallow to offer much protection from the gliders. The lieutenant lifted his head and surveyed the scene. It looked like Feretti was right.

The aerial assault had taken them completely by surprise. The unit, hodgepodge to begin with, was now scattered on both sides of the ramp, hiding in whatever passed as a foxhole. They had no radios, no common language, and, worst of all, no plan.

The gliders cruised overhead strafing the area with shattering explosive pulses. On each pass they met with less ground fire and, for the moment at least, seemed more intent on keeping the invaders pinned down than in polishing them off. Or maybe not. Hurtling out of nowhere, one of the gliders sent a shot whirring toward them. It hit the ramp less than ten feet away, blowing a pothole into the structure as if it were made of Styrofoam.

"We're sitting ducks out here, man. And these guys know it."

"Don't worry, I've got a plan," Kawalsky mumbled absently.

"Plan!?" Feretti thought that was hilarious. "We're completely exposed, under heavy visual-contact fire, our formation is broken, we're totally outgunned, and nearest available backup is pretty damn far away. Whatever you've got in mind, I'd think twice before using the word plan to describe it."

Kawalsky tried to ignore the tirade. He peeked over the edge of the ramp and looked toward where the line of quartz wagons stood between the obelisks.

"Okay, you wanna see a plan? Watch this!" he shouted. He jumped out of the ditch and hauled ass across the sand, dodging power bursts as he went.

"Jackson, the Gate." O'Neil put a hand on Daniel's shoulder and gave him a friendly shake.

"There's no time. We've got to get you back to the silo. Jackson?" O'Neil was getting nowhere.

For a minute, he stood back and watched Daniel, his arms wound tight around Sha'uri's body. He understood what it meant to grieve like that, to hold on long past the point when you knew it was over. He'd been holding on for more than two years. But he couldn't let Daniel have that same luxury. He pried one set of fingers loose and then the other, forcing Daniel to his feet. Then he regurgitated the hollow, reassuring advice he'd heard so often.

"It's over, Jackson. She's gone. Clear your mind and keep going. We need you to get through."

Daniel didn't need to clear his mind. The shock of losing Sha'uri had done that for him. He stood unsteadily at the mouth of the StarGate, unable to remember who he was and what he was doing there.

"Looks like we've got company," he heard O'Neil say.

A crisp sting of quartz blue light shot from the floor of the medallion room up to the ceiling, then began to spread sideways. When Daniel turned and saw it, he could think of only one thing—the sarcophagus. If it had brought him back to life, it could do the same for Sha'uri.

O'Neil moved to the edge of the stairs at the base of the huge ring, toward the table to retrieve his gun. But he didn't stop there. Daniel shoved him off the edge sending him crashing onto the table then spilling, along with the bomb, off the other side.

By the time O'Neil jumped up and made it to the medallion, Daniel was already standing behind the glittering curtain of blue light holding Sha'uri in his arms. Unaware of the danger, Daniel let Sha'uri's legs dangle perilously close to the beam. Where the light closed into a transparent cylinder, a fold of Sha'uri's robe was hanging beyond the perimeter. The beam moved right through the cloth, slicing it off cleanly. O'Neil watched it drop to the floor.

"Jackson, what the hell are you doing? The bomb!"

Beginning to disappear, Daniel spoke to O'Neil through the glittering curtain of blue light. No sound penetrated the barrier, but the colonel was sure Daniel's lips had made the words "wait for me."

Then he was gone, disintegrating in an upward flare of light.

O'Neil turned to check the clock: 11:08.

Smash, O'Neil took a hard shot right in the chin that landed him on his ass. When he looked up, all the short hairs on his neck sprang to attention. This was the moment he knew would come. Standing over him, poised for the kill was the gnarled fossil he'd meditated about in the silo, the huge armored warrior with the jackal's head, Ra's champion warrior, Anubis.

Somehow he needed to reach the bomb and abort the countdown to give Jackson enough time. Otherwise, Anubis would get there first and send it through to Earth.

Kawalsky strained against the weight but couldn't tip the cart by himself. When the first two shepherds came out of the dunes to help him, Kawalsky crouched against the side of the cart and explained his strategy as quickly as he could.

"First, we're going to turn this cart over. Then we're gonna go turn that one over, drag it back over here, and build ourselves a little fort, okay?"

"Oh-khay," they agreed enthusiastically.

Kawalsky looked at them again. "You didn't understand a word I said, did you?"

True, neither of them had captured the finer nuances of the big man's plan. But they'd understood the gist of what he'd told them: something's going to happen, and you're going to help.

When the sky was clear, Kawalsky jumped up, positioned the boys on either side of him, and together, they tipped the vehicle on its side, spilling the quartz into the sand. After dragging the cart a little way and turning it belly-up, they dashed for the second cart.

Skaara and Feretti both arrived in time to help. They easily jettisoned the load of quartz, tipped the rig belly-up, then ducked underneath to avoid the next barrage from the gliders.

On his hands and knees, Kawalsky tested the weight of the cart, then like Atlas, he slowly stood up, shouldering his end of the vehicle into the air. The others followed his lead and lifted the cart above their heads. Then they marched back between the obelisks, moving like a gigantic Saharan millipede.

When the temporary command post had been established, Skaara called for the rest of the shepherds to join them. While Kawalsky and Feretti provided cover, several of the kids made it in from the surrounding dunes, dodging the gliders.

"*Nabeh! Anda ni, andu ni,*" Skaara yelled.

Nabeh was still at the top of the ramp, almost a hundred yards away. After more encouragement, he started motoring bowlegged straight down the center of the ramp at full speed, no gliders in sight. But halfway home, one of the pilots spotted him and swooped down at the ramp.

Skaara tried to warn him. "*Khem eem, khem een!*" Jump off, jump off. But Nabeh, feeling paralyzed within the motion of his run, continued to come. Skaara scrambled out into the open before anyone could stop him, running and pointing for Nabeh to get off the open ramp.

Before he could do any good, the small plane fired twice in quick succession. The ground in front of Nabeh erupted in an upward shatter of rock and dust. Skaara felt the wave of ambient heat roll past his cheeks a full second before he was hit by the first flying chip.

The breeze moved the dust straight at the rebels. When it finally cleared, there was no sign of Nabeh or what had happened to him. Their only clue was the misshapen green helmet. It came rolling out of the smoke like a drunken spare tire.

Skaara called desperately for his friend, then suddenly found himself moving backward. Kawalsky's meaty hand was cuffed around the boy's wrist, dragging him like a doll back to the barricade.

Kawalsky pinned Skaara under the cart and restrained him until he stopped fighting. He conferred with Feretti about their options. It only took a minute to agree that they didn't have any.

"Well at least let's concentrate all our firepower at the same target," Kawalsky urged, holding up the grenade launcher salvaged by the shepherds. "This baby's gotta be able to take out those toy jets."

Feretti rolled onto his back and pulled three grenades out of his long desert robe.

"Under normal circumstances, I would explain why that is not, technically, a plan. I'd give you a list of reasons why it's really a pathetic substitute for a plan. But, at this particular moment, it sounds like a plan. So let's do it."

As soon as the plan was explained, one of the gliders came slowly prowling toward them, squeezing off a series of carefully aimed shots. The soldiers pointed to the glider, and the boys understood.

"Now!" Kawalsky gave the order. Ten conventional rifles plus Feretti at the trigger of the grenade launcher suddenly sprung out from the bunker, took aim, and started blasting a hole in the sky.

The minnow-size jet took a grenade in the tail. The shot did no structural damage, but did succeed in knocking it slightly out of control. For a moment, it seemed the swerving *udajeet* would wreck itself into the carts, but the pilot stabilized the craft and sailed it a few feet above their heads. A violent crash ensued when the plane's wing clipped one of the obelisks, then spun like a ninja's throwing star out into the dunes, demolishing itself into a fireball.

* * *

Daniel arrived in the palace standing nose to nose with the polished sculpture of the ram god Khnum. He spun around ready to face whoever he had to, but the room was completely empty.

He picked Sha'uri up and galloped straight ahead into the magnificent throne room. The colossal stone figures carved into the pillars seemed to follow his progress through the room. The thudding of his boots echoed off the walls as he turned down the short passageway leading to the sarcophagus, that had somehow restored his own life.

It was open.

He lifted Sha'uri onto the hard bed at the center of the device then stepped back as the machine ground into action. He watched as Sha'uri was lowered deeper into the healing grave and the thick walls of the lid slid to a close. As she disappeared, Daniel realized how stupid this was. He had no idea how long the process would take—or even if the machine had to be switched on. Now he was trapped in Ra's stronghold with no way to get out. As he had carried Sha'uri to the medallion below, he had some vague notion of reasoning with Ra, pleading with him, striking some sort of bargain. Now, with more time to think, he realized how ludicrous that idea was.

Hiding behind the golden box, he tried not to think about the implications of what he had done. He looked down and saw he was still holding the scrap of notepaper with the coordinates for Earth. He banged his head backward against the sarcophagus. He'd squandered the chance to get back to the silo and slam the lid on this Pandora's Box before it could spill its demons into the Colorado mountains.

He turned to examine the side of the sarcophagus, hoping to find some clue there. Etched into the long gold panels was the story of Osiris. Hacked to pieces by his enemies, his body was spread to the far corners of the Nile. His wife, Isis, wandered the land slowly gathering his parts. She put the body back together then wrapped it in cloth and paper. The last section of the etching showed Osiris reborn.

Daniel looked up and noticed Ra, blazing gold skin, standing calmly at the foot of the mysterious coffin. Daniel recoiled to the other end of the box, then moved several steps across the floor to the door. Ra made no attempt to stop him. At the mouth of the passage, Daniel saw the children coming out of Ra's chamber and down the stairs past the throne. His first impulse was to run, but then he remembered the bomb set to explode below. There was nowhere to go.

Ra stepped between Daniel and where Sha'uri lay hidden, puzzled.

"Why?" he rasped softly. "Why come here now?"

Daniel didn't move, didn't respond.

"For this?" Ra looked over at the sarcophagus, then back at Daniel. "Have you put something inside?"

Daniel lunged at Ra, but was quickly and violently subdued. Ra opened his palm to expose the lethal coin-size medallion he was so fond of experimenting with. Before he even got close, the small jewel knocked him backward like he'd stepped in front of a bus. It sent a stinging burn across his skin, a sensation he remembered from his trip through the StarGate.

Ra smiled and strolled to the machine. He ran his hand over the lid, fascinated to watch the anxiety rise in Daniel's face. The coffin's lid slowly opened to reveal Sha'uri, sleeping peacefully. The scab over her eyebrow, earned when Ra's soldiers had invaded and burned Nagada, was almost completely healed.

"Hana'i hana'e," Ra whispered. The phrase, which Daniel did not know, translated to something like "how romantic." He reached into the sarcophagus and ran the backs of his golden fingers delicately over the girl's lovely features.

"Very, very clever." He seemed truly impressed with Daniel, adding, "Now you can die together."

O'Neil's instincts took over. Before his opponent could react, the colonel had wedged the five-foot-long staff into the throat of Anubis's helmet, driving him backward. He slammed the bigger man against the wall of the narrow hallway and yanked back on the rifle. But Anubis's grip was too strong. The weapon refused to budge, and the next moment the jackal's iron glove came crashing down on the side of O'Neil's face, knocking him to the ground.

Even before he hit the floor, O'Neil was on the move to

avoid the pulse blast he knew was coming. He rolled away with a sudden change of direction. Sure enough, the spot where he had landed exploded a second later.

The hallway was just small enough for O'Neil to plant his palms against the wall and still reach back with his feet to kick Anubis in the head. The impact drove the monstrous combatant a step inside the StarGate room, but didn't knock him down. He regained his balance and leveled the rifle for another shot at O'Neil.

When O'Neil saw what was happening, he dove around the corner of the hallway into the Grand Gallery. The shot hit the stones of the arched doorway and caromed off into the darkness. Then O'Neil did the only sensible thing: he ran away.

The Grand Gallery behind him was blacker than squid ink and the colonel hoped it would allow him to get the drop on Anubis. He ran as far as he could into the vacuum of light before he started to lose his balance. He turned and saw the big soldier calmly step into the StarGate room. He was probably checking for Daniel and the others.

Soon enough, Anubis came hunting for O'Neil, but not as quickly as the colonel wanted him to. Crouching fifty feet out in the lake of darkness, O'Neil watched the large jackal head bobbing toward him into the darkness. After only a few steps, the hunter reached up to the collar of his helmet, made an adjustment, then came deeper into the hallway. Just before he disappeared, O'Neil saw the helmet retract down into its collar.

The barely audible scrape of armor against armor came closer, then stopped. O'Neil fought to control his breathing, listening like he never had. Then suddenly much closer, a continuous scraping sound filled the hall. By the time O'Neil figured out what was happening, it was too late. The staff, raking across the floor like a blind man's cane, knocked against the colonel's leg.

O'Neil found his feet and retreated a couple of steps, listening, waiting. With no warning, the blunt end of the staff poked him in the mouth, splitting his lip open against his teeth. O'Neil continued to retreat in a new direction, moving his hands in frantic circles through the air, trying to protect against the next invisible blow. A whistling sound

made him jerk his head backward. The weapon moved past
his face like an ax at full speed. As Anubis followed through
with the swing, O'Neil stepped in and brought his elbow
down with a crack onto his opponent's nose.

He heard the rifle clatter to the ground, and dove toward
the sound. Groping everywhere, he got a hand on the
weapon just as Anubis reached out to retrieve it. O'Neil
tried to twist the gun away, but the man was too strong.

Knowing that whoever seized control of the weapon first
would kill the other, the two of them began a kicking,
punching, head-butting gladiator contest. O'Neil was using
every trick in his book, and just breaking even.

O'Neil finally decided that this game was too dangerous
and too time-consuming. He waited for the right moment
before suddenly releasing the weapon. As he sprinted
toward the light of the StarGate room, he heard Anubis
falling flat on his ass.

5:20. 5:19. 5:18.

One of the planes came zipping around the corner of the
pyramid, five hundred yards away, and went onto an attack
dive. Kawalsky locked everyone onto the plane and counted
backwards from five real slow.

No one noticed his partner skimming in low over the
dunes. On the word "go" they all came out blasting. The
boys, despite Kawalsky's crystal-clear orders, strayed several steps away from cover. The first plane suddenly banked
off, leaving them open to his partner's swift attack.

The spray of white pulses killed five of the kids instantly.
Another died accidentally, when one of the boys wheeled
around firing wildly. He mowed down the boy standing in
front of him. Realizing what he had done, the boy fell to his
knees while the more shells exploded around him. Feretti
crabbed out to get the kid and brought him back inside. He
was crying hysterically, the last thing anyone needed.

A few minutes later, the gliders tried the same trick again.
This time, instead of one decoy, there were two. The second
plane would come in over the dunes as before but then
accelerate over the carts, and bank right to avoid the
pyramid.

Bad idea. The situation under the carts was so chaotic

that Kawalsky couldn't communicate with his untrained fighters. They jumped into the same trap they'd fallen into for only a minute before.

Feretti, however, understood what was going on. He waited for the first plane to bank to safety, then exploded out from below the cart with the grenade launcher aimed.

The second pilot, concentrating on the sharp turn he had to make, never fired a shot. He accelerated over the carts just as Feretti let their last shell fly. The projectile erupted into the bottom of the craft, cracking its fuselage like a cheap pair of eyeglasses.

"Back underneath. Get down!" Kawalsky got them herded to safety before the remaining third plane could swoop in for the kill.

The broken glider continued to speed forward, straight at the pyramid. The plane raked into a vertical climb at the last second, narrowly averting the massive wall of stone as it rocketed upward. But it hit the overhanging edge of the spacecraft perched atop. The craft disintegrated in a wicked roar of fire and crackling blue light.

As the flaming wreckage tumbled down the side of the pyramid, the boys jumped out once more, cheering like mad men and firing at the fireball until their guns were empty.

O'Neil raced straight for the contents of the overturned table. He began searching everywhere in the jumble of captured supplies for the access card. He glanced at the bomb: 3:39, 3:38.

From the doorway came the distinctive metallic click of a pulse rifle cocking to the ready position. Totally exposed, there was nowhere to hide. No time to even turn and look. Just as the shot was fired, O'Neil lifted the big silver tray as a shield. The platter's mirrorlike surface deflected the brunt of the power ball, bending the shot back in the direction it came from. O'Neil stood and whipped the tray like a flying saw blade toward the door. Anubis, easily stepped behind the door, but when he ducked back in for a second shot, he was welcomed by both of O'Neil's boots delivering a flying stomp to his chest.

The jackal crashed belly-first to the ground. He tried to push himself up to his feet, but two knees landed between his shoulder blades, forcing him back down in a heap. The next moment he felt the snout of his helmet being yanked violently to the side. O'Neil was trying to break his neck, not realizing that the quartz-based helmet prevented this from happening.

O'Neil saw the long rifle laying nearby and made a decision. Without leaving Anubis's back, he reached out and kicked the rifle into the darkness of the Grand Gallery. He would defuse the bomb and deal with his opponent later.

As swiftly as he had attacked, O'Neil was gone. Anubis stumbled up to his feet, his neck throbbing from the kick and spun around to confront O'Neil. But he had disappeared once again into the StarGate room.

Before following him inside, Anubis adjusted the scarab mounting on the back of his hand armor. Four razor-sharp claws spit out of the pad following the natural curve of his hand. Like his helmet, the knives were made of powdered quartz held to shape in a gaseous membrane. Anubis turned his wrist bracelet, focusing the claws, then marched into the StarGate where O'Neil was on his hands and knees.

Both men looked up when they heard the explosion.

Ra was patiently coaxing Daniel closer to the sarcophagus, promising not to harm Sha'uri if Daniel would only come a little closer. The game was interrupted by the ear-piercing explosion of the glider into the side of its mothership.

Everyone inside was badly startled, but none more than Ra. He dropped down behind the sarcophagus shrieking and cowering, his head buried between his arms for several seconds. When he finally stopped, he looked at Daniel strangely. His expression seemed to be asking for sympathy, as if this frightening attack on his citadel should naturally be a cause of concern to everyone.

When he came away from the sarcophagus at a shuffling run, Daniel darted away to the other side of the room. But Ra wasn't interested in him. He posed no threat and could be dealt with later.

Daniel saw the strange golden man run up the stairs and go into the doorway behind his throne.

Seizing the opportunity, Daniel raced to the sarcophagus where Sha'uri was beginning to stir. The sarcophagus had done enough to bring her back, but it hadn't finished the job. Daniel scooped her into his arms and bulled past the children out into the throne room.

From his window, Ra could see both the fiery wreckage of the glider and the tiny figures celebrating between the obelisks. As he watched them exult, he realized he would be forced to spend much more time than he wished in this desolate, insignificant corner of his empire. The entire population would have to be exterminated and another brought to replace it. He looked out over the rolling desert and remembered why he hated this colony, his first: it reminded him too much of home.

When he was sure the pilots were still in command, he turned with new purpose and strode off to kill Daniel.

Kawalsky and company were fresh out of ammo, and the glider pilots knew it. Prowling slowly overhead, they practically invited ground fire. The only resistance they encountered was angry shouting from the boys.

The *udajeet*, flying in tandem, coasted out across the empty desert. Just when it looked like they were leaving, they gently touched down on the lip of the vast amphitheater of sand surrounding the pyramid. A minute later, the large hatch doors opened and the two Horuses stepped out. They retrieved pulse rifles from their planes, then began marching toward the obelisks.

O'Neil heard the footsteps and knew Anubis had followed him into the room, but he kept working. Exhibiting nerves of steel or perhaps his old suicidal recklessness, he had just begun to punch in the command to abort when he looked up to see Anubis's death claw swiping down at him.

The claws cut deeply, but not into the colonel. They sunk into Daniel's 1931 edition of *Aegypticus* by Sir A. E. Wallis Budge. Anubis looked down at the shredded book, his claws buried deep within its tortuously dull chapters. O'Neil allowed him no time to read. With a violent twist, he forced Anubis to turn, then jacked his arm up behind him. He brought the bones almost to the breaking point, then leaned forward and whispered into the jackal's ear.

"Bad dog."

There was a wet hollow pop as the arm said good-bye to its socket. Howling in pain, Anubis felt O'Neil's boot in his back. Anubis spun back around just in time to eat a fist full of knuckles. Like a power punching heavy-weight contender, O'Neil drove Anubis backward with a rapid flurry of punches. Snapping Anubis's head from side to side, O'Neil kept the pressure on till Anubis had stumbled back into the medallion room.

Teetering on weak legs, Anubis tried to shake it off. O'Neil, bending him over, snapped his own knee up into Anubis's already dazed head. He wrapped a leg behind Anubis and slammed him down to the floor, hard.

O'Neil fell on him, pinning him down, his body laying half on the medallion on the floor, half off.

Daniel had Sha'uri slumped over his shoulder as he carried her over to the palace medallion. Gently he laid her down on top of the medallion as he began searching frantically for some way to turn it on. He ran his fingers over the sinister statue of Khnum searching for a hidden panel, a button, anything. Frustrated, he turned to the children who had trailed after him down the hall, curious to see what this amazing visitor would do next.

"Help us," he urged them, his eyes wild with terror. The children only looked at him like a circus freak and backed farther away. "Don't be scared," he stepped off the platform moving closer, trying to show them a kinder face.

"*Semmoun*," he said gesturing to himself. "*Semmoun, friend.*"

The children understood what he was trying to say, and a couple of them giggled nervously at the way his pronunciation butchered the words.

"*Ya'ani!*" Ra's scream filled the hall. At once, the children scattered in every direction away from the spot.

"The time for games is over," he said, already moving toward them.

Like a grim image from some long-forgotten dream, Daniel watched the golden pharaoh, this brutal and immortal child, stalking toward him, his golden sandals clicking across the cold mosaic floor at an even, inexorable tempo. Daniel turned back to Sha'uri, who barely stirred up atop the medallion. Somehow he would buy enough time to get her through.

Ra was almost to the medallion when Daniel plowed forward to attack. Effortlessly, Ra reversed the man's momentum. He simply opened his hand and sent Daniel crashing backward, tumbling down next to Sha'uri on the medallion.

Undaunted, Daniel turned back to Ra, attempting once again to rush him. This time, the consequences were more severe. Ra caught Daniel with the full paralyzing force of the device. His head and arms snapped backward in pain as Ra lowered his hand onto Daniel's head, forcing him down submissively to his knees. A moment later, Daniel's face began to ripple like the reflection in a liquid mirror. Every bone and organ in his body began to swell and contract, warping into new shapes as the quartz jewel, a weaker version of the StarGate, began to break him down at the molecular level. In a matter of seconds, Daniel would be dead.

Still pinned over the medallion below, Anubis tried to buck the colonel off of him. But as O'Neil pressed Anubis back down, he noticed the wrist device on the back plate of Anubis's hand and remembered seeing him use it to activate the medallion when they had been captured before. This was his chance to end this once and for all.

"Give my regards to King Tut, asshole."

Quickly O'Neil lifted Anubis's wrist up and slammed it back down, hard to the floor. The impact activated the device set into the scarab mounting. Immediately, the cold blue laser pierced into the air, inches from Anubis's head.

When Anubis saw the beam spreading around the disk on the ceiling, he forgot the pain shooting from his arm and went absolutely wild. Twisting and bucking and screaming in pain, he desperately tried to find the leverage he needed to throw O'Neil aside. O'Neil remembered the way Sha'uri's haik had been sliced away and held Anubis down, partially over the medallion. He concentrated on holding Anubis and waited to see what would happen when the blade of light completed its circuit.

* * *

When the blue beam speared into the air next to him, Ra reacted, easing up, ever so slightly on the torture to Daniel as Ra attempted to retreat. Even through the intense pain, Daniel realized what was happening. O'Neil. He was at the medallion below, trying to show him and Sha'uri the way to safety.

With every once of energy Daniel had left, he reached up and grabbed Ra's hand, holding it in place. Ra couldn't understand. Why would Daniel hold him there, continuing the torture? He pressed down and increased the intensity to force Daniel's hands open, but it was to no avail. Daniel held on tight.

Ra was in more trouble than he knew. The cylinder of blue light was three-quarters complete. When Daniel saw how close they were, he started thinking he might win. He raised both hands and locked on to Ra's wrist.

"Release the hand!" he commanded. Ra was so startled he'd shut his hand before trying to yank it free.

Daniel's head began to clear. When he saw the laser only a foot away from completion, he tightened his grip on Ra's arm, picturing himself as a pit bull, his teeth deep into the soft part of a bone. As his eyesight refocused, he blinked up at the devil and saw something swinging from Ra's neck—the sun disk Catherine had given him for luck.

When Daniel saw it, his hand shot out and snapped the disk away, ripping it from Ra's neck just as the curtain completed its arc and sealed. Once in place the wall held Ra's arm frozen in place, held perfectly immobile. Daniel backed away, staring at Ra, who was held tight against the medallion, struggling in vain to free himself.

As Daniel and Sha'uri began to vanish, so did part of Ra's arm. The beam cut a clean path through his forearm. Ra tumbled backward and looked like he was shrieking over and over again, pain blistering through the stump of his arm, as he watched.

In exchange, the machine delivered the freshly severed head of his one truly able warrior, Anubis, the muscles in his jaw still twitching with life.

Ra collapsed and began calling for help. He had to get to the sarcophagus. He knew from his experiments the machine would eventually grow back severed limbs. But it was knowledge that would do him no good if he bled to death on the floor.

Again, he screamed for his servants. But the children had either fled the room or were keeping themselves well hidden. Enraged by this unsubordination, Ra got to his feet and wrapped his arm in the folds of his golden skirt. He staggered toward the throne, shouting angrily as he went. Over and over, he promised that he would severely punish all who had ignored his call.

23

SUPREME POWER

O'Neil instantly recognized the severed hand as Ra's; the torturing device still clutched in its palm. But as O'Neil looked away from the headless Anubis, he discovered that Sha'uri and Daniel were out cold, exhausted and beaten.

O'Neil turned back to the bomb in a panic.

03:46 and counting down.

Even if Daniel were conscious, it would take him longer than that to activate the StarGate. O'Neil knew he must shut the bomb down and revive Daniel.

Sprinting, O'Neil raced over to the bomb and quickly punched in the abort code. With the last of the numbers activated, O'Neil punched the "ENTER" button and breathed a sigh of relief.

His respite was premature as the counter continued to click downward.

03:22 . . . 03:21 . . .

Shocked, O'Neil searched through his memory. What could he have forgotten? Why didn't it work? Again he tried the abort codes, and again they failed to work.

Frustrated, O'Neil grabbed for the electronic key snapped on the top of the bomb. Violently he yanked it out of its housing. Yet still, the bomb ticked down.

* * *

Ammunition out, scattered casualties, and down to the knives and bayonets, Kawalsky was out of options. With the exception of Skaara, who wanted to fight to the finish, the rest of the shepherd boys were beaten and exhausted.

The gliders had already landed, and the two Horus guards were marching closer. Kawalsky knew any attempt to resist them would be futile.

"We've got to surrender," Kawalsky groaned.

"Say what?" barked Feretti.

"We'll lose any fight we start out here. We've got to surrender and hope O'Neill's still alive."

"If O'Neil's still alive, he's in Colorado by now."

"I'm not worried about us, Feretti. It's the kids. If we don't resist, they may just take them prisoner."

This was the one option Feretti was never willing to accept: surrender. It had been drilled into his head ever since his early Special Forces training days, no surrender. But when Feretti looked over at the wounded children, he realized that Kawalsky was right.

Kawalsky tossed his empty rifle aside and marched out past the obelisks into the sand toward the two Horus soldiers. Skaara couldn't believe what he was seeing. Feretti, too, tossed his weapon away and followed Kawalsky, raising their arms in the air.

One by one the shepherds followed suit, walking away from the barrier, arms in the air. Tried as he might, Skaara could not convince them to fight to the death. As the last of the boys passed him, Skaara finally resigned himself, tossing away his pistol and reluctantly following the others out.

They walked several yards away from the barricades and dropped to their knees. Kawalsky hoped this would save them from execution. The Horus guards were over fifty yards away when suddenly they snapped the housings of their weapons open, ready to fire. In desert silence the action sounded much closer. The hawks leveled their weapons, ready to execute the team on the spot. Maybe if the boys saw the soldiers fall, they'd finally run. Kawalsky strode forward to take the first shot, but the next second his heart and his feet stopped together.

It was the sound of drums. The soldiers looked around at the ring of dunes, empty as the deafening sonic mayhem pounded the desert. It sounded like thousands of drums, all being hit with excessive force by people uninterested in tempo or rhythm.

One of the Horuses turned and fired twice at the survivors and their carts. They all hit the deck a full second before the pulse burned a crisp hiss over their heads. By the time they looked up again, a thousand men from Nagada were standing on the hillside, looking down on the scene. About a hundred more came up behind them as the noise continued to build in volume and in fury.

The two Horus soldiers held their ground, staring back at these new intruders, their unease growing. The hawk heads turned as another group of a hundred came over a ridge, and formed a human wall between the pilots and their planes. Hundreds more came banging kettles with spoons, waving mining tools in the air, brandishing knives and brooms and paving stones. They came to the top of every dune, not in hundreds but in thousands, each one making their share of the noise. Exuberant young men danced from side to side, laughing and screaming, feeling the exhilaration of becoming a mob for the first time in their lives. Like a strong animal held in reins too long, they were surging with energy, ready to explode into action.

Suddenly Kasuf appeared at the top of the highest dune. All attention was riveted to him as he raised his arms. Kasuf's order for the drumming to cease was sent through the crowd, and a few seconds later everything began to fall quiet. Kasuf got out in front of the giant horde. If he wanted to stop them, he would need a miracle. He walked halfway down the big slope and turned back to the crowd, signaling for them to be calm.

One of the Horuses used the moment to invoke the fear of Ra. Repeating a catechism he and the people both knew well, he shouted:

"*Aten-Re, tiyi harukha khare na'aran sa, Henten-Re.*" Ra, Lord of the Sun, repays both piety and disrespect many times over, Ra, Lord of Justice."

Kasuf responded by lifting his staff high above his head and shouting as loud as he could, "*Bani dharam Ka!*" Supreme power!

At once, the people spilled down the dunes from all sides,

crashing like a tidal wave into the empty basin of sand. Both Horuses squeezed off deadly shots as quickly as their weapons would fire, doing nothing to slow the mad rush. A long sustained battle cry rose out of the crowd. No one had planned it, but now that the whole population was screaming the same note, it became a source of strength. The fierce song reminded them that they were one people, swarming to achieve a common goal. They came in overwhelming numbers, like a vengeful sea.

Ra hurried to the sarcophagus and threw himself onto the stone table inside. Trembling uncontrollably, he reached for the shroud and covered himself as the lid slowly closed above him. The hushed hum of the machine sounded as soothing as a lullaby. It meant the ghastly pain in his arm would stop, that he would wake up with a healthy stump that would in time grow to be a hand. But there was more. Being in the machine meant undisturbed comfort and the voluptuous sleep of the dead. The sarcophagus was the nearest thing he had to affection. He crawled inside when he needed treatment of his chronic ailment, loneliness.

Ra had no peers, no relationships. He mistrusted everyone except the children, who were so poorly educated, they made terrible companions. They were his pets. But there was no one to talk to. He hadn't lost an argument for thousands of years, even over something small. On his master's advice, he'd prohibited all writing and all organized study pre-slavery culture. Less than a hundred years into his rule, his subjects were effectively lobotomized. Commander of his own fate, the world around him reflected who he was. And the world around him was barren. There were consequences to being so old.

Just before the lid closed above him like an infant reentering the womb, he heard the giant noise of voices erupt outside.

Alarmed, he climbed out of the sarcophagus and staggered back to his private chamber. He went to the giant window and saw the ferocious spectacle being improvised in the sand. When his soldiers fell to the stampede, Ra had seen enough. Now it was a matter of escaping.

He went to a control panel and readjusted the instruments.

At once, the lifters began to whistle, the huge quartz hoops pushing more and more air down the sides of the pyramid. As the great golden sections of the spacecraft's wall began rumbling closed, some of the children had gathered in the arms of Khnum, stomping on the medallion as they had seen Daniel do. They were trying to escape before Ra could make good on his promise to punish them.

Like a swam of piranha, the crowd flooded in from all sides and fell upon the soldiers, tearing them limb from limb. The attack continued until the gods were nothing but bloody stains on the people's hands.

At the same time, a thousand others crowded up the ramp and rushed for the massive stone door. Working together under Kawalsky's direction, they easily lifted it high and stacked loose stones into piles to prop it open. Most of those who went under the door hovered near the entrance, not yet bold enough to rush into the pitch-black for a confrontation with Ra himself.

There had been no particular plan of attack, only a running march across the desert to stop Ra from harming Sha'uri, the shepherds and the visitors. Once the obvious target, the Horus guards, had been dispatched the scene outside the entrance quickly devolved to chaos. Kasuf huddled in urgent discussion with the other Elders.

A loud crack shot from the sky, silencing the crowd in a heartbeat. It was followed immediately by the deep rumbling of the spacecraft's internal machinery jolting into action. The long claws of the stabilizing arms unanchored themselves while the megalithic window panels rolled to a close.

Ra was running away.

The Nagadans had won. As they slowly realized, a wild joyful cry exploded out of them, the celebrate shout of unintended conquerors. Unintended because they hadn't come here today expecting to win a victory. They came to protect the visitors and the shepherd boys, all of them heroes of the town.

But at a deeper level, they came because they could. For the first time in their collective memory, they felt they had a choice. When Ra's soldiers had come to the city indiscriminately killing and burning, no one had challenged them. Not even the strongest man, seeing his child killed before him, had imagined striking back. Then the visitors, the first in their history, had arrived and turned everything upside down. Along with two of Kasuf's own children, they had killed the vicious Horus, then bravely set out to confront Ra in his temple. If a miracle is an event that unexpectedly and massively expands the definition of what is humanly possible, the arrival of the Dan-yer and the soldiers qualified as a miracle. As news of their exploits spread, an exhilarating feeling swept through the city, the feeling that suddenly, anything was possible. They had come in order to hit back at Ra.

A blindfold had been torn away, and the people's habit of obedience was quickly overwhelmed by an instinct for justice.

Daniel's entire face was a huge purple and blue bruise. So were his hands and shoulders, all the areas that had taken the brunt of the jewel's painful, atom-shifting power. The blood coming from his nose and ears indicated the likelihood of internal hemorrhaging. But all his vital signs were normal. The injuries appeared worse than they actually were; there wasn't enough time for the device to achieve its critical mass and liquefy Daniel from the inside out. Once he had broken free of the small medallion's dark magic, the damage had ceased.

The rumbling of the spacecraft taking off woke Daniel, and his eyes creaked open, bloodshot. He smiled over at Sha'uri, who was just stirring to consciousness herself. They looked like hell. She smiled back at him, grateful they were still alive.

Suddenly Daniel's memory rushed back at him. Where was O'Neil? The bomb? Daniel sat up and looked across the room at O'Neil standing over the bomb, working every control panel he could find. The bomb was still counting down.

00:41. 00:40. 00:39.

Daniel jumped to his feet and rushed over to O'Neil in a panic, stumbling as the room began to shake ever violently.

00:32. 00:31. 00:30.

"Turn it off! He's leaving! We've won!" Daniel demanded.

"I'm trying! It's been rigged. It won't abort."

"Rigged? By who?"

A grim and ugly truth that O'Neil wished was just a joke.

"Military intelligence," O'Neil explained.

00:22. 00:21. 00:20.

Both men looked at the bomb, stunned. Then they looked at each other and began speaking at the same time. They both had the same idea.

The moment the massive spacecraft lifted away from the pyramid, the thousands in the crowd went berserk with joy, they went completely stark-raving lunatic hog wild, dancing insanely, jumping headfirst into the sand, singing, taunting the ship with their mining implements. People were jumping on each other, hugging, tackling each other. Anything to express the wild physical joy erupting from within.

The only person in the entire triumphant crowd who just couldn't enjoy the victory was Skaara. He knew they'd won and knew it was all worth it. But he'd lost his friend, Nabeh.

Through the throngs of people, Skaara spotted the helmet laying near the base of the ramp. Skaara decided he must have it as a last momento. Aggressively he pushed through the crowd, attempting to make his way over to the helmet before one of the jubilant Nagadans picked it up.

The man didn't get two feet before a burned-up hand reached out and locked on to the helmet. Skarra pushed closer to get a better look.

When he found was Nabeh, scorched and bloodied, but alive, wrestling with the last of his strength until he retrieved his coveted helmet. Skaara knocked people aside to get to him. He grabbed his big friend and squeezed him tight in his arms.

"Did you see me, Skaara? I was flying."

Skaara smiled through tears of happiness.

"I saw you, Nabeh."

The other victorious shepherd boys spotted Nabeh and came rushing over. Kawalsky and Feretti, both caught up in the excitement of the moment finally saw young Nabeh and ran over.

Quickly Kawalsky checked Nabeh's injuries. Trained for battle injury medical care, Kawalsky examined Nabeh closely. Feretti looked over to Kawalsky, worried.

"It's not as bad as it looks. He's going to be okay."

Skaara and Nabeh both looked back at Kawalsky, not understanding. Though they didn't understand the words, Kawalsky knew they'd understand the tone in his voice.

"You're going to be fine. You're a tough little guy."

Enjoying the victory, Kasuf had nearly forgotten about Skaara when he saw the boys gathered around Nabeh. Kasuf rushed over and saw that the young Nabeh was still alive. Returning his attention to Skaara, the old man's plan to be stern with the child suddenly melted. He grabbed the boy and wrapped him up in his arms, lifting him like he was still a baby, whooping along with the others.

Ra's children came running from every direction. The oldest girl made a mad dash for the bathing room where she knew the young ones were hiding. She gathered them quickly and hurried them to the medallion. The last of the children jumped onto the medallion just as Ra came out of his chamber and slumped against his throne, his proud form was bent over the severed hand in pain. He knew it was too late to stop the beam. Slowly, he straightened up and came down the stairs toward the children, tears welling up in his yellow and amber eyes.

"You cannot leave me!" he screamed, the light flaring from deep within his eyes.

It was partly a command, partly a plea. But it was too late. The merciless wall of blue light was about to seal, and as soon as it did, the children disappeared in a downward rush of light.

In their place, O'Neil's bomb materialized. It was the last thing Ra would ever see. The red countdown numbers were blinking on the twin canisters, impudently sending Ra the news of his own destruction. In a futile attempt to escape, the creature within the boy wrenched itself free from it's human host. The body of the boy Ra collapsed, lifeless. As it hit the ground and without the creature within, the skin,

bone hair, and teeth aged instantly returning to its natural
state. Within the time it took to fall to the ground, Ra's
body finally looked it's age.

00:09. 00:08. 00.07.

Free of its shell, the creature wanted to rush past the
bomb and beam away through the rings. If he was quick
enough, he could attach himself to another host body before
his natural one would expire. But before he could move an
inch, the bomb ticked down to its final count. The creature
screamed out one last ghoulish howl.

00:02. 00:01. And in a flash, it was over. The light-like
creature turned solid, then burst into a million tiny particles.

Daniel, Sha'uri, and O'Neil stumbled out of the pyramid
entrance just in time to watch Ra's craft disappear from
view. The crowd below staring intensely at the craft as it
began to vanish.

"He's gone," Daniel announced.

The craft was already miles away, speeding toward the
vanishing point when the timer flashed to zero. Even at that
distance, if it hadn't been moving away at such terrific
speed, the white burst of light would have blinded everyone
on the ground. What they got instead, after that initial
brilliant pulsation, was a fireworks show like none ever seen
on Earth. Not only from the nuclear reaction itself, but as a
result of the temperature climbing past the meltdown point
of the quartz. It shattered chameleon into long fiery arcs
across the sky.

"And he's not coming back," O'Neill added. When the
people realized that Sha'uri, Daniel, and O'Neil had made it
safely back outside, another roar spread through the crowd.

Following them onto the landing were the thinly clad
children, Ra's young slaves. They looked and felt desperately out of place among the rough-hewn people of the
mines. O'Neil wanted to send a signal to any who might
want to attack these kids as a symbol of Ra. He carried one
of the youngest on his hip, his pistol prominently displayed
in the other.

Kasuf and his entourage knelt to offer a prayer, but
Skaara ran past his father until he was halfway up the ramp,
facing O'Neil and the others. Wearing a big grin smeared

across his face, Skaara slowly lifted his hand to his brow in a pretty decent military salute. Something about this simple pleasure got to O'Neil, who stared at the boy, speechless. Slowly, one by one, the entire team of shepherd boys walked up behind Skaara and saluted.

Kawalsky and Feretti ate it up. They loved these kids for all they had done for them. Kawalsky, then Feretti, joined the shepherd boys as they all saluted the colonel.

O'Neil found himself choked up. He knew it was silly, yet it still got to him. Ever so slowly O'Neil lifted his hand and returned young Skaara's salute.

Sha'uri turned and took Daniel's hand and raised it high in the air. The thousands roared back, each and every one of them raising their fists in solidarity with the fair-haired one they once feared as a god, but now respected as a man and a friend.

Daniel turned to Sha'uri and kissed her. For the first time in Daniel's entire life, he felt like he belonged. That someone had needed him and that he came through for them.

The noisy throng stood and cheered Daniel for several minutes, until, swept up in their adulation, they lifted him and Sha'uri onto their soldiers and paraded them away from the scene.

As they buoyed the couple out into the desert, Daniel saw, with mixed emotion, his favorite smelly *mastadge,* Little Bit, pacing back and forth on a dune top waiting for his turn to congratulate the hero of the day.

Sha'uri saw Daniel's expression turn sour as he looked at the mangiest beast he'd known on either planet. Sha'uri saw this and shouted instructions over the din to the man carrying Daniel on their shoulders. Laughing and cheering, they ran Daniel straight toward the bad breath and slimy affection of the braying mongrel. Just before the beast's hot tongue slathering up the side of his face, he shot a look at Sha'uri, a look that translated the same way in any language: "I'll get you back for this."

Epilogue

"IT BROUGHT ME LUCK"

Daniel held a flare in one hand, his notebook in the other. Under his direction, Kawalsky turned the heavy inner ring of the StarGate, sliding the appropriate constellations up to the top in their prescribed order. As soon as the final symbol was wheeled into place and registered with a click, the strange machine began to operate under its own power. Daniel tossed the flare, and the two men hightailed it to join the others waiting in the medallion room.

The narrow medallion hall and the giant sloping Grand Gallery behind it were crowded with spectators, lit by the torches brought from Nagada. Even though they'd seen it before, Daniel, Feretti, Kawalsky, and O'Neil were peeking around the corner like a bunch of boys who'd snuck into the movies. The show was fantastic.

The light came pouring from the ring's seven hooded clamps like ropes of water spilling upward against gravity, slowly filling the ring's center, becoming the shimmering white surface of a turbulent pool.

But this time it wasn't the ring's light show that was the star of the show. It was the music. They'd heard it before in the antiseptic silo, from behind safety glass and computers and asbestos doors. This time, sitting in mellowing torchlight surrounded by the stone cathedral walls of the pyramid, they understood that the ring's music was more than a sharpening of a sound frequency. It was a song of slow variations and rising power, a twelve-tone rhapsody produced by this naturally occurring organic synthesizer. Here in the StarGate's natural setting, the ring's music was truly awesome.

As the song reached the top of its power, and the seething pool of light began sloshing over the rim of the Gate, Daniel pulled Sha'uri safely behind the doorjamb. A second later came the moment the Americans were waiting for: the sudden and violent eruption of energy, the liquid light splashing out into the room, like the grasping hand of God. Or gods. Even the people far back in the Gallery gasped and jumped backward at the terrifying power of the *mysterious* machine. When they peeked out from around their corners, or lifted their arms away from their eyes, the light had already been sucked back through the ring, the energy tearing off the perimeter of the device like a wind sock one hundred yards from a nuclear explosion. The circular tube of energy disappeared into the thick stone pyramid wall less than thirty feet behind the ring.

The Americans stood up and came into the room. It was time to go. Skaara moved from the crowd over to O'Neil. Skaara lifted his hand, but unlike the first meeting with Colonel O'Neil, this time Skaara didn't run shrieking when O'Neil took his hand and shook it. In fact, Skaara would never run shrieking from anything ever again.

As O'Neil stood there shaking his hand, he understood that. He also understood that somehow, in his own way, he too had been running. And now, partially through the courage of this young man, he'd never run away again, either. O'Neil smiled a good-bye.

As the team walked to the short flights of stairs that led up to the Gate, Feretti turned to Daniel.

"Hey, by the way," he said over the StarGate's sublime humming, "did you ever get those books back?"

"Actually I did. One of them got a little mauled"—he glanced at O'Neil, then back—"but yes I did, thank you."

"And I want you to know"—Feretti leaned in with a conspiratorial whisper—"I always knew you'd get us back," Feretti said, badly stretching the truth.

"Yeah, right," the big lieutenant commented dryly. He

reached out to shake Daniel's hand and said, simply, "Thanks."

Daniel nodded a "your welcome," then turned to face the soldier in the black beret.

"You gonna be okay?" O'Neil said, even though he knew the answer.

Daniel turned to Sha'uri and smiled. Sha'uri, standing right next to him, understood more or less what they were talking about. Daniel turned back to O'Neil.

"Yeah. I think so." Pointedly, Daniel returned the question. "And you?"

O'Neil knew exactly what Daniel was referring to and didn't mind answering him. Daniel had been right on the money when they were in the cave. O'Neil was not in a hurry to die. Not today. Today he was thinking about Sarah. About getting back to her as fast as he could. Maybe it wasn't too late. Maybe there was still time to save their marriage.

No matter what, O'Neil was at least ready to try. To try and live again.

"Yeah. I'll be okay," he answered. And just with those few words, Daniel knew it was the truth. O'Neil was going to be okay.

"This place seems to suit you, Jackson. You'll probably be down in those catacombs for the next six months."

"You'll come and visit, won't you?" Even as the words left his lips, Daniel felt funny saying them. How casually he invited his new friend to come visit him, only several million light-years away from home. Amazing.

"What can I tell you?" O'Neil shouted. "The decision won't be made by me. That'll be up to my superiors."

"Military intelligence?" Daniel asked.

"Goddamn contradiction in terms." O'Neil smiled.

"Do me a favor"—Daniel handed over Catherine's medallion—"tell Catherine it brought me luck."

"You bet." Before he let himself do anything too emotional, O'Neil turned away, walked up the steps directly into the StarGate's beam.

Kawalsky and Feretti followed suit, their images hanging frozen in mid-step for a moment before rushing away in a blur. Each time one of the men stepped into the intense white streaking pool of light, the assembled Nagadans gasped. Then they were gone.

Skaara, Daniel, and Sha'uri watched long after the soldiers had disappeared, until the ring spun and shut down and the bowels of the pyramid returned to the darkness of torchlight. Then they led the procession through the pyramid and out into the desert where the last of the three suns was setting on the horizon.

As they began the long walk back to the city, Little Bit wandered up to the top of a tall dune. Standing between the Nagadans and the planet's oblong moon, she sounded a beautiful, plaintive cry.